A FASCINATING—AND
AWARD-WINNING—COLLECTION!

- **FIRE WATCH** by Connie Willis
  The story that established her amazing career.
  Winner of the Hugo and Nebula Awards

- **HARDFOUGHT** by Greg Bear
  A "breakthrough" novella by the author of *Blood Music*.
  Winner of the Nebula Award

- **THE END OF LIFE AS WE KNOW IT** by Lucius Shepard
  The popular Nebula Award-nominated story by the author of
  *Green Eyes. Winner of the John W. Campbell Award in 1985
  for Best New Writer*

- **BLOODCHILD** by Octavia E. Butler
  A powerful and controversial story by the author of *Clay's
  Ark. Winner of the Hugo and Nebula Awards*

- **PRESS ENTER ■** by John Varley
  An acclaimed favorite by the bestselling author of *Titan,
  Wizard,* and *Demon. Winner of the Hugo and Nebula Awards*

- **HER FURRY FACE** by Leigh Kennedy
  One of the most controversial stories to appear in *Isaac
  Asimov's SF Magazine.*

- **THE PEACEMAKER** by Gardner Dozois
  The award-winning anthologist's remarkable contribution.
  Winner of the Nebula Award

THE BEST OF *ISAAC ASIMOV'S*
SCIENCE FICTION MAGAZINE

THE BEST OF ISAAC ASIMOV'S SCIENCE FICTION MAGAZINE

EDITED BY GARDNER DOZOIS

ACE BOOKS, NEW YORK

THE BEST OF *ISAAC ASIMOV'S SCIENCE FICTION MAGAZINE*

An Ace Book/published by arrangement with
Davis Publications, Inc.

PRINTING HISTORY
Ace edition/February 1988

ISBN: 0-441-05498-6

Ace Books are published by
The Berkley Publishing Group,
200 Madison Avenue, New York, New York 10016.
The name "Ace" and the "A" logo are
trademarks belonging to Charter Communications, Inc.

PRINTED IN THE UNITED STATES OF AMERICA

10 9 8 7 6 5 4 3 2 1

CONTENTS

FOREWORD
Isaac Asimov's Science Fiction Magazine
by Gardner Dozois

Ten years ago, in the lost and fabled days of 1976—gone now with the dodo and the dinosaur—*Isaac Asimov's Science Fiction Magazine* was born, the result of a series of discussions between Isaac Asimov and Joel Davis, President of Davis Publications, Inc. George Scithers was hired as Editor, he hired me as Associate Editor, and *IAsfm* was launched. The almost unanimous critical opinion of the day was that the magazine could not possibly last, that the climate of the SF publishing world had changed to such a degree that it was no longer possible to found a successful SF magazine. The most optimistic of the commentators gave us six months.

They were wrong. I parted company with *IAsfm* after the first year or so, four issues, more or less (we were quarterly then), but the magazine itself continued on for years under the editorship of George Scithers, who remained at the helm until the 51st issue. This was the first great Age of the magazine, the Scitherian Era, and so far George holds the record for the longest editorial regime. Under George, *IAsfm* became an established and accepted part of the science fiction scene, progressing from a quarterly to a monthly publication. (We are now actually a tetraweekly publication, publishing thirteen issues a year, but never mind about that.) After George stepped down, there was a brief period in which Kathleen Moloney was in charge. Then Shawna McCarthy (who had already been associated with the magazine for many years, first as assistant, and then, later, as Managing Editor) was named as *IAsfm*'s new Editor, and the curtain rose on the second great Age of the magazine—the McCarthy Age. During Shawna's regime, IAsfm achieved its greatest critical successes, becoming accepted by many commentators as the most prestigious of all SF magazines, perhaps the foremost showcase of the field. Stories purchased by Shawna won eight Nebula Awards, five Hugos, and a World Fantasy Award, and Shawna herself won a well-deserved Hugo as Best Professional Editor.

Evolution never stops, however, and the McCarthy Age came to an end with our 100th issue, the January 1986 issue, when Shawna stepped down and was replaced as Editor by me, Gardner Dozois—feeling a bit odd about being back with and this time at the helm of a magazine I'd helped to launch so many years before, but delighted to give it my best shot. It is perhaps premature to speak of the Dozois Period (the Dozoisian Age? The Dozoisite Era? the Dozoiscine?), but it should be interesting at some indeterminate time down the road to examine the geological strata laid down and see just exactly what it was that I did. As I said, evolution *never* stops.

Meanwhile, this anthology. Until recently, there were regularly issued, non-theme IAsfm anthologies, drawn from the contents of the magazine—so that the Scitherian Era, for instance, has been fairly well documented. There *is* a gap in the fossil record, however. For a few years now there have been no systematically issued, general, non-theme IAsfm anthologies (Shawna did edit several anthologies during this period, two of which—*Space of Her Own* and *Fantasy*—will later be issued by Ace, but those were *theme* anthologies), so that much of that period remains undocumented. *This* anthology, designed to remedy that situation, covers (more or less) the period from 1982 to early 1985, roughly convergent with the McCarthy Age. I have cheated a little, to get "Fire Watch" in on one end and "The End of Life As We Know It" in on the other, but, for the most part, I have concentrated on the years 1983 and 1984, deciding arbitrarily, for reasons of anthology length, not to use anything from 1985, Shawna's last year—material which I hope to save for possible future anthologies. (Yes, I know, the Shepard story appeared in the January 1985 issue, but, as Emerson once said, a foolish consistency is the hobgoblin of little minds. So *there . . .*) Circumstances forced other choices, and other omissions, even of award-winning stories. Connie Willis's Nebula-winning "A Letter From the Clearys" appears in *Space of Her Own,* for instance, and Scott Baker's World Fantasy Award–winning "Still Life With Scorpion" appears in *Fantasy,* and I didn't want to duplicate the contents of those anthologies. Similarly, Octavia Butler's "Speech Sounds" won a Hugo, but I've used her story "Bloodchild" instead . . . and so on. Some first-rate stories were simply too long to fit into this book with the stuff that *had* to be here. For the last few years, *IAsfm* has been one of the last natural refuges of that endangered literary lifeform, the novella, and many fine novellas have appeared there, but the problem with novellas is that they are—after all—*long,* and that means that you can't fit too many of them into one book all at once.

Since almost no one outside of the publishing world understands the long lead-times involved in publishing a magazine, I should emphasize again that the stories in this anthology were purchased either by George or (mostly) by Shawna. No material purchased by me showed up in *IAsfm* until the January 1986 issue of the magazine.

In closing, I'd like to thank George and Shawna for having the good taste to buy this material in the first place (Shawna in particular for supplying me with historical detail); thank Managing Editor Sheila Williams (who has labored behind the scenes on *IAsfm* for many years and played a part in the decision-making process involved in the buying of some of these stories); Editorial Assistant Tina Lee (who did much of the thankless scut-work involved in producing this anthology); Cynthia Manson (who set up this deal); and especially my own editor on this project, Susan Allison.

—*Gardner Dozois*

THE END OF LIFE AS WE KNOW IT

by Lucius Shepard

"The End of Life As We Know It" was purchased by
Shawna McCarthy and appeared in the January 1985
issue of IAsfm, with a luminous cover and interior illustrations by J.K. Potter. It went on to become one of
the most popular and critically acclaimed stories of the
year, although it was edged out of a spot on that year's
Final Nebula Ballot by another Shepard story from a
competing magazine, "The Jaguar Hunter." Shepard
made his first sale to IAsfm with the powerful novella
"A Traveller's Tale," in the July 1984 issue, and since
then has become one of the mainstays of the magazine.
Pleasingly prolific, Shepard has made more than a
dozen sales to IAsfm in the last couple of years . . . and
we are pleased to announce that we still have several
major stories by Shepard in inventory. We hope to bring
you lots more of him in the future.

Born in Lynchburg, Virginia, Lucius Shepard has
traveled widely in the Middle East, Europe, Latin
America, and the Caribbean, places that often serve as
gritty and authentic settings for his fiction. Shepard
began publishing in 1983, and in a very short time has

become one of the most popular and prolific new writers to enter the genre in many years. In 1985, Shepard won the John W. Campbell Award as the year's Best New Writer, as well as being on the Nebula Award final ballot an unprecedented three times, in three separate categories. He has also showed up on the Hugo final ballot, as well as being a finalist for the British Fantasy Award, the John W. Campbell Memorial Award, and the Philip K. Dick Award, and the World Fantasy Award. His acclaimed first novel, Green Eyes, *was an Ace Special. His most recent books are a major new novel,* Life During Wartime, *from Bantam's New Fiction line, and a collection,* The Jaguar Hunter, *from Arkham House. In 1987, he won the Nebula Award for his novella "R & R," another* IAsfm *story.*

What Lisa hated most about Mexico were the flies, and Richard said, Yeah, the flies were bad, but it was the lousy attitude of the people that did him in, you know, the way the waiters ignored you and the taxi drivers sneered, the sour expressions of desk clerks—as if they were doing you a big favor by letting you stay in their fleabag hotels. All that. Lisa replied that she couldn't blame the people, because they were probably irritated by the flies; this set Richard to laughing, and though Lisa had not meant it to be funny, after a moment she joined in. They needed laughter. They had come to Mexico to Save Their Marriage, and things were not going well . . . except in bed, where things had always gone well. Lisa had never been less than ardent with Richard, even during her affair.

They were an attractive couple in their thirties, the sort to whom a healthy sex life seems an essential of style, a trendy accessory to pleasure like a Jacuzzi or a French food processor. She was a tall, fey-looking brunette with fair skin, an aerobically nurtured slimness, and a face that managed to express both sensuality and intelligence ("hooker eyes and Vassar bones," Richard had told her); he was lean from handball and weights, with an executive touch of gray in his black hair and the bland, firm-jawed handsomeness of a youthful anchorman. Once they had held to the illusion that they kept fit and beautiful for one another, but all their illusions had been tarnished and they no longer understood their reasons for maintaining them.

For a while they made a game of hating Mexico, pretending it was a new bond between them, striving to outdo each other in pointing out instances of filth and native insensitivity; finally they realized that what they hated most about the country were their own perceptions of it, and they headed south to Guatemala where—they had been informed—the atmosphere was conducive to romance. They were leery about the reports of guerrilla activity, but their informant had assured them that the dangers were overstated. He was a seasoned traveler, an elderly Englishman who had spent his last twelve winters in Central America; Richard thought he was colorful, a Graham Greene character, whereas Lisa described him in her journal as "a deracinated old fag."

"You mustn't miss Lake Atitlán," he'd told them. "It's absolutely breath-taking. Revolution there is an aesthetic impossibility."

Before boarding the plane Richard bought the latest Miami Herald, and he entertained himself during the flight by bemoaning the decline of Western civilization. It was his conviction that the United States was becoming part of the Third World and that their grandchildren would inhabit a mildly poisoned earth and endure lives of back-breaking drudgery under an increasingly Orwellian government. Though this conviction was hardly startling, it being evident from the newspaper that such a world was close upon them, Lisa accorded his viewpoint the status of wisdom; in fact, she had relegated wisdom in general to be his preserve, staking claim herself to the traditional feminine precincts of soulfulness and caring. Sometimes back in Connecticut, while teaching her art class at the Y or manning the telephones for PBS or Greenpeace or whatever cause had enlisted her soulfulness, looking around at the other women, all—like her—expensively kept and hopeless and with an eye cocked for the least glimmer of excitement, then she would see how marriage had decreased her wattage; and yet, though she had fallen in love with another man, she had clung to the marriage for almost a year thereafter, unable to escape the fear that this was the best she could hope for, that no matter what steps she took to change her situation, her life would always be ruled by a canon of mediocrity. That she had recently stopped clinging did not signal a slackening of fear, only that her fingers were slipping, her energy no longer sufficient to maintain a good grip.

As the plane came down into Guatemala City, passing over rumpled green hills dotted with shacks whose colors looked deceptively bright and cheerful from a height, Richard began talking about his various investments, saying he was glad he'd bought this and that, because things were getting worse every day. "The shitstorm's a 'comin', babe," he said, patting her knee. "But we're gonna be awright." It annoyed Lisa no end that whenever he was feeling particularly accomplished his language became countrified, and she only shrugged in response.

After clearing customs they rented a car and drove to Panajachel, a village on the shores of Lake Atitlán. There was a fancy hotel on the shore, but in the spirit of "roughing it" Richard insisted they stay at a cheaper place on the edge of town—an old green stucco building with red trim and an arched entranceway and a courtyard choked with ferns; it catered to what he called "the bleeding-ear set," a reference to the loud rock 'n' roll that blasted from the windows. The other guests were mostly college-age vacationers, a mixture of French and Scandinavians and Americans, and as soon as they had unpacked, Lisa changed into jeans and a work shirt so she would fit in among them. They ate dinner in the hotel dining room, which was cramped and furnished with red wooden tables and chairs and had the menu painted on the wall in English and Spanish. Richard appeared to be enjoying himself; he was relaxed, and his speech was peppered with slang that he hadn't used in almost a decade. Lisa liked listening to the glib chatter around them, talk of dope and how the people treat you in Huehuetenango and watch out if you're goin' to Bogota, man, 'cause they got packs of street kids will pick you clean. . . . These conversations reminded her of the world in which she had traveled at Vassar before Richard had snatched her up during her junior year. He had been just back from Vietnam, a medic, full of anguish at the horrors he had seen, yet strong for having seen them; he had seemed to her a source of strength, a shining knight, a rescuer. After the wedding, though, she had not been able to recall why she had wanted to be rescued; she thought now that she had derived some cheap thrill from his aura of recent violence and had applied it to herself out of a romantic need to feel imperiled.

They lingered over dinner, watching the younger guests drift off into the evening and being watched themselves—at least in Lisa's case—by a fortyish Guatemalan man with a pencil-line mustache, a dark suit, and patent-leather hair. He stared at her as he chewed, ducking his eyes each time he speared a fresh bite, then resuming his stare. Ordinarily Lisa would have been irritated, but she found the man's conspicuous anonymity appealing and she adopted a flirtatious air, laughing too loudly and fluttering her hands, in hopes that she was frustrating him.

"His name's Raoul," said Richard. "He's a white slaver in the employ of the Generalissimo, and he's been commissioned to bring in a new *gringa* for the harem."

"He's somebody's uncle," said Lisa. "Here to settle a family dispute. He's married to a dumpy Indian woman, has seven kids, and he's wearing his only suit to impress the Americans."

"God, you're a romantic!" Richard sipped his coffee, made a face and set it down.

Lisa bit back a sarcastic reply. "I think he's very romantic. Let's say he's staring at me because he wants me. If that's true, right now he's probably thinking how to do you in, or maybe wondering if he could trade you his truck, his means of livelihood, for a night with me. That's real romance. Passionate stupidity and bloody consequences."

"I guess," said Richard, unhappy with the definition; he took another sip of coffee and changed the subject.

At sunset they walked down to the lake. The village was charming enough—the streets cobbled, the houses whitewashed and roofed with tile; but the rows of tourist shops and the American voices acted to dispel the charm. The lake, however, was beautiful. Ringed by three volcanoes, bordered by palms, Indians poling canoes toward scatters of light on the far shore. The water was lacquered with vivid crimson and yellow reflection, and silhouetted against an equally vivid sky, the palms and volcanic cones gave the place the look of a prehistoric landscape. As they stood at the end of a wooden pier, Richard drew her into a kiss and she felt again the explosive dizziness of their first kiss; yet she knew it was a sham, a false magic born of geography and their own contrivance. They could keep traveling, keep filling their days with exotic sights, lacquering their lives with reflection, but when they stopped they would discover that they had merely been preserving the forms of the marriage. There was no remedy for their dissolution.

Roosters crowing waked her to gray dawn light. She remembered a dream about a faceless lover, and she stretched and rolled onto her side. Richard was sitting at the window, wearing jeans and a T-shirt; he glanced at her, then turned his gaze to the window, to the sight of a pale green volcano wreathed in mist. "It's not working," he said, and when she failed to respond, still half-asleep, he buried his face in his hands, muffling his voice. "I can't make it without you, babe."

She had dreaded this moment, but there was no reason to put it off. "That's the problem," she said. "You used to be able to." She plumped the pillows and leaned back against them.

He looked up, baffled. "What do you mean?"

"Why should *I* have to explain it? You know it as well as I do. We weaken each other, we exhaust each other, we depress each other." She lowered her eyes, not wanting to see his face. "Maybe it's not even us. Sometimes I think marriage is this big pasty spell of cakes and veils that shrivels everything it touches."

"Lisa, you know there isn't anything I wouldn't . . ."

"What? What'll you do?" Angrily, she wadded the sheet. "I don't understand how we've managed to hurt each other so much. If I did I'd try to fix it. But there's nothing left to do. Not together, anyway."

He let out a long sigh—the sigh of a man who has just finished defusing a bomb and can allow himself to breathe again. "It's him, right? You still want to be with him."

It angered her that he would never say the name, as if the name were what counted. "No," she said stiffly. "It's not *him*."

"But you still love him."

"That's not the point! I still love you, but love . . ." She drew up her legs and rested her forehead on her knees. "Christ, Richard. I don't know what more to tell you. I've said it all a hundred times."

"Maybe," he said softly, "maybe this discussion is premature."

"Oh, Richard!"

"No, really. Let's go on with the trip."

"Where next? The Mountains of the Moon? Brazil? It won't change anything."

"You can't be sure of that!" He came toward the bed, his face knitted into lines of despair. "We'll just stay a few more days. We'll visit the villages on the other side of the lake, where they do the weaving."

"Why, Richard? God, I don't even understand why you still want me . . ."

"Please, Lisa. Please. After eleven years you can try for a few more days."

"All right," she said, weary of hurting him. "A few days."

"And you'll try?"

I've always tried, she wanted to say; but then, wondering if it were true, as true as it should be, she merely said, "Yes."

The motor launch that ran back and forth across the lake between Panajachel and San Augustín had seating room for fifteen, and nine of those places were occupied by Germans, apparently members of a family—kids, two sets of parents, and a pair of portly, red-cheeked grandparents. They reeked of crudity and good health, and made Lisa feel refined by comparison. The young men snapped their wives' bra straps—grandpa almost choked with laughter each time this happened; the kids whined; the women were heavy and hairy-legged. They spent the entire trip taking pictures of one another. They must have understood English, because when Richard cracked a joke about them they frowned and whispered and became standoffish. Lisa and Richard moved to the stern, a superficial union imposed, and watched the shore glide past. Though it was still early, the sun reflected a dynamited white glare on the water; in the daylight the volcanoes looked depressingly real, their slopes covered by patchy grass and scrub and stunted palms.

San Augustín was situated at the base of the largest volcano, and was probably like what Panajachel had been before tourism. Weeds grew between the cobblestones, the white-wash was flaked away in places, and grimy, naked toddlers sat in the doorways, chewing sugar cane and drooling. Inside the houses it was the Fourteenth Century. Packed dirt floors, iron cauldrons suspended over fires, chickens pecking and pigs asleep. Gnomish old Indian women worked at hand looms, turning out strange tapestries—as, for example, a design of black cranelike birds against a backdrop of purple sky and green trees, the image repeated over and over—and bolts of dress material, fabric that on first impression seemed to be of a hundred colors, all in perfect harmony. Lisa wanted to be sad for the women, to sympathize with their poverty and par-ticular female plight, and to some extent she managed it; but the women were uncomplaining and appeared reasonably con-tent and their weaving was better work than she had ever done, even when she had been serious about art. She bought several yards of the material, tried to strike up a conversation with one of the women, who spoke neither English or Span-ish, and then they returned to the dock, to the village's only bar-restaurant—a place right out of a spaghetti western, with a hitching rail in front and skinned sapling trunks propping up the porch roof and a handful of young, long-haired American men standing along the bar, having an early-morning beer. "Holy marijuana!" said Richard, winking. "Hippies! I won-dered where they'd gone." They took a table by the rear win-dow so they could see the slopes of the volcano. The scarred varnish of the table was dazzled by sunlight; flies buzzed against the heated panes.

"So what do you think?" Richard squinted against the glare.

"I thought we were going to give it a few days," she said testily.

"Jesus, Lisa! I meant, what do you think about the weav-ing?" He adopted a pained expression.

"I'm sorry." She touched his hand, and he shook his head ruefully. "It's beautiful . . . I mean, the weaving's beautiful. Oh, God, Richard. I don't intend to be so awkward."

"Forget it." He stared out the window, deadpan, as if he were giving serious consideration to climbing the volcano, sizing up the problems involved. "What did you think of it?"

"It was beautiful," she said flatly. The buzzing of the flies intensified, and she had the notion that they were telling her to try harder. "I know it's corny to say, but watching her work . . . What was her name?"

"Expectación."

"Oh, right. Well, watching her I got the feeling I was watching something magical, something that went on and on . . ." She trailed off, feeling foolish at having to legitimize with conversation what had been a momentary whimsy; but she could think of nothing else to say. "Something that went on forever," she continued. "With different hands, of course, but always that something the same. And the weavers, while they had their own lives and problems, that was less important than what they were doing. You know, like the generations of weavers were weaving something through time as well as space. A long, woven magic." She laughed, embarrassed.

"It's not corny. I know what you're talking about." He pushed back his chair and grinned. "How about I get us a couple of beers?"

"Okay," she said brightly, and smiled until his back was turned. He thought he had her now. That was his plan—to get her a little drunk, not drunk enough for a midday hangover, just enough to get her happy and energized, and then that afternoon they'd go for a ride to the next village, the next exotic attraction, and more drinks and dinner and a new hotel. He'd keep her whirling, an endless date, an infinitely prolonged seduction. She pictured the two of them as a pair of silhouetted dancers tangoing across the borders of map-colored countries. Whirling and whirling, and the thing was, the very sad thing was, that sooner or later, if he kept her whirling, she would lose her own momentum and be sucked into the spin, into that loving-the-spin-I'm-in-old-black-magic routine. Then final rinse. Final spin. Then the machine would stop and she'd be plastered to the side of the marriage like a wet blouse, needing a hand to lift her out. She should do what had to be done right now. Right this moment. Cause a scene, hit him. Whatever it took. Because if she didn't . . . He *thunked* down a bottle of beer in front of her, and her smile twitched by reflex into place.

"Thanks," she said.

"Por nada." He delivered a gallant bow and sat down. "Listen . . ."

There was a clatter from outside, and through the door she saw a skinny, bearded man tying a donkey to the hitching rail. He strode on in, dusting off his jeans cowboy-style, and ordered a beer. Richard turned to look and chuckled. The man was worth a chuckle. He might have been the Spirit of the Sixties, the Wild Hippie King. His hair was a ratty brown thatch hanging to his shoulders, and braided into it were long gray feathers that dangled still lower; his jeans were festooned with painted symbols, and there were streaks of what appeared to be green dye in his thicket of a beard. He noticed them staring, waved, and came toward them.

"Mind if I join you folks?" Before they could answer, he dropped into a chair. "I'm Dowdy. Believe it or not, that's a name, not a self-description." He smiled, and his blue eyes crinkled up. His features were sharp, thin to the point of being wizened. It was hard to tell his age because of the beard, but Lisa figured him for around thirty-five. Her first reaction had been to ask him to leave; the instant he had started talking, though, she had sensed a cheerful kind of sanity about him that intrigued her. "I live up yonder," he went on, gesturing at the volcano. "Been there goin' on four years."

"Inside the volcano?" Lisa meant it for a joke.

"Yep! Got me a little shack back in under the lip. Hot in the summer, freezin' in the winter, and none of the comforts of home. I got to bust my tail on Secretariat there—he waved at the donkey—"just to haul water and supplies." In waving he must have caught a whiff of his underarm—he gave it an ostentatious sniff. *"And* to get me a bath. Hope I ain't too ripe for you folks." He chugged down a third of his beer. "So! How you like Guatemala?"

"Fine," said Richard. "Why do you live in a volcano?"

"Kinda peculiar, ain't it," said Dowdy by way of response; he turned to Lisa. "And how you like it here?"

"We haven't seen much," she said. "Just the lake."

"Oh, yeah? Well, it ain't so bad 'round here. They keep it nice for the tourists. But the rest of the country . . . whooeee! Violent?" Dowdy made a show of awed disbelief. "You got your death squads, your guerrillas, your secret police, not to mention your basic crazed killers. Hell, they even got a political party called the Party of Organized Violence. Bad dudes. They like to twist people's arms off. It ain't that they're evil, though. It's just the land's so full of blood and brimstone and Mayan weirdness, it fumes up and freaks 'em out. That's how come we got volcanoes. Safety valves to blow off the excess poison. But things are on the improve."

"Really?" said Richard, amused.

"Yes, indeed!" Dowdy tipped back in his chair, propping the beer bottle on his stomach; he had a little pot belly like that of a cartoon elf. "The whole world's changing. I s'pose y'all have noticed the way things are goin' to hell back in the States?"

Lisa could tell that the question had mined Richard's core of political pessimism, and he started to frame an answer; but Dowdy talked through him.

"That's part of the change," he said. "All them scientists say they figured out reasons for the violence and pollution and economic failure, but what them things really are is just the sound of consensus reality scrapin' contrary to the flow of the change. They ain't nothin' but symptoms of the real change, of everything comin' to an end."

Richard made silent speech with his eyes, indicating that it was time to leave.

"Now, now," said Dowdy, who had caught the signal. "Don't get me wrong. I ain't talkin' Apocalypse, here. And I for sure ain't no Bible basher like them Mormons you see walkin' 'round the village. Huh! Them suckers is so scared of life they travel in pairs so's they can keep each other from bein' corrupted. 'Watch it there, Billy! You're steppin' in some sin!'" Dowdy rolled his eyes to the ceiling in a parody of prayer. "'Sweet Jesus gimme the strength to scrape this sin off my shoe!' Then off they go, purified, a couple of All-American haircuts with souls stuffed fulla white-bread gospel and crosses 'round their necks to keep off the vampire women. Shit!" he leaned forward, resting his elbows on the table. "But I digress. I got me a religion all right. Not Jesus, though. I'll tell you 'bout it if you want, but I ain't gonna force it down your throat."

"Well," Richard began, but Lisa interrupted.

"We've got an hour until the boat," she said. "Does your religion have anything to do with your living in the volcano?"

"Sure does." Dowdy pulled a hand-rolled cigar from his shirt pocket, lit it, and blew out a plume of smoke that boiled into a bluish cloud against the windowpanes. "I used to smoke, drink"—he flourished his beer—"and I was a bear for the ladies. Praise God, religion ain't changed that none!" He laughed, and Lisa smiled at him. Whatever it was that had put Dowdy in such good spirits seemed to be contagious. "Actually," he said, "I wasn't a hell-raiser at all. I was a painfully shy little fella, come from backwoods Tennessee. Like my daddy'd say, town so small you could spit between the city limits signs. Anyway, I was shy but I was smart, and with that combination it was a natural for me to end up in computers. Gave me someone I could feel comfortable talkin' to. After college I took a job designin' software out in Silicon Valley, and seven years later there I was . . . Livin' in an apartment tract with no real friends, no pictures on the walls, and a buncha terminals. A real computer nerd. Wellsir! Somehow I got it in mind to take a vacation. I'd never had one. Guess I figured I'd just end up somewhere weird, sittin' in a room and thinkin' 'bout computers, so what was the point? But I was determined to do it this time, and I came to Panajachel. First few days I did what you folks probably been doin'. Wanderin', not meetin' anyone, buyin' a few gee-gaws. Then I caught the launch across the lake and ran into ol' Murcielago." He clucked his tongue against his teeth. "Man, I didn't know what to make of him at first. He was the oldest human bein' I'd ever seen. Looked centuries old. All hunched up, white-haired, as wrinkled as a walnut shell. He couldn't speak no English, just Cakchiquel, but he had this mestizo fella with him who did his interpretin', and it was through him I learned that Murcielago was a *brujo*."

"A wizard," said Lisa, who had read Casteneda, to Richard, who hadn't.

"Yep," said Dowdy. "'Course I didn't believe it. Thought it was some kinda hustle. But he interested me, and I kept hangin' 'round just to see what he was up to. Well, one night he says to me—through the mestizo fella—'I like you,' he said. 'Ain't nothin' wrong with you that a little magic wouldn't cure. I'd be glad to make you a gift if you got no objections.' I said to myself, 'Oh-oh, here it comes.' But I reckoned it couldn't do me no harm to let him play his hand, and I told him to go ahead. So he does some singin' and rubs powder on my mouth and mutters and touches me, and that was it. 'You gonna be fine now,' he tells me. I felt sorta strange, but no finer than I had. Still, there wasn't any hustle, and that same night I realized that his magic was doin' its stuff. Confused the hell out of me, and the only thing I could think to do was to hike on up to the volcano, where he lived, and ask him about it. Murcielago was waitin' for me. The mestizo had gone, but he'd left a note explainin' the situation. Seems he'd learned all he could from Murcielago and had taken up his own post, and it was time the ol' man had a new apprentice. He told me how to cook for him, wished me luck, and said he'd be seein' me around." Dowdy twirled his cigar and watched smoke rings float up. "Been there ever since and ain't regretted it a day."

Richard was incredulous. "You gave up a job in Silicon Valley to become a sorcerer's apprentice?"

"That's right." Dowdy pulled at one of the feathers in his hair. "But I didn't give up nothin' real, Richard."

"How do you know my name?"

"People grow into their names, and if you know how to look for it, it's written everywhere on 'em. 'Bout half of magic is bein' able to see clear."

Richard snorted. "You read our names off the passenger manifest for the launch."

"I don't blame you for thinkin' that," said Dowdy. "It's hard to accept the existence of magic. But that ain't how it happened." He drained the dregs of his beer. "You were easy to read, but Lisa here was sorta hard 'cause she never liked her name. Ain't that so?"

Lisa nodded, surprised.

"Yeah, see, when a person don't like their name it muddies up the writin' so to speak, and you gotta scour away a lotta half-formed names to see down to the actual one." Dowdy heaved a sigh and stood. "Time I'm takin' care of business, but tell you what! I'll bring ol' Murcielago down to the bar around seven o'clock and you can check him out. You can catch the nine o'clock boat back. I know he'd like to meet you."

"*How* do you know?" asked Richard.

"It ain't my place to explain. Look here, Rich. I ain't

gonna twist your arm, but if you go back to Panajachel you're just gonna wander 'round and maybe buy some garbage. If you stay, well, whether or not you believe Murcielago's a *brujo,* you'll be doin' somethin' out of the ordinary. Could be he'll give you a gift."

"What gift did he give you?" asked Lisa.

"The gift of gab," said Dowdy. "Surprised you ain't deduced that for yourself, Lisa, 'cause I can tell you're a perceptive soul. 'Course that was just part of the gift. The gift wrappin', as it were. It's like Murcielago says, a real gift ain't known by its name." He winked at her. "But it took pretty damn good, didn't it?"

As soon as Dowdy had gone, Richard asked Lisa if she wanted a last look at the weaving before heading back, but she told him she would like to meet Murcielago. He argued briefly, then acquiesced. She knew what he was thinking. He had no interest in the *brujo,* but he would humor her; it would be an Experience, a Shared Memory, another increment of momentum added to the spin of their marriage. To pass the time she bought a notebook from a tiny store, whose entire inventory would have fit in her suitcases, and sat outside the bar sketching the volcanoes, the people, the houses. Richard *oohed* and *ahhed* over the sketches, but in her judgment they were lifeless—accurate, yet dull and uninspired. She kept at it, though; it beat her other options.

Toward four o'clock black thunderheads muscled up from behind the volcano, drops of cold rain splattered down, and they retreated into the bar. Lisa did not intend to get drunk, but she found herself drinking to Richard's rhythm. He would nurse each beer for a while, shearing away the label with his thumbnail; once the label had been removed he would empty the bottle in a few swallows and bring them a couple more. After four bottles she was tipsy, and after six walking to the bathroom became an adventure in vertigo. Once she stumbled against the only other customer, a long-haired guy left over from the morning crowd, and caused him to spill his drink. "My pleasure," he said when she apologized, leering, running his hands along her hips as he pushed her gently away. She wanted to pose a vicious comeback, but was too fuddled. The bathroom served to make her drunker. It was a chamber of

horrors, a hole in the middle of the floor with a ridged foot-
print on either side, scraps of brown paper strewn about, dark
stains everywhere, reeking. There was a narrow window
which—if she stood on tip-toe—offered a view of two volcanoes and the lake. The water mirrored the grayish-black of the
sky. She stared through the smeared glass, watching waves
pile in toward shore, and soon she realized that she was staring at the scene with something like longing, as if the storm
held a promise of resolution. By the time she returned to the
bar, the bartender had lit three kerosene lamps; they added a
shabby glory to the place, casting rich gleams along the coun-
tertop and gemmy orange reflections in the windowpanes.
Richard had brought her a fresh beer.

"They might not come, what with the rain," he said.

"Maybe not." She downed a swallow of beer, beginning to
like its sour taste.

"Probably for the best," he said. "I've been thinking, and
I'm sure he was setting us up for a robbery."

"You're paranoid. If he were going to rob us, he'd pick a
spot where there weren't any soldiers."

"Well, he's got something in mind...though I have to
admit that was a clever story he told. All that stuff about his
own doubts tended to sandbag any notion that he was hustling
us."

"I don't believe he was hustling us. Maybe he's deluded,
but he's not a criminal."

"How the hell could you tell that?" He picked at a stubborn
fleck of beer label. "Feminine intuition? God, he was only
here a few minutes."

"You know," she said angrily, "I deserve that. I've been
buying that whole feminine intuition chump ever since we
were married. I've let you play the intelligent one, while I"—
she affected a southern accent and a breathy voice—"I just get
these little flashes. I swear I don't know where they come
from, but they turn out right so often I must be psychic or
somethin'. Jesus!"

"Lisa, please."

He looked utterly defeated but she was drunk and sick of
all the futile effort and she couldn't stop. "Any idiot could've
seen that Dowdy was just a nice, weird little guy. Not a threat!
But you had to turn him into a threat so you could feel you

were protecting me from dangers I was too naïve to see.
What's that do for you? Does it wipe out the fact that I've
been unfaithful, that I've walked all over your self-respect?
Does it restore your masculine pride?"

His face worked, and she hoped he would hit her, punctu-
ate the murkiness of their lives with a single instance of shock
and clarity. But she knew he wouldn't. He relied on his sadness to defeat her. "You must hate me," he said.

She bowed her head, her anger emptying into the hollow
created by his dead voice. "I don't hate you. I'm just tired."

"Let's go home. Let's get it over with."

She glanced up, startled. His lips were thinned, a muscle
clenching in his jaw.

"We can catch a flight tomorrow. If not tomorrow, the next
day. I won't try to hold you anymore."

She was amazed by the panic she felt; she couldn't tell if it
resulted from surprise, the kind you feel when you haven't
shut the car door properly and suddenly there you are, hanging
out the side, unprepared for the sight of the pavement flowing
past; or if it was that she had never really wanted freedom,
that all her protest had been a means of killing boredom.
Maybe, she thought, this was a new tactic on his part, and
then she realized that everything between them had become
tactical. They played each other without conscious effort, and
their games bordered on the absurd. To her further amazement
she heard herself say in a tremulous voice, "Is that what *you*
want?"

"Hell, no!" He smacked his palm against the table, rattling
the bottles. "I want you! I want children, eternal love . . . all
those dumb bullshit things we wanted in the beginning! But
you don't want them anymore, do you?"

She saw how willingly she had given him an opening in
which to assert his masculinity, his moral position, combining
them into a terrific left hook to the heart. *Oh, Jesus, they were
pathetic!* Tears started from her eyes, and she had a dizzying
sense of location, as if she were looking up from a well-
bottom through the strata of her various conditions. Drunk, in
a filthy bar, in Guatemala, shadowed by volcanos, under a
stormy sky, and—spanning it all, binding it all together—the
strange webs of their relationship.

"Do you?" He frowned at her, demanding that she finish

the game, speak her line, admit to the one verity that prevented them from ever truly finishing—her uncertainty.

"I don't know," she answered; she tried to say it in a neutral tone, but it came out hopeless.

The storm's darkness passed, and true darkness slipped in under cover of the final clouds. Stars pricked out above the rim of the volcano. The food in the bar was greasy—fried fish, beans, and a salad that she was afraid to eat (stains on the lettuce)—but eating steadied her, and she managed to start a conversation about their recent meals. Remember the weird Chinese place in Mérida, hot sauce in the Lobster Cantonese? Or what had passed for crepes at their hotel in Zihuatenejo? Things like that. The bartender hauled out a portable record player and put on an album of romantic ballads sung by a man with a sexy voice and a gaspy female chorus; the needle kept skipping, and finally, with an apologetic smile and a shrug, the bartender switched it off. It came to be seven-thirty, and they talked about Dowdy not showing, about catching the eight o'clock boat. Then there he was. Standing in the door next to a tiny, shrunken old man, who was leaning on a cane. He was deeply wrinkled, skin the color of weathered mahogany, wearing grungy white trousers and a gray blanket draped around his shoulders. All his vitality seemed to have collected in an astounding shock of thick white hair that—to Lisa's drunken eyes—looked like a white flame licking up from his skull.

It took the old man almost a minute to hobble the length of the room, and a considerable time thereafter to lower himself, wheezing and shaking, into a chair. Dowdy hauled up another chair beside him; he had washed the dye from his beard, and his hair was clean, free of feathers. His manner, too, had changed. He was no longer breezy, but subdued and serious, and even his grammar had improved.

"Now listen," he said. "I don't know what Murcielago will say to you, but he's a man who speaks his mind and sometimes he tells people things they don't like to hear. Just remember he bears you no ill-will and don't be upset. All right?"

Lisa gave the old man a reassuring smile, not wanting him to think that they were going to laugh; but upon meeting his eyes all thought of reassuring him vanished. They were ordinary eyes. Dark, wet-looking under the lamplight. And yet they were compelling—like an animal's eyes, they radiated strangeness and pulled you in. They made the rest of his ruined face seem irrelevant. He muttered to Dowdy.

"He wants to know if you have any questions," said Dowdy.

Richard was apparently as fascinated by the old man as was Lisa; she had expected him to be glib and sardonic, but instead he cleared his throat and said gravely, "I'd like to hear about how the world's changing."

Dowdy repeated the question in Cakchiquel, and Murcielago began to speak, staring at Richard, his voice a gravelly whisper. At last he made a slashing gesture, signaling that he was finished, and Dowdy turned to them. "It's like this," he said. "The world is not one but many. Thousands upon thousands of worlds. Even those who do not have the power of clear sight can perceive this if they consider the myriad realities of the world they do see. It's easiest to imagine the thousands of worlds as different-colored lights all focused on a single point, having varying degrees of effectiveness as to how much part they play in determinin' the character of that point. What's happenin' now is that the strongest light—the one most responsible for determinin' this character—is startin' to fade and another is startin' to shine bright and dominate. When it has gained dominance, the old age will end and the new begin."

Richard smirked, and Lisa realized that he had been putting the old man on. "If that's the case," he said snottily, "then . . ."

Murcielago broke in with a burst of harsh, angry syllables.

"He doesn't care if you believe him," said Dowdy. "Only that you understand his words. Do you?"

"Yes." Richard mulled it over. "Ask him what the character of the new age will be."

Again, the process of interpretation.

"It'll be the first age of magic," said Dowdy. "You see, all the old tales of wizards and great beasts and warriors and undyin' kings, they aren't fantasy or even fragments of a distant past. They're visions, the first unclear glimpses seen long ago of a future that's now dawnin'. This place, Lake Atitlán, is one of those where the dawn has come early, where the light

of the new age shines the strongest and its forms are visible to
those who can see." The old man spoke again, and Dowdy
arched an eyebrow. "Hmm! He says that because he's tellin'
you this, and for reasons not yet clear to him, you will be
more a part of the new age than the old."

Richard gave Lisa a nudge under the table, but she chose to
ignore it. "Why hasn't someone noticed this change?" he
asked.

Dowdy translated and in a moment had a response. "Murcielago says he has noticed it, and asks if you have not noticed
it yourself. For instance, have you not noticed the increased
interest in magic and other occult matters in your own land?
And surely you must have noticed the breakdown of systems,
economies, governments. This is due to the fact that the light
that empowered them is fadin', not to any other cause. The
change comes slowly. The dawn will take centuries to brighten
into day, and then the sorrows of this age will be gone from
the memories of all but those few who have the ability to draw
upon the dawnin' power and live long in their mortal bodies.
Most will die and be reborn. The change comes subtly, as
does twilight change to dusk, an almost imperceptible merging of light into dark. It will be noticed and it will be recorded. Then, just as the last age, it will be forgotten."

"I don't mean to be impertinent," said Richard, giving Lisa
another nudge, "but Murcielago looks pretty frail. He can't
have much of a role to play in all this."

The old man rapped the floor with his cane for emphasis as
he answered, and Dowdy's tone was peeved. "Murcielago is
involved in great struggles against enemies whose nature he's
only beginnin' to discern. He has no time to waste with fools.
But because you're not a total fool, because you need instruction, he will answer. Day by day his power grows, and at
night the volcano is barely able to contain his force. Soon he
will shed this fraility and flow between the forms of his spirit.
He will answer no more of your questions." Dowdy looked to
Lisa. "Do you have a question?"

Murcielago's stare burned into her, and she felt disoriented, as insubstantial as one of the gleams slipping across
his eyes. "I don't know," she said. "Yes. What does he think
about us?"

"This is a good question," said Dowdy after consulting

with Murcielago, "because it concerns self-knowledge, and all important answers relate to the self. I will not tell you what you are. You know that, and you have shame in the knowledge. What you will be is manifest, and soon you will know that. Therefore I will answer the question you have not asked, the one that most troubles you. You and the man will part and come together, part and come together. Many times. For though you are lovers, you are not true companions and you both must follow your own ways. I will help you in this. I will free the hooks that tear at you and give you back your natures. And when this is done, you and the man may share each other, may part and come together without sadness or weakness."

Murcielago fumbled for something under his blanket, and Dowdy glanced back and forth between Richard and Lisa. "He wants to make you a gift," he said.

"What kind of gift?" asked Richard.

"A gift is not known by its name," Dowdy reminded him. "But it won't be a mystery for long."

The old man muttered again and stretched out a trembling hand to Richard; in his palm were four black seeds.

"You must swallow them one at a time," said Dowdy. "And as you do, he will channel his power through them."

Richard's face tightened with suspicion. "It's some sort of drug, right? Take four and I won't care what happens."

Dowdy reverted to his ungrammatical self. "Life is a drug, man. You think me and the ol' boy are gonna get you high and boost your traveler's checks. Shit! You ain't thinkin' clear."

"Maybe that's exactly what you're going to do," said Richard stonily. "And I'm not falling for it."

Lisa slipped her hand into his. "They're not going to hurt us. Why don't you try it?"

"You believe this old fraud, don't you?" He disengaged his hand, looking betrayed. "You believe what he said about us?"

"I'd like to believe it," she said. "It would be better than what we have, wouldn't it?"

The lamplight flickered, and a shadow veered across his face. Then the light steadied, and so it seemed did he. It was as if the orange glow were burning away eleven years of wrong-thinking, and the old unparanoid, sure-of-himself Richard was shining through. Christ, she wanted to say, you're really in there!

"Aw, hell! He who steals my purse steals only forty cents on the dollar, right?" He plucked the seeds from Murcielago's hand, picked one up and held it to his mouth. "Anytime."

Before letting Richard swallow the seeds, Murcielago sang for a while. The song made Lisa think of a comic fight in a movie, the guy carrying on a conversation in between ducking and throwing punches, packing his words into short, rushed phrases. Murcielago built it to a fierce rhythm, signaled Richard, and grunted each time a seed went down, putting—Lisa thought—some magical English on it.

"God!" said Richard afterward, eyes wide with mock awe. "I had no idea! The colors, the infinite harmony! If only. . ." He broke it off and blinked, as if suddenly waking to an unaccustomed thought.

Murcielago smiled and gave out with a growly, humming noise that Lisa assumed was a sign of satisfaction. "Where are mine?" she asked.

"It's different for you," said Dowdy. "He has to anoint you, touch you."

At this juncture Richard would normally have cracked a joke about dirty old men but he was gazing out the window at shadowy figures on the street. She asked if he were okay, and he patted her hand. "Yeah, don't worry. I'm just thinking."

Murcielago had pulled out a bottle of iodine-colored liquid and was dipping his fingers into it, wetting the tips. He began to sing again—a softer, less hurried song with the rhythm of fading echoes—and Dowdy had Lisa lean forward so the old man wouldn't have to strain to reach her. The song seemed to be all around her, turning her thoughts slow and drifty. Calloused brown fingers trembled in front of her face; the callouses were split, and the splits crusted with grime. She shut her eyes. The fingers left wet, cool tracks on her skin, and she could feel the shape he was tracing. A mask. Widening her eyes, giving her a smile, drawing curlicues on her cheeks and forehead. She had the idea that he was tracing the conformation of her real face, doing what the lamplight had done for Richard. Then his fingers brushed her eyelids. There was a stinging sensation, and dazzles exploded behind her eyes.

"Keep 'em shut," advised Dowdy. "It'll pass."

When at last she opened them, Dowdy was helping Murcielago to his feet. The old man nodded but did not smile at her as he had with Richard; from the thinned set of his mouth she took it that he was either measuring her or judging his work.

"That's all folks!" said Dowdy, grinning. "See? No dirty tricks, nothin' up his sleeve. Just good ol' new-fangled, stick-to-your-soul magic." He waved his arms high like an evangelist. "Can you feel it, brothers and sisters? Feel it wormin' its way through your bones?"

Richard mumbled affirmatively. He seemed lost in himself, studying the pattern of rips his thumb had scraped on the label of the beer bottle, and Lisa was beginning to feel a bit lost herself. "Do we pay him anything?" she asked Dowdy; her voice sounded small and metallic, like a recorded message.

"There'll come a day when the answer's yes," said Dowdy. "But not now." The old man hobbled toward the door, Dowdy guiding him by the arm.

"Goodbye," called Lisa, alarmed by their abrupt exit.

"Yeah," said Dowdy over his shoulder, paying more attention to assisting Murcielago. "See ya."

They were mostly silent while waiting for the launch, limiting their conversation to asking how the other was doing and receiving distracted answers; and later, aboard the launch, the black water shining under the stars and the motor racketing, their silence deepened. They sat with their hips pressed together, and Lisa felt close to Richard; yet she also felt that the closeness wasn't important; or if it was, it was of memorial importance, a tribute to past closeness, because things were changing between them. That, too, she could feel. Old postures were being redefined, webs were tearing loose, shadowy corners of their souls were coming to light. She knew this was happening to Richard as well as herself, and she wondered how she knew, whether it was her gift to know these things. But the first real inkling she had of her gift was when she noticed that the stars were shining different colors—red, yellow, blue, and white—and there were pale gassy shapes passing across them. Clouds, she realized. Very high clouds that she would not ordinarily have seen. The sight frightened her, but a calm presence inside her would not admit to fright; and this presence, she further realized, had been there all along. Just like the true colors of the stars. It was her fearful self that was relatively new, an obscuring factor, and it—like the clouds—was passing. She considered telling Richard, but decided that he would be busy deciphering *his* gift. She concentrated on her own, and as they walked from the pier to the hotel, she saw halos around leaves, gleams coursing along electrical wires, and opaque films shifting over people's faces.

They went straight up to their room and lay without talking in the dark. But the room wasn't dark for Lisa. Pointillistic fires bloomed and faded in mid-air, seams of molten light spread along the cracks in the wall, and once a vague human shape—she identified it as a ghostly man wearing robes—crossed from the door to the window and vanished. Every piece of furniture began to glow golden around the edges, brighter and brighter, until it seemed they each had a more ornate shape superimposed. There came to be so much light that it disconcerted her, and though she was unafraid, she wished she could have a moment's normalcy just to get her bearings. And her wish was granted. In a wink the room had reverted to dim bulky shadows and a rectangle of streetlight slanting onto the floor from the window. She sat bolt upright, astonished that it could be controlled with such ease. Richard pulled her back down beside him and asked, "What is it?" She told him some of what she had seen, and he said, "It sounds like hallucinations."

"No, that's not how it feels," she said. "How about you?"

"I'm not hallucinating, anyway. I feel restless, penned in, and I keep thinking that I'm going somewhere. I mean, I have this sense of motion, of speed, and I can almost tell where I am and who's with me. I'm full of energy; it's like I'm sixteen again or something." He paused. "And I'm having these thoughts that ought to scare me but don't."

"What, for instance?"

"For instance"—he laughed—"and this really the most important 'for instance', I'll be thinking about us and I'll understand that what the old guy said about us parting is true, and I don't want to accept it. But I can't help accepting it. I know it's true, for the best. All that. And then I'll have this feeling of motion again. It's like I'm sensing the shape of an event or . . ." He shook his head, befuddled. "Maybe they did drug us, Lisa. We sound like a couple of acidheads out of the Sixties."

"I don't think so," she said; and then, after a silence, she asked, "Do you want to make love?"

He trailed his fingers along the curve of her stomach. "No offense, but I'm not sure I could concentrate on it just now."

"All right. But . . ."

He rolled onto his side and pressed against her, his breath warm on her cheeks. "You think we might not have another chance?"

Embarrassed, she turned her face into his chest. "I'm just horny is all."

"God, Lisa. You pick the weirdest times to get aroused."

"You've picked some pretty weird times yourself."

"I've always been absolutely correct in my behavior toward you, madam," he said in an English accent.

"Really? What about the time in Jim and Karen's bathroom?"

"I was drunk."

"Well? I'm nervous now. You know how that affects me."

"A common glandular condition, fraulein." German accent this time. "Correctable by simple surgery." He laughed and dropped the accent. "I wonder what Karen and Jim would be doing in our shoes."

For a while they told stories about what their various friends might do, and afterward they lay quietly, arms around each other. Richard's heart jolted against Lisa's breast, and she thought back to the first time they had been together this way. How protected she had felt, yet how fragile the strength of his heartbeat had made him seem. She'd had the idea that she could reach into his chest and touch his heart. And she could have. You had that much power over your lover; his heart was in your care, and at moments like this it was easy to believe that you would always be caring. But the moments failed you. They were peaks, and from them you slid into a mire where caring dissolved into mistrust and selfishness, where you saw that your feeling of being protected was illusory, and the moments were few and far-between. Marriage sought to institutionalize those moments, by law, to butter them over a ridiculous number of years; but all it did was lessen their intensity and open you up to a new potential for failure. Everyone talked about "good marriages," ones that evolved into hallowed friendships, an emeritus passion of the spirit. Maybe they did exist. Maybe there were—as Murcielago had implied—true companions. But most of the old marrieds Lisa had known were simply exhausted, weary of struggling, and had reached an accommodation with their mates based upon mutual despair. If Murcielago were right, if the world were changing, possibly the condition of marriage would change. Lisa doubted it, though. Hearts would have to be changed as well, and not even magic could affect their basic nature. Like with seashells, you could put your ear to one and hear the sad truth of an ocean breaking on a deserted shore. They were always empty, always unfulfilled. *Deeds fill them,* said an almost-voice inside her head, and she almost knew whose voice it had been; she pushed the knowledge aside, wanting to hold onto the moment.

Somebody shrieked in the courtyard. Not unusual. Groups of people frequently hung around the courtyard at night, smoking dope and exchanging bits of travel lore; the previous night two French girls and an American boy had been fighting with water pistols, and the girls had shrieked whenever they were hit. But this time the shriek was followed by shouts in Spanish and in broken English, a scream of pure terror, then silence. Richard sprang to his feet and cracked the door. Lisa moved up behind him. Another shout in Spanish—she recognized the word *doctor*. Richard put a finger to his lips and slipped out into the hall. Together they edged along the wall and peeked down into the courtyard. About a dozen guests were standing against the rear wall, some with their hands in the air; facing them, carrying automatic rifles, were three young men and a girl. Teenagers. Wearing jeans and polo shirts. A fourth man lay on the ground, his hands and head swathed in bandages. The guests were very pale—at this distance their eyes looked like raisins in uncooked dough—and a couple of the women were sobbing. One of the gunmen was wounded, a patch of blood staining his side; he was having to lean on the girl's shoulder, and his rifle barrel was wavering back and forth. With all the ferns sprouting around them, the pots of flowers hanging from the green stucco wall, the scene had an air of mythic significance—a chance meeting between good and evil in the Garden of Eden.

"Sssst!" A hiss behind Lisa's shoulder. It was the Guatemalan man who had watched her during dinner the night before; he had a machine pistol in one hand, and in the other he was flapping a leather card case. ID. He beckoned, and they moved after him down the hall. *"Policia!"* he whispered, displaying the ID; in the photograph he was younger, his mustache so black it appeared to have been painted on for a joke. His nervous eyes and baggy suit and five o'clock shadow reminded Lisa of 1940s movie heavies, the evil flunky out to kill George Sanders or Humphrey Bogart; but the way his breath whined through his nostrils, the oily smell of the gun, his radiation of callous stupidity, all that reduced her romantic impression. *"Malos!"* he said, pointing to the courtyard. *"Communistas! Guerrillas!"* He patted the gun barrel.

"Okay," said Richard, holding up both hands to show his neutrality, his non-involvement. But as the man crept toward the courtyard, toward the balcony railing, Richard locked his hands together and brought them down on the back of the man's neck, then fell atop him, kneeing and pummeling him. Lisa was frozen by the attack, half-disbelieving that Richard was capable of such decisive action. He scrambled to his feet, breathing hard, and tossed the machine pistol down into the courtyard, "Amigos!" he shouted, and turned to Lisa, his mouth still open from the shout.

Their eyes met, and that stare was a divorce, an acknowledgement that something was happening to separate them, happening right now, and though they weren't exactly sure what, they were willing to accept the fact and allow it to happen. "I couldn't let him shoot," said Richard. "I didn't have a choice." He sounded amazed, as if he hadn't known until this moment why he had acted.

Lisa wanted to console him, to tell him he'd done the right thing, but her emotions were locked away, under restraint, and she sensed a gulf between them that nothing could bridge—all their intimate connections were withdrawing, receding. Hooks, Murcielago had called them.

One of the guerrillas, the girl, was sneaking up the stairs, gun at the ready. She was pretty but on the chubby side, with shiny wings of black hair falling over her shoulders. She motioned for them to move back and nudged the unconscious man with her toe. He moaned, his hand twitched. "You?" she said, pointing at Richard and then to the man.

"He was going to shoot," said Richard hollowly.

From the girl's blank expression Lisa could tell that she hadn't understood. She rummaged in the man's jacket, pulled out the ID case and shouted in rapid-fire Spanish. *"Vamanos!"* she said to them, indicating that they should precede her down the stairs. As Lisa started down there was a short burst of automatic fire from the hall; startled, she turned to see the girl lifting the barrel of her rifle from the man's head, a stippling of red droplets on the green stucco. The girl frowned and trained the rifle on her, and Lisa hurried after Richard, horrified. But before her emotional reaction could mature into fear, her vision began to erode.

Glowing white flickers were edging every figure in the room, with the exception of the bandaged man, and as they grew clearer, she realized that they were phantom human shapes; they were like the afterimages of movement you see on benzedrine, yet sharper and slower to fade, and the movements were different from those of their originals—an arm flailing, a half-formed figure falling or running off. Each time one vanished another would take its place. She tried to banish them, to will them away, but was unsuccessful, and she found that watching them distracted her from thinking about the body upstairs.

The tallest of the guerrillas—a gangly kid with a skull face and huge dark eyes and a skimpy mustache—entered into conversation with the girl, and Richard dropped to his knees beside the bandaged man. Blood had seeped through the layers of wrapping, producing a grotesque striping around the man's head. The gangly kid scowled and prodded Richard with his rifle.

"I'm a medic," Richard told him. *"Como un doctor."* Gingerly, he peeled back some layers of bandage and looked away, his face twisted in disgust. "Jesus Christ!"

"The soldiers torture him." The kid spat into the ferns. "They think he is *guerrillero,* because he's my cousin."

"And is he?" Richard was probing for a pulse under the bandaged man's jaw.

"No." The kid leaned over Richard's shoulder. "He studies at San Carlos University. But because we have killed the soldiers, now he will have to fight." Richard sighed, and the kid faltered. "It is good you are here. We think a friend is here, a

doctor. But he's gone." He made a gesture toward the street.
"Pasado."

Richard stood and cleaned his fingers on his jeans. "He's
dead."

One of the women who had been sobbing let out a wail,
and the kid snapped his rifle into firing position and shouted,
"Cayete, gringa!" His face was stony, the vein in his temple
throbbed. A balding, bearded man wearing an embroidered
native shirt embraced the woman, muting her sobs, and glared
fiercely at the kid; one of his afterimages raised a fist. The rest
of the imprisoned guests were terrified, their Adam's apples
working, eyes darting about; and the girl was arguing with the
kid, pushing his rifle down. He kept shaking her off. Lisa felt
detached from the tension, out of phase with existence, as if
she were gazing down from a higher plane.

With what seemed foolhardy bravado, the bearded guy
called out to Richard. "Hey, you! The American! You with
these people or somethin'?"

Richard had squatted beside the wounded guerrilla—a boy
barely old enough to shave—and was probing his side. "Or
something," he said without glancing up. The boy winced and
gritted his teeth and leaned on his friend, a boy not much
older.

"You gonna let 'em kill us?" said the bearded guy. "That's
what's happenin', y'know. The girl's sayin' to let us go, but
the dude's tellin' her he wants to make a statement." Panic
seeped into his voice. "Y'understand that, man? The dude's
lookin' to waste us so he can make a statement."

"Take it easy." Richard got to his feet. "The bullet needs to
come out," he said to the gangly kid. "I . . ."

The kid swiped at Richard's head with the rifle barrel, and
Richard staggered back, clutching his brow; when he straightened up, Lisa saw blood welling from his hairline. "Your
friend's going to die," he said stubbornly. "The bullet needs to
come out." The kid jammed the muzzle of the rifle into Richard's throat, forcing him to tip back his head.

With a tremendous effort of will Lisa shook off the fog that
had enveloped her. The afterimages vanished. "He's trying to
help you," she said, going toward the kid. "Don't you understand?" The girl pushed her back and aimed her rifle at Lisa's
stomach. Looking into her eyes, Lisa had an intimation of the

depth of her seriousness, the ferocity of her commitment. "He's trying to help," Lisa repeated. The girl studied her, and after a moment she called over her shoulder to the kid. Some of the hostility drained from the kid's face and was replaced by suspicion.

"Why?" the kid asked Richard. "Why you help us?"

Richard seemed confused, and then he started to laugh; he wiped his forehead with the back of his hand, smearing the blood and sweat, and laughed some more. The kid was puzzled at first, but a few seconds later he smiled and nodded as if he and Richard were sharing a secret male joke. "Okay," he said. "Okay. You help him. But here is danger. We go now."

"Yeah," said Richard, absorbing this. "Yeah, okay." He stepped over to Lisa and drew her into a smothering hug. She gripped his shoulders hard, and she thought her emotions were going to break free; but when he stepped back, appearing stunned, she sensed again that distance between them. . . . He put his arm around the wounded boy and helped him through the entrance; the others were already peering out the door. Lisa followed. The rows of tourist shops and restaurants looked unreal—a deserted stage set—and the colors seemed streaky and too bright. Parked under a streetlight near the entrance, gleaming toylike in the yellow glare, was a Suzuki mini-truck, the kind with a canvas-draped frame over the rear. Beyond it the road wound away into darkened hills. The girl vaulted the tailgate and hauled the wounded boy after her; the other two climbed into the cab and fired the engine. Only Richard was left standing on the cobblestones.

"Dase prisa!" The girl banged on the tailgate.

As Richard hesitated there was a volley of shots. The noise sent Lisa scuttling away from the entrance toward the lake. Three policemen were behind a parked car on the opposite side of the street. More shots. The girl returned their fire, blowing out the windshield of the car, and they ducked out of sight. Another shot. Sparks and stone chips were kicked up near Richard's feet. Still he hesitated.

"Richard!" Lisa had intended the shout as a caution, but the name floated out of her, not desperate-sounding at all—it had the ring of an assurance. He dove for the tailgate. The girl helped him scramble inside, and the truck sped off over the first rise. The policemen ran after it, firing; then, like Keystone Kops, they put on the brakes and ran in the opposite direction.

Lisa had a flash-feeling of anguish that almost instantly began to subside, as if it had been the freakish firing of a nerve. Dazedly, she moved further away from the hotel entrance. A jeep stuffed with policemen came swerving past, but she hardly noticed. The world was dissolving in golden light, every source of light intensifying and crumbling the outlines of things. Streetlights burned like novas, sunbursts shone from windows, and even the cracks in the sidewalk glowed; misty shapes were fading into view, overlaying the familiar with tall, peak-roofed houses and carved wagons and people dressed in robes. All rippling, illusory. It was as if a fantastic illustration were coming to life, and she was the only real-life character left in the story, a contemporary Alice with designer jeans and turquoise earrings, who had been set to wander through a golden fairytale. She was entranced, and yet at the same time she resented the fact that the display was cheating her of the right to sadness. She needed to sort herself out, and she continued toward the lake, toward the pier where she and Richard had kissed. By the time she reached it, the lake itself had been transformed into a scintillating body of light and out on the water the ghost of a sleek sailboat, its canvas belling, glided past for an instant and was gone.

She sat at the end of the pier, dangling her feet over the edge. The cool roughness of the planks was a comfort, a proof against the strangeness of the world . . . or was it *worlds?* The forms of the new age. Was that what she saw? Weary of seeing it, she willed the light away and before she could register whether or not she had been successful, she shut her eyes and tried to think about Richard. And, as if thought were a vehicle for sight, she saw him. A ragged-eyed patch of vision appeared against the darkness of her closed eyes, like a hole punched through black boards. He was sitting on the oil-smeared floor of the truck, cradling the wounded boy's head in his lap; the girl was bending over the boy, mopping his forehead, holding onto Richard's shoulder so the bouncing of the truck wouldn't throw her off-balance. Lisa felt a pang of jealousy, but she kept watching for a very long time. She didn't wonder how she saw them. It all meant something, and she knew that meaning would come clear.

When she opened her eyes, she found it had grown pitch-dark. She couldn't see her hand in front of her face and she panicked, thinking she had gone blind; but accompanying the panic was a gradual brightening, and she realized that she must have willed away all light. Soon the world had returned to normal. Almost. Though the slopes of the volcanos were unlighted—shadows bulking against the stars—above each of their cones blazed a nimbus of ruby glow, flickering with an inconstant rhythm. The glow above Murcielago's volcano was the brightest—at least it was for a few seconds. Then it faded, and in its place a fan of rippling white radiance sprayed from the cone, penetrating high into the dark. It was such an eerie sight, she panicked. Christ, what was she doing just sitting here and watching pretty lights? And what was she going to do? Insecurity and isolation combined into an electricity that jolted her to her feet. Maybe there was an antidote for this, maybe the thing to do would be to go see Murcielago . . . And she remembered Dowdy's story. How he'd been afraid and had gone to Murcielago, only to find that the old apprentice had taken up his own post, leaving a vacancy. She looked back at the other two volcanos, still pulsing with their ruby glow. Dowdy and the mestizo? It had to be. The white light was Murcielago's vacancy sign. The longer she stared at it, the more certain that knowledge became.

Stunned by the prospect of setting out on such an eccentric course, by the realization that everything she knew was dissolving in light or fleeing into darkness, she walked away from the pier, following the shoreline. She wanted to hold onto Richard, to sadness—her old familiar and their common woe—but with each step her mood brightened, and she couldn't even feel guilty about not being sad. Four or five hours would take her to the far side of the lake. A long walk, alone, in the dark, hallucinations lurking behind every bush. She could handle it, though. It would give her time to work at controlling her vision, to understand some of what she saw, and when she had climbed the volcano she'd find a rickety cabin back in under the lip, a place as quirky as Dowdy himself. She saw it the same way she had seen Richard and the girl. Tilting walls; ferns growing from the roof; a door made from the side of a packing crate, with the legend THIS END UP upside down. Tacked to the door was a piece of paper, probably Dowdy's note explaining the care and feeding of wizards. And inside, the thousandfold forms of his spirit compacted into a gnarled shape, a nugget of power (she experienced an upwelling of sadness, and then she felt that power surging through her, nourishing her own strength, making her aware of the thousands of bodies of light she was, all focused upon this moment in her flesh), there Murcielago would be waiting to teach her power's usage and her purpose in the world. *Oh, God, Richard, goodbye.*

THE PEACEMAKER

by Gardner Dozois

The appearance of "The Peacemaker" in these pages is somewhat embarassing to me, since an anthologist who includes his own work in his own anthology is leaving himself wide-open to charges of shooting fish in a barrel. My original impulse, therefore, was to leave "The Peacemaker" out of this anthology, but, after some argument, I am bowing to pressure from Isaac, Sheila Williams, Shawna, Susan Allison, Cynthia Manson, and others, and am, somewhat reluctantly, putting it in the book after all. So, it is All Their Fault. Nevertheless, I'm sure I'll get letters, and I'll just have to hope that the fact that the story was an important one for the magazine is enough to justify its inclusion.

"The Peacemaker" was purchased by Shawna McCarthy, and appeared in the August 1983 issue of IAsfm, with an evocative cover by Val Lakey and a beautiful interior illustration by Bob Walters. It won the Nebula Award for 1983, and was also a Hugo Finalist that year.

In addition to editing IAsfm, I am the author or editor of twenty-two books, including the novel **Strangers**

33

and the short-story collection The Visible Man. *I am also
the editor of the annual anthology series* The Year's Best
Science Fiction, *from St. Martin's Press, and, with Jack
Dann, of the "Magic Tales" anthology series, from Ace.
My most recent books are* The Year's Best Science Fic-
tion, Fourth Annual Collection, *and, with Jack Dann, the
anthologies* Sorcerers! *and* Demons! *My story "Morning
Child" won another Nebula in 1984.*

Roy had dreamed of the sea, as he often did. When he woke
up that morning, the wind was sighing through the trees outside with a sound like the restless murmuring of surf, and for a
moment he thought that he was home, back in the tidy brick
house by the beach, with everything that had happened un-
done, and hope opened hotly inside him, like a wound.

"Mom?" he said. He sat up, straightening his legs, expect-
ing his feet to touch the warm mass that was his dog, Toby.
Toby always slept curled at the foot of his bed, but already
everything was breaking up and changing, slipping away, and
he blinked through sleep-gummed eyes at the thin blue light
coming in through the attic window, felt the hardness of the
old Army cot under him, and realized that he wasn't home,
that there was no home anymore, that for him there could
never be a home again.

He pushed the blankets aside and stood up. It was bitterly
cold in the big attic room—winter was dying hard, the most
terrible winter he could remember—and the rough wood
planking burned his feet like ice, but he couldn't stay in bed
anymore, not now.

None of the other kids were awake yet; he threaded his way
through the other cots—accidently bumping against one of
them so that its occupant tossed and moaned and began to
snore in a higher register—and groped through cavernous
shadows to the single high window. He was just tall enough to
reach it, if he stood on tiptoe. He forced the window open, the
old wood of its frame groaning in protest, plaster dust puffing,
and shivered as the cold dawn wind poured inward, hitting
him in the face, tugging with ghostly fingers at his hair,

sweeping past him to rush through the rest of the stuffy attic like a restless child set free to play.

The wind smelled of pine resin and wet earth, not of salt flats and tides, and the bird-sound that rode in on that wind was the burbling of wrens and the squawking of bluejays, not the raucous shrieking of seagulls ... but even so, as he braced his elbows against the window frame and strained up to look out, his mind still full of the broken fragments of dreams, he half-expected to see the ocean below, stretched out to the horizon, sending patient wavelets to lap against the side of the house. Instead he saw the nearby trees holding silhouetted arms up against the graying sky, the barn and the farmyard, all still lost in shadow, the surrounding fields, the weathered macadam line of the road, the forested hills rolling away into distance. Silver mist lay in pockets of low ground, retreated in wraithlike streamers up along the ridges.

Not yet. The sea had not chased him here—yet.

Somewhere out there to the east, still invisible, were the mountains, and just beyond those mountains was the sea that he had dreamed of, lapping quietly at the dusty Pennsylvania hill towns, coal towns, that were now, suddenly, seaports. There the Atlantic waited, held at bay, momentarily at least, by the humpbacked wall of the Appalachians, still perhaps forty miles from here, although closer now by leagues of swallowed land and drowned cities than it had been only three years before.

He had been down by the seawall that long-ago morning, playing some forgotten game, watching the waves move in slow oily swells, like some heavy, dull metal in liquid form, watching the tide come in ... and come in ... and come in. ... He had been excited at first, as the sea crept in, way above the high-tide line, higher than he had ever seen it before, and then, as the sea swallowed the beach entirely and began to lap patiently against the base of the seawall, he had become uneasy, and *then*, as the sea continued to rise up toward the top of the seawall itself, he had begun to be afraid. ... The sea had just kept coming in, rising slowly and inexorably, swallowing the land at a slow walking pace, never stopping, always coming *in*, always rising higher. ... By the time the sea had swallowed the top of the seawall and begun to creep up the short grassy slope toward his house, sending glassy fingers probing almost to his feet, he had started to scream, and as the first thin sheet of water rippled up to soak his sneakers, he had whirled and run frantically up the slope, screaming hysterically for his parents, and the sea had followed patiently at his heels. . . .

A "marine transgression," the scientists called it. Ordinary people called it, inevitably, the Flood. Whatever you called it, it had washed away the old world forever. Scientists had been talking about the possibility of such a thing for years—some of them even pointing out that it was already as warm as it had been at the peak of the last interglacial, and getting warmer—but few had suspected just how *fast* the Antarctic ice could melt. Many times during those chaotic weeks, one scientific King Canute or another had predicted that the worst was over, that the tide would rise this high and no higher . . . but each time the sea had come inexorably on, pushing miles and miles further inland with each successive high-tide, rising almost 300 feet in the course of one disastrous summer, drowning lowlands around the globe until there *were* no lowlands anymore. In the United States alone, the sea had swallowed most of the East Coast east of the Appalachians, the West Coast west of the Sierras and the Cascades, much of Alaska and Hawaii, Florida, the Gulf Coast, East Texas, taken a big wide scoop out of the lowlands of the Mississippi Valley, thin fingers of water penetrating north to Iowa and Illinois, and caused the St. Lawrence and the Great Lakes to overflow and drown their shorelines. The Green Mountains, the White Mountains, the Adirondacks, the Poconos and the Catskills, the Ozarks, the Pacific Coast Ranges—all had been transformed to archipelagos, surrounded by the invading sea.

The funny thing was . . . that as the sea pursued them relentlessly inland, pushing them from one temporary refuge to another, he had been unable to shake the feeling that *he* had caused the Flood: that he had done something that day while playing atop the seawall, inadvertently stumbled on some magic ritual, some chance combination of gesture and word that had untied the bonds of the sea and sent it sliding up over the land . . . that it was chasing *him*, personally. . . .

A dog was barking out there now, somewhere out across the fields toward town, but it was not *his* dog. His dog was dead, long since dead, and its whitening skull was rolling along the ocean floor with the tides that washed over what had once been Brigantine, New Jersey, three hundred feet down.

Suddenly he was covered with gooseflesh, and he shivered, rubbing his hands over his bare arms. He returned to his cot and dressed hurriedly—no point in trying to go back to bed, Sara would be up to kick them all out of the sack in a minute or two anyway. The day had begun; he would think no further ahead than that. He had learned in the refugee camps to take life one second at a time.

As he moved around the room, he thought that he could feel hostile eyes watching him from some of the other bunks. It was much colder in here now that he had opened the window, and he had inevitably made a certain amount of noise getting dressed, but although they all valued every second of sleep they could scrounge, none of the other kids would dare to complain. The thought was bittersweet, bringing both pleasure and pain, and he smiled at it, a thin, brittle smile that was almost a grimace. No, they would watch sullenly from their bunks, and pretend to be asleep, and curse him under their breath, but they would say nothing to anyone about it. Certainly they would say nothing to *him*.

He went down through the still-silent house like a ghost, and out across the farmyard, through fugitive streamers of mist that wrapped clammy white arms around him and beaded his face with dew. His uncle Abner was there at the slit-trench before him. Abner grunted a greeting, and they stood pissing side by side for a moment in companionable silence, their urine steaming in the gray morning air.

Abner stepped backward and began to button his pants. "You start playin' with yourself yet, boy?" he said, not looking at Roy.

Roy felt his face flush. "No," he said, trying not to stammer, "no sir."

"You growin' hair already," Abner said. He swung himself slowly around to face Roy, as if his body was some ponderous machine that could only be moved and aimed by the use of pulleys and levers. The hard morning light made his face look harsh as stone, but also sallow and old. Tired, Roy thought. Unutterably weary, as though it took almost more effort than he could sustain just to stand there. Worn out, like the over-taxed fields around them. Only the eyes were alive in the eroded face; they were hard and merciless as flint, and they looked at you as if they were looking right through you to some distant thing that nobody else could see. "I've tried to explain to you about remaining pure," Abner said, speaking slowly. "About how important it is for you to keep yourself pure, not to let yourself be sullied in any way. I've tried to explain that, I hope you could understand—"

"Yes, sir," Roy said.

Abner made a groping hesitant motion with his hand, fingers spread wide, as though he were trying to sculpt meaning from the air itself. "I mean—it's important that you understand, Roy. Everything has to be *right*. I mean, everything's got to be just . . . *right* . . . or nothing else will mean anything. You got to be right in your *soul,* boy. You got to let the Peace of God into your soul. It all depends on *you* now—you got to let that Peace inside yourself, no one can do it for you. And it's so important . . ."

"Yes, sir," Roy said quietly, "I understand."

"I wish . . . ," Abner said, and fell silent. They stood there for a minute, not speaking, not looking at each other. There was wood-smoke in the air now, and they heard a door slam somewhere on the far side of the house. They had instinctively been looking out across the open land to the east, and now, as they watched, the sun rose above the mountains, splitting the plum-and-ash sky open horizontally with a long wedge of red, distinguishing the rolling horizon from the lowering clouds. A lance of bright white sunlight hit their eyes, thrusting straight in at them from the edge of the world.

"You're going to make us proud, boy, I know it," Abner said, but Roy ignored him, watching in fascination as the molten disk of the sun floated free of the horizon-line, squinting against the dazzle until his eyes watered and his sight blurred. Abner put his hand on the boy's shoulder. The hand felt heavy and hot, proprietary, and Roy shook it loose in annoyance, still not looking away from the horizon. Abner sighed, started to say something, thought better of it, and instead said, "Come on in the house, boy, and let's get some breakfast inside you."

Breakfast—when they finally did get to sit down to it, after the usual rambling grace and invocation by Abner—proved to be unusually lavish. For the brethren, there were hickory-nut biscuits, and honey, and cups of chicory, and even the other refugee kids—who on occasion during the long bitter winter had been fed as close to nothing at all as law and appearances would allow—got a few slices of fried fatback along with their habitual cornmeal mush. Along with his biscuits and honey, Roy got wild turkey eggs, Indian potatoes, and a real pork chop. There was a good deal of tension around the big table that morning: Henry and Luke were stern-faced and tense, Raymond was moody and preoccupied, Albert actually looked frightened; the refugee kids were round-eyed and silent, doing their best to make themselves invisible; the jolly Mrs. Crammer was as jolly as ever, shoveling her food in with gusto, but the grumpy Mrs. Zeigler, who was feared and disliked by all the kids, had obviously been crying, and ate little or nothing; Abner's face was set like rock, his eyes were hard and bright, and he looked from one to another of the brethren, as if daring them to question his leadership and spiritual guidance. Roy ate with good appetite, unperturbed by the emotional convection currents that were swirling around him, calmly but deliberately concentrating on mopping up every morsel of food on his plate—in the last couple of months he had put back some of the weight he had lost, although by the old standards, the ones his Mom would have applied four years ago, he was still painfully thin. At the end of the meal, Mrs. Reardon came in from the kitchen and, beaming with the well-justified pride of someone who is about to do the impossible, presented Roy with a small, rectangular object wrapped in shiny brown paper. He was startled for a second, but yes, by God, it *was:* a Hershey bar, the first one he'd seen in years. A black market item, of course, difficult to get hold of in the impoverished East these days, and probably expensive as hell. Even some of the brethren were looking at him enviously now, and the refugee kids were frankly gaping. As he picked up the Hershey bar and slowly and caressingly peeled the wrapper back, exposing the pale chocolate beneath, one of the other kids actually began to drool.

After breakfast, the other refugee kids—"wetbacks," the townspeople sometimes called them, with elaborate irony— were divided into two groups. One group would help the brethren work Abner's farm that day, while the larger group would be loaded onto an ox-drawn dray (actually an old flatbed truck, with the cab knocked off) and sent out around the countryside to do what pretty much amounted to slave labor: road work, heavy farm work, helping with the quarrying or the timbering, rebuilding houses and barns and bridges damaged or destroyed in the chaotic days after the Flood. The federal government—or what was left of the federal government, trying desperately, and not always successfully, to keep a battered and Balkanizing country from flying completely apart, struggling to put the Humpty Dumpty that was America back together again—the federal government paid Abner (and others like him) a yearly allowance in federal scrip or promise-of-merchandise notes for giving room and board to refugees from the drowned lands . . . but times being as tough as they were, no one was going to complain if Abner also helped ease the burden of their upkeep by hiring them out locally to work for whomever could come up with the scrip, or sufficient barter goods, or an attractive work-swap offer; what was left of the state and town governments also used them on occasion (and the others like them, adult or child), gratis, for work-projects "for the common good, during this time of emergency . . ."

Sometimes, hanging around the farm with little or nothing to do, Roy almost missed going out on the work-crews, but only almost: he remembered too well the back-breaking labor performed on scanty rations . . . the sickness, the accidents, the staggering fatigue . . . the blazing sun and the swarms of mosquitoes in summer, the bitter cold in winter, the snow, the icy wind . . . He watched the dray go by, seeing the envious and resentful faces of kids he had once worked beside—Stevie, Enrique, Sal—turn toward him as it passed, and, reflexively, he opened and closed his hands. Even two months of idleness and relative luxury had not softened the thick and roughened layers of callus that were the legacy of several seasons spent on the crews. . . . No, boredom was infinitely preferable.

By mid-morning, a small crowd of people had gathered in the road outside the farmhouse. It was hotter now; you could smell the promise of summer in the air, in the wind, and the sun that beat down out of a cloudless blue sky had a real sting to it. It must have been uncomfortable out there in the open, under that sun, but the crowd made no attempt to approach—

they just stood there on the far side of the road and watched the house, shuffling their feet, occasionally muttering to each other in voices that, across the road, were audible only as a low wordless grumbling.

Roy watched them for a while from the porch door; they were townspeople, most of them vaguely familiar to Roy, although none of them belonged to Abner's sect, and he knew none of them by name. The refugee kids saw little of the townspeople, being kept carefully segregated for the most part. The few times that Roy had gotten into town he had been treated with icy hostility—and God help the wetback kid who was caught by the town kids on a deserted stretch of road! For that matter, even the brethren tended to keep to themselves, and were snubbed by certain segments of town society, although the sect had increased its numbers dramatically in recent years, nearly tripling in strength during the past winter alone; there were new chapters now in several of the surrounding communities.

A gaunt-faced woman in the crowd outside spotted Roy, and shook a thin fist at him. "Heretic!" she shouted. "Blasphemer!" The rest of the crowd began to buzz ominously, like a huge angry bee. She spat at Roy, her face contorting and her shoulders heaving with the ferocity of her effort, although she must have known that the spittle had no chance of reaching him. "Blasphemer!" she shouted again. The veins stood out like cords in her scrawny neck.

Roy stepped back into the house, but continued to watch from behind the curtained front windows. There was shouting inside the house as well as outside—the brethren had been cloistered in the kitchen for most of the morning, arguing, and the sound and ferocity of their argument carried clearly through the thin plaster walls of the crumbling old house. At last the sliding door to the kitchen slammed open, and Mrs. Zeigler strode out into the parlor, accompanied by her two children and her scrawny, pasty-faced husband, and followed by two other families of brethren—about nine people altogether. Most of them were carrying suitcases, and a few had backpacks and bindles. Abner stood in the kitchen doorway and watched them go, his anger evident only in the whiteness of his knuckles as he grasped the doorframe. "*Go,* then," Abner said scornfully. "We spit you up out of our mouths!

Don't ever think to come back!" He swayed in the doorway, his voice tremulous with hate. "We're better off without you, you hear? You *hear* me? We don't *need* the weak-willed and the short-sighted."

Mrs. Zeigler said nothing, and her steps didn't slow or falter, but her homely hatchet-face was streaked with tears. To Roy's astonishment—for she had a reputation as a harridan—she stopped near the porch door and threw her arms around him. "Come with us," she said, hugging him with smothering tightness, "Roy, *please* come with us! You can, you know—we'll find a place for you, everything will work out fine." Roy said nothing, resisting the impulse to squirm—he was uncomfortable in her embrace; in spite of himself, it touched some sleeping corner of his soul he had thought was safely bricked-over years before, and for a moment he felt trapped and panicky, unable to breathe, as though he were in sudden danger of wakening from a comfortable dream into a far more terrible and less desirable reality. "Come *with* us," Mrs. Zeigler said again, more urgently, but Roy shook his head gently and pulled away from her. "You're a goddamned fool then!" she blazed, suddenly angry, her voice ringing harsh and loud, but Roy only shrugged, and gave her his wistful, ghostly smile. "Damn it—" she started to say, but her eyes filled with tears again, and she whirled and hurried out of the house, followed by the other members of her party. The children—wetbacks were kept pretty much segregated from the children of the brethren as well, and he had seen some of these kids only at meals—looked at Roy with wide, frightened eyes as they passed.

Abner was staring at Roy now, from across the room; it was a hard and challenging stare, but there was also a trace of desperation in it, and in that moment Abner seemed uncertain and oddly vulnerable. Roy stared back at him serenely, unblinkingly meeting his eyes, and after a while some of the tension went out of Abner, and he turned and stumbled out of the room, listing to one side like a church steeple in the wind.

Outside, the crowd began to buzz again as Mrs. Zeigler's party filed out of the house and across the road. There was much discussion and arm-waving and head-shaking when the two groups met, someone occasionally gesturing back toward the farmhouse. The buzzing grew louder, then gradually died away. At last, Mrs. Zeigler and her group set off down the road for town, accompanied by some of the locals. They trudged away dispiritedly down the center of the dusty road, lugging their shabby suitcases, only a few of them looking back.

Roy watched them until they were out of sight, his face still and calm, and continued to stare down the road after them long after they were gone.

About noon, a carload of reporters arrived outside, driving up in one of the bulky new methane-burners that were still rarely seen east of Omaha. They circulated through the crowd of townspeople, pausing briefly to take photographs and ask questions, working their way toward the house, and Roy watched them as if they were unicorns, strange remnants from some vanished cycle of creation. Most of the reporters were probably from State College or the new state capital at Altoona—places where a few small newspapers were again being produced—but one of them was wearing an armband that identified him as a bureau man for one of the big Denver papers, and that was probably where the money for the car had come from. It was strange to be reminded that there were still areas of the country that were . . . not unchanged, no place in the world could claim that . . . and not rich, not by the old standards of affluence anyway . . . but, at any rate, better off than *here*. The whole western part of the country—from roughly the 95th meridian on west to approximately the 122nd—had been untouched by the flooding, and although the west had also suffered severely from the collapse of the national economy and the consequent social upheavals, at least much of their industrial base had remained intact. Denver—one of the few large American cities built on ground high enough to have been safe from the rising waters—was the new federal capital, and, if poorer and meaner, it was also bigger and busier than ever.

Abner went out to herd the reporters inside and away from the unbelievers, and after a moment or two Roy could hear Abner's voice going out there, booming like a church organ. By the time the reporters came in, Roy was sitting at the dining room table, flanked by Raymond and Aaron, waiting for them.

They took photographs of him sitting there, while he stared calmly back at them, and they took photographs of him while he politely refused to answer questions, and then Aaron handed him the pre-prepared papers, and he signed them, and repeated the legal formulas that Aaron had taught him, and they took photographs of that, too. And then—able to get nothing more out of him, and made slightly uneasy by his blank composure and the remoteness of his eyes—they left.

Within a few more minutes, as though everything were over, as though the departure of the reporters had drained all possible significance from anything else that might still happen, most of the crowd outside had drifted away also, only one or two people remaining behind to stand quietly waiting, like vultures, in the once-again empty road.

Lunch was a quiet meal. Roy ate heartily, taking seconds of everything, and Mrs. Crammer was as jovial as ever, but everyone else was subdued, and even Abner seemed shaken by the schism that had just sundered his church. After the meal, Abner stood up and began to pray aloud. The brethren sat resignedly at the table, heads partially bowed, some listening, some not. Abner was holding his arms up toward the big blackened rafters of the ceiling, sweat runneling his face, when Peter came hurriedly in from outside and stood hesitating in the doorway, trying to catch Abner's eye. When it became obvious that Abner was going to keep right on ignoring him, Peter shrugged, and said in a loud flat voice, "Abner, the sheriff is here."

Abner stopped praying. He grunted, a hoarse, exhausted sound, the kind of sound a baited bear might make when, already pushed beyond the limits of endurance, someone jabs it yet again with a spear. He slowly lowered his arms and was still for a long moment, and then he shuddered, seeming to shake himself back to life. He glanced speculatively—and, it almost seemed, beseechingly—at Roy, and then straightened his shoulders and strode from the room.

They received the sheriff in the parlor, Raymond and Aaron and Mrs. Crammer sitting in the battered old armchairs, Roy sitting unobtrusively to one side of the stool from a piano that no longer worked, Abner standing a little to the fore with his arms locked behind him and his boots planted solidly on the oak planking, as if he were on the bridge of a schooner that was heading into a gale. County Sheriff Sam Braddock glanced at the others—his gaze lingering on Roy for a moment—and then ignored them, addressing himself to Abner as if they were alone in the room. "Mornin', Abner," he said.

"Mornin', Sam," Abner said quietly. "You here for some reason other than just t'say hello, I suppose."

Braddock grunted. He was a short, stocky, grizzled man with iron-gray hair and a tired face. His uniform was shiny and old and patched in a dozen places, but clean, and the huge old revolver strapped to his hip looked worn but serviceable. He fidgeted with his shapeless old hat, turning it around and around in his fingers—he was obviously embarrassed, but he was determined as well, and at last he said, "The thing of it is, Abner, I'm here to talk you out of this damned tomfoolery."

"Are you, now?" Abner said.

"We'll do whatever we damn well want to do—" Raymond burst out, shrilly, but Abner waved him to silence. Braddock glanced lazily at Raymond, then looked back at Abner, his tired old face settling into harder lines. "I'm not going to allow it," he said, most harshly. "We don't want this kind of thing going on in this county."

Abner said nothing.

"There's not a thing you can do about it, sheriff," Aaron said, speaking a bit heatedly, but keeping his melodious voice well under control. "It's all perfectly legal, all the way down the line."

"Well, now," Braddock said, "I don't know about that . . ."

"Well, I *do* know, sheriff," Aaron said calmly. "As a legally sanctioned and recognized church, we are protected by law all the way down the line. There is ample precedent, most of it recent, most of it upheld by appellate decisions within the last year: Carlton *versus* the State of Vermont, Trenholm *versus* the State of West Virginia, the Church of Souls *versus* the State of New York. There was that case up in Tylersville, just last year. Why, the Freedom of Worship Act *alone* . . ."

Braddock sighed, tacitly admitting that he knew Aaron was right—perhaps he had hoped to bluff them into obeying. "The 'Flood Congress' of '93," Braddock said, with bitter contempt. "They were so goddamned panic-stricken and full of sick chatter about Armageddon that you could've rammed *any* nonsense down their throats. That's a bad law, a pisspoor law . . ."

"Be that as it may, sheriff, you have no authority whatsoever—"

Abner suddenly began to speak, talking with a slow heavy deliberateness, musingly, almost reminiscently, ignoring the conversation he was interrupting—and indeed, perhaps he had not even been listening to it. "My grandfather lived right here on this farm, and *his* father before him—you know that, Sam? *They* lived by the old ways, and they survived and prospered. Greatgranddad, there wasn't hardly anything he needed from the outside world, anything he needed to *buy*, except maybe nails and suchlike, and he could've made them himself, too, if he'd needed to. Everything they needed, everything they ate, or wore, or used, they got from the woods, or from out of the soil of this farm, right here. *We* don't know how to do that anymore. We forgot the old ways, we turned our faces away, which is why the Flood came on us as a Judgment, a Judgment and a scourge, a scouring, a winnowing. The Old Days have come back again, and we've forgotten so goddamned *much*, we're almost helpless now that there's no goddamned K-mart down the goddamned street. We've got to go back to the old ways, or we'll pass from the earth, and be seen no more in it . . ." He was sweating now, staring earnestly at Braddock, as if to compel him by force of will alone to share the vision. "But it's so *hard*, Sam. . . . We have to *work* at relearning the old ways, we have to reinvent them as we go, step by step . . ."

"Some things we were better off without," Braddock said grimly.

"Up at Tylersville, they *doubled* their yield last harvest. Think what that could mean to a county as hungry as this one has been—"

Braddock shook his iron-gray head and held up one hand, as if he were directing traffic. "I'm telling you, Abner, the town won't stand for this—I'm bound to warn you that some of the boys just might decide to go outside the law to deal with this thing." He paused. "And, unofficially of course, I just might be inclined to give them a hand. . . ."

Mrs. Crammer laughed. She had been sitting quietly and taking all of this in, smiling good-naturedly from time to time, and her laugh was a shocking thing in that stuffy little room, harsh as a crow's caw. "You'll do *nothing*, Sam Braddock," she said jovially. "And neither will anybody else. More than half the county's with us already, nearly all the country folk, and a good part of the town, too." She smiled pleasantly at him, but her eyes were small and hard. "Just you remember, we *know* where *you* live, Sam Braddock. And we know where your sister lives, too, and your sister's child, over to Framington . . ."

"Are you threatening an officer of the law?" Braddock said, but he said it in a weak voice, and his face, when he turned it away to stare at the floor, looked sick and old. Mrs. Crammer laughed again, and then there was silence.

Braddock kept his face turned down for another long moment, and then he put his hat back on, squashing it down firmly on his head, and when he looked up he pointedly ignored the brethren and addressed his next remark to Roy. "You don't have to stay with these people, son," he said. *"That's* the law, too." He kept his eyes fixed steadily on Roy. "You just say the word, son, and I'll take you straight out of here, right now." His jaw was set, and he touched the butt of his revolver, as if for encouragement. "They can't stop us. How about it?"

"No, thank you," Roy said quietly. "I'll stay."

That night, while Abner wrung his hands and prayed aloud, Roy sat half-dozing before the parlor fire, unconcerned, watching the firelight throw Abner's gesticulating shadow across the white-washed walls. There was something in the wine they kept giving him, Roy knew, maybe somebody's saved-up Quääludes, but he didn't need it. Abner kept exorting him to let the Peace of God into his heart, but he didn't need that either. He didn't need anything. He felt calm and self-possessed and remote, disassociated from everything that went on around him, as if he were looking down on the world through the wrong end of a telescope, feeling only a mild scientific interest as he watched the tiny mannequins swirl and pirouette. . . . Like watching television with the sound off. If this were the Peace of God, it had settled down on him months ago, during the dead of that terrible winter, while he had struggled twelve hours a day to load foundation-stone in the face of icestorms and the razoring wind, while they had all, wetbacks and brethren alike, come close to starving. About the same time that word of the goings-on at

Tylersville had started to seep down from the brethren's parent church upstate, about the same time that Abner, who until then had totally ignored their kinship, had begun to talk to him in the evenings about the old ways. . . .

Although perhaps the great dead cold had started to settle in even earlier, that first day of the new world, while they were driving off across foundering Brigantine, the water already up over the hubcaps of the Toyota, and he had heard Toby barking frantically somewhere behind them. . . . His dad had died that day, died of a heart-attack as he fought to get them onto an overloaded boat that would take them across to the "safety" of the New Jersey mainland. His mother had died months later in one of the sprawling refugee camps, called "Floodtowns," that had sprung up on high ground everywhere along the new coastlines. She had just given up—sat down in the mud, rested her head on her knees, closed her eyes, and died. Just like that. Roy had seen the phenomenon countless times in the Floodtowns, places so festeringly horrible that even life on Abner's farm, with its Dickensian bleakness, forced labor, and short rations, had seemed—and was—a distinct change for the better. It was odd, and wrong, and sometimes it bothered him a little, but he hardly ever thought of his mother and father anymore—it was as if his mind shut itself off every time he came to those memories; he had never even cried for them, but all he had to do was close his eyes and he could see Toby, or his cat, Basil, running toward him and meowing with his tail held up over his back like a flag, and grief would come up like black bile at the back of his throat. . . .

It was still dark when they left the farmhouse. Roy and Abner and Aaron walked together, Abner carrying a large tattered carpetbag. Hank and Raymond ranged ahead with shotguns, in case there was trouble, but the last of the afternoon's gawkers had been driven off hours before by the cold and the road was empty, a dim charcoal line through the slowly lightening darkness. No one spoke, and there was no sound other than the sound of boots crunching on gravel. It was chilly again that morning, and Roy's bare feet burned against the macadam, but he trudged along stoically, ignoring the bite of cinders and pebbles. Their breath steamed faintly against the paling stars. The fields stretched dark and formless around them to either side of the road, and once they heard the rustling of some unseen animal fleeing away from them through the stubble. Mist flowed slowly down the road to meet them, sending out gleaming silver fingers to curl around their legs.

The sky was graying to the east, where the sea slept behind the mountains. Roy could imagine the sea rising higher and higher until it found its patient way around the roots of the hills and came spilling into the tableland beyond, flowing steadily forward like the mist, spreading out into a placid sheet of water that slowly swallowed the town, the farmhouse, the fields, until only the highest branches of the trees remained, held up like the beckoning arms of the drowned, and then they too would slide slowly, peacefully, beneath the water. . . .

A bird was crying out now, somewhere in the darkness, and they were walking through the fields, away from the road, cold mud squelching underfoot, the dry stubble crackling around them. Soon it would be time to sow the spring wheat, and after that, the corn. . . .

They stopped. Wind sighed through the dawn, muttering in the throat of the world. Still no one had spoken. Then hands were helping him remove the old bathrobe he'd been wearing. . . . Before leaving the house, he had been bathed, and annointed with a thick fragrant oil, and with a tiny silver scissors Mrs. Reardon had clipped a lock of his hair for each of the brethren.

Suddenly he was naked, and he was being urged forward again, his feet stumbling and slow.

They had made a wide ring of automobile flares here, the flares spitting and sizzling luridly in the wan dawn light, and in the center of the ring, they had dug a hollow in the ground.

He lay down in the hollow, feeling his naked back and buttocks settle into the cold mud, feeling it mat the hair on the back of his head. The mud made little sucking noises as he moved his arms and legs, settling in, and then he stretched out and lay still. The dawn breeze was cold, and he shivered in the mud, feeling it take hold of him like a giant's hand, tightening around him, pulling him down with a grip old and cold and strong. . . .

They gathered around him, seeming, from his low perspective, to tower miles into the sky. Their faces were harsh and angular, gouged with lines and shadows that made them look like something from a stark old woodcut. Abner bent down to rummage in the carpetbag, his harsh woodcut face close to Roy's for a moment, and when he straightened up again he had the big fine-honed hunting knife in his hand.

Abner began to speak now, groaning out the words in a loud, harsh voice, but Roy was no longer listening. He watched calmly as Abner lifted the knife high into the air, and then he turned his head to look last, as if he could somehow see across all the intervening miles of rock and farmland and forest to where the sea waited behind the mountains. . . .

Is this enough? he thought disjointedly, ignoring the towering scarecrow figures that were swaying in closer over him, straining his eyes to look last, to where the Presence lived . . . speaking now only to that Presence, to the sea, to that vast remorseless deity, bargaining with it cannily, hopefully, shrewdly, like a country housewife at market, proffering it the fine rich red gift of his death. Is this enough? Will this do?

Will you stop now?

FIRE WATCH

by Connie Willis

"Fire Watch" was purchased by George Scithers to-
ward the end of his reign as editor and appeared in the
February 15, 1982 issue of IAsfm, with interior illus-
trations by James Odbert. Willis had appeared on the
Hugo final ballot the year before with her story "Daisy,
In The Sun," but "Fire Watch" was the story that finally
established her reputation, going on to win both the
Nebula and the Hugo Award in 1982. Her story "A
Letter From The Clearys," purchased a few months
later during the McCarthy regime, also won a Nebula
Award that year, making Willis one of the few writers
ever to win two Nebulas in the same year. Over the next
few years other IAsfm stories by Willis also appeared
on the final award ballots: "The Sidon in the Mirror"
on both Nebula and Hugo ballots in 1983, and "Blued
Moon" on the Hugo ballot in 1984—and she would
become one of the magazine's major talents. As I write
this, several more stories by her are in inventory at
IAsfm.

Connie Willis lives in Greeley, Colorado, with a
husband, a teenage daughter, and a bulldog. Her first

novel, written in collaboration with Cynthia Felice, was Water Witch, *and another collaborative novel with Felice,* Light Raid, *is coming up from Ace. Her most recent books are* Fire Watch, *a collection of her short fiction, and* Lincoln's Dreams, *her first solo novel.*

"History hath triumphed over time, which besides it nothing but eternity hath triumphed over."
—Sir Walter Raleigh

September 20—Of course the first thing I looked for was the fire-watch stone. And of course it wasn't there yet. It wasn't dedicated until 1951, accompanying speech by the Very Reverend Dean Walter Matthews, and this is only 1940. I knew that. I went to see the fire-watch stone only yesterday, with some kind of misplaced notion that seeing the scene of the crime would somehow help. It didn't.

The only things that would have helped were a crash course in London during the Blitz and a little more time. I had not gotten either.

"Travelling in time is not like taking the tube, Mr. Bartholomew," the esteemed Dunworthy had said, blinking at me through those antique spectacles of his. "Either you report on the twentieth or you don't go at all."

"But I'm not ready," I'd said. "Look, it took me four years to get ready to travel with St. Paul. *St. Paul.* Not St. Paul's. You can't expect me to get ready for London in the Blitz in two days."

"Yes," Dunworthy had said. "We can." End of conversation.

"Two days!" I had shouted at my roommate, Kivrin. "All because some computer adds an *apostrophe s*. And the esteemed Dunworthy doesn't even bat an eye when I tell him. 'Time travel is not like taking the tube, young man,' he said. 'I'd suggest you get ready. You're leaving the day after tomorrow.' The man's a total incompetent."

"No," she said. "He isn't. He's the best there is. He wrote the book on St. Paul's. Maybe you should listen to what he says."

I had expected Kivrin to be at least a little sympathetic. She had been practically hysterical when she got her practicum changed from fifteenth to fourteenth century England, and how did either century qualify as a practicum? Even counting infectious diseases they couldn't have been more than a five. The Blitz is an eight, and St. Paul's itself is, with my luck, a ten.

"You think I should go see Dunworthy again?" I said.

"Yes."

"And then what? I've got two days. I don't know the money, the language, the history. Nothing."

"He's a good man," Kivrin said. "I think you'd better listen to him while you can." Good old Kivrin. Always the sympathetic ear.

The good man was responsible for my standing just inside the propped-open west doors, gawking like the country boy I was supposed to be, looking for a stone that wasn't there. Thanks to the good man, I was about as unprepared for my practicum as it was possible for him to make me.

I couldn't see more than a few feet into the church. I could see a candle gleaming feebly a long way off and a closer blur of white moving toward me. A verger, or possibly the Very Reverend Dean himself. I pulled out the letter from my clergyman uncle in Wales that was supposed to gain me access to the Dean, and patted my back pocket to make sure I hadn't lost the microfiche *Oxford English Dictionary, Revised, with Historical Supplements*, I'd smuggled out of the Bodleian. I couldn't pull it out in the middle of the conversation, but with luck I could muddle through the first encounter by context and look up the words I didn't know later.

"Are you from the ayarpee?" he said. He was no older than I am, a head shorter and much thinner. Almost ascetic looking. He reminded me of Kivrin. He was not wearing white, but clutching it to his chest. In other circumstances I would have thought it was a pillow. In other circumstances I would know what was being said to me, but there had been no time to unlearn sub-Mediterranean Latin and Jewish law and learn Cockney and air-raid procedures. Two days, and the esteemed Dunworthy, who wanted to talk about the sacred burdens of the historian instead of telling me what the ayarpee was.

"Are you?" he demanded again.

I considered shipping out the *OED* after all on the grounds that Wales was a foreign country, but I didn't think they had microfilm in 1940. Ayarpee. It could be anything, including a nickname for the fire watch, in which case the impulse to say no was not safe at all. "No," I said.

He lunged suddenly toward and past me and peered out the open doors. "Damn," he said, coming back to me. "Where are they then? Bunch of lazy bourgeois tarts!" And so much for getting by on context.

He looked at me closely, suspiciously, as if he thought I was only pretending not to be with the ayarpee. "The church is closed," he said finally.

I held up the envelope and said, "My name's Bartholomew. Is Dean Matthews in?"

He looked out the door a moment longer, as if he expected the lazy bourgeois tarts at any moment and intended to attack them with the white bundle, then he turned and said, as if he were guiding a tour, "This way, please," and took off into the gloom.

He led me to the right and down the south aisle of the nave. Thank God I had memorized the floor plan or at that moment, heading into total darkness, led by a raving verger, the whole bizarre metaphor of my situation would have been enough to send me out the west doors and back to St. John's Wood. It helped a little to know where I was. We should have been passing number twenty-six: Hunt's painting of "The Light of the World"—Jesus with his lantern—but it was too dark to see it. We could have used the lantern ourselves.

He stopped abruptly ahead of me, still raving. "We weren't asking for the bloody Savoy, just a few cots. Nelson's better off than we are—at least he's got a pillow provided." He brandished the white bundle like a torch in the darkness. It was a pillow after all. "We asked for them over a fortnight ago, and here we still are, sleeping on the bleeding generals from Trafalgar because those bitches want to play tea and crumpets with the tommies at Victoria and the Hell with us!"

He didn't seem to expect me to answer his outburst, which was good, because I had understood perhaps one key word in three. He stomped on ahead, moving out of sight of the one pathetic altar candle and stopping again at a black hole. Number twenty-five: stairs to the Whispering Gallery, the

Dome, the library (not open to the public). Up the stairs, down a hall, stop again at a medieval door and knock. "I've got to go wait for them," he said. "If I'm not there they'll likely take them over to the Abbey. Tell the Dean to ring them up again, will you?" and he took off down the stone steps, still holding his pillow like a shield against him.

He had knocked, but the door was at least a foot of solid oak, and it was obvious the Very Reverend Dean had not heard. I was going to have to knock again. Yes, well, and the man holding the pinpoint had to let go of it, too, but even knowing it will all be over in a moment and you won't feel a thing doesn't make it any easier to say, "Now!" So I stood in front of the door, cursing the history department and the esteemed Dunworthy and the computer that had made the mistake and brought me here to this dark door with only a letter from a fictitious uncle that I trusted no more than I trusted the rest of them.

Even the old reliable Bodleian had let me down. The batch of research stuff I cross-ordered through Balliol and the main terminal is probably sitting in my room right now, a century out of reach. And Kivrin, who had already done her practicum and should have been bursting with advice, walked around as silent as a saint until I begged her to help me.

"Did you go to see Dunworthy?" she said.

"Yes. You want to know what priceless bit of information he had for me? 'Silence and humility are the sacred burdens of the historian.' He also told me I would love St. Paul's. Golden gems from the master. Unfortunately, what I need to know are the times and places of the bombs so one doesn't fall on me." I flopped down on the bed. "Any suggestions?"

"How good are you at memory retrieval?" she said.

I sat up. "I'm pretty good. You think I should assimilate?"

"There isn't time for that," she said. "I think you should put everything you can directly into long-term."

"You mean endorphins?" I said.

The biggest problem with using memory-assistance drugs to put information into your long-term memory is that it never sits, even for a micro-second, in your short-term memory, and that makes retrieval complicated, not to mention unnerving. It gives you the most unsettling sense of *déjà vu* to suddenly know something you're positive you've never seen or heard before.

The main problem, though, is not eerie sensations but retrieval. Nobody knows exactly how the brain gets what it wants out of storage, but short-term is definitely involved. That brief, sometimes microscopic, time information spends in short-term is apparently used for something besides tip-of-the-tongue availability. The whole complex sort-and-file process of retrieval is apparently centered in short-term; and without it, and without the help of the drugs that put it there or artificial substitutes, information can be impossible to retrieve. I'd used endorphins for examinations and never had any difficulty with retrieval, and it looked like it was the only way to store all the information I needed in anything approaching the time I had left, but it also meant that I would *never* have known any of the things I needed to know, even for long enough to have forgotten them. If and when I could retrieve the information, I would know it. Till then I was as ignorant of it as if it were not stored in some cobwebbed corner of my mind at all.

"You can retrieve without artificials, can't you?" Kivrin said, looking skeptical.

"I guess I'll have to."

"Under stress? Without sleep? Low body endorphin levels?" What exactly had her practicum been? She had never said a word about it, and undergraduates are not supposed to ask. Stress factors in the Middle Ages? I thought everybody slept through them.

"I hope so," I said. "Anyway, I'm willing to try this idea if you think it will help."

She looked at me with that martyred expression and said, "Nothing will help." Thank you, St. Kivrin of Balliol.

But I tried it anyway. It was better than sitting in Dunworthy's rooms having him blink at me through his historically accurate eyeglasses and tell me I was going to love St. Paul's. When my Bodleian requests didn't come, I overloaded my credit and bought out Blackwell's. Tapes on World War II, Celtic literature, history of mass transit, tourist guidebooks, everything I could think of. Then I rented a high-speed recorder and shot up. When I came out of it, I was so panicked by the feeling of not knowing any more than I had when I started that I took the tube to London and raced up Ludgate Hill to see if the firewatch stone would trigger any memories. It didn't.

"Your endorphin levels aren't back to normal yet," I told myself and tried to relax, but that was impossible with the prospect of the practicum looming up before me. And those are real bullets, kid. Just because you're a history major doing his practicum doesn't mean you can't get killed. I read history books all the way home on the tube and right up until Dunworthy's flunkies came to take me to St. John's Wood this morning.

Then I jammed the microfiche *OED* in my back pocket and went off feeling as if I would have to survive by my native wit and hoping I could get hold of artificials in 1940. Surely I could get through the first day without mishap, I thought; and now here I was, stopped cold by almost the first word that was spoken to me.

Well, not quite. In spite of Kivrin's advice that I not put anything in short-term, I'd memorized the British money, a map of the tube system, a map of my own Oxford. It had gotten me this far. Surely I would be able to deal with the Dean.

Just as I had almost gotten up the courage to knock, he opened the door, and as with the pinpoint, it really was over quickly and without pain. I handed him my letter, and he shook my hand and said something understandable like, "Glad to have another man, Bartholomew." He looked strained and tired and as if he might collapse if I told him the Blitz had just started. I know, I know: Keep your mouth shut. The sacred silence, etc.

He said, "We'll get Langby to show you round, shall we?" I assumed that was my Verger of the Pillow, and I was right. He met us at the foot of the stairs, puffing a little but jubilant.

"The cots came," he said to Dean Matthews. "You'd have thought they were doing us a favor. All high heels and hoity-toity. 'You made us miss our tea, luv,' one of them said to me. 'Yes, well, and a good thing, too,' I said. 'You look as if you could stand to lose a stone or two.'"

Even Dean Matthews looked as though he did not completely understand him. He said, "Did you set them up in the crypt?" and then introduced us. "Mr. Bartholomew's just got

in from Wales," he said. "He's come to join our volunteers."
Volunteers, not fire watch.

Langby showed me around, pointing out various dimnesses
in the general gloom and then dragged me down to see the ten
folding canvas cots set up among the tombs in the crypt, also
in passing Lord Nelson's black marble sarcophagus. He told
me I didn't have to stand a watch the first night and suggested
I go to bed, since sleep is the most precious commodity in the
raids. I could well believe it. He was clutching that silly pillow to his breast like his beloved.

"Do you hear the sirens down here?" I asked, wondering if
he buried his head in it.

He looked round at the low stone ceilings. "Some do, some
don't. Brinton has to have his Horlich's. Bence-Jones would
sleep if the roof fell in on him. I have to have a pillow. The
important thing is to get your eight in no matter what. If you
don't, you turn into one of the walking dead. And then you
get killed."

On that cheering note he went off to post the watches for
tonight, leaving his pillow on one of the cots with orders for
me to let nobody touch it. So here I sit, waiting for my first
air-raid siren and trying to get all this down before I turn into
one of the walking or non-walking dead.

I've used the stolen *OED* to decipher a little Langby. Mid-
dling success. A tart is either a pastry or a prostitute (I assume
the latter, although I was wrong about the pillow). Bourgeois
is a catchall term for all the faults of the middle class. A
Tommy's a soldier. Ayarpee I could not find under any spell-
ing and I had nearly given up when something in the long-
term about the use of acronyms and abbreviations in wartime
popped forward (bless you, St. Kivrin) and I realized it must
be an abbreviation. ARP. Air Raid Precautions. Of course.
Where else would you get the bleeding cots from?

September 21—Now that I'm past the first shock of being
here, I realize that the history department neglected to tell me
what I'm supposed to do in the three-odd months of this practicum. They handed me this journal, the letter from my uncle,
and a ten-pound note, and sent me packing into the past. The
ten pounds (already depleted by train and tube fares) is supposed to last me until the end of December and get me back to

St. John's Wood for pickup when the second letter calling me back to Wales to sick uncle's bedside comes. Till then I live here in the crypt with Nelson, who, Langby tells me, is pickled in alcohol inside his coffin. If we take a direct hit, will he burn like a torch or simply trickle out in a decaying stream onto the crypt floor, I wonder. Board is provided by a gas ring, over which are cooked wretched tea and indescribable kippers. To pay for all this luxury I am to stand on the roofs of St. Paul's and put out incendiaries.

I must also accomplish the purpose of this practicum, whatever it may be. Right now the only purpose I care about is staying alive until the second letter from uncle arrives and I can go home.

I am doing makework until Langby has time to "show me the ropes." I've cleaned the skillet they cook the foul little fishes in, stacked wooden folding chairs at the altar end of the crypt (flat instead of standing because they tend to collapse like bombs in the middle of the night), and tried to sleep.

I am apparently not one of the lucky ones who can sleep through the raids. I spent most of the night wondering what St. Paul's risk rating is. Practica have to be at least a six. Last night I was convinced this was a ten, with the crypt as ground zero, and that I might as well have applied for Denver.

The most interesting thing that's happened so far is that I've seen a cat. I am fascinated, but trying not to appear so since they seem commonplace here.

September 22—Still in the crypt. Langby comes dashing through, periodically cursing various government agencies (all abbreviated) and promising to take me up on the roofs. In the meantime, I've run out of makework and taught myself to work a stirrup pump. Kivrin was overly concerned about my memory retrieval abilities. I have not had any trouble so far. Quite the opposite. I called up fire-fighting information and got the whole manual with pictures, including instructions on the use of the stirrup pump. If the kippers set Lord Nelson on fire, I shall be a hero.

Excitement last night. The sirens went early and some of the chars who clean offices in the City sheltered in the crypt with us. One of them woke me out of a sound sleep, going like an air raid siren. Seems she'd seen a mouse. We had to go whacking at tombs and under the cots with a rubber boot to persuade her it was gone. Obviously what the history department had in mind: murdering mice.

September 24—Langby took me on rounds. Into the choir, where I had to learn the stirrup pump all over again, assigned rubber boots and a tin helmet. Langby says Commander Allen is getting us asbestos firemen's coats, but hasn't yet, so it's my own wool coat and muffler and very cold on the roofs even in September. It feels like November and looks it, too, bleak and cheerless with no sun. Up to the dome and onto the roofs which should be flat, but in fact are littered with towers, pinnacles, gutters, and statues, all designed to catch and hold incendiaries out of reach. Shown how to smother an incendiary with sand before it burns through the roof and sets the church on fire. Shown the ropes (literally) lying in a heap at the base of the dome in case somebody has to go up one of the west towers or over the top of the dome. Back inside and down to the Whispering Gallery.

Langby kept up a running commentary through the whole tour, part practical instruction, part church history. Before we went up into the Gallery he dragged me over to the south door to tell me how Christopher Wren stood in the smoking rubble of Old St. Paul's and asked a workman to bring him a stone from the graveyard to make the cornerstone. On the stone was written in Latin, "I shall rise again," and Wren was so impressed by the irony that he had the words inscribed above the door. Langby looked as smug as if he had not told me a story every first-year history student knows, but I suppose without the impact of the firewatch stone, the other is just a nice story.

Langby raced me up the steps and onto the narrow balcony circling the Whispering Gallery. He was already halfway round to the other side, shouting dimensions and acoustics at me. He stopped facing the wall opposite and said softly, "You can hear me whispering because of the shape of the dome. The sound waves are reinforced around the perimeter of the dome. It sounds like the very crack of doom up here during a raid. The dome is one hundred and seven feet across. It is eighty feet above the nave."

I looked down. The railing went out from under me and the black-and-white marble floor came up with dizzying speed. I hung onto something in front of me and dropped to my knees, staggered and sick at heart. The sun had come out, and all of St. Paul's seemed drenched in gold. Even the carved wood of the choir, the white stone pillars, the leaden pipes of the organ, all of it golden, golden.

Langby was beside me, trying to pull me free. "Bartholomew," he shouted, "What's wrong? For God's sake, man."

I knew I must tell him that if I let go, St. Paul's and all the past would fall in on me, and that I must not let that happen because I was an historian. I said something, but it was not what I intended because Langby merely tightened his grip. He hauled me violently free of the railing and back onto the stairway, then let me collapse limply on the steps and stood back from me, not speaking.

"I don't know what happened in there," I said. "I've never been afraid of heights before."

"You're shaking," he said sharply. "You'd better lie down." He led me back to the crypt.

September 25—Memory retrieval: ARP manual. Symptoms of bombing victims. Stage one—shock; stupefaction; unawareness of injuries; words may not make sense except to victim. Stage two—shivering; nausea; injuries, losses felt; return to reality. Stage three—talkativeness that cannot be controlled; desire to explain shock behavior to rescuers.

Langby must surely recognize the symptoms, but how does he account for the fact there was no bomb? I can hardly explain my shock behavior to him, and it isn't just the sacred silence of the historian that stops me.

He has not said anything, in fact assigned me my first watches for tomorrow night as if nothing had happened, and he seems no more preoccupied than anyone else. Everyone I've met so far is jittery (one thing I had in short-term was how calm everyone was during the raids) and the raids have not come near us since I got here. They've been mostly over the East End and the docks.

There was a reference tonight to a UXB, and I have been thinking about the Dean's manner and the church being closed when I'm almost sure I remember reading it was open through the entire Blitz. As soon as I get a chance, I'll try to retrieve the events of September. As to retrieving anything else, I don't see how I can hope to remember the right information until I know what it is I am supposed to do here, if anything.

There are no guidelines for historians, and no restrictions either. I could tell everyone I'm from the future if I thought they would believe me. I could murder Hitler if I could get to Germany. Or could I? Time paradox talk abounds in the history department, and the graduate students back from their practica don't say a word one way or the other. Is there a tough, immutable past? Or is there a new past every day and do we, the historians, make it? And what are the consequences of what we do, if there are consequences? And how do we dare do anything without knowing them? Must we interfere boldly, hoping we do not bring about all our downfalls? Or must we do nothing at all, not interfere, stand by and watch St. Paul's burn to the ground if need be so that we don't change the future?

All those are fine questions for a late-night study session. They do not matter here. I could no more let St. Paul's burn down than I could kill Hitler. No, that is not true. I found that out yesterday in the Whispering Gallery. I could kill Hitler if I caught him setting fire to St. Paul's.

September 26—I met a young woman today. Dean Matthews has opened the church, so the watch have been doing duties as chars and people have started coming in again. The young woman reminded me of Kivrin, though Kivrin is a good deal taller and would never frizz her hair like that. She looked as if she had been crying. Kivrin has looked like that since she got back from her practicum. The Middle Ages were too much for her. I wonder how she would have coped with this. By pouring out her fears to the local priest, no doubt, as I sincerely hoped her lookalike was not going to do.

"May I help you?" I said, not wanting in the least to help. "I'm a volunteer."

She looked distressed. "You're not paid?" she said and wiped at her reddened nose with a handkerchief. "I read about St. Paul's and the fire watch and all and I thought, perhaps there's a position there for me. In the canteen, like, or something. A paying position." There were tears in her red-rimmed eyes.

"I'm afraid we don't have a canteen," I said as kindly as I

could, considering how impatient Kivrin always makes me, "and it's not actually a real shelter. Some of the watch sleep in the crypt. I'm afraid we're all volunteers, though."

"That won't do, then," she said. She dabbed at her eyes with the handkerchief. "I love St. Paul's, but I can't take on volunteer work, not with my little brother Tom back from the country." I was not reading this situation properly. For all the outward signs of distress, she sounded quite cheerful and no closer to tears than when she had come in. "I've got to get us a proper place to stay. With Tom back, we can't go on sleeping in the tubes."

A sudden feeling of dread, the kind of sharp pain you get sometimes from involuntary retrieval, went over me. "The tubes?" I said, trying to get at the memory.

"Marble Arch, usually," she went on. "My brother Tom saves us a place early and I go—" She stopped, held the handkerchief close to her nose, and exploded into it. "I'm sorry," she said, "this awful cold!"

Red nose, watering eyes, sneezing. Respiratory infection. It was a wonder I hadn't told her not to cry. It's only by luck that I haven't made some unforgivable mistake so far, and this is not because I can't get at the long-term memory. I don't have half the information I need even stored: cats and colds and the way St. Paul's looks in full sun. It's only a matter of time before I am stopped cold by something I do not know. Nevertheless, I am going to try for retrieval tonight after I come off watch. At least I can find out whether and when something is going to fall on me.

I have seen the cat once or twice. He is coal-black with a white patch on his throat that looks as if it were painted on for the blackout.

September 27—I have just come down from the roofs. I am still shaking.

Early in the raid the bombing was mostly over the East End. The view was incredible. Searchlights everywhere, the sky pink from the fires and reflecting in the Thames, the exploding shells sparkling like fireworks. There was a constant, deafening thunder broken by the occasional droning of the planes high overhead, then the repeating stutter of the ack-ack guns.

About midnight the bombs began falling quite near with a horrible sound like a train running over me. It took every bit of will I had to keep from flinging myself flat on the roof, but Langby was watching. I didn't want to give him the satisfaction of watching a repeat performance of my behavior in the dome. I kept my head up and my sandbucket firmly in hand and felt quite proud of myself.

The bombs stopped roaring past about three, and there was a lull of about half an hour, and then a clatter like hail on the roofs. Everybody except Langby dived for shovels and stirrup pumps. He was watching me. And I was watching the incendiary.

It had fallen only a few meters from me, behind the clock tower. It was much smaller than I had imagined, only about thirty centimeters long. It was sputtering violently, throwing greenish-white fire almost to where I was standing. In a minute it would simmer down into a molten mass and begin to burn through the roof. Flames and the frantic shouts of firemen, and then the white rubble stretching for miles, and nothing, nothing left, not even the firewatch stone.

It was the Whispering Gallery all over again. I felt that I had said something, and when I looked at Langby's face he was smiling crookedly.

"St. Paul's will burn down," I said. "There won't be anything left."

"Yes," Langby said. "That's the idea, isn't it? Burn St. Paul's to the ground? Isn't that the plan?"

"Whose plan?" I said stupidly.

"Hitler's, of course," Langby said. "Who did you think I meant?" and, almost casually, picked up his stirrup pump.

The page of the ARP manual flashed suddenly before me. I poured the bucket of sand around the still sputtering bomb, snatched up another bucket and dumped that on top of it. Black smoke billowed up in such a cloud that I could hardly find my shovel. I felt for the smothered bomb with the tip of it and scooped it into the empty bucket, then shovelled the sand in on top of it. Tears were streaming down my face from the acrid smoke. I turned to wipe them on my sleeve and saw Langby.

He had not made a move to help me. He smiled. "It's not a bad plan, actually. But of course we won't let it happen.

That's what the fire watch is here for. To see that it doesn't happen. Right, Bartholomew?"

I know now what the purpose of my practicum is. I must stop Langby from burning down St. Paul's.

September 28—I must try to tell myself I was mistaken about Langby last night, that I misunderstood what he said. Why would he want to burn down St. Paul's unless he is a Nazi spy? How can a Nazi spy have gotten on the fire watch? I think about my faked letter of introduction and shudder.

How can I find out? If I set him some test, some fatal thing that only a loyal Englishman in 1940 would know, I fear I am the one who would be caught out. I *must* get my retrieval working properly.

Until then, I shall watch Langby. For the time being at least that should be easy. Langby has just posted the watches for the next two weeks. We stand every one together.

September 30—I know what happened in September. Langby told me.

Last night in the choir, putting on our coats and boots, he said, "They've already tried once, you know."

I had no idea what he meant. I felt as helpless as that first day when he asked me if I was from the ayarpee.

"The plan to destroy St. Paul's. They've already tried once. The tenth of September. A high explosive bomb. But of course you didn't know about that. You were in Wales.

I was not even listening. The minute he had said, "High explosive bomb," I had remembered it all. It had burrowed in under the road and lodged on the foundations. The bomb squad had tried to defuse it, but there was a leaking gas main. They decided to evacuate St. Paul's, but Dean Matthews refused to leave, and they got it out after all and exploded it in Barking Marshes. Instant and complete retrieval.

"The bomb squad saved her that time," Langby was saying. "It seems there's always somebody about."

"Yes," I said. "There is," and walked away from him.

October 1—I thought last night's retrieval of the events of September tenth meant some sort of breakthrough, but I have been lying here on my cot most of the night trying for Nazi

spies in St. Paul's and getting nothing. Do I have to know
exactly what I'm looking for before I can remember it? What
good does that do me?

Maybe Langby is not a Nazi spy. Then what is he? An
arsonist? A madman? The crypt is hardly conducive to
thought, being not at all as silent as a tomb. The chars talk
most of the night and the sound of the bombs is muffled,
which somehow makes it worse. I find myself straining to
hear them. When I did get to sleep this morning, I dreamed
about one of the tube shelters being hit, broken mains, drowning people.

October 4—I tried to catch the cat today. I had some idea
of persuading it to dispatch the mouse that has been terrifying
the chars. I also wanted to see one up close. I took the water
bucket I had used with the stirrup pump last night to put out
some burning shrapnel from one of the anti-aircraft guns. It
still had a bit of water in it, but not enough to drown the cat,
and my plan was to clamp the bucket over him, reach under,
and pick him up, then carry him down to the crypt and point
him at the mouse. I did not even come close to him.

I swung the bucket, and as I did so, perhaps an inch of
water splashed out. I thought I remembered that the cat was a
domesticated animal, but I must have been wrong about that.
The cat's wide complacent face pulled back into a skull-like
mask that was absolutely terrifying, vicious claws extended
from what I had thought were harmless paws, and the cat let
out a sound to top the chars.

In my surprise I dropped the bucket and it rolled against
one of the pillars. The cat disappeared. Behind me, Langby
said, "That's no way to catch a cat."

"Obviously," I said and bent to retrieve the bucket.

"Cats hate water," he said, still in that expressionless
voice.

"Oh," I said and started in front of him to take the bucket
back to the choir. "I didn't know that."

"Everybody knows it. Even the stupid Welsh."

October 8—We have been standing double watches for a
week—bomber's moon. Langby didn't show up on the roofs,
so I went looking for him in the church. I found him standing

by the west doors talking to an old man. The man had a newspaper tucked under his arm and he handed it to Langby, but Langby gave it back to him. When the man saw me, he ducked out. Langby said, "Tourist. Wanted to know where the Windmill Theater is. Read in the paper the girls are starkers."

I know I looked as if I didn't believe him because he said, "You look rotten, old man. Not getting enough sleep, are you? I'll get somebody to take the first watch for you tonight."

"No," I said coldly. "I'll stand my own watch. I like being on the roofs," and added silently, *where I can watch you.*

He shrugged and said, "I suppose it's better than being down in the crypt. At least on the roofs you can hear the one that gets you."

October 10—I thought the double watches might be good for me, take my mind off my inability to retrieve. The watched pot idea. Actually, it sometimes works. A few hours of thinking about something else, or a good night's sleep, and the fact pops forward without any prompting, without any artificials.

The good night's sleep is out of the question. Not only do the chars talk constantly, but the cat has moved into the crypt and sidles up to everyone, making siren noises and begging for kippers. I am moving my cot out of the transept and over by Nelson before I go on watch. He may be pickled, but he keeps his mouth shut.

October 11—I dreamed Trafalgar, ships' guns and smoke and falling plaster and Langby shouting my name. My first waking thought was that the folding chairs had gone off. I could not see for all the smoke.

"I'm coming," I said, limping toward Langby and pulling on my boots. There was a heap of plaster and tangled folding chairs in the transept. Langby was digging in it. "Bartholomew!" he shouted, flinging a chunk of plaster aside. "Bartholomew!"

I still had the idea it was smoke. I ran back for the stirrup pump and then knelt beside him and began pulling on a splintered chair back. It resisted, and it came to me suddenly, *there is a body under here. I will reach for a piece of the ceiling and find it is a hand*. I leaned back on my heels, determined not to be sick, then went at the pile again.

Langby was going far too fast, jabbing with a chair leg. I grabbed his hand to stop him, and he struggled against me as if I were a piece of rubble to be thrown aside. He picked up a large flat square of plaster, and under it was the floor. I turned and looked behind me. Both chars huddled in the recess by the altar. "Who are you looking for?" I said, keeping hold of Langby's arm.

"Bartholomew," he said and swept the rubble aside, his hands bleeding through the coating of smoky dust.

"I'm here," I said. "I'm all right." I choked on the white dust. "I moved my cot out of the transept."

He turned sharply to the chars and then said quite calmly, "What's under here?"

"Only the gas ring," one of them said timidly from the shadowed recess, "and Mrs. Galbraith's pocketbook." He dug through the mess until he had found them both. The gas ring was leaking at a merry rate, though the flame had gone out.

"You've saved St. Paul's and me after all," I said, standing there in my underwear and boots, holding the useless stirrup pump. "We might all have been asphyxiated."

He stood up. "I shouldn't have saved you," he said.

Stage one: shock, stupefaction, unawareness of injuries, words may not make sense except to victim. He would not know his hand was bleeding yet. He would not remember what he had said. He had said he shouldn't have saved my life.

"I shouldn't have saved you," he repeated. "I have my duty to think of."

"You're bleeding," I said sharply. "You'd better lie down." I sounded just like Langby in the Gallery.

October 13—It was a high explosive bomb. It blew a hole in the choir roof; and some of the marble statuary is broken; but the ceiling of the crypt did not collapse, which is what I thought at first. It only jarred some plaster loose.

I do not think Langby has any idea what he said. That should give me some sort of advantage, now that I am sure where the danger lies, now that I am sure it will not come crashing down from some other direction. But what good is all this knowing, when I do not know what he will do? Or when?

Surely I have the facts of yesterday's bomb in long-term, but even falling plaster did not jar them loose this time. I am not even trying for retrieval now. I lie in the darkness waiting for the roof to fall in on me. And remembering how Langby saved my life.

October 15—The girl came in again today. She still has the cold, but she has gotten her paying position. It was a joy to see her. She was wearing a smart uniform and open-toed shoes, and her hair was in an elaborate frizz around her face. We are still cleaning up the mess from the bomb, and Langby was out with Allen getting wood to board up the choir, so I let the girl chatter at me while I swept. The dust made her sneeze, but at least this time I knew what she was doing.

She told me her name is Enola and that she's working for the WVS, running one of the mobile canteens that are sent to the fires. She came, of all things, to thank me for the job. She said that after she told the WVS that there was no proper shelter with a canteen for St. Paul's, they gave her a run in the City. "So I'll just pop in when I'm close and let you know how I'm making out, won't I just?"

She and her brother Tom are still sleeping in the tubes. I asked her if that was safe and she said probably not, but at least down there you couldn't hear the one that got you and that was a blessing.

October 18—I am so tired I can hardly write this. Nine incendiaries tonight and a land mine that looked as though it were going to catch on the dome till the wind drifted its parachute away from the church. I put out two of the incendiaries. I have done that at least twenty times since I got here and helped with dozens of others, and still it is not enough. One incendiary, one moment of not watching Langby, could undo it all.

I know that is partly why I feel so tired. I wear myself out every night trying to do my job and watch Langby, making sure none of the incendiaries falls without my seeing it. Then I go back to the crypt and wear myself out trying to retrieve something, anything, about spies, fires, St. Paul's in the fall of 1940, anything. It haunts me that I am not doing enough, but I do not know what else to do. Without the retrieval, I am as helpless as these poor people here, with no idea what will happen tomorrow.

If I have to, I will go on doing this till I am called home. He cannot burn down St. Paul's so long as I am here to put out the incendiaries. "I have my duty," Langby said in the crypt.

And I have mine.

October 21—It's been nearly two weeks since the blast and I just now realized we haven't seen the cat since. He wasn't in the mess in the crypt. Even after Langby and I were sure there was no one in there, we sifted through the stuff twice more. He could have been in the choir, though.

Old Bence-Jones says not to worry. "He's all right," he said. "The jerries could bomb London right down to the ground and the cats would waltz out to greet them. You know why? They don't love anybody. That's what gets half of us killed. Old lady out in Stepney got killed the other night trying to save her cat. Bloody cat was in the Anderson."

"Then where is he?"

"Someplace safe, you can bet on that. If he's not around St. Paul's, it means we're for it. That old saw about the rats deserting a sinking ship, that's a mistake, that is. It's cats, not rats."

October 25—Langby's tourist showed up again. He cannot still be looking for the Windmill Theatre. He had a newspaper under his arm again today, and he asked for Langby, but Langby was across town with Allen, trying to get the asbestos firemen's coats. I saw the name of the paper. It was *The Worker*. A Nazi newspaper?

November 2—I've been up on the roofs for a week straight, helping some incompetent workmen patch the hole the bomb made. They're doing a terrible job. There's still a great gap on one side a man could fall into, but they insist it'll be all right because, after all, you wouldn't fall clear through but only as far as the ceiling, and "the fall can't kill you." They don't seem to understand it's a perfect hiding place for an incendiary.

And that is all Langby needs. He does not even have to set a fire to destroy St. Paul's. All he needs to do is let one burn uncaught until it is too late.

I could not get anywhere with the workmen. I went down into the church to complain to Matthews and saw Langby and his tourist behind a pillar, close to one of the windows. Langby was holding a newspaper and talking to the man. When I came down from the library an hour later, they were still there. So is the gap. Matthews says we'll put planks across it and hope for the best.

November 5—I have given up trying to retrieve. I am so far behind on my sleep I can't even retrieve information on a newspaper whose name I already know. Double watches the permanent thing now. Our chars have abandoned us altogether (like the cat), so the crypt is quiet, but I cannot sleep.

If I do manage to doze off, I dream. Yesterday I dreamed Kivrin was on the roofs, dressed like a saint. "What was the secret of your practicum?" I said. "What were you supposed to find out?"

She wiped her nose with a handkerchief and said, "Two things. One, that silence and humility are the sacred burdens of the historian. Two," she stopped and sneezed into the handkerchief. "Don't sleep in the tubes."

My only hope is to get hold of an artificial and induce a trance. That's a problem. I'm positive it's too early for chemical endorphins and probably hallucinogens. Alcohol is definitely available, but I need something more concentrated than ale, the only alcohol I know by name. I do not dare ask the watch. Langby is suspicious enough of me already. It's back to the *OED*, to look up a word I don't know.

November 11—The cat's back. Langby was out with Allen again, still trying for the asbestos coats, so I thought it was safe to leave St. Paul's. I went to the grocer's for supplies and hopefully, an artificial. It was late, and the sirens sounded before I had even gotten to Cheapside, but the raids do not usually start until after dark. It took awhile to get all the groceries and to get up my courage to ask whether he had any alcohol—he told me to go to a pub—and when I came out of the shop, it was as if I had pitched suddenly into a hole.

I had no idea where St. Paul's lay, or the street, or the shop I had just come from. I stood on what was no longer the sidewalk, clutching my brown-paper parcel of kippers and bread with a hand I could not have seen if I held it up before my face. I reached up to wrap my muffler closer about my neck and prayed for my eyes to adjust, but there was no reduced light to adjust to. I would have been glad of the moon, for all St. Paul's watch curses it and calls it a fifth columnist. Or a bus, with its shuttered headlights giving just enough light to orient myself by. Or a searchlight. Or the kickback flare of an ack-ack gun. Anything.

Just then I did see a bus, two narrow yellow slits a long way off. I started toward it and nearly pitched off the curb. Which meant the bus was sideways in the street, which meant it was not a bus. A cat meowed, quite near, and rubbed against my leg. I looked down into the yellow lights I had thought belonged to the bus. His eyes were picking up light from somewhere, though I would have sworn there was not a light for miles, and reflecting it flatly up at me.

"A warden'll get you for those lights, old tom," I said, and then as a plane droned overhead, "or a jerry."

The world exploded suddenly into light, the searchlights and a glow along the Thames seeming to happen almost simultaneously, lighting my way home.

"Come to fetch me, did you, old tom?" I said gaily. "Where've you been? Knew we were out of kippers, didn't you? I call that loyalty." I talked to him all the way home and gave him half a tin of the kippers for saving my life. Bence-Jones said he smelled the milk at the grocer's.

November 13—I dreamed I was lost in the blackout. I could not see my hands in front of my face, and Dunworthy came and shone a pocket torch at me, but I could only see where I had come from and not where I was going.

"What good is that to them?" I said. "They need a light to show them where they're going."

"Even the light from the Thames? Even the light from the fires and the ack-ack guns?" Dunworthy said.

"Yes. Anything is better than this awful darkness." So he came closer to give me the pocket torch. It was not a pocket torch, after all, but Christ's lantern from the Hunt picture in the south nave. I shone it on the curb before me so I could find my way home, but it shone instead on the firewatch stone and I hastily put the light out.

November 20—I tried to talk to Langby today. "I've seen you talking to the old gentleman," I said. It sounded like an accusation. I meant it to. I wanted him to think it was and stop whatever he was planning.

"Reading," he said. "Not talking." He was putting things in order in the choir, piling up sandbags.

"I've seen you reading then," I said belligerently, and he dropped a sandbag and straightened.

"What of it?" he said. "It's a free country. I can read to an old man if I want, same as you can talk to that little WVS tart."

"What do you read?" I said.

"Whatever he wants. He's an old man. He used to come home from his job, have a bit of brandy and listen to his wife read the papers to him. She got killed in one of the raids. Now I read to him. I don't see what business it is of yours."

It sounded true. It didn't have the careful casualness of a lie, and I almost believed him, except that I had heard the tone of truth from him before. In the crypt. After the bomb.

"I thought he was a tourist looking for the Windmill," I said.

He looked blank only a second, and then he said, "Oh, yes, that. He came in with the paper and asked me to tell him where it was. I looked it up to find the address. Clever, that. I didn't guess he couldn't read it for himself." But it was enough. I knew that he was lying.

He heaved a sandbag almost at my feet. "Of course you wouldn't understand a thing like that, would you? A simple act of human kindness?"

"No," I said coldly. "I wouldn't."

None of this proves anything. He gave away nothing, except perhaps the name of an artificial, and I can hardly go to Dean Matthews and accuse Langby of reading aloud.

I waited till he had finished in the choir and gone down to the crypt. Then I lugged one of the sandbags up to the roof and over to the chasm. The planking has held so far, but everyone walks gingerly around it, as if it were a grave. I cut the sandbag open and spilled the loose sand into the bottom. If it has occurred to Langby that this is the perfect spot for an incendiary, perhaps the sand will smother it.

November 21—I gave Enola some of "uncle's" money today and asked her to get me the brandy. She was more reluctant than I thought she'd be so there must be societal complications I am not aware of, but she agreed.

I don't know what she came for. She started to tell me about her brother and some prank he'd pulled in the tubes that got him in trouble with the guard, but after I asked her about the brandy, she left without finishing the story.

November 25—Enola came today, but without bringing the brandy. She is going to Bath for the holidays to see her aunt. At least she will be away from the raids for awhile. I will not have to worry about her. She finished the story of her brother and told me she hopes to persuade this aunt to take Tom for the duration of the Blitz but is not at all sure the aunt will be willing.

Young Tom is apparently not so much an engaging scape-grace as a near-criminal. He has been caught twice picking pockets in the Bank tube shelter, and they have had to go back to Marble Arch. I comforted her as best I could, told her all boys were bad at one time or another. What I really wanted to say was that she needn't worry at all, that young Tom strikes me as a true survivor type, like my own tom, like Langby, totally unconcerned with anybody but himself, well equipped to survive the Blitz and rise to prominence in the future.

Then I asked her whether she had gotten the brandy.

She looked down at her open-toed shoes and muttered un-happily, "I thought you'd forgotten all about that."

I made up some story about the watch taking turns buying a bottle, and she seemed less unhappy, but I am not convinced she will not use this trip to Bath as an excuse to do nothing. I will have to leave St. Paul's and buy it myself, and I don't dare leave Langby alone in the church. I made her promise to bring the brandy today before she leaves. But she is still not back, and the sirens have already gone.

* * *

December 28—Enola came this morning while I was on the west porch, picking up the Christmas tree. It has been knocked over three nights running by concussion. I righted the tree and was bending down to pick up the scattered tinsel when Enola appeared suddenly out of the fog like some cheerful saint. She stooped quickly and kissed me on the cheek. Then she straightened up, her nose red from her perennial cold, and handed me a box wrapped in colored paper.

"Merry Christmas," she said. "Go on then, open it. It's a gift."

My reflexes are almost totally gone. I knew the box was far too shallow for a bottle of brandy. Nevertheless, I believed she had remembered, had brought me my salvation. "You darling," I said, and tore it open.

It was a muffler. Gray wool. I stared at it for fully half a minute without realizing what it was. "Where's the brandy?" I said.

She looked shocked. Her nose got redder and her eyes started to blur. "You need this more. You haven't any clothing coupons and you have to be outside all the time. It's been so dreadful cold."

"I *needed* the brandy," I said angrily.

"I was only trying to be kind," she started, and I cut her off.

"Kind?" I said. "I asked you for brandy. I don't recall ever saying I needed a muffler." I shoved it back at her and began untangling a string of colored lights that had shattered when the tree fell.

She got that same holy martyr look Kivrin is so wonderful at. "I worry about you all the time up here," she said in a rush. "They're *trying* for St. Paul's, you know. And it's so close to the river. I didn't think you should be drinking. I . . . it's a crime when they're trying so hard to kill us all that you won't take care of yourself. It's like you're in it with them. I worry someday I'll come up to St. Paul's and you won't be here."

"Well, and what exactly am I supposed to do with a muffler? Hold it over my head when they drop the bombs?"

She turned and ran, disappearing into the gray fog before she had gone down two steps. I started after her, still holding the string of broken lights, tripped over it, and fell almost all the way to the bottom of the steps.

Langby picked me up. "You're off watches," he said grimly.

"You can't do that," I said.

"Oh, yes, I can. I don't want any walking dead on the roofs with me."

I let him lead me down here to the crypt, make me a cup of tea, put me to bed, all very solicitous. No indication that this is what he has been waiting for. I will lie here till the sirens go. Once I am on the roofs he will not be able to send me back without seeming suspicious. Do you know what he said before he left, asbestos coat and rubber boots, the dedicated fire watcher? "I want you to get some sleep." As if I could sleep with Langby on the roofs. I would be burned alive.

December 30—The sirens woke me, and old Bence-Jones said, "That should have done you some good. You've slept the clock round."

"What day is it?" I said, going for my boots.

"The twenty-ninth," he said, and as I dived for the door, "No need to hurry. They're late tonight. Maybe they won't come at all. That'd be a blessing, that would. The tide's out."

I stopped by the door to the stairs, holding onto the cool stone. "Is St. Paul's all right?"

"She's still standing," he said. "Have a bad dream?"

"Yes," I said, remembering the bad dreams of all the past weeks—the dead cat in my arms in St. John's Wood, Langby with his parcel and his *Worker* under his arm, the fire-watch stone garishly lit by Christ's lantern. Then I remembered I had not dreamed at all. I had slept the kind of sleep I had prayed for, the kind of sleep that would help me remember.

Then I remembered. Not St. Paul's, burned to the ground by the Communists. A headline from the dailies. "Marble Arch hit. Eighteen killed by blast." The date was not clear except for the year. 1940. There were exactly two more days left in 1940. I grabbed my coat and muffler and ran up the stairs and across the marble floor.

"Where the hell do you think you're going?" Langby shouted to me. I couldn't see him.

"I have to save Enola," I said, and my voice echoed in the dark sanctuary. "They're going to bomb Marble Arch."

"You can't leave now," he shouted after me, standing where the fire-watch stone would be. "The tide's out. You dirty..."

I didn't hear the rest of it. I had already flung myself down the steps and into a taxi. It took almost all the money I had, the money I had so carefully hoarded for the trip back to St. John's Wood. Shelling started while we were still in Oxford Street, and the driver refused to go any farther. He let me out into pitch blackness, and I saw I would never make it in time.

Blast. Enola crumpled on the stairway down to the tube, her open-toed shoes still on her feet, not a mark on her. And when I try to lift her, jelly under the skin. I would have to wrap her in the muffler she gave me, because I was too late. I had gone back a hundred years to be too late to save her.

I ran the last blocks, guided by the gun emplacement that had to be in Hyde Park, and skidded down the steps into Marble Arch. The woman in the ticket booth took my last shilling for a ticket to St. Paul's Station. I stuck it in my pocket and raced toward the stairs.

"No running," she said placidly. "To your left, please." The door to the right was blocked off by wooden barricades, the metal gates beyond pulled to and chained. The board with names on it for the stations was X-ed with tape, and a new sign that read, "All trains," was nailed to the barricade, pointing left.

Enola was not on the stopped escalators or sitting against the wall in the hallway. I came to the first stairway and could not get through. A family had set out, just where I wanted to step, a communal tea of bread and butter, a little pot of jam sealed with waxed paper, and a kettle on a ring like the one Langby and I had rescued out of the rubble, all of it spread on a cloth embroidered at the corners with flowers. I stood staring down at the layered tea, spread like a waterfall down the steps.

"I... Marble Arch..." I said. Another twenty killed by flying tiles. "You shouldn't be here."

"We've as much right as anyone," the man said belligerently, "and who are you to tell us to move on?"

A woman lifting saucers out of a cardboard box looked up at me, frightened. The kettle began to whistle.

"It's you that should move on," the man said. "Go on then." He stood off to one side so I could pass. I edged past the embroidered cloth apologetically.

"I'm sorry," I said. "I'm looking for someone. On the platform."

"You'll never find her in there, mate," the man said thumbing in that direction. I hurried past him, nearly stepping on the teacloth, and rounded the corner into hell.

It was not hell. Shopgirls folded coats and leaned back against them, cheerful or sullen or disagreeable, but certainly not damned. Two boys scuffled for a shilling and lost it on the tracks. They bent over the edge, debating whether to go after it, and the station guard yelled to them to back away. A train rumbled through, full of people. A mosquito landed on the guard's hand and he reached out to slap it and missed. The boys laughed. And behind and before them, stretching in all directions down the deadly tile curves of the tunnel like casualties, backed into the entrance-ways and onto the stairs, were people. Hundreds and hundreds of people.

I stumbled back into the hall, knocking over a teacup. It spilled like a flood across the cloth.

"I told you, mate," the man said cheerfully. "It's Hell in there, ain't it? And worse below."

"Hell," I said. "Yes." I would never find her. I would never save her. I looked at the woman mopping up the tea, and it came to me that I could not save her either. Enola or the cat or any of them, lost here in the endless stairways and cul-de-sacs of time. They were already dead a hundred years, past saving. The past is beyond saving. Surely that was the lesson the history department sent me all this way to learn. Well, fine, I've learned it. Can I go home now?

Of course not, dear boy. You have foolishly spent all your money on taxicabs and brandy, and tonight is the night the Germans burn the City. (Now it is too late, I remember it all. Twenty-eight incendiaries on the roofs.) Langby must have his chance, and you must learn the hardest lesson of all and the one you should have known from the beginning. You cannot save St. Paul's.

I went back out onto the platform and stood behind the yellow line until a train pulled up. I took my ticket out and held it in my hand all the way to St. Paul's Station. When I got there, smoke billowed toward me like an easy spray of water. I could not see St. Paul's.

"The tide's out," a woman said in a voice devoid of hope, and I went down in a snake pit of limp cloth hoses. My hands came up covered with rank-smelling mud, and I understood finally (and too late) the significance of the tide. There was no water to fight the fires.

A policeman barred my way and I stood helplessly before him with no idea what to say. "No civilians allowed up there," he said. "St. Paul's is for it." The smoke billowed like a thundercloud, alive with sparks, and the dome rose golden above it.

"I'm fire watch," I said, and his arm fell away, and then I was on the roofs.

My endorphin levels must have been going up and down like an air raid siren. I do not have any short-term from then on, just moments that do not fit together: the people in the church when we brought Langby down, huddled in a corner playing cards, the whirlwind of burning scraps of wood in the dome, the ambulance driver who wore open-toed shoes like Enola and smeared salve on my burned hands. And in the center, the one clear moment when I went after Langby on a rope and saved his life.

I stood by the dome, blinking against the smoke. The City was on fire and it seemed as if St. Paul's would ignite from the heat, would crumble from the noise alone. Bence-Jones was by the northwest tower, hitting at an incendiary with a spade. Langby was too close to the patched place where the bomb had gone through, looking toward me. An incendiary clattered behind him. I turned to grab a shovel, and when I turned back, he was gone.

"Langby!" I shouted, and could not hear my own voice. He had fallen into the chasm and nobody saw him or the incendiary. Except me. I do not remember how I got across the roof. I think I called for a rope. I got a rope. I tied it around my waist, gave the ends of it into the hands of the fire watch, and went over the side. The fires lit the walls of the hole almost all the way to the bottom. Below me I could see a pile of whitish rubble. He's under there, I thought, and jumped free of the wall. The space was so narrow there was nowhere to throw the rubble. I was afraid I would inadvertently stone him, and I

tried to toss the pieces of planking and plaster over my
shoulder, but there was barely room to turn. For one awful
moment I thought he might not be there at all, that the pieces
of splintered wood would brush away to reveal empty pavement, as they had in the crypt.

I was numbed by the indignity of crawling over him. If he
was dead I did not think I could bear the shame of stepping on
his helpless body. Then his hand came up like a ghost's and
grabbed my ankle, and within seconds I had whirled and had
his head free.

He was the ghastly white that no longer frightens me. "I
put the bomb out," he said. I stared at him, so overwhelmed
with relief I could not speak. For one hysterical moment I
thought I would even laugh, I was so glad to see him. I finally
realized what it was I was supposed to say.

"Are you all right?" I said.

"Yes," he said and tried to raise himself on one elbow. "So
much the worse for you."

He could not get up. He grunted with pain when he tried to
shift his weight to his right side and lay back, the uneven
rubble crunching sickeningly under him. I tried to lift him
gently so I could see where he was hurt. He must have fallen
on something.

"It's no use," he said, breathing hard. "I put it out."

I spared him a startled glance, afraid that he was delirious,
and went back to rolling him onto his side.

"I know you were counting on this one," he went on, not
resisting me at all. "It was bound to happen sooner or later
with all these roofs. Only I went after it. What'll you tell your
friends?"

His asbestos coat was torn down the back in a long gash.
Under it his back was charred and smoking. He had fallen on
the incendiary. "Oh, my God," I said, trying frantically to see
how badly he was burned without touching him. I had no way
of knowing how deep the burns went, but they seemed to
extend only in the narrow space where the coat had torn. I
tried to pull the bomb out from under him, but the casing was
as hot as a stove. It was not melting, though. My sand and
Langby's body had smothered it. I had no idea if it would start
up again when it was exposed to the air. I looked around, a

little wildly, for the bucket and stirrup pump Langby must have dropped when he fell.

"Looking for a weapon?" Langby said, so clearly it was hard to believe he was hurt at all. "Why not just leave me here? A bit of overexposure and I'd be done for by morning. Or would you rather do your dirty work in private?"

I stood up and yelled to the men on the roof above us. One of them shone a pocket torch down at us, but its light didn't reach.

"Is he dead?" somebody shouted down to me.

"Send for an ambulance," I said. "He's been burned."

I helped Langby up, trying to support his back without touching the burn. He staggered a little and then leaned against the wall, watching me as I tried to bury the incendiary, using a piece of the planking as a scoop. The rope came down and I tied Langby to it. He had not spoken since I helped him up. He let me tie the rope around his waist, still looking steadily at me. "I should have let you smother in the crypt," he said.

He stood leaning easily, almost relaxed against the wood supports, his hands holding him up. I put his hands on the slack rope and wrapped it once around them for the grip I knew he didn't have. "I've been onto you since that day in the Gallery. I knew you weren't afraid of heights. You came down here without any fear of heights when you thought I'd ruined your precious plans. What was it? An attack of conscience? Kneeling there like a baby, whining. 'What have we done? What have we done?' You made me sick. But you know what gave you away first? The cat. Everybody knows cats hate water. Everybody but a dirty Nazi spy."

There was a tug on the rope. "Come ahead," I said, and the rope tautened.

"That WVS tart? Was she a spy, too? Supposed to meet you in Marble Arch? Telling me it was going to be bombed. You're a rotten spy, Bartholomew. Your friends already blew it up in September. It's open again."

The rope jerked suddenly and began to lift Langby. He twisted his hands to get a better grip. His right shoulder scraped the wall. I put up my hands and pushed him gently so that his left side was to the wall. "You're making a big mistake, you know," he said. "You should have killed me. I'll tell."

I stood in the darkness, waiting for the rope. Langby was unconscious when he reached the roof. I walked past the fire watch to the dome and down to the crypt.

This morning the letter from my uncle came and with it a ten-pound note.

December 31—Two of Dunworthy's flunkies met me in St. John's Wood to tell me I was late for my exams. I did not even protest. I shuffled obediently after them without even considering how unfair it was to give an exam to one of the walking dead. I had not slept in—how long? Since yesterday when I went to find Enola. I had not slept in a hundred years.

Dunworthy was at his desk, blinking at me. One of the flunkies handed me a test paper and the other one called time. I turned the paper over and left an oily smudge from the ointment on my burns. I stared uncomprehendingly at them. I had grabbed at the incendiary when I turned Langby over, but these burns were on the backs of my hands. The answer came to me suddenly in Langby's unyielding voice. "They're rope burns, you fool. Don't they teach you Nazi spies the proper way to come up a rope?"

I looked down at the test. It read, "Number of incendiaries that fell on St. Paul's. Number of land mines. Number of high explosive bombs. Method most commonly used for extinguishing incendiaries. Land mines. High explosive bombs. Number of volunteers on first watch. Second watch. Casualties. Fatalities." The questions made no sense. There was only a short space, long enough for the writing of a number, after any of the questions. Method most commonly used for extinguishing incendiaries. How would I ever fit what I knew into that narrow space? Where were the questions about Enola and Langby and the cat?

I went up to Dunworthy's desk. "St. Paul's almost burned down last night," I said. "What kind of questions are these?"

"You should be answering questions, Mr. Bartholomew, not asking them."

"There aren't any questions about the people," I said. The outer casing of my anger began to melt.

"Of course there are," Dunworthy said, flipping to the second page of the test. "Number of casualties, 1940. Blast, shrapnel, other."

"Other?" I said. At any moment the roof would collapse on me in a shower of plaster dust and fury. "Other? Langby put out a fire with his own body. Enola has a cold that keeps getting worse. The cat..." I snatched the paper back from him and scrawled "one cat" in the narrow space next to "blast." "Don't you care about them at all?"

"They're important from a statistical point of view," he said, "but as individuals, they are hardly relevant to the course of history."

My reflexes were shot. It was amazing to me that Dunworthy's were almost as slow. I grazed the side of his jaw and knocked his glasses off. "Of course they're relevant!" I shouted "They *are* the history, not all these bloody numbers!"

The reflexes of the flunkies were very fast. They did not let me start another swing at him before they had me by both arms and were hauling me out of the room.

"They're back there in the past with nobody to save them. They can't see their hands in front of their faces and there are bombs falling down on them and you tell me they aren't important? You call that being an historian?"

The flunkies dragged me out the door and down the hall. "Langby saved St. Paul's. How much more important can a person get? You're no historian! You're nothing but a..." I wanted to call him a terrible name, but the only curses I could summon up were Langby's. "You're nothing but a dirty Nazi spy!" I bellowed. "You're nothing but a lazy bourgeois tart!"

They dumped me on my hands and knees outside the door and slammed it in my face. "I wouldn't be an historian if you paid me!" I shouted and went to see the fire-watch stone.

December 31—I am having to write this in bits and pieces. My hands are in pretty bad shape, and Dunworthy's boys didn't help matters much. Kivrin comes in periodically, wearing her St. Joan look, and smears so much salve on my hands that I can't hold a pencil.

St. Paul's Station is not there, of course, so I got out at Holborn and walked, thinking about my last meeting with Dean Matthews on the morning after the burning of the City. This morning.

"I understand you saved Langby's life," he said. "I also understand that between you, you saved St. Paul's last night."

I showed him the letter from my uncle and he stared at it as if he could not think what it was. "Nothing stays saved forever," he said, and for a terrible moment I thought he was going to tell me Langby had died. "We shall have to keep on saving St. Paul's until Hitler decides to bomb the countryside."

The raids on London are almost over, I wanted to tell him. He'll start bombing the countryside in a matter of weeks. Canterbury, Bath, aiming always at the cathedrals. You and St. Paul's will both outlast the war and live to dedicate the fire-watch stone.

"I am hopeful, though," he said. "I think the worst is over."

"Yes, sir." I thought of the stone, its letters still readable after all this time. No, sir, the worst is not over.

I managed to keep my bearings almost to the top of Ludgate Hill. Then I lost my way completely, wandering about like a man in a graveyard. I had not remembered that the rubble looked so much like the white plaster dust Langby had tried to dig me out of. I could not find the stone anywhere. In the end I nearly fell over it, jumping back as if I had stepped on a grave.

It is all that's left. Hiroshima is supposed to have had a handful of untouched trees at ground zero, Denver the capitol steps. Neither of them says, "Remember the men and women of St. Paul's Watch who by the grace of God saved this cathedral." The grace of God.

Part of the stone is sheared off. Historians argue there was another line that said, "for all time," but I do not believe that, not if Dean Matthews had anything to do with it. And none of the watch it was dedicated to would have believed it for a minute. We saved St. Paul's every time we put out an incendiary, and only until the next one fell. Keeping watch on the danger spots, putting out the little fires with sand and stirrup pumps, the big ones with our bodies, in order to keep the whole vast complex structure from burning down. Which sounds to me like a course description for History Practicum 401. What a fine time to discover what historians are for when I have tossed my chance for being one out the windows as easily as they tossed the pinpoint bomb in! No, sir, the worst is not over.

There are flash burns on the stone, where legend says the Dean of St. Paul's was kneeling when the bomb went off. Totally apocryphal, of course, since the front door is hardly an appropriate place for prayers. It is more likely the shadow of a tourist who wandered in to ask the whereabouts of the Windmill Theatre, or the imprint of a girl bringing a volunteer his muffler. Or a cat.

Nothing is saved forever, Dean Matthews; and I knew that when I walked in the west doors that first day, blinking into the gloom, but it is pretty bad nevertheless. Standing here knee-deep in rubble out of which I will not be able to dig any folding chairs or friends, knowing that Langby died thinking I was a Nazi spy, knowing that Enola came one day and I wasn't there. It's pretty bad.

But it is not as bad as it could be. They are both dead, and Dean Matthews, too; but they died without knowing what I knew all along, who sent me to my knees in the Whispering Gallery, sick with grief and guilt: that in the end none of us saved St. Paul's. And Langby cannot turn to me, stunned and sick at heart, and say, "Who did this? Your friends the Nazis?" And I would have to say, "No. The Communists." That would be the worst.

I have come back to the room and let Kivrin smear more salve on my hands. She wants me to get some sleep. I know I should pack and get gone. It will be humiliating to have them come and throw me out, but I do not have the strength to fight her. She looks so much like Enola.

January 1—I have apparently slept not only through the night, but through the morning mail drop as well. When I woke up just now, I found Kivrin sitting on the end of the bed holding an envelope. "Your grades came," she said.

I put my arm over my eyes. "They can be marvelously efficient when they want to, can't they?"

"Yes," Kivrin said.

"Well, let's see it," I said, sitting up. "How long do I have before they come and throw me out?"

She handed the flimsy computer envelope to me. I tore it along the perforation. "Wait," she said. "Before you open it, I want to say something." She put her hand gently on my burns. "You're wrong about the history department. They're very good."

It was not exactly what I expected her to say. "Good is not the word I'd use to describe Dunworthy," I said and yanked the inside slip free.

Kivrin's look did not change, not even when I sat there with the printout on my knees where she could surely see it.

"Well," I said.

The slip was hand-signed by the esteemed Dunworthy. I have taken a first. With honors.

January 2—Two things came in the mail today. One was Kivrin's assignment. The history department thinks of everything—even to keeping her here long enough to nursemaid me, even to coming up with a prefabricated trial by fire to send their history majors through.

I think I wanted to believe that was what they had done, Enola and Langby only hired actors, the cat a clever android with its clockwork innards taken out for the final effect, not so much because I wanted to believe Dunworthy was not good at all, but because then I would not have this nagging pain at not knowing what had happened to them.

"You said your practicum was England in 1300?" I said, watching her as suspiciously as I had watched Langby.

"1349," she said, and her face went slack with memory. "The plague year."

"My God," I said. "How could they do that? The plague's a ten."

"I have a natural immunity," she said and looked at her hands.

Because I could not think of anything to say, I opened the other piece of mail. It was a report on Enola. Computer-printed, facts and dates and statistics, all the numbers the history department so dearly loves, but it told me what I thought I would have to go without knowing: that she had gotten over her cold and survived the Blitz. Young Tom had been killed in the Baedaker raids on Bath, but Enola had lived until 2006, the year before they blew up St. Paul's.

I don't know whether I believe the report or not, but it does not matter. It is, like Langby's reading aloud to the old man, a simple act of human kindness. They think of everything.

Not quite. They did not tell me what happened to Langby. But I find as I write this that I already know: I saved his life. It does not seem to matter that he might have died in hospital next day; and I find, in spite of all the hard lessons the history department has tried to teach me, I do not quite believe this one: that nothing is saved forever. It seems to me that perhaps Langby is.

January 3—I went to see Dunworthy today. I don't know what I intended to say—some pompous drivel about my willingness to serve in the fire-watch of history, standing guard against the falling incendiaries of the human heart, silent and saintly.

But he blinked at me nearsightedly across his desk, and it seemed to me that he was blinking at that last bright image of St. Paul's in sunlight before it was gone forever and that he knew better than anyone that the past cannot be saved, and I said instead, "I'm sorry that I broke your glasses, sir."

"How did you like St. Paul's?" he said, and like my first meeting with Enola, I felt I must be somehow reading the signals all wrong, that he was not feeling loss, but something quite different.

"I loved it, sir," I said.

"Yes," he said. "So do I."

Dean Matthews is wrong. I have fought with memory my whole practicum only to find that it is not the enemy at all, and being an historian is not some saintly burden after all. Because Dunworthy is not blinking against the fatal sunlight of the last morning, but into the gloom of that first afternoon, looking in the great west doors of St. Paul's at what is, like Langby, like all of it, every moment, in us, saved forever.

HER FURRY FACE

by Leigh Kennedy

"Her Furry Face" was purchased by Shawna McCarthy, and appeared in the Mid-December 1983 issue of IAsfm, with an illustration by John Piebard. Although buried inconspicuously in the middle of the magazine, "Her Furry Face" managed to attract attention anyway—it quickly became one of the most controversial stories of the year, and remains one of the most controversial stories the magazine has ever run. "Her Furry Face" was another editorial gamble on Shawna's part—and another one that paid off, for "Her Furry Face" may well have been the best story to appear in IAsfm that year, and was almost certainly the best story of its length. Two other stories by Kennedy appeared in IAsfm that year—"Belling Martha" and "Greek"—and both of them might well have attracted similar attention in a year that didn't have "Her Furry Face" in it.

Born in Denver, Colorado, Leigh Kennedy spent some years in Austin as an honorary Texan, and now lives in England. She sold her first story in 1978 and has since become a frequent contributor to most of the major SF magazines and anthologies. Her first novel,

The Journal of Nicholas the American, *was published last year by the Atlantic Monthly Press and was a Finalist for the 1986 Nebula award. Upcoming is a short-story collection,* Faces, *which will also be published by the Atlantic Monthly Press.*

Douglas was embarrassed when he saw Annie and Vernon mating.

He'd seen hours of sex between orangutans, but this time was different. He'd never seen *Annie* doing it. He stood in the shade of the pecan tree for a moment, shocked, iced tea glasses sweating in his hand, then he backed around the corner of the brick building. He was confused. The cicadas seemed louder than usual, the sun hotter, and the squeals of pleasure from the apes strange.

He walked back to the front porch and sat down. His mind still saw the two giant mounds of red-orange fur moving together like one being.

When the two orangs came back around, Douglas thought he saw smugness in Vernon's face. Why not, he thought? I guess I would be smug, too.

Annie flopped down on the grassy front yard and crossed one leg over the other, her abdomen bulging high; she gazed upward into the heavy white sky.

Vernon bounded toward Douglas. He was young and red-chocolate colored. His face was still slim, without the older orangutan jowls yet.

"Be polite," Douglas warned him.

"Drink tea, please?" Vernon signed rapidly, the fringe on his elbows waving. "Dry as bone."

Douglas handed Vernon one of the glasses of tea, though he'd brought it out for Annie. The handsome nine-year-old downed it in a gulp. "Thank you," he signed. He touched the edge of the porch and withdrew his long fingers. "Could fry egg," he signed, and instead of sitting, swung out hand-over-hand on the ropes between the roof of the schoolhouse and the trees. It was a sparse and dry substitute for the orang's native rain forest.

He's too young and crude for Annie, Douglas thought.

"Annie," Douglas called. "Your tea."

Annie rolled onto one side and lay propped on an elbow, staring at him. She was lovely. Fifteen years old, her fur was glossy and coppery, her small yellow eyes in the fleshy face expressive and intelligent. She started to raise up toward him, but turned toward the road.

The mail jeep was coming down the highway.

In a blurred movement, she set off at a four-point gallop down the half-mile drive toward the mailbox. Vernon swung down from his tree and followed, making a small groan.

Reluctant to go out in the sun, Douglas put down the tea and followed the apes down the drive. By the time he got near them, Annie was sitting with mail sorted between her toes, holding an opened letter in her hands. She looked up with an expression on her face that he'd never seen—it could have been fear, but it wasn't.

She handed the letter to Vernon, who pestered her for it. "Douglas," she signed, "they want to buy my story."

Therese lay in the bathwater, her knees sticking up high, her hair floating beside her face. Douglas sat on the edge of the tub; as he talked to her he was conscious that he spoke a double language—the one with his lips and the other with his hands.

"As soon as I called Ms. Young, the magazine editor, and told her who Annie was, she got really excited. She asked me why we didn't send a letter explaining it with the story, so I told her that Annie didn't want anyone to know first."

"Did Annie decide that?" Therese sounded skeptical, as she always seemed to when Douglas talked about Annie.

"We talked about it and she wanted it that way." Douglas felt that resistance from Therese. Why she never understood, he didn't know, unless she did it to provoke him. She acted as though she thought an ape was still just an ape, no matter what he or she could do. "Anyway," he said, "she talked about doing a whole publicity thing to the hilt—talk shows, autograph parties. You know. But Dr. Morris thinks it would be better to keep things quiet."

"Why?" Therese sat up; her legs went underwater and she soaped her arms.

"Because she'd be too nervous. Annie, I mean. It might

disrupt her education to become a celebrity. Too bad. Even Dr. Morris knows that it would be great for fund-raising. But I guess we'll let the press in some."

Therese began to shampoo her hair. "I brought home that essay that Sandy wrote yesterday. The one I told you about. If she were an orangutan instead of just a deaf kid, she could probably get it published in *Fortune*." Therese smiled.

Douglas stood. He didn't like the way Therese headed for the old argument—no matter what one of Therese's deaf students did, if Annie could do it one-one-hundredth as well, it was more spectacular. Douglas knew it was true, but why Therese was so bitter about it, he didn't understand.

"That's great," he said, trying to sound enthusiastic.

"Will you wash my back?" she asked.

He crouched and absently washed her. "I'll never forget Annie's face when she read that letter."

"Thank you," Therese said. She rinsed. "Do you have any plans for this evening?"

"I've got work to do," he said, leaving the bathroom. "Would you like me to work in the bedroom so you can watch television?"

After a long pause, she said, "No, I'll read."

He hesitated in the doorway. "Why don't you go to sleep early? You looked tired."

She shrugged. "Maybe I am."

In the playroom at the school, Douglas watched Annie closely. It was still morning, though late. In the recliner across the room from him, she seemed a little sleepy. Staring out the window, blinking, she marked her place in Pinkwater's *Fat Men From Space* with a long brown finger.

He had been thinking about Therese, who'd been silent and morose that morning. Annie was never morose, though often quiet. He wondered if Annie were quiet today because she sensed that Douglas was not happy. When he'd come to work, she'd given him an extra hug.

He wondered if Annie could have a crush on him, like many schoolgirls have on their teachers. Remembering her mating with Vernon days before, he idly wandered into a fantasy of touching her and gently, gently moving inside her.

The physical reaction to his fantasy embarrassed him. *God, what am I thinking?* He shook himself out of the reverie, averting his gaze for a few moments, until he'd gotten control of himself again.

"Douglas," Annie signed. She walked erect, towering, to him and sat down on the floor at his feet. Her flesh folded onto her lap like dough.

"What?" he asked, wondering suddenly if orangutans were telepathic.

"Why you say my story children's?"

He looked blankly at her.

"Why not send *Harper's?*" she asked, having to spell out the name of the magazine.

He repressed a laugh, knowing it would upset her. "It's . . . it's the kind of story children would like."

"Why?"

He sighed. "The level of writing is . . . *young*. Like you, sweetie." He stroked her head, looking into the small intense eyes. "You'll get more sophisticated as you grow."

"I smart as you," she signed. "You understand me always because I talk smart."

Douglas was dumbfounded by her logic.

She tilted her head and waited. When Douglas shrugged, she seemed to assume victory and returned to her recliner.

Dr. Morris came in. "Here we go," she said, handing him the paper and leaving again.

Douglas skimmed the page until he came to an article about the "ape author." He scanned it. It contained one of her flashpoints; this, and the fact that she was irritable from being in estrus, made him consider hiding it. But that wouldn't be right.

"Annie," he said softly.

She looked up.

"There's an article about you."

"Me read," she signed, putting her book on the floor. She came and crawled up on the sofa next to him. He watched her eyes as they jerked across every word. He grew edgy. She read on.

Suddenly she took off as if from a diving board. He ran after her as she bolted out the door. The stuffed dog which had always been a favorite toy was being shredded in those powerful hands even before he knew she had it. Annie screamed as she pulled the toy apart, running into the yard.

Terrified by her own aggression, she ran up the tree with stuffing falling like snow behind her.

Douglas watched as the shade filled with foam rubber and fake fur. The tree branches trembled. After a long while, she stopped pummeling the tree and sat quietly.

She spoke to herself with her long ape hand. "Not animal," she said, "not animal."

Douglas suddenly realized that Therese was afraid of the apes.

She watched Annie warily as the four of them strolled along the edge of the school acreage. Douglas knew that Therese didn't appreciate the grace of Annie's muscular gait as he did; the sign language that passed between them was as similar to the Amslan that Therese used for her deaf children as British to Jamaican. Therese couldn't appreciate Annie in creative conversation.

It wasn't good to be afraid of the apes, no matter how educated they were.

He had invited her out, hoping it would please her to be included in his world here. She had only visited briefly twice before.

Vernon lagged behind them, snapping pictures now and then with the expensive but hardy camera modified for his hands. Vernon took several pictures of Annie and one of Douglas, but only when Therese had separated from him to peer between the rushes at the edge of the creek.

"Annie," Douglas called, pointing ahead. "A cardinal. The red bird."

Annie lumbered forward. She glanced back to see where Douglas pointed, then stood still, squatting. Douglas walked beside her and they watched the bird.

It flew.

"Gone," Annie signed.

"Wasn't it pretty, though?" Douglas asked.

They ambled on. Annie stopped often to investigate shiny bits of trash or large bugs. They didn't come this far from the school much. Vernon whizzed past them, a dark auburn streak of youthful energy.

Remembering Therese, Douglas turned. She sat on a stump far behind. He was annoyed. He'd told her to wear her jeans and a straw hat because there would be grass burrs and hot sun. But there she sat, bareheaded, wearing shorts, miserably rubbing at her ankles.

He grunted impatiently. Annie looked up at him. "Not you," he said, stroking her fur. She patted his butt.

"Go on," Douglas said, turning back. When he came to Therese, he said, "What's the problem?"

"No problem." She stood and started forward without looking at him. "I was just resting."

Annie had paused to poke at something on the ground with a stick. Douglas quickened his step. Even though his students were smart. they had orangutan appetites. He always worried that they would eat something that would sicken them. "What is it?" he called.

"Dead cat," Vernon signed back. He took a picture as Annie flipped the carcass with her stick.

Therese hurried forward. "Oh, poor kitty..." she said, kneeling.

Annie had seemed too absorbed in poking the cat to notice Therese approach; only a quick eye could follow her leap. Douglas was stunned.

Both screamed. It was over.

Annie clung to Douglas's legs, whimpering.

"Shit!" Therese said. She lay on the ground, rolling from side to side, holding her left arm. Blood dripped from between her fingers.

Douglas pushed Annie back. "That was bad, *very bad,*" he said. "Do you hear me?"

Annie sank down on her rump and covered her head. She hadn't gotten a child-scolding for a long time. Vernon stood beside her, shaking his head, signing, "Not wise, baboon-face."

"Stand up," Douglas said to Therese. "I can't help you right now."

Therese was pale, but dry-eyed. Clumsily, she stood and grew even paler. A hunk of flesh hung loosely from above her elbow, meaty and bleeding. "Look."

"Go on. Walk back to the house. We'll come right behind

you." He tried to keep his voice calm, holding a warning hand on Annie's shoulder.

Therese moaned, catching her breath. "It hurts," she said, but stumbled on.

"We're coming," Douglas said sternly. "Just walk and—Annie, don't you dare step out of line."

They walked silently, Therese ahead, leaving drops of blood in the dirt. The drops got larger and closer together. Once, Annie dipped her finger into a bloody spot and sniffed her fingertip.

Why can't things just be easy and peaceful, he wondered. Something always happens. *Always.* He should have known better than to bring Therese around Annie. Apes didn't understand that vulnerable quality that Therese was made of. He himself didn't understand it, though at one time he'd probably been attracted to it. No—maybe he'd never really seen it until it was too late. He'd only thought of Therese as "sweet" until their lives were too tangled up to keep clear of it.

Why couldn't she be as tough as Annie? Why did she always take everything so seriously?

They reached the building. Douglas sent Annie and Vernon to their rooms and guided Therese to the infirmary. He watched as Jim, their all-purpose nurse and veterinary assistant, examined her arm. "I think you should probably have stitches."

He left the room to make arrangements.

Therese looked at Douglas, holding the gauze over her still-bleeding arm. "Why did she bite me?" she asked.

Douglas didn't answer. He couldn't think off how to say it.

"Do you have any idea?" she asked.

"You asked for it, all your wimping around."

"*I* . . ."

Douglas saw the anger rising in her. He didn't want to argue now. He wished he'd never brought her. He'd done it for her, and she ruined it. All ruined.

"Don't start," he said simply, giving her a warning look.

"But, Douglas, I didn't do anything."

"Don't start," he repeated.

"I see now," she said coldly. "Somehow it's my fault again."

Jim returned with his supplies.

"Do you want me to stay?" Douglas asked. He suddenly felt a pang of guilt, realizing that she was actually hurt enough for all this attention.

"No," she said softly.

And her eyes looked far, far from him as he left her.

On the same day that the largest donation ever came to the school, a television news team came out to tape.

Douglas could tell that everyone was excited. Even the chimps that lived on the north half of the school hung on the fence and watched the TV van being unloaded. The reporter decided upon the playroom as the best location for the taping, though she didn't seem to relish sitting on the floor with the giant apes. People went over scripts, strung cords, microphones, set up hot lights, and discussed angles and sound while pointing at the high ceiling's jungle-gym design. All this to talk to a few people and an orangutan.

They brought Annie's desk into the playroom, contrary to Annie's wishes. Douglas explained that it was temporary, that these people would go away after they talked a little. Douglas and Annie stayed outside as long as possible and played Tarzan around the big tree. He tickled her. She grabbed him as he swung from a limb. "Kagoda?" she signed, squeezing him with one arm.

"Kagoda!" he shouted, laughing.

They relaxed on the grass. Douglas was hot. He felt flushed all over. "Douglas," Annie signed, "they read story?"

"Not yet. It isn't published yet."

"Why come talk?" she asked.

"Because you wrote it and sold it and people like to interview famous authors." He groomed her shoulder. "Time to go in," he said, seeing a wave from inside.

Annie picked him up in a big hug and carried him in.

"Here it is!" Douglas called to Therese and turned on the video recorder.

First, a long shot of the school from the dusty drive, looking only functional and square, without personality. The reporter's voice said, "Here, just southeast of town, is a special school with unusual young students. The students here have little prospect for employment when they graduate, but millions of dollars each year fund this institution."

A shot of Annie at her typewriter, picking at the keyboard with her long fingers; a sheet of paper is slowly covered with large block letters.

"This is Annie, a fifteen-year-old orangutan, who has been a student with the school for five years. She graduated with honors from another 'ape school' in Georgia before coming here. And now Annie has become a writer. Recently, she sold a story to a children's magazine. The editor who bought the story didn't know that Annie was an orangutan until after she had selected the story for publication."

Annie looked at the camera uncertainly.

"Annie can read and write, and understand spoken English, but she cannot speak. She uses a sign language similar to the one hearing-impaired use." Change in tone from narrative to interrogative. "Annie, how did you start writing?"

Douglas watched himself on the small screen watching Annie sign, "Teacher told me write." He saw himself grin, eyes shift slightly toward the camera, but generally watching Annie. His name and "Orangutan Teacher" appeared on the screen. The scene made him uneasy.

"What made you send in Annie's story for publication?" the reporter asked.

Douglas signed to Annie, she came to him for a hug, and turned a winsome face to the camera. "Our administrator, Dr. Morris, and I both read it. I commented that I thought it was as good as any kid's story, so Dr. Morris said, 'Send it in.' The editor liked it." Annie made a "pee" sign to Douglas.

Then, a shot of Dr. Morris in her office, a chimp on her lap, clapping her brown hands.

"Dr. Morris, your school was established five years ago by grants and government funding. What is your purpose here?"

"Well, in the last few decades, apes—mostly chimpanzees like Rose here—have been taught sign language experimentally. Mainly to prove that apes could indeed use language." Rosie put the tip of her finger through the gold hoop in Dr. Morris's ear. Dr. Morris took her hand away gently. "We were established with the idea of *educating* apes, a comparable education to the primary grades." She looked at the chimp. "Or however far they will advance."

"Your school has two orangutans and six chimpanzees. Are there differences in their learning?" the reporter asked.

Dr. Morris nodded emphatically. "Chimpanzees are very clever, but the orang has a different brain structure which allows for more abstract reasoning. Chimps learn many things quickly, orangs are slower. But the orangutan has the ability to learn in greater depth."

Shot of Vernon swinging in the ropes in front of the school.

Assuming that Vernon is Annie, the reporter said, "Her teacher felt from the start that Annie was an especially promising student. The basic sentences that she types out on her typewriter are simple but original entertainment."

Another shot of Annie at the typewriter.

"If you think this is just monkey business, you'd better think again. Tolstoy, watch out!"

Depressed by the lightness, brevity, and the stupid "monkey-business" remark, Douglas turned off the television.

He sat for a long time. Whenever Therese had gone to bed, she had left him silently. After a half hour of staring at the blank screen, he rewound his video recorder and ran it soundlessly until Annie's face appeared.

And then froze it. He could almost feel again the softness of her halo of red hair against his chin.

He couldn't sleep.

Therese had rumpled her way out of the sheet and lay on her side, her back to him. He looked at the shape of her shoulder and back, downward to the dip of the waist, up the curve of her hip. Her buttocks were round ovals, one atop the other. Her skin was sleek and shiny in the filtered streetlight coming through the window. She smelled slightly of shampoo and even more slightly of female.

What he felt for her anyone would call "love," when he thought of her generally. And yet, he found himself helplessly angry with her most of the time. When he thought he could amuse her, it would end with her feelings being hurt for some obscure reason. He heard cruel words come barging out of an otherwise gentle mouth. She took everything seriously; mishaps and misunderstandings occurred beyond his control, beyond his repair.

Under this satiny skin, she was troubled and tense. A lot of sensitivity and fear. He had stopped trying to gain access to what had been the happier parts of her person, not understanding where they had gone. He had stopped wanting to love her, but he didn't *not* want to love her, either. It just didn't seem to matter.

Sometimes, he thought, it would be easier to have someone like Annie for a wife.

Annie.

He loved her furry face. He loved the unconditional joy in her face when she saw him. It was always there. She was bright and warm and unafraid. She didn't read things into what he said, but listened and talked with him. They were so natural together. Annie was so filled with vitality.

Douglas withdrew his hand from Therese, whose skin seemed a bare blister of dissatisfaction.

He lay on the floor of the apes' playroom with the fan blowing across his chest. He held Annie's report on Lawrence's *Sons and Lovers* by diagonal corners to keep it from flapping.

Annie lazily swung from bars criss-crossing the ceiling.

"Paul wasn't happy at work because the boss looked over his shoulder at his handwriting," she had written. "But he was happy again later. His brother died and his mother was sad. Paul got sick. He was better and visited his friends again. His mother died and his friends didn't tickle him anymore."

Douglas looked over the top of the paper at Annie. True, it was the first time she'd read an "adult" novel, but he'd expected something better than this. He considered asking her if Vernon had written the report for her, but thought better of it.

"Annie," he said, sitting up. "What do you think this book is really about?"

She swung down and landed on the sofa. "About man," she said.

Douglas waited. There was no more. "But what about it? Why this man instead of another? What was special about him?"

Annie rubbed her hands together, answerless.

"What about his mother?"

"She help him," Annie answered in a flurry of dark fingers. "Especially when he paint."

Douglas frowned. He looked at the page again, disappointed.

"What I do?" Annie asked, worried.

He tried to brighten up. "You did just fine. It was a hard book."

"Annie smart," the orang signed. "Annie smart."

Douglas nodded. "I know."

Annie rose, then stood on her legs, looking like a two-story fuzzy building, teetering from side to side. "Annie smart. Writer. Smart," she signed. "Write book. Bestseller."

Douglas made a mistake. He laughed. Not as simple as a human laughing at another, this was an act of aggression. His bared teeth and uncontrolled guff-guff struck out at Annie. He tried to stop.

She made a gulping sound and galloped out of the room.

"Wait, Annie!" He chased after her.

By the time he got outside she was far ahead. He stopped running when his chest hurt and trotted slowly through the weeds toward her. She sat forlornly far away and watched him come.

When he was near, she signed "hug" three times.

Douglas collapsed, panting, his throat raw. "Annie, I'm sorry," he said. "I didn't mean it." He put his arms around her.

She held onto him.

"I love you, Annie. I love you so much I don't want ever to hurt you. Ever, ever, ever. I want to be with you all the time. Yes, you're smart and talented and good." He kissed her tough face.

Whether forgotten or forgiven, the hurt of his laughter was gone from her eyes. She held him tighter, making a soft sound in her throat, a sound for him.

They lay together in the crackling yellow weeds, clinging. Douglas felt his love physically growing for her. More passionately than ever before in his life, he wanted to make love to her. He touched her. He felt that she understood what she wanted, that her breath on his neck was anticipation. A consummation as he'd never imagined, the joining of their species in language and body. Not dumb animal-banging but mutual love . . . He climbed over her and hugged her back.

Annie went rigid when he entered her.

Slowly, she rolled away from him, but he held onto her.

"No." A horrible grimace came across her face that raised the hairs on the back of Douglas's neck. "Not you," she said.

She's going to kill me, he thought.

His passion declined; Annie disentangled herself and walked away.

He sat for a moment, stunned at what he'd done, stunned at what had happened, wondering what he would do the rest of his life with the memory of it. Then he zipped up his pants.

Staring at his dinner plate, he thought, it's just the same as if I had been rejected by a woman. I'm not the kind that goes for bestiality. I'm not some farm boy who can't find someplace to put it.

His hands could still remember the matted feel of her fur; tucked in his groin was the memory of being in an alien place. It had made him throw up out in the field that afternoon, and after that he'd come straight home. He hadn't even said goodnight to the orangs.

"What's the matter?" Therese asked.

He shrugged.

She half-rose out of her chair to kiss him on the temple. "You don't have a fever, do you?"

"No."

"Can I do something to make you feel better?" Her hand slid along his thigh.

He stood up. "Stop it."

She sat still. "Are you in love with another woman?"

Why can't she just leave me alone? "No. I have a lot on my mind. There's a lot going on."

"It never was like this, even when you were working on your thesis."

"Therese," he said, with what he felt was undeserved patience, "just leave me alone. It doesn't help with you at me all the time."

"But I'm scared, I don't know what to do. You act like you don't want me around."

"All you do is criticize me." He stood and took his dishes to the sink.

Slowly, she trailed after him, carrying her plate. "I'm just trying to understand. It's my life, too."

He said nothing and she walked away as if someone had told her not to leave footsteps.

In the bathroom, he stripped and stood under the shower a long time. He imagined that Annie's smell clung to him. He felt that Therese could smell it on him.

What have I done, what have I done...

And when he came out of the shower, Therese was gone.

He had considered calling in sick, but he knew that it would be just as miserable to stay around the house and think about Annie, think about Therese, and worse, to think about himself.

He dressed for work but couldn't eat breakfast. Realizing that his pain showed, he straightened his shoulders but found them drooping again as he got out of the car at work.

With some fear, he came through the office. The secretary greeted him with rolled eyes. "Someone's given out our number again," she said as the phone buzzed. Another line was on hold. "This morning there was a man standing at the window watching me until Gramps kicked him off the property."

Douglas shook his head in sympathy with her and approached the orang's door. He felt nauseated again.

Vernon sat at the typewriter, most likely composing captions for his photo album. He didn't get up to greet Douglas but gave him an evaluative stare.

Douglas patted his shoulder. "Working?" he asked.

"Like dog," Vernon said and resumed typing.

Annie sat outside on the back porch. Douglas opened the door and stood beside her. She looked up at him, but—like Vernon—made no move toward the customary hug. The morning was still cool, the shadow of the building still long in front of them. Douglas sat down.

"Annie," he said softly. "I'm sorry. I'll never do it again. You see, I felt..." He stopped. It wasn't any easier than it had been to talk to Oona, or Wendy, or Shelley, or Therese.... He realized that he didn't understand her any more than he'd understood them. Why had she rejected him? What was she thinking? What would happen from now on? Would they be friends again?

"Oh, hell," he said. He stood. "It won't happen again."

Annie gazed away into the trees.

He felt strained all over, especially in his throat. He stood by her for a long time.

"I don't want write stories," she signed.

Douglas stared at her. "Why?"

"Don't want." She seemed to shrug.

Douglas wondered what had happened to the confident ape who'd planned to write a bestseller the day before. "Is that because of me?"

She didn't answer.

"I don't understand," he said. "Do you want to write it down for me? Could you explain it that way?"

"No," she signed, "can't explain. Don't want."

He signed. "What *do* you want?"

"Sit tree. Eat bananas, chocolate. Drink brandy." She looked at him seriously. "Sit tree. Day, day, day, week, month, year."

Christ almighty, he thought, she's having a goddamned existential crisis. All the years of education. All the accomplishments. All the hopes of an entire field of primatology. All shot to hell because of a moody ape. It can't just be me. This would have happened sooner or later, but maybe . . . He thought of all the effort he would have to make to repair their relationship. It made him tired.

"Annie, why don't we just ease up a little on your work. You can rest. Today. You can go sit in the tree all of today and I'll bring you a glass of wine."

She shrugged again.

Oh, I've botched it, he thought. What an idiot. He felt a pain coming back, a pain like poison, without a focal point but shooting through his heart and hands, making him dizzy and short of breath.

At least she doesn't hate me, he thought, squatting to touch her hand.

She bared her teeth.

Douglas froze. She slid away from him and headed for the trees.

He sat alone at home and watched the newscast. In a small midwestern town they burned the issues of the magazine with Annie's story in it.

A heavy woman in a windbreaker was interviewed with the bonfire in the background. "I don't want my children reading things that weren't even written by humans. I have human children and this godless ape is not going to tell its stories to them."

A quick interview with Dr. Morris, who looked even more tired and introverted than usual. "The story is a very innocent tale, told by an innocent personality. Annie is not a beast. I really don't think she has any ability for, or intention of, corruption . . ."

He turned the television off. He picked up the phone and dialed one of Therese's friends. "Jan, have you heard from Therese yet?"

"No, sure haven't."

"Well, let me know, okay?"

"Sure."

He thought vaguely about trying to catch her at work, but he left earlier in the morning and came home later in the evening than she did.

Looking at her picture on the wall, he thought of when they had first met, first lived together. There had been a time when he'd loved her so much he'd been bursting with it. Now he felt empty, but curious about where she was. He didn't want her to hate him, but he still didn't know if he could talk to her about what had happened. The idea that she would sit and listen to him didn't seem realistic.

Even Annie wouldn't listen to him anymore.

He was alone. He'd done a big, dumb, terrible thing and wished he hadn't. It would have been different if Annie had reciprocated, if somehow they could have become lovers. Then it would have been them against the world, a new kind of relationship. The first intelligent interspecial love affair . . .

But Annie didn't seem any different than Therese, after all. Annie was no child. She'd given him all those signals, flirting, then not carrying through. Acting like he'd raped her or something. She didn't really have any more interest in him than Dr. Morris would in Vernon. I couldn't have misunderstood, could I? he wondered.

He was alone. And without Annie's consent, he was just a jerk who'd screwed an ape.

"I made a mistake," he said aloud to Therese's picture. "So let's forget it."

But even he couldn't forget.

"Dr. Morris wants to see you," the secretary said as he came in.

"Okay." He changed course for the administrative office. He whistled. In the past few days, Annie had been cool, but he felt that everything would settle down eventually. He felt better. Wondering what horrors or marvels Dr. Morris had to share with him, he knocked at her door and peered through the glass window. Probably another magazine burning, he thought.

She signaled him to come in. "Hello, Douglas."

Annie, he thought, *something's happened.*

He stood until she motioned him to sit down. She looked at his face several seconds. "This is difficult for me," she said.

She's discovered me, he thought. But he put that aside, figuring it was a paranoia that made him worry. There's no way. No way. I have to calm down or I'll show it.

She held up a photograph.

There it was—a dispassionate and cold document of that one moment in his life. She held it up to him like an accusation. It shocked him as if it hadn't been himself.

Defiance forced him to stare at the picture instead of looking for compassion in Dr. Morris's eyes. He knew exactly where the picture had come from.

Vernon and his new telephoto lens.

He imagined the image of his act rising up in a tray of chemicals. Slowly, he looked away from it. Dr. Morris could not know how he had changed since that moment. He could make no protest or denial.

"I have no choice," Dr. Morris said flatly. "I'd always thought that even if you weren't good with people, at least you worked well with the apes. Thank God, Henry, who does Vernon's darkroom work, has promised not to say anything."

Douglas was rising from the chair. He wanted to tear the picture out of her hands because she still held it up to him. He didn't want to see it. He wanted her to ask him if he had changed, that it would never happen again, that he understood he'd been wrong.

But her eyes were flat and shuttered against him. "We'll send your things," she said.

He paused at his car and saw two big red shapes—one coppery orange, one chocolate red—sitting in the trees. Vernon bellowed out a groan that ended with an alien burbling. It was a wild sound full of the jungle and steaming rain.

Douglas watched Annie scratch herself and looked toward chimps walking the land beyond their boundary fence. As she started to turn her gaze his direction he ducked into his car.

Angrily driving away, Douglas thought, why should an ape understand me any better than a human?

HARDFOUGHT

by Greg Bear

"Hardfought" was purchased by Shawna McCarthy toward the beginning of her regime and appeared in the February 1983 issue of IAsfm, with illustrations by H.R. Van Dongen. It was the first IAsfm story to carry a "warning label"—usually a notice that the story contains explicit sexual material and/or "hard" language; in the case of "Hardfought," it was not so much used for that as to warn people that what they were about to read was wildly unlike anything that had ever appeared in IAsfm before—vauntingly ambitious, stunningly complex, and staggering in scope. The purchase of "Hardfought" was a real gamble on McCarthy's part— and one that paid off handsomely. "Hardfought" became one of the most critically acclaimed stories of the year, hailed everywhere as a "breakthrough" novella, a step forward in the evolution of the genre. It went on to win a Nebula Award that year, as did Bear's "Blood Music," from our sister publication, Analog. Bear has not appeared subsequently in IAsfm, alas, but we intend to Keep After Him.

Born in San Diego, California, Greg Bear made his

first sale at the age of fifteen to Robert Lowndes' Famous
Science Fiction, *and has subsequently established himself
as one of the top young professionals in the genre. His
books include the novels* Hegira, Psychlone, Beyond
Heaven's River, Strength of Stones, The Infinity Ccon-
certo, *and the collection* The Wind From a Burning
Woman. *His most recent books are the novels* Blood
Music, *an expanded version of his Nebula-winning story,*
Eon, The Serpent Mage, *and* The Forge of God.

Humans called it the Medusa. Its long twisted ribbons of gas
strayed across fifty parsecs, glowing blue, yellow, and car-
mine. Its central core was a ghoulish green flecked with wa-
tery black. Half a dozen protostars circled the core, and as
many more dim conglomerates pooled in dimples in the nebula's magnetic field. The Medusa was a huge womb of stars
—and disputed territory.

Whenever Prufrax looked at it in displays or through the
ship's ports, it seemed malevolent, like a zealous mother displaying an ominous face to protect her children. Prufrax had
never had a mother, but she had seen them in some of the fibs.

At five, Prufrax was old enough to know the *Mellangee*'s
mission and her role in it. She had already been through four
ship-years of indoctrination. Until her first battle she would be
educated in both the Know and the Tell. She would be exer-
cised and trained in the Mocks; in sleep she would dream of
penetrating the huge red-and-white Senexi seedships and finding the brood mind. "Zap, Zap," she went with her lips, silent
so the tellman wouldn't think her thoughts were straying.

The tellman peered at her from his position in the center of
the spherical classroom. Her mates stared straight at the
center, all focusing somewhere around the tellman's spiderlike
teaching desk, waiting for the trouble, some fidgeting. "How
many branch individuals in the Senexi brood mind?" he asked.
He looked around the classroom. Peered face by face. Focused on her again. "Pru?"

"Five," she said. Her arms ached. She had been pumped
full of moans the wake before. She was already three meters
tall, in elfstate, with her long, thin limbs not nearly adequately

fleshed out and her fingers still crisscrossed with the surgery done to adapt them to the gloves.

"What will you find in the brood mind?" the tellman pursued, his impassive face stretched across a hammerhead as wide as his shoulders. Some of the fems thought tellmen were attractive. Not many—and Pru was not one of them.

"Yoke," she said.

"What is in the brood-mind yoke?"

"Fibs."

"More specifically? And it really isn't all fib, you know."

"Info. Senexi data."

"What will you do?"

"Zap," she said, smiling.

"Why, Pru?"

"Yoke has team gens-memory. Zap yoke, spill the life of the team's five branch inds."

"Zap the brood, Pru?"

"No," she said solemnly. That was a new instruction, only in effect since her class's inception. "Hold the brood for the supreme overs." The tellmen did not say what would be done with the Senexi broods. That was not her concern.

"Fine," said the tellman. "You tell well, for someone who's always half-journeying."

She was already five, soon six. Old. Some saw Senexi by the time they were four.

"Zap, Zap," she went with her lips.

Aryz skidded through the thin layer of liquid ammonia on his broadest pod, considering his new assignment. He knew the Medusa by another name, one that conveyed all the time and effort the Senexi had invested in it. The protostar nebula held few mysteries for him. He and his four branch-mates, who along with the all-important brood mind made up one of the six teams aboard the seedship, had patrolled the nebula for ninety-three orbits, each orbit—including the timeless periods outside status geometry—taking some one hundred and thirty human years. They had woven in and out of the tendrils of gas, charting the infalling masses and exploring the rocky accretion disks of stars entering the main sequence. With each measure and update, the brood minds refined their view of the nebula as it would be a hundred generations hence when the Senexi plan would finally mature.

The Senexi were nearly as old as the galaxy. They had achieved spaceflight during the time of the starglobe when the galaxy had been a sphere. They had not been a quick or brilliant race. Each great achievement had taken thousands of generations, and not just because of their intellectual handicaps. In those times elements heavier than helium had been rare, round only around stars that had greedily absorbed huge amounts of primeval hydrogen, burned fierce and blue, and exploded early, permeating the ill-defined galactic arms with carbon and nitrogen, lithium and oxygen. Elements heavier than iron had been almost nonexistent. The biologies of cold gas-giant worlds had developed with a much smaller palette of chemical combinations in producing the offspring of the primary Population II stars.

Aryz, even with the limited perspective of a branch ind, was aware that, on the whole, the humans opposing the seedship were more adaptable, more vital. But they were not more experienced. The Senexi with their billions of years had often matched them. And Aryz's perspective was expanding with each day of his new assignment.

In the early generations of the struggle, Senexi mental stasis and cultural inflexibility had made them avoid contact with the Population I species. They had never begun a program of extermination of the younger, newly life-forming worlds; the task would have been monumental and probably useless. So when spacefaring cultures developed, the Senexi had retreated, falling back into the redoubts of old stars even before engaging with the new kinds. They had retreated for three generations, about thirty thousand human years, raising their broods on cold nestworlds around red dwarfs, conserving, holding back for the inevitable conflicts.

As the Senexi had anticipated, the younger Population I races had found need of even the aging groves of the galaxy's first stars. They had moved in savagely, voraciously, with all the strength and mutability of organisms evolved from a richer soup of elements. Biology had, in some ways, evolved in its own right and superseded the Senexi.

Aryz raised the upper globe of his body, with its five silicate eyes arranged in a cross along the forward surface. He had memory of those times, and times long before, though his team hadn't existed then. The brood mind carried memories selected from the total store of nearly twelve billion years' experience, an awesome amount of knowledge, even to a Senexi. He pushed himself forward with his rear pods.

Through the brood mind Aryz could share the memories of a hundred thousand past generations, yet the brood mind itself was younger than its branch individuals. For a time in their youth, in their liquid-dwelling larval form, the branch inds carried their own sacs of data, each a fragment of the total necessary for complete memory. The branch inds swam through ammonia seas and wafted through thick warm gaseous zones, protoplasmic blobs three to four meters in diameter, developing their personalities under the weight of the past—and not even a complete past. No wonder they were inflexible, Aryz thought. Most branch inds were aware enough to see that—especially when they were allowed to compare histories with the Population I species, as he was doing—but there was nothing to be done. They were content the way they were. To change would be unspeakably repugnant. Extinction was preferable . . . almost.

But now they were pressed hard. The brood mind had begun a number of experiments. Aryz's team had been selected from the seedship's contingent to oversee the experiments, and Aryz had been chosen as the chief investigator. Two orbits past, they had captured six human embryos in a breeding device, as well as a highly coveted memory storage center. Most Senexi engagements had been with humans for the past three or four generations. Just as the Senexi dominated Population II species, humans were ascendant among their kind.

Experiments with the human embryos had already been conducted. Some had been allowed to develop normally; others had been tampered with, for reasons Aryz was not aware of. The tamperings had not been very successful.

The newer experiments, Aryz suspected, were going to take a different direction, and the seedship's actions now focused on him; he believed he would be given complete authority over the human shapes. Most branch inds would have dissipated under such a burden, but not Aryz. He found the human shapes rather interesting, in their own horrible way. They might, after all, be the key to Senexi survival.

The moans were toughening her elfstate. She lay in pain for a wake, not daring to close her eyes; her mind was changing and she feared sleep would be the end of her. Her nightmares were not easily separated from life; some, in fact, were sharper.

Too often in sleep she found herself in a Senexi trap, struggling uselessly, being pulled in deeper, her hatred wasted against such power...

When she came out of the rigor, Prufrax was given leave by the subordinate tellman. She took to the *Mellangee*'s greenroads, walking stiffly in the shallow gravity. Her hands itched. Her mind seemed almost empty after the turmoil of the past few wakes. She had never felt so calm and clear. She hated the Senexi double now; once for their innate evil, twice for what they had made her overs put her through to be able to fight them. She was growing more mature wake by wake. Fight-budding, the tellman called it, hate coming out like blooms, synthesizing the sunlight of his teaching into pure fight.

The greenroads rose temporarily beyond the labyrinth shields and armor of the ship. Simple transparent plastic-and-steel geodesic surfaces formed a lacework over the gardens, admitting radiation necessary to the vegetation growing along the paths.

Prufrax looked down on the greens to each side of the paths without much comprehension. They were *beautiful*. Yes, one should say that, think that, but what did it mean? Pleasing? She wasn't sure what being pleased meant, outside of thinking Zap. She sniffed a flower that, the signs explained, bloomed only in the light of young stars not yet fusing. They were near such a star now, and the greenroads were shiny black and electric green with the blossoms. Lamps had been set out for other plants unsuited to such darkened conditions. Some technic allowed suns to appear in selected plastic panels when viewed from certain angles. Clever, the technicals.

She much preferred the looks of a technical to a tellman, but she was common in that. She wished a technical were on the greenroads with her. The moans had the effect of making her receptive—what she saw, looking in mirrors, was a certain shine in her eyes—but there was no chance of a breeding liaison. She was quite unreproductive in this moment of elf-state.

She looked up and saw a figure at least a hundred meters away, sitting on an allowed patch near the path. She walked casually, as gracefully as possible with the stiffness. Not a technical, she saw soon, but she was not disappointed. Too calm.

"Over," he said as she approached.

"Under," she replied. But not by much—he was probably six or seven ship-years old and not easily classifiable.

"Such a fine elfstate," he commented. His hair was black. He was shorter than she, but something in his build reminded her of the glovers. He motioned for her to sit, and she did so with a whuff, massaging her knees.

"Moans?" he asked.

"Bad stretch," she said.

"You're a glover." He was looking at the fading scars on her hands.

"Can't tell what you are," she said.

"Noncombat," he said. "Tuner of the mandates."

She knew very little about the mandates, except that law decreed every ship carry one, and few of the crew were ever allowed to peep. "Noncombat, hm?" She mused. She didn't despise him for that; one never felt strongs negatives for a crew member.

"Been working on ours this wake," he said. "Too hard, I guess. Told to talk." Overzealousness in work was considered an erotic trait aboard the *Mellangee*. Still, she didn't feel too receptive toward him.

"Glovers walk after a rough growing," she said.

He nodded. "My name's Clevo."

"Prufrax."

"Combat soon?"

"Hoping. Waiting forever."

"I know. Just been allowed access to the mandate for a half-dozen wakes. All new to me. Very happy."

"Can you talk about it?" she asked. Information about the ship not accessible in certain rates was excellent barter.

"Not sure," he said, frowning. "I've been told caution."

"Well, I'm listening."

He could come from glover stock, she thought, but probably not from technical. He wasn't very muscular, but he wasn't as tall as a glover, or as thin, either.

"If you'll tell me about gloves."

With a smile she held up her hands and wriggled the short, stumpy fingers. "Sure."

The brood mind floated weightless in its tank, held in place by buffered carbon rods. Metal was at a premium aboard the Senexi ships, more out of tradition than actual material limitations.

Aryz floated before the brood mind, all these thoughts coursing through his tissues. He had no central nervous system, no truly differentiated organs except those that dealt with the outside world—limbs, eyes, permea. The brood mind, however, was all central nervous system, a thinly buffered sac of viscous fluids about ten meters wide.

"Have you investigated the human memory device yet?" the brood mind asked.

"I have."

"Is communication with the human shapes possible for us?"

"We have already created interfaces for dealing with their machines. Yes, it seems likely we can communicate."

"Does it strike you that in our long war with humans, we have made no attempt to communicate before?"

This was a complicated question. It called for several qualities that Aryz, as a branch ind, wasn't supposed to have. Inquisitiveness, for one. Branch inds did not ask questions. They exhibited initiative only as offshoots of the brood mind.

He found, much to his dismay, that the question had occurred to him. "We have never captured a human memory store before," he said, by way of incomplete answer. "We could not have communicated without such an extensive source of information."

"Yet, as you say, even in the past we have been able to use human machines."

"The problem is vastly more complex."

The brood mind paused. "Do you think the teams have been prohibited from communicating with humans?"

Aryz felt the closest thing to anguish possible for a branch ind. Was he being considered unworthy? Accused of conduct inappropriate to a branch ind? His loyalty the brood mind was unshakeable. "Yes."

"And what might our reasons be?"

"Avoidance of pollution."

"Correct. We can no more communicate with them and remain untainted than we can walk on their worlds, breathe their atmosphere." Again, silence. Aryz lapsed into a mode of inactivity. When the brood mind readdressed him, he was instantly aware.

"Do you know how you are different?" it asked.

"I am not . . ." Again, hesitation. Lying to the brood mind was impossible for him. He signaled his distress.

"You are useful to the team," the brood mind said. Aryz calmed instantly. His thoughts became sluggish, receptive. There was a possibility of redemption. But how was he different? "You are to attempt communication with the shapes yourself. You will not engage in any discourse with your fellows while you are so involved." He was banned. "And after completion of this mission and transfer of certain facts to me, you will dissipate."

Aryz struggled with the complexity of the orders. "How am I different, worthy of such a commission?"

The surface of the brood mind was as still as an undisturbed pool. The indistinct black smudges that marked its radiating organs circulated slowly within the interior, then returned, one above the other, to focus on him. "You will grow a new branch ind. It will not have your flaws, but, then again, it will not be useful to me should such a situation come a second time. Your dissipation will be a relief, but it will be regretted."

"How am I different?"

"I think you know already," the brood mind said. "When the time comes, you will feed the new branch ind all your memories but those of human contact. If you do not survive to that stage of its growth, you will pick your fellow who will perform that function for you."

A small pinkish spot appeared on the back of Aryz's globe. He floated forward and placed his largest permeum against the brood mind's cool surface. The key and command were passed, and his body became capable of reproduction. Then the signal of dismissal was given. He left the chamber.

Flowing through the thin stream of liquid ammonia lining the corridor, he felt ambiguously stimulated. His was a position of privilege and anathema. He had been blessed—and condemned. Had any other branch ind experienced such a thing?

Then he knew the brood mind was correct. He was different from his fellows. None of them would have asked such questions. None of them could have survived the suggestion of communicating with human shapes. If this task hadn't been given to him, he would have had to dissipate anyway.

The pink spot grew larger, then began to make grayish flakes. It broke through the skin, and casually, almost without thinking, Aryz scraped it off against a bulkhead. It clung, made a radio-frequency emanation something like a sigh, and began absorbing nutrients from the ammonia.

Aryz went to inspect the shapes.

She was intrigued by Clevo, but the kind of interest she felt was new to her. She was not particularly receptive. Rather, she felt a mental gnawing as if she were hungry or had been injected with some kind of brain moans. What Clevo told her about the mandates opened up a topic she had never considered before. How did all things come to be—and how did she figure in them?

The mandates were quite small, Clevo explained, each little more than a cubic meter in volume. Within them was the entire history and culture of the human species, as accurate as possible, culled from all existing sources. The mandate in each ship was updated whenever the ship returned to a contact station.

Clevo had been assigned small tasks—checking data and adding ship records—that had allowed him to sample bits of the mandate. "It's mandated that we have records," he explained, "and what we have, you see, is *man-data*." He smiled. "That's a joke," he said. "Sort of."

Prufrax nodded solemnly. "So where do we come from?"

"Earth, of course," Clevo said. "Everyone knows that."

"I mean, where do *we* come from—you and I, the crew."

"Breeding division. Why ask? You know."

"Yes." She frowned, concentrating. "I mean, we don't come from the same place as the Senexi. The same way."

"No, that's foolishness."

She saw that it was foolishness—the Senexi were different all around. What was she struggling to ask? "Is their fib like our own?"

"Fib? History's not a fib. Not most of it, anyway. Fibs are for unreal. History is over fib."

She knew, in a vague way, that fibs were unreal. She didn't like to have their comfort demeaned, though. "Fibs are fun," she said. "They teach Zap."

"I suppose," Clevo said dubiously. "Being noncombat, I don't see Zap fibs."

Fibs without Zap were almost unthinkable to her. "Such dull," she said.

"Well, of course you'd say that. I might find Zap fibs dull —think of that?"

"We're different," she said. "Like Senexi are different."

Clevo's jaw hung open. "No way. We're crew. We're human. Senexi are . . ." He shook his head as if fed bitters.

"No, I mean . . ." She paused, uncertain whether she was entering unallowed territory. "You and I, we're fed different, given different moans. But in a big way we're different from Senexi. They aren't made, nor act, as you and I. But . . ." Again it was difficult to express. She was irritated. "I don't want to talk to you anymore."

A tellman walked down the path, not familiar to Prufrax. He held out his hand for Clevo, and Clevo grasped it. "It's amazing," the tellman said, "how you two gravitate to each other. Go, elfstate," he addressed Prufrax. "You're on the wrong greenroad."

She never saw the young researcher again. With glover training under way, the itches he aroused soon faded, and Zap resumed its overplace.

The Senexi had ways of knowing humans were near. As information came in about fleets and individual cruisers less than one percent nebula diameter distant, the seedship seemed warmer, less hospitable. Everything was UV with anxiety, and the new branch ind on the wall had to be shielded by a special silicate cup to prevent distortion. The brood mind grew a corniculum automatically, though the toughened outer membrane would be of little help if the seedship was breached.

Aryz had buried his personal confusion under a load of work. He had penetrated the human memory store deeply enough to find instructions on its use. It called itself a *mandate* and even the simple preliminary directions were difficult for Aryz. It was like swimming in another family's private sea, though of course infinitely more alien; how could he connect with experiences never had, problems and needs never encountered by his kind?

He observed the new branch ind once or twice each watch period. Never before had he seen an induced replacement. The normal process was for two brood minds to exchange plasm and form new team buds, then to exchange and nurture the buds. The buds were later cast free to swim as individual larvae. While the larvae swam through the liquid and gas atmosphere of a Senexi world often for thousands, even tens of thousands of kilometers, inevitably they returned to gather with the other buds of their team. Replacements were selected from a separately created pool of "generic" buds only if one or more originals had been destroyed during their wanderings. The destruction of a complete team meant reproductive failure.

In a mature team, only when a branch ind was destroyed did the brood mind induce a replacement. In essence, then, Aryz was already considered dead.

Yet he was still useful. That amused him, if the Senexi emotion could be called amusement. Restricting himself from his fellows was difficult, but he filled the time by immersing himself, through the interface, in the mandate.

The humans were also connected with the mandate through their surrogate parent, and in this manner they were quiescent.

He reported infrequently to the broodmind. Until he had established communication, there was little to report.

And throughout his turmoil, like the others he could sense a fight was coming. It could determine the success or failure of all their work in the nebula. In the grand scheme, failure here might not be crucial. But the Senexi had taken the long view too often in the past.

And he knew himself well enough to doubt he would fail.

He could feel an affinity for the humans already, peering at them through the thick glass wall in their isolated chamber, his skin paling at the thought of their heat, their poisonous chemistry. A diseased affinity. He hated himself for it. And reveled in it. It was what made him particularly useful to the team. If he was defective, and this was the only way he could serve, then so be it.

The other branch inds observed his passings from a distance, making no judgments. Aryz was dead, though he worked and moved. His sacrifice had been fearful. Yet he would not be a hero. His kind could never be emulated.

It was a horrible time, a horrible conflict.

She floated in language, learned it in a trice; there were no distractions. She floated in history and picked up as much as she could, for the source seemed inexhaustible. She tried to distinguish between eyes-open—the barren, pale gray-brown chamber with the thick green wall, beyond which floated a murky roundness—and eyes-shut, when she dropped back into language and history with no fixed foundation.

Eyes-open, she saw the Mam with its comforting limbs and its soft voice, its tubes and extrusions of food and its hissings and removal of waste. Through Mam's wires she learned. Mam also tended another like herself, and another unlike either of them, more like the shape beyond the green wall.

She was very young, and it was all a mystery.

At least she knew her name. And what she was supposed to do. She took small comfort in that.

They fitted Prufrax with her gloves, and she went into the practice chamber, dragged by her gloves almost, for she hadn't yet knitted the plug-in nerves in her right index digit and her pace control was uncertain.

There, for six wakes straight, she flew with the other glovers back and forth across the dark spaces like elfstate comets. Constellations and nebula aspects flashed at random on the distant walls, and she oriented to them like a night-flying bird. Her glovemates were Ornin, an especially slender male, and Ban, a red-haired female, and the special-projects sisters Ya, Trice, and Damu, new from the breeding division.

When she let the gloves have their way, she was freer than she had ever felt before. Control was somewhere uncentered,

behind her eyes and beyond her fingers, as if she were drawn
on a beautiful silver wire where it was best to go. Doing what
was best to do. She barely saw the field that flowed from the
grip of the thick, solid gloves or felt its caressing, life-
sustaining influence. Truly, she hardly saw or felt anything but
situations, targets, opportunities, the success or failure of the
Zap. Failure was an acute pain. She was never reprimanded
for failure; the reprimand was in her blood, and she felt as if
she wanted to die. But then the opportunity would improve,
the Zap would succeed, and everything around her—stars,
Senexi seedship, the *Mellangee*, everything—seemed part of
a beautiful dream all her own.

She was intense in the Mocks.

Their initial practice over, the entry play began.

One by one, the special-projects sisters took their hyper-
bolic formation. Their glove fields threw out extensions, and
they combined force. In they went, the mock Senexi seedship
brilliant red and white and UV and radio and hateful before
them. Their tails swept through the seedship's outer shields
and swirled like long silky hair laid on water; they absorbed
fantastic energies, grew bright like violent little stars against
the seedship outline. They were engaged in the drawing of the
shields, and sure as topology, the spirals of force had to have a
dimple on the opposite side that would iris wide enough to let
in glovers. The sisters twisted the forces and Prufrax could see
the dimple stretching out under them—

The exercise ended. The elfstate glovers were cast into
sudden dark. Prufrax came out of the mock unprepared, her
mind still bent on the Zap. The lack of orientation drove her as
mad as a moth suddenly flipped from night to day. She car-
eened until gently mitted and channeled. She flowed down a
tube, the field slowly neutralizing, and came to a halt still
gloved, her body jerking and tingling.

"What the breed happened?" she screamed, her hands beginning to hurt.

"Energy conserve," a mechanical voice answered. Behind
Prufrax the other elfstate glovers lined up in the catch tube, all
but the special-projects sisters. Ya, Trice, and Damu had been
taken out of the exercise early and replaced by simulations.
There was no way their functions could be mocked. They

entered the tube ungloved and helped their comrades adjust to the overness of the real.

As they left the mock chamber, another batch of glovers, even younger and fresher in elfstate, passed them. Ya held her hands up, and they saluted in return. "Breed more every day," Prufrax grumbled. She worried about having so many crew she'd never be able to conduct a satisfactory Zap herself. Where would the honor of being a glover go if everyone was a glover?

She wriggled into her cramped bunk, feeling exhilarated and irritated. She replayed the mocks and added in the missing Zap, then stared gloomily at her small narrow feet.

Out there the Senexi waited. Perhaps they were in the same state as she—ready to fight, testy at being reined in. She pondered her ignorance, her inability to judge whether such things were even possible among the enemy. She thought of the researcher, Clevo. "Blank," she murmured. "Blank, blank." Such thoughts were unnecessary, and humanizing Senexi was unworthy of a glover.

Aryz looked at the instrument, stretched a pod into it, and willed. Vocal human language came out the other end, thin and squeaky in the helium atmosphere. The sound disgusted and thrilled him. He removed the instrument from the gelatinous strands of the engineering wall and pushed it into his interior through a stretched permeum. He took a thick draft of ammonia and slid to the human-shapes chamber again.

He pushed through the narrow port into the observation room. Adjusting his eyes to the heat and bright light beyond the transparent wall, he saw the round mutated shape first—the result of their unsuccessful experiments. He swung his sphere around and looked at the others.

For a time he couldn't decide which was uglier—the mutated shape or the normals. Then he thought of what it would be like to have humans tamper with Senexi and try to make them into human forms. . . . He looked at the round human and shrank as if from sudden heat. Aryz had had nothing to do with the experiments. For that, at least, he was grateful.

Aryz placed the tip of the vocalizer against a sound-transmitting plate and spoke.

"Zello," came the sound within the chamber. The mutated

shape looked up. It lay on the floor, great bloated stomach backed by four almost useless pods. It usually made high-pitched sounds continuously. Now it stopped and listened, straining on the tube that connected it to the breed-supervising device.

"Hello," replied the *male*. It sat on a ledge across the chamber, having unhooked itself.

The machine that served as surrogate parent and instructor stood in one corner, an awkward parody of a human, with limbs too long and head too small. Aryz could see the unwillingness of the designing engineers to examine human anatomy too closely.

"I am called—" Aryz said, his name emerging as a meaningless stretch of white noise. He would have to do better than that. He compressed and adapted the frequencies. "I am called Aryz."

"Hello," the young female said.

"What are your names?" He knew them well enough, having listened many times to their conversations.

"Prufrax," the female said. "I'm a glover."

The human shapes contained very little genetic memory. As a kind of brood marker, Aryz supposed, they had been equipped with their name, occupation, and the rudiments of environmental knowledge.

"I'm a teacher, Prufrax," Aryz said.

"I don't understand you," the female replied.

"You teach me, I teach you."

"We have the Mam," the male said, pointing to the machine. "She teaches us." The Mam, as they called it, was hooked into the mandate.

"Do you know where you are?" Aryz asked.

"Where we live," Prufrax said. "Eyes-open."

"Don't talk to it," the male said. "Mam talks to us." Aryz consulted the mandate for some understanding of the name they had given to the breed-supervising machine. Mam, it explained, was probably a natural expression for womb-carrying parent. Aryz severed the machine's power.

"Mam is no longer functional," he said. He would have the engineering wall put together another less identifiable machine to link them to the mandate and to their nutrition. He wanted them to associate comfort and completeness with nothing but himself.

The machine slumped, and the female shape pulled herself free of the hookup. She started to cry, a reaction quite mysterious to Aryz. His link with the mandate had not been intimate enough to answer questions about the wailing and moisture from the eyes. After a time the male and female lay down and became dormant.

The mutated shape made more soft sounds and tried to approach the transparent wall. It held up its thin arms as if beseeching. The others would have nothing to do with it; now it wished to go with him. Perhaps the biologists had partially succeeded in their attempt at transformation; perhaps it was more Senexi than human.

Aryz quickly backed out through the port, into the cool and security of the corridor beyond.

It was an endless orbital dance, this detection and matching of course, moving away and swinging back, deceiving and revealing, between the *Mellangee* and the Senexi seedship.

Filled with her skill and knowledge, Prufrax waited, feeling like a ripe fruit about to fall from the tree. At this point in their training, just before the application, elfstates were most receptive. She was allowed to take a lover, and they were assigned small separate quarters near the outer greenroads.

The contact was satisfactory, as far as it went. Her mate was an older glover named Kumnax, and as they lay back in the cubicle, soothed by air-dance fibs, he told her stories about past battles, special tactics, how to survive.

"Survive?" she asked, puzzled.

"Of course." His long brown face was intent on the view of the greenroads through the cubicle's small window.

"I don't understand," she said.

"Most glovers don't make it," he said patiently.

"I will."

He turned to her. "You're six," he said. "You're very young. I'm ten. I've seen. You're about to be applied for the first time, you're full of confidence. But most glovers won't make it. They breed thousands of us. We're expendable. We're based on the best glovers of the past but even the best don't survive."

"I will," Prufrax repeated, her jaw set.

"You always say that," he murmured.

Prufrax stared at him for a moment.

"Last time I knew you," he said, "you kept saying that. And here you are, fresh again."

"What last time?"

"Master Kumnax," a mechanical voice interrupted.

He stood, looking down at her. "We glovers always have big mouths. They don't like us knowing, but once we know, what can they do about it?"

"You are in violation," the voice said. "Please report to **S**."

"But now, if you last, you'll know more than the tellman tells."

"I don't understand," Prufrax said slowly, precisely, looking him straight in the eye.

"I've paid my debt," Kumnax said. "We glovers stick. Now I'm going to go get my punishment." He left the cubicle. Prufrax didn't see him again before her first application.

The seedship buried itself in a heating protostar, raising shields against the infalling ice and stone. The nebula had congealed out of a particularly rich cluster of exploded fourth- and fifth-generation stars, thick with planets, the detritus of which now fell on Aryz's ship like hail.

Aryz had never been so isolated. No other branch ind addressed him; he never even saw them now. He made his reports to the brood mind, but even there the reception was warmer and warmer, until he could barely endure to communicate. Consequently—and he realized this was part of the plan—he came closer to his charges, the human shapes.

The brood mind was interested in one question: how successfully could they be planted aboard a human ship? Would they be accepted until they could carry out their sabotage, or would they be detected? Already Senexi instructions were being coded into their teachings.

"I think they will be accepted in the confusion of an engagement," Aryz answered. He had long since guessed the general outlines of the brood mind's plans. Communication with the human shapes was for one purpose only, to use them as decoys, insurgents. They were weapons. Knowledge of human activity and behavior was not an end in itself; seeing what was happening to him, Aryz fully understood why the brood mind wanted such study to proceed no further.

He would lose them soon, he thought, and his work would be over. He would be much too human-tainted. He would end, and his replacement would start a new existence, very little different from Aryz's—but, he reasoned, adjusted. The replacement would not have Aryz's peculiarity.

He approached his last meeting with the brood mind, preparing himself for his final work, for the ending. In the cold liquid-filled chamber, the great red-and-white sac waited, the center of his team, his existence. He adored it. There was no way he could criticize its action.

Yet—

"We are being sought," the brood mind radiated. "Are the shapes ready?"

"Yes," Aryz said. "The new teaching is firm. They believe they are fully human." And, except for the new teaching, they were. "They defy sometimes." He said nothing about the mutated shape. It would not be used. If they won this encounter, it would probably be placed with Aryz's body in a fusion torch for complete purging.

"Then prepare them," the brood mind said. "They will be delivered to the vector for positioning and transfer."

Darkness and waiting. Prufrax nested in her delivery tube like a freshly chambered round. Through her gloves she caught distant communications murmurs that resembled voices down hollow pipes. The *Mellangee* was coming to full readiness.

Huge as her ship was, Prufrax knew that it would be dwarfed by the seedship. She could recall some hazy details about the seedship's structure, but most of that information was stored securely away from interference by her conscious mind.

More information would be fed to her just before the launch, but she knew the general procedure. The seedship was deep in a protostar, hiding behind the distortion of geometry and the complete hash of electromagnetic energy. The *Mellangee* would approach, collide if need be. Penetrate. Release. Find. Zap. Her fingers ached. Sometime before the launch she would also be fed her final moans—the tempers—and she would be primed to leave elfstate. She would be a mature glover. She would be a woman.

If she returned

will return.

Her fingers ached worse.

The tempers came, moans tiding in, then the battle data. As it passed into her subconscious, she caught a flash of—

Rocks and ice, a thick cloud of dust and gas glowing red but seeming dark, no stars, no constellation guides this time. The beacon came on. That would be her only way to orient once the gloves stopped inertial and locked onto the target.

The seedship

was like

a shadow within a shadow

twenty-two kilometers across, yet

carrying

only six

teams

LAUNCH *she flies!*

Data: The *Mellangee* has buried herself in the seedship, plowed deep into the interior like a carnivore's muzzle looking for vitals

Instruction a swarm of seeks is dashing through the seedship, looking for the brood minds, for the brood chambers, for branch inds. The glovers will follow.

Prufrax sees herself clearly now. She is the great avenging comet, bringer of omen and doom, like a knife moving through the glass and ice and thin, cold helium as if they weren't there, the chambered round fired and tearing at hundreds of kilometers an hour through the Senexi vessel, following the seeks.

The seedship cannot withdraw into higher geometries now. It is pinned by the *Mellangee*. It is hers.

Information floods her, pleases her immensely. She swoops down orange-and-gray corridors, buffeting against the walls like a ricocheting bullet. Almost immediately she comes across a branch ind, sliding through the ammonia film against the outrushing wind, trying to reach an armored cubicle. Her first Zap is too easy, not satisfying, nothing like what she thought. In her wake the branch ind becomes scattered globules of plasma. She plunges deeper.

Aryz delivers his human charges to the vectors that will launch them. They are equipped with simulations of the human weapons, their hands encased in the hideous gray gloves.

The seedship is in deadly peril; the battle has almost been lost at one stroke. The seedship cannot remain whole. It must self-destruct, taking the human ship with it, leaving only a fragment with as many teams as can escape.

The vectors launch the human shapes. Aryz tries to determine which part of the ship will be elected to survive; he must not be there. His job is over, and he must die.

The glovers fan out through the seedship's central hollow, demolishing the great cold drive engines, bypassing the shielded fusion flare and the reprocessing plant, destroying machinery built before their Earth was formed.

The special-projects sisters take the lead. Suddenly they are confused. They have found a brood mind, but it is not heavily protected. They surround it, prepare for the Zap—

It is sacrificing itself, drawing them into an easy kill and away from another portion of the seedship. Power is concentrating elsewhere. Sensing that, they kill quickly and move on.

Aryz's brood mind prepares for escape. It begins to wrap itself in flux bind as it moves through the ship toward the frozen fragment. Already three of its five branch inds are dead; it can feel other brood minds dying. Aryz's bud replacement has been killed as well.

Following Aryz's training, the human shapes rush into corridors away from the main action. The special-projects sisters encounter the decoy male, allow it to fly with them . . . until it aims its weapons. One Zap almost takes out Trice. The others fire on the shape immediately. He goes to his death weeping, confused from the very moment of his launch.

The fragment in which the brood mind will take refuge encompasses the chamber where the humans had been nurtured, where the mandate is still stored. All the other brood minds are dead, Aryz realizes; the humans have swept down on them so quickly. What shall he do?

Somewhere, far off, he feels the distressed pulse of another branch ind dying. He probes the remains of the seedship. He is the last. He cannot dissipate now; he must ensure the brood mind's survival.

Prufrax, darting through the crumbling seedship, searching for more opportunities, comes across an injured glover. She calls for a mediseek and pushes on.

The brood mind settles into the fragment. Its support system is damaged; it is entering the time-isolated state, the flux bind, more rapidly than it should. The seals of foamed electric ice cannot quite close off the fragment before Ya, Trice, and Damu slip in. They frantically call for bind cutters and preservers; they have instructions to capture the last brood mind, if possible.

But a trap falls upon Ya, and snarling fields tear her from her gloves. She is flung down a dark distintegrating shaft, red cracks opening all around as the seedship's integrity fails. She trails silver dust and freezes, hits a barricade, shatters.

The ice seals continue to close. Trice is caught between them and pushes out frantically, blundering into the region of the intensifying flux bind. Her gloves break into hard bits, and she is melded into an ice wall like an insect trapped on the surface of a winter lake.

Damu sees that the brood mind is entering the final phase of flux bind. After that they will not be able to touch it. She begins a desperate Zap.

and is too late.

Aryz directs the subsidiary energy of the flux against her. Her Zap deflects from the bind region, she is caught in an interference pattern and vibrates until her tiniest particles stop their knotted whirlpool spins and she simply becomes

space and searing light.

The brood mind, however, has been damaged. It is losing information from one portion of its anatomy. Desperate for storage, it looks for places to hold the information before the flux bind's last wave.

Aryz directs an interface onto the brood mind's surface. The silvery pools of time binding flicker around them both. The brood mind's damaged sections transfer their data into the last available storage device—the human mandate.

Now it contains both human and Senexi information.

The silvery pools unite, and Aryz backs away. No longer can he sense the brood mind. It is out of reach but not yet safe. He must propel the fragment from the remains of the seedship. Then he must wrap the fragment in its own flux bind, cocoon it in physics to protect it from the last ravages of the humans.

Aryz carefully navigates his way through the few remaining corridors. The helium atmosphere has almost completely dissipated, even there.. He strains to remember all the procedures. Soon the seedship will explode, destroying the human ship. By then they must be gone.

Angry red, Prufrax follows his barely sensed form, watching him behind barricades of ice, approaching the moment of a most satisfying Zap. She gives her gloves their way

and finds a shape behind her, wearing gloves that are not gloves, not like her own, but capable of grasping her in tensed fields, blocking the Zap, dragging them together. The fragment separates, heat pours in from the protostar cloud. They are swirled in their vortex of power, twin locked comets—one red, one sullen gray.

"Who are you?" Prufrax screams as they close in on each other in the fields. Their environments meld. They grapple. In the confusion, the darkening, they are drawn out of the cloud with the fragment, and she sees the other's face.

Her own.

The seedship self-destructs. The fragment is propelled from the protostar, above the plane of what will become planets in their orbits, away from the crippled and dying *Mellangee*.

Desperate, Prufrax uses all her strength to drill into the fragment. Helium blows past them, and bits of dead branch inds.

Aryz catches the pair immediately in the shapes chamber, rearranging the fragment's structure to enclose them with the mutant shape and mandate. For the moment he has time enough to concentrate on them. They are dangerous. They are almost equal to each other, but his shape is weakening faster than the true glover. They float, bouncing from wall to wall in the chamber, forcing the mutant to crawl into a corner and howl with fear.

There may be value in saving the one and capturing the other. Involved as they are, the two can be carefully dissected from their fields and induced into a crude kind of sleep before the glover has a chance to free her weapons. He can dispose of the gloves—fake and real—and hook them both to the Mam, reattach the mutant shape as well. Perhaps something can be learned from the failure of the experiment.

The dissection and capture occur faster than the planning. His movement slows under the spreading flux bind. His last action, after attaching the humans to the Mam, is to make sure the brood mind's flux bind is properly nested within that of the ship.

The fragment drops into simpler geometries.

It is as if they never existed.

The battle was over. There were no victors. Aryz became aware of the passage of time, shook away the sluggishness, and crawled through painfully dry corridors to set the environmental equipment going again. Throughout the fragment, machines struggled back to activity.

How many generations? The constellations were unrecognizable. He made star traces and found familiar spectra and types, but advanced in age. There had been a malfunction in the overall flux bind. He couldn't find the nebula where the battle had occurred. In its place were comfortably middle-aged stars surrounded by young planets.

Aryz came down from the makeshift observatory. He slid through the fragment, established the limits of his new home, and found the solid mirror surface of the brood mind's cocoon. It was still locked in flux bind, and he knew of no way to free it. In time the bind would probably wear off—but that might require life spans. The seedship was gone. They had lost the brood chamber, and with it the stock.

He was the last branch ind of his team. Not that it mattered now; there was nothing he could initiate without a brood mind. If the flux bind was permanent, then he might as well be dead.

He closed his thoughts around him and was almost completely submerged when he sensed an alarm from the shapes chamber. The interface with the mandate had turned itself off; the new version of the Mam was malfunctioning. He tried to repair the equipment, but without the engineer's wall he was almost helpless. The best he could do was rig a temporary nutrition supply through the old human-form Mam. When he was done, he looked at the captive and the two shapes, then at the legless, armless Mam that served as their link to the interface and life itself.

She had spent her whole life in a room barely eight by ten meters, and not much taller than her own height. With her had been Grayd and the silent round creature whose name—if it had any—they had never learned. For a time there had been Mam, then another kind of Mam not nearly as satisfactory. She was hardly aware that her entire existence had been miserable, cramped, in one way or another incomplete.

Separated from them by a transparent partition, another round shape had periodically made itself known by voice or gesture.

Grayd had kept her sane. They had engaged in conspiracy. Removing themselves from the interface—what she called "eyes-shut"—they had held onto each other, tried to make sense out of what they knew instinctively, what was fed them through the interface, and what the being beyond the partition told them.

First, they knew their names, and they knew that they were glovers. They knew that glovers were fighters. When Aryz passed instruction through the interface on how to fight, they had accepted it eagerly but uneasily. It didn't seem to jibe with instructions locked deep within their instincts.

Five years under such conditions had made her introspective. She expected nothing, sought little beyond experience in the eyes-shut. Eyes-open with Grayd seemed scarcely more than a dream. They usually managed to ignore the peculiar round creature in the chamber with them; it spent nearly all its time hooked to the mandate and the Mam.

Of one thing only was she completely sure. Her name was Prufrax. She said it in eyes-open and eyes-shut, her only certainty.

Not long before the battle, she had been in a condition resembling dreamless sleep, like a robot being given instructions. The part of Prufrax that had taken on personality during eyes-shut and eyes-open for five years had been superseded by the fight instructions Aryz had programmed. She had flown as glovers must fly (though the gloves didn't seem quite right).

She had fought, grappling (she thought), with herself, but who could be certain of anything?

She had long since decided that reality was not to be sought too avidly. After the battle she fell back into the mandate—into eyes-shut—all too willingly.

But a change had come to eyes-shut, too. Before the battle, the information had been selected. Now she could wander through the mandate at will. She seemed to smell the new information, completely unfamiliar, like a whiff of ocean. She hardly knew where to begin. She stumbled across:

—**that all vessels carry one, no matter what their size or class, just as every individual carries the map of a species. The mandate shall contain all the information of our kind, including accurate, and uncensored history, for if we have learned anything, it is that censored and untrue accounts distort the eyes of the leaders. Unders are told lies. Leaders must seek and be provided with accounts as accurate as possible, or we will be weakened and fall—**

What wonderful dreams the *leaders* must have had. And they possessed some intrinsic gift called *truth,* through the use of the *mandate*. Prufrax could hardly believe that. As she made her tentative explorations through the new fields of eyes-shut, she began to link the word *mandate* with what she experienced. That was where she was.

And she was alone. Once, she had explored with Grayd. Now there was no sign of Grayd.

She learned quickly. Soon she walked along a beach on Earth, then a beach on a world called Myriadne, and other beaches, fading in and out. By running through the entries rapidly, she came up with a blurred *eidos* and so learned what a beach was in the abstract. It was a boundary between one kind of eyes-shut and another, between water and land, neither of which had any corollary in eyes-open.

Some beaches had sand. Some had clouds—the *eidos* of clouds was quite attractive. And one—

had herself running scared, screaming.

She called out, but the figure vanished. Prufrax stood on a beach under a greenish-yellow star, on a world called Kyrene, feeling lonelier than ever.

She explored further, hoping to find Grayd, if not the figure that looked like herself. Grayd wouldn't flee from her. Grayd would—

The round thing confronted her, its helpless limbs twitching. Now it was her turn to run, terrified. Never before had she met the round creature in eyes-shut. It was mobile; it had a purpose. Over land, clouds, trees, rocks, wind, air, equations, and an edge of physics she fled. The farther she went, the more distant from the round one with hands and small head, the less afraid she was.

She never found Grayd.

The memory of the battle was fresh and painful. She remembered the ache of her hands, clumsily removed from the gloves. Her environment had collapsed and been replaced by something indistinct. Prufrax had fallen into a deep slumber and had dreamed.

The dreams were totally unfamiliar to her. If there was a left-turning in her arc of sleep, she dreamed of philosophies and languages and other things she couldn't relate to. A right-turning led to histories and sciences so incomprehensible as to be nightmares.

It was a most unpleasant sleep, and she was not at all sorry to find she wasn't really asleep.

The crucial moment came when she discovered how to slow her turnings and the changes of dream subject. She entered a pleasant place of which she had no knowledge but which did not seem threatening. There was a vast expanse of water, but it didn't terrify her. She couldn't even identify it as water until she scooped up a handful. Beyond the water was a floor of shifting particles. Above both was an open expanse, not black but obviously space, drawing her eyes into intense pale blue-green. And there was that figure she had encountered in the seedship. Herself. The figure pursued. She fled.

Right over the boundary into Senexi information. She knew then that what she was seeing couldn't possibly come from within herself. She was receiving data from another source. Perhaps she had been taken captive. It was possible she was now being forcibly debriefed. The tellman had discussed such possibilities, but none of the glovers had been taught how to defend themselves in specific situations. Instead it had been stated—in terms that brooked no second thought

—that self-destruction was the only answer. So she tried to kill herself.

She sat in the freezing cold of a red-and-white room, her feet meeting but not touching a fluid covering on the floor. The information didn't fit her senses—it seemed blurred, inappropriate. Unlike the other data, this didn't allow participation or motion. Everything was locked solid.

She couldn't find an effective means of killing herself. She resolved to close her eyes and simply will herself into dissolution. But closing her eyes only moved her into a deeper or shallower level of deception—other categories, subjects, visions. She couldn't sleep, wasn't tired, couldn't die.

Like a leaf on a stream, she drifted. Her thoughts untangled, and she imagined herself floating on the water called ocean. She kept her eyes open. It was quite by accident that she encountered:

Instruction. Welcome to the introductory use of the mandate. As a noncombat processor, your duties are to maintain and, if necessary, protect or destroy the mandate. The mandate is your immediate over. If it requires maintenance, you will oblige. Once linked with the mandate, as you are now, you may explore any aspect of the information by requesting delivery. To request delivery, indicate the core of your subject—

Prufrax! she shouted silently. What is Prufrax?

A voice with different tone immediately took over.

Ah, now that's quite a story. I was her biographer, the organizer of her life tapes (ref. GEORGE MACKNAX), AND KNEW HER WELL IN THE LAST YEARS OF HER LIFE. SHE WAS BORN IN THE FERMENT 26468. HERE ARE SELECTED LIFE TAPES. CHOOSE EMPHASIS. ANALYSES FOLLOW.

—Hey! Who are you? There's someone here with me. . . .

—Shh! Listen. Look at her. Who is she?

They looked, listened to the information.

—Why, she's *me* . . . sort of.

—She's *us*.

She stood two and a half meters tall. Her hair was black and thick, though cut short; her limbs well muscled though drawn out by the training and hormonal treatments. She was

seventeen years old, one of the few birds born in the solar
system, and for the time being she had a chip on her shoulder.
Everywhere she went, the birds asked about her mother, Jay-
ax. "You better than her?"

Of course not! Who could be? But she was good; the in-
structors said so. She was just about through training, and
whether she graduated to hawk or remained bird she would do
her job well. Asking Prufrax about her mother was likely to
make her set her mouth tight and glare.

On Mercior, the Grounds took up four thousand hectares
and had its own port. The Grounds was divided into Land,
Space, and Thought, and training in each area was mandatory
for fledges, those birds embarking on hawk training. Prufrax
was fledge three. She had passed Land—though she loathed
downbound fighting—and was two years into Space. The
tough part, everyone said, was not passing Space, but lasting
through four years of Thought after the action in nearorbit and
planetary.

Since she had been a little girl, no more than five—

—Five! Five what?

and had seen her mother's ships and fightsuits and fibs, she
had known she would never be happy until she had ventured
far out and put a seedship in her sights, had convinced a Senexi of the overness of end—

—The Zap! She's talking the Zap!

—What's that?

—You're me, you should know.

—I'm not you, and we're not her.

The Zap, said the mandate, and the data shifted.

"Tomorrow you receive your first implants. These will
allow you to coordinate with the zero-angle phase engines and
find your targets much more rapidly than you ever could with
simple biologic. Are there any questions?"

"Yes, sir." Prufrax stood at the top of the spherical
classroom, causing the hawk instructor to swivel his platform.
"I'm having problems with the zero-angle phase maths. Reduction of the momenta of the real."

Other fledge threes piped up that they, too, had had trouble
with those maths. The hawk instructor sighed. "We don't want
to install cheaters in all of you. It's bad enough needing implants to supplement biologic. Individual learning is much

more desirable. Do you request cheaters?" That was a challenge. They all responded negatively, but Prufrax had a secret smile. She knew the subject. She just took delight in having the maths explained again. She could reinforce an already thorough understanding. Others not so well versed would benefit. She wasn't wasting time. She was in the pleasure of her weapon—the weapon she would be using against the Senexi.

"Zero-angle phase is the temporary reduction of the momenta of the real." Equations and plexes appeared before each student as the instructor went on. "Nested unreals can conflict if a barrier is placed between the participator princip and the assumption of the real. The effectiveness of the participator can be determined by a convenience model we call the angle of phase. Zero-angle phase is achieved by an opaque probability field according to modified Fourier of the separation of real waves. This can also be caused by the reflection of the beam —an effective counter to zero-angle phase, since the beam is always compoundable and the compound is always time-reversed. Here are the true gedanks—"

—Zero-angle phase. She's learning the Zap.

—She hates them a lot, doesn't she?

—The Senexi? They're Senexi.

—I think . . . eyes-open is the world of the Senexi. What does that mean?

—That we're prisoners. You were caught before me.

—Oh.

The news came as she was in recovery from the implant. Seedships had violated human space again, dropping cuckoos on thirty-five worlds. The worlds had been young colonies, and the cuckoos had wiped out all life, then tried to reseed with Senexi forms. The overs had reacted by sterilizing the planets' surfaces. No victory, loss to both sides. It was as if the Senexi were so malevolent they didn't care about success, only about destruction.

She hated them. She could imagine nothing worse.

Prufrax was twenty-three. In a year she would be qualified to hawk on a cruiser/raider. She would demonstrate her hatred.

Aryz felt himself slipping into endthought, the mind set that always preceded a branch ind's self-destruction. What was there for him to do? The fragment had survived, but at

what cost, to what purpose? Nothing had been accomplished.
The nebula had been lost, or he supposed it had. He would
likely never know the actual outcome.

He felt a vague irritation at the lack of a spectrum of re-
sponses. Without a purpose, a branch ind was nothing more
than excess plasm.

He looked in on the captive and the shapes, all hooked to
the mandate, and wondered what he would do with them.
How would humans react to the situation he was in? More
vigorously, probably. They would fight on. They always had.
Even without leaders, with no discernible purpose, even in
defeat. What gave them such stamina? Were they superior,
more deserving? If they were better, then was it right for the
Senexi to oppose their triumph?

Aryz drew himself tall and rigid with confusion. He had
studied them too long. They had truly infected him. But here
at least was a hint of purpose. A question needed to be answered.

He made preparations. There were signs the brood mind's
flux bind was not permanent, was in fact unwinding quite
rapidly. When it emerged, Aryz would present it with a judgment, an answer.

He realized, none too clearly, that by Senexi standards he
was now a raving lunatic.

He would hook himself into the mandate, improve the
somewhat isolating interface he had used previously to search
for selected answers. He, the captive, and the shapes would be
immersed in human history together. They would be like
young suckling on a Population I mother-animal—just the
opposite of the Senexi process, where young fed nourishment
and information into the brood mind.

The mandate would nourish, or poison. Or both.

—Did she love?
—What—you mean, did she receive?
—No, did she—we—I—give?
—I don't know what you mean.
—I wonder if *she* would know what I mean. . . .
Love, said the mandate, and the data proceeded.
Prufrax was twenty-nine. She had been assigned to a

cruiser in a new program where superior but untested fighters were put into thick action with no preliminary.

The Cruiser was a million-ton raider, with a hawk contingent of fifty-three and eighty regular crew. She would be used in a secondwave attack, following the initial hardfought.

She was scared. That was good; fright improved basic biologic, if properly managed. The cruiser would make a raid into Senexi space and retaliate for past cuckoo-seeding programs. They would come up against thornships and seedships, probably.

The fighting was going to be fierce.

The raider made its final denial of the overness of the real and pipsqueezed into an arduous, nasty sponge space. It drew itself together again and emerged far above the galactic plane.

Prufrax sat in the hawks wardroom and looked at the simulated rotating snowball of stars. Red-coded numerals flashed along the borders of known Senexi territory, signifying where they had first come to power when the terrestrial sun had been a mist-wrapped youngster. A green arrow showed the position of the raider.

She drank sponge-space supplements with the others but felt isolated because of her firstness, her fear. Everyone seemed so calm. Most were fours or fives—on their fourth or fifth battle call. There were ten ones and an upper scatter of experienced hawks with nine to twenty-five battles behind them. There were no thirties. Thirties were rare in combat; the few that survived so many engagements were plucked off active and retired to PR service under the polinstructors. They often ended up in fibs, acting poorly, looking unhappy.

Still, when she had been more naive, Prufrax's heros had been a man-and-woman thirty team she had watched in fib after fib—Kumnax and Arol. They had been better actors than most.

Day in, day out, they drilled in their fightsuits. While the crew bustled, hawks were put through implant learning, what slang was already calling the Know, as opposed to the Tell, of classroom teaching. Getting background, just enough to tickle her curiosity, not enough to stimulate morbid interest.

—There it is again. Feel?

—I know it. Yes. The round one, part of eyes-open . . .

—Senexi?

—No, brother without name.

—Your . . . brother?

—No . . . I don't know.

Still, there were items of information she had never received before, items privileged only to the fighters, to assist
them in their work. Older hawks talked about the past, when
data had been freely available. Stories circulated in the wardroom about the Senexi, and she managed to piece together
something of their origins and growth.

Senexi worlds, according to a twenty, had originally been
large, cold masses of gas circling bright young suns nearly
metal-free. Their gas-giant planets had orbited the suns at
hundreds of millions of kilometers and had been dusted by the
shrouds of neighboring dead stars; the essential elements carbon, nitrogen, silicon, and fluorine had gathered in sufficient
quantities on some of the planets to allow Population II biology.

In cold ammonia seas, lipids had combined in complex
chains. A primal kind of life had arisen and flourished. Across
millions of years, early Senexi forms had evolved. Compared
with evolution on Earth, the process at first had moved quite
rapidly. The mechanisms of procreation and evolution had
been complex in action, simple in chemistry.

There had been no competition between life forms of different genetic bases. On Earth, much time had been spent
selecting between the plethora of possible ways to pass on
genetic knowledge.

And among the early Senexi, outside of predation there had
been no death. Death had come about much later, self-im-
posed for social reasons. Huge colonies of protoplasmic individuals had gradually resolved into the team-forms now
familiar.

Soon information was transferred through the budding of
branch inds; cultures quickly developed to protect the integrity
of larvae, to allow them to regroup and form a new brood
mind. Technologies had been limited to the rare heavy mate-
rials available, but the Senexi had expanded for a time with
very little technology. They were well adapted to their environment, with few predators and no need to hunt, absorbing
stray nutrients from the atmosphere and from layers of liquid
ammonia. With perceptions attuned to the radio and micro-

wave frequencies, they had before long turned groups of branch inds into radio telescope chains, piercing the heavy atmosphere and probing the universe in great detail, especially the very active center of the young galaxy. Huge jets of matter, streaming from other galaxies and emitting high-energy radiation, had provided laboratories for their vicarious observations. Physics was a primitive science to them.

Since little or no knowledge was lost in breeding cycles, cultural growth was rapid at times; since the dead weight of knowledge was often heavy, cultural growth often slowed to a crawl.

Using water as a building material, developing techniques that humans still understood imperfectly, they prepared for travel away from their birthworlds.

Prufrax wondered, as she listened to the older hawks, how humans had come to know all this. Had Senexi been captured and questioned? Was it all theory? Did anyone really know— anyone she could ask?

—She's weak.

—Why weak?

—Some knowledge is best for glovers to ignore. Some questions are best left to the supreme overs.

—Have you thought that in here, you can answer her questions, our questions?

—No. No. Learn about me—us—first.

In the hour before engagement, Prufrax tried to find a place alone. On the raider, this wasn't difficult. The ship's size was overwhelming for the number of hawks and crew aboard. There were many areas where she could put on an environs and walk or drift in silence, surrounded by the dark shapes of equipment wrapped in plexerv.

She pulled herself through the cold G-less tunnels, feeling slightly awed by the loneness, the quiet. One tunnel angled outboard, toward the hull of the cruiser. She hesitated, peering into its length with her environs beacon, when a beep warned her she was near another crew member. She was startled to think someone else might be as curious as she. She scooted expertly up the tunnel, spreading her arms and tucking her legs as she would in a fightsuit.

The tunnel was filled with a faint milky green mist, absorbing her environs beam. It couldn't be much more than a couple of hundred meters long, however, and it was quite straight. The signal beeped louder.

Ahead she could make out a dismantled weapons blister. That explained the fog: a plexerv aerosol diffused in the low pressure. Sitting in the blister was a man, his environs glowing a pale violet. He had deopaqued a section of the blister and was staring out at the stars. He swiveled as she approached and looked her over dispassionately. He seemed to be a hawk—he had fightform, tall, thin with brown hair above hull-white skin, large eyes with pupils so dark she might have been looking through his head into space beyond.

"Under," she said as their environs met and merged.

"Over. What are you doing here?"

"I was about to ask you the same."

"You should be getting ready for the fight," he admonished.

"I am. I need to be alone for a while."

"Yes." He turned back to the stars. "I used to do that, too."

"You don't fight now?"

He shook his head. "Retired. I'm a researcher."

She tried not to look impressed. Crossing rates was almost impossible. A bitalent was unusual in the service.

"What kind of research?" she asked.

"I'm here to correlate enemy finds."

"Won't find much of anything, after we've done with the zero phase."

It would have been polite for him to say, "Power to that," or offer some other encouragement. He said nothing.

"Why would you want to research them?"

"To fight an enemy properly, you have to know what they are. Ignorance is defeat."

"You research tactics?"

"Not exactly."

"What, then?"

"You'll be in tough hardfought this wake. Make you a proposition. You fight well, observe, come to me, and tell me what you see. Then I'll answer your questions."

"Brief you before my immediate overs?"

"I have the authority," he said. No one had ever lied to her; she didn't even suspect he would. "You're eager?"

"Very."

"You'll be doing what?"

"Engaging Senexi fighters, then hunting down branch inds and brood minds."

"How many fighters going in?"

"Twelve."

"Big target, eh?"

She nodded.

"While you're there, ask yourself—what are they fighting for? Understand?"

"I—"

"Ask, what are they fighting for. Just that. Then come back to me."

"What's your name?"

"Not important," he said. "Now go."

She returned to the prep center as the sponge-space warning tones began. Overhawks went among the fighters in the lineup, checking gear and giveaway body points for mental orientation. Prufrax submitted to the molded sensor mask being slipped over her face. "Ready!" the overhawk said. "Hardfought!" He clapped her on the shoulder. "Good luck."

"Thank you, sir." She bent down and slid into her fightsuit. Along the launch line, eleven other hawks did the same. The overs and other crew left the chamber, and twelve red beams delineated the launch tube. The fightsuits automatically lifted and aligned on their individual beams. Fields swirled around them like silvery tissue in moving water, then settled and hardened into cold scintillating walls, pulsing as the launch energy built up.

The tactic came to her. The ship's sensors became part of her information net. She saw the Senexi thornship—twelve kilometers in diameter, cuckoos lacing its outer hull like maggots on red fruit, snakes waiting to take them on.

She was terrified and exultant, so worked up that her body temperature was climbing. The fightsuit adjusted her balance.

At the count of ten and nine, she switched from biologic to cyber. The implant—after absorbing much of her thought processes for weeks—became Prufrax.

For a time there seemed to be two of her. Biologic continued, and in that region she could even relax a bit, as if watching a fib.

With almost dreamlike slowness, in the electronic time of

cyber, her fightsuit followed the beam. She saw the stars and oriented herself to the cruiser's beacon, using both for reference, plunging in the sword-flower formation to assault the thornship. The cuckoos retreated in the vast red hull like worms withdrawing into an apple. Then hundreds of tiny black pinpoints appeared in the quadrant closest to the sword flower.

Snakes shot out, each piloted by a Senexi branch ind. "Hardfought!" she told herself in biologic before that portion gave over completely to cyber.

Why were we flung out of dark
through ice and fire, a shower
of sparks? a puzzle;
Perhaps to build hell.

We strike here, there;
Set brief glows, fall through
and cross round again.

By our dimming, we see what
Beatitude we have.
In the circle, kindling
together, we form an
exhausted Empyrean.
We feel the rush of
igniting winds but still
grow dull and wan.

New rage flames, new light,
dropping like sun through muddy
ice and night and fall
Close, spinning blue and bright.

In time they, too,
Tire. Redden.
We join, compare pasts
cool in huddled paths,
turn gray.

And again.
We are a companion flow
of ash, in the slurry,
out and down.
We sleep.

Rivers form above and below.
Above, iron snakes twist,
clang and slice, chime,
helium eyes watching, seeing
Snowflake hawks,
signaling adamant muscles and
energy teeth. What hunger
compels our venom spit?

It flies, strikes the crystal
flight, making mist gray-green
with ammonia rain.

Sleeping we glide,
and to each side
unseen shores wait
with the moans of an
unseen tide.

> —She wrote that. We. One of her—our—poems.
> —Poem?
> —A kind of fib, I think.
> —I don't see what it says.
> —Sure you do! She's talking hardfought.
> —Do you understand it?
> —Not at all . . .

She lay back in the bunk, legs crossed, eyes closed, feeling the receding dominance of the implant—the overness of cyber—and the almost pleasant ache in her back. She had survived her first. The thornship had retired, severely damaged, its surface seared and scored so heavily it would never release cuckoos again.

It would become a hulk, a decoy. Out of action. *Satisfaction/out of action/Satisfaction . . .*

Still, with eight of the twelve fighters lost, she didn't quite feel the exuberance of the rhyme. The snakes had fought very well. Bravely, she might say. They lured, sacrificed, cooperated, demonstrating teamwork as fine as that in her own group. Strategy was what made the cruiser's raid successful. A superior approach, an excellent tactic. And perhaps even surprise, though the final analysis hadn't been posted yet.

Without those advantages, they might have all died.

She opened her eyes and stared at the pattern of blinking lights in the ceiling panel, lights with their secret codes that repeated every second, so that whenever she looked at them, the implant deep inside was debriefed, reinstructed. Only when she fought would she know what she was now seeing.

She returned to the tunnel as quickly as she was able. She floated up toward the blister and found him there, surrounded by packs of information from the last hardfought. She waited until he turned his attention to her.

"Well?" he said.

"I asked myself what they are fighting for. And I'm very angry."

"Why?"

"Because I don't know. I *can't* know. They're Senexi."

"Did they fight well?"

"We lost eight. Eight." She cleared her throat.

"Did they fight well?" he repeated, an edge to his voice.

"Better than I was ever told they could."

"Did they die?"

"Enough of them."

"How many did you kill?"

"I don't know." But she did. Eight.

"You killed eight," he said, pointing to the packs. "I'm analyzing the battle now."

"You're behind what we read, what gets posted?" she asked.

"Partly," he said. "You're a good hawk."

"I knew I would be," she said, her tone quiet, simple.

"Since they fought bravely—"

"How can Senexi be brave?" she asked sharply.

"Since," he repeated, "they fought bravely, why?"

"They want to live, to do their . . . work. Just like me."

"No," he said. She was confused, moving between extremes in her mind, first resisting, then giving in too much. "They're Senexi. They're not like us."

"What's your name?" she asked, dodging the issue.

"Clevo."

Her glory hadn't even begun yet, and already she was well into her fall.

Aryz made his connection and felt the brood mind's emergency cache of knowledge in the mandate grow up around him like ice crystals on glass. He stood in a static scene. The transition from living memory to human machine memory had resulted in either a coding of data or a reduction of detail; either way, the memory was cold, not dynamic. It would have to be compared, recorrelated, if that would ever be possible.

How much human data had had to be dumped to make space for this?

He cautiously advanced into the human memory, calling up topics almost at random.

He backed away from sociological data, trying to remain within physics and mathematics. There he could make conversions to fit his understanding without too much strain.

Then something unexpected happened. He felt the brush of another mind, a gentle inquiry from a source made even stranger by the hint of familiarity. It made what passed for a Senexi greeting, but not in the proper form, using what one branch ind of a team would radiate to a fellow; a gross breach, since it was obviously not from his team or even from his family. Aryz tried to withdraw. How was it possible for minds to meet in the mandate? As he retreated, he pushed into a broad region of incomprehensible data. It had none of the characteristics of the other human regions he had examined.

—This is for machines, the other said. —Not all cultural data are limited to biologic. You are in the area where programs and cyber designs are stored. They are really accessible only to a machine hooked into the mandate.

—What is your family? Aryz asked, the first step-question in the sequence Senexi used for urgent identity requests.

—I have no family. I am not a branch ind. No access to active brood minds. I have learned from the mandate.

—Then what are you?

—I don't know, exactly. Not unlike you.

"Well, finally!"

"The Senexi," Clevo continued, unperturbed, "long ago needed only gas-giant planets like their homeworlds. They lived in peace for billions of years before our world was formed. But as they moved from star to star, they learned uses for other types of worlds. We were most interested in rocky Earth-like planets. Gradually we found uses for gas giants, too. By the time we met, each of us encroached on the other's territory. Their technology is so improbable, so unlike ours, that when we first encountered them we thought they must come from another geometry."

"Where did you learn all this?" Prufrax squinted at him suspiciously.

"I'm no longer a hawk," he said, "but I was too valuable just to discard. My experience was too broad, my abilities too useful. So I was placed in research. It seems a safe place for me. Little contact with my comrades." He looked directly at her. "We must try to know our enemy, at least a little."

"That's dangerous," Prufrax said, almost instinctively.

"Yes, it is. What you know, you cannot hate."

"We must hate," she said. "It makes us strong. Senexi hate."

"They might," he said. "But, sometime, wouldn't you like to . . . sit down and talk with one, after a battle? Talk with a fighter? Learn its tactic, how it bested you in one move, compare—"

"No!" Prufrax shoved off rapidly down the tube. "We're shifting now. We have to get ready."

—She's smart. She's leaving him. He's crazy.

—Why do you think that?

—He would stop the fight, end the Zap.

—But he was a hawk.

—And hawks became glovers, I guess. But glovers go wrong, too. Like you.

—?

—Did you know they used you? How you were used?

—That's all blurred now.

—She's doomed if she stays around him. Who's that?

—Someone is listening with us.

* * *

The next battle was bad enough to fall into the hellfought. Prufrax was in her fightsuit, legs drawn up as if about to kick off. The cruiser exited sponge space and plunged into combat before sponge space supplements could reach full effectiveness. She was dizzy, disoriented. The overhawks could only hope that a switch from biologic to cyber would cure the problem.

She didn't know what they were attacking. Tactic was flooding the implant, but she was only receiving the wash of that; she hadn't merged yet. She sensed that things were confused. That bothered her. Overs did not feel confusion.

The cruiser was taking damage. She could sense at least that, and she wanted to scream in frustration. Then she was ordered to merge with the implant. Biologic became cyber. She was in the Know.

The cruiser had reintegrated above a gas-giant planet. They were seventy-nine thousand kilometers from the upper atmosphere. The damage had come from ice mines—chunks of Senexi-treated water ice, altered to stay in sponge space until a human vessel integrated near by. Then they emerged, packed with momentum and all the residual instability of an unsuccessful return to status geometry. Unsuccessful for a ship, that is—very successful for a weapon.

The ice mines had given up the overness of the real within range of the cruiser and had blasted out whole sections of the hull. The launch lanes had not been damaged. The fighters lined up on their beams and were peppered out into space, spreading in the famous sword flower.

The planet was a cold nest. Over didn't know what the atmosphere contained, but Senexi activity had been high in the star system, concentrating on this world. Over had decided to take a chance. Fighters headed for the atmosphere. The cruiser began planting singularity eggs. The eggs went ahead of the fighters, great black grainy ovoids that seemed to leave a trail of shadow—the wake of a birthing disruption in status geometry that could turn a gas giant into a short-lived sun.

Their time was limited. The fighters would group on entry sleds and descend to the liquid water regions where Senexi commonly kept their upwelling power plants. The fighters would first destroy any plants, loop into the liquid ammonia regions to search for hidden cuckoos, then see what was so important about the world.

She and five other fighters mounted the sled. Growing closer, the hazy clear regions of the atmosphere sparked with Senexi sensors. Spiderweb beams shot from the six sleds to down the sensors. Buffet began. Scream, heat, then a second flower from the sled at a depth of two hundred kilometers. The sled slowed and held station. It would be their only way back. The fightsuits couldn't pull out of such a large gravity well.

She descended deeper. The pale, bloated beacon of the red star was drooping below the second cloudtops, limning the strata in orange and purple. At the liquid ammonia level she was instructed to key in permanent memory of all she was seeing. She wasn't "seeing" much, but other sensors were recording a great deal, all of it duly processed in her implant. "There's life here," she told herself. Indigenous life. Just another example of Senexi disregard for basic decency: they were interfering with a world developing its own complex biology.

The temperature rose to ammonia vapor levels, then to liquid water. The pressure on the fightsuit was enormous, and she was draining her stores much more rapidly than expected. At this level the atmosphere was particularly thick with organics.

Senexi snakes rose from below, passed them in altitude, then doubled back to engage. Prufrax was designated the deep diver; the others from her sled would stay at this level in her defense. As she fell, another sled group moved in behind her to double the cover.

She searched for the characteristic radiation curve of an upwelling plant. At the lower boundary of the liquid water level, below which her suit could not safely descend, she found it.

The Senexi were tapping the gas giant's convection from greater depths than usual. Above the plant, almost indetectable, was another object with an uncharacteristic curve. They were separated by ten kilometers. The power plant was feeding its higher companion with tight energy beams.

She slowed. Two other fighters, disengaged from the brief skirmish above, took positions as backups a few dozen kilometers higher than she. Her implant searched for an appropriate tactic. She would avoid the zero-angle phase for the moment, go in for reconnaissance. She could feel sound pouring from the plant and its companion—rhythmic, not waste noise, but deliberate. And homing in on that sound were waves of large vermiform organisms, like chains of gas-filled sausage. They were dozens of meters long, two meters at their greatest thickness, shaped vaguely like the Senexi snake fighters. The vermiforms were native, and they were being lured into the uppermost floating structure. None were merging. Her backups spread apart, descended, and drew up along her flanks.

She made her decision almost immediately. She could see a pattern in the approach of the natives. If she fell into the pattern, she might be able to enter the structure unnoticed.

—It's a grinder. She doesn't recognize it.

—What's a grinder?

—She should make the Zap! It's an ugly thing; Senexi use them all the time. Net a planet with grinders, like a cuckoo, but for larger operations.

The creatures were being passed through separator fields. Their organics fell from the bottom of the construct, raw material for new growth—Senexi growth. Their heavier elements were stored for later harvest.

With Prufrax in their midst, the vermiforms flew into the separator. The interior was hundreds of meters wide, lead-white walls with flat gray machinery floating in a dust haze, full of hollow noise, the distant bleats of vermiforms being slaughtered. Prufrax tried to retreat, but she was caught in a selector field. Her suit bucked and she was whirled violently, then thrown into a repository for examination. She had been screened from the separator; her plan to record, then destroy, the structure had been foiled by an automatic filter.

"Information sufficient." Command logic programmed into the implant before launch was now taking over. "Zero-angle phase both plant and adjunct." She was drifting in the repository, still slightly stunned. Something was fading. Cyber was hissing in and out; the over logic-commands were being scrambled. Her implant was malfunctioning and was returning control to biologic. The selector fields had played havoc with all cyber functions, down to the processors in her weapons.

Cautiously she examined the down systems one by one, determining what she could and could not do. This took as much as thirty seconds—an astronomical time on the implant's scale.

She still could use the phase weapon. If she was judicious and didn't waste her power, she could cut her way out of the repository, maneuver and work with her escorts to destroy both the plant and the separator. By the time they returned to the sleds, her implant might have rerouted itself and made sufficient repairs to handle defense. She had no way of knowing what was waiting for her if—when—she escaped, but that was the least of her concerns for the moment.

She tightened the setting of the phase beam and swung her fightsuit around, knocking a cluster of junk ice and silty phosphorescent dust. She activated the beam. When she had a hole large enough to pass through, she edged the suit forward, beamed through more walls and obstacles, and kicked herself out of the repository into free fall. She swiveled and laid down a pattern of wide-angle beams, at the same time relaying a message on her situation to the escorts.

The escorts were not in sight. The separator was beginning to break up, spraying debris through the almost opaque atmosphere. The rhythmic sound ceased, and the crowds of vermiforms began to disperse.

She stopped her fall and thrust herself several kilometers higher—directly into a formation of Senexi snakes. She had barely enough power to reach the sled, much less fight and turn her beams on the upwelling plant.

Her cyber was still down.

The sled signal was weak. She had no time to calculate its direction from the inertial guidance cyber. Besides, all cyber was unreliable after passing through the separator.

Why do they fight so well? Clevo's question clogged her thoughts. Cursing, she tried to blank and keep all her faculties available for running the fightsuit. *When evenly matched, you cannot win against your enemies unless you understand them. And if you truly understand, why are you fighting and not talking?* Clevo had never told her that—not in so many words. But it was part of a string of logic all her own.

Be more than an automaton with a narrow range of choices. Never underestimate the enemy. Those were old

Grounds dicta, not entirely lost in the new training, but only emphasized by Clevo.

If they fight as well as you, perhaps in some ways they fight-think like you do. Use that.

Isolated, with her power draining rapidly, she had no choice. They might disregard her if she posed no danger. She cut her thrust and went into a diving spin. Clearly she was on her way to a high-pressure grave. They would sense her power levels, perhaps even pick up the lack of field activity if she let her shields drop. She dropped the shields. If they let her fall and didn't try to complete the kill—if they concentrated on active fighters above—she had enough power to drop into the water vapor regions, far below the plant, and silently ride a thermal into range. With luck, she could get close enough to lay a web of zero-angle phase and take out the plant.

She had minutes in which to agonize over her plan. Falling, buffeted by winds that could knock her kilometers out of range, she spun like a vagrant flake of snow.

She couldn't even expend the energy to learn if they were scanning her, checking out her potential.

Perhaps she underestimated them. Perhaps they would be that much more thorough and take her out just to be sure. Perhaps they had unwritten rules of conduct like the ones she was using, taking hunches into account. Hunches were discouraged in Grounds training—much less reliable than cyber.

She fell. Temperature increased. Pressure on her suit began to constrict her air supply. She used fighter trancing to cut back on her breathing.

Fell.

And broke the trance. Pushed through the dense smoke of exhaustion. Planned the beam web. Counted her reserves. Nudged into an updraft beneath the plant. The thermal carried her, a silent piece of paper in a storm, drifting back and forth beneath the objective. The huge field intakes pulsed above, lightning outlining their invisible extension. She held back on the beam.

Nearly faded out. Her suit interior was almost unbearably hot.

She was only vaguely aware of laying down the pattern. The beams vanished in the murk. The thermal pushed her through a layer of haze, and she saw the plant, riding high above clear-atmosphere turbulence. The zero-angle phase had pushed through the field intakes, into their source nodes and the plant body, surrounding it with bright blue Tcherenkov. First, the surface began to break up, then the middle layers, and finally key supports. Chunks vibrated away with the internal fury of their molecular, then atomic, then particle disruption. Paraphrasing Grounds description of beam action, the plant became less and less convinced of its reality. "Matter dreams," an instructor had said a decade before. "Dreams it is real, maintains the dream by shifting rules with constant results. Disturb the dreams, the shifting of the rules results in inconstant results. Things cannot hold."

She slid away from the updraft, found another, wondered idly how far she would be lifted. Curiosity at the last. Let's just see, she told herself; a final experiment.

Now she was cold. The implant was flickering, showing signs of reorganization. She didn't use it. No sense expanding the amount of time until death. No sense at all.

The sled, maneuvered by one remaining fighter, glided up beneath her almost unnoticed.

Aryz waited in the stillness of a Senexi memory, his thinking temporarily reduced to a faint susurrus. What he waited for was not clear.

—Come.

The form of address was wrong, but he recognized the voice. His thoughts stirred, and he followed the nebulous presence out of Senexi territory.

—Know your enemy.

Prufrax . . . the name of one of the human shapes sent out against their own kind. He could sense her presence in the mandate, locked into a memory store. He touched on the store and caught the essentials—the grinder, the updraft plant, the fight from Prufrax's viewpoint.

—Know how your enemy knows you.

He sensed a second presence, similar to that of Prufrax. It took him some time to realize that the human captive was another form of the shape, a reproduction of the . . .

Both were reproductions of the female whose image was in the memory store. Aryz was not impressed by threes—Senexi mysticism, what had ever existed of it, had been preoccupied with fives and sixes—but the coincidence was striking.

—Know how your enemy sees you.

He saw the grinder processing organics—the vermiform natives—in preparation for a widespread seeding of deuterium gatherers. The operation had evidently been conducted for some time; the vermiform populations were greatly reduced from their usual numbers. Vermiforms were a common type-species on gas giants of the sort depicted. The mutated shape nudged him into a particular channel of the memory, that which carried the original Prufrax's emotions. She had reacted with *disgust* to the Senexi procedure. It was a reaction not unlike what Aryz might feel when coming across something forbidden in Senexi behaviour. Yet eradication was perfectly natural, analogous to the human cleansing of *food* before *eating*.

—It's in the memory. The vermiforms are intelligent. They have their own kind of civilization. Human action on this world prevented their complete extinction by the Senexi.

—So what matter they were *intelligent?* Aryz responded. They did not behave or think like Senexi, or like any species Senexi find compatible. They were therefore not desirable. Like humans.

—You would make humans extinct?

—We would protect ourselves from them.

—Who damages the other most?

Aryz didn't respond. The line of questioning was incomprehensible. Instead he flowed into the memory of Prufrax, propelled by another aspect of complete freedom, confusion.

The implant was replaced. Prufrax's damaged limbs and skin were repaired or regenerated quickly, and within four wakes, under intense treatment usually reserved only for overs, she regained all her reflexes and speed. She requested liberty of the cruiser while it returned for repairs. Her request was granted.

She first sought Clevo in the designated research area. He wasn't there, but a message was, passed on to her by a smiling young crew member. She read it quickly:

"You're free and out of action. Study for a while, then

come find me. The old place hasn't been damaged. It's less private, but still good. Study! I've marked highlights."

She frowned at the message, then handed it to the crew member, who duly erased it and returned to his duties. She wanted to talk with Clevo, not study.

But she followed his instructions. She searched out highlighted entries in the ship's memory store. It was not nearly as dull as she had expected. In fact, by following the highlights, she felt she was learning more about Clevo and about the questions he asked.

Old literature was not nearly as graphic as fibs, but it was different enough to involve her for a time. She tried to create imitations of what she read but erased them. Nonfib stories were harder than she suspected. She read about punishment, duty; she read about places called heaven and hell, from a writer who had died tens of thousands of years before. With ed supplement guidance, she was able to comprehend most of what she read. Plugging the store into her implant, she was able to absorb hundreds of volumes in an hour.

Some of the stores were losing definition. They hadn't been used in decades, perhaps centuries.

Halfway through, she grew impatient. She left the research area. Operating on another hunch, she didn't go to the blister as directed, but straight to memory central, two decks inboard the research area. She saw Clevo there, plugged into a data pillar, deep in some aspect of ship history. He noticed her approach, unplugged, and swiveled on his chair. "Congratulations," he said, smiling at her.

"Hardfought," she acknowledged, smiling.

"Better than that, perhaps," he said.

She looked at him quizzically. "What do you mean, better?"

"I've been doing some illicit tapping on over channels."

"So?"

—He *is dangerous!*

"For what?"

"You may have a valuable genetic assortment. Overs think you behaved remarkably well under impossible conditions."

"Did I?"

He nodded. "Your type may be preserved."

"Which means?"

"There's a program being planned. They want to take the best fighters and reproduce them—clone them—to make uniform top-grade squadrons. It was rumored in my time—you haven't heard?"

She shook her head.

"It's not new. It's been done, off and on, for tens of thousands of years. This time they believe they can make it work."

"You were a fighter, once," she said. "Did they preserve your type?"

Clevo nodded. "I had something that interested them, but not, I think, as a fighter."

Prufrax looked down at her stubby-fingered hands. "It was grim," she said. "You know what we found?"

"An extermination plant."

"You want me to understand them better. Well, I can't. I refuse. How could they do such things?" She looked disgusted and answered her own question. "Because they're Senexi."

"Humans," Clevo said, "have done much the same, sometimes worse."

"No!"

—No!

"Yes," he said firmly. He sighed. "We've wiped Senexi worlds, and we've even wiped worlds with intelligent species like our own. Nobody is innocent. Not in this universe."

"We were never taught that."

"It wouldn't have made you a better hawk. But it might make a better human of you to know. Greater depth of character. Do you want to be more aware?"

"You mean, study more?"

He nodded.

"What makes you think *you* can teach me?"

"Because you thought about what I asked you. About how Senexi thought. And you survived where some other hawk might not have. The overs think it's in your genes. It might be. But it's also in your head."

"Why not tell the overs?"

"I have," he said. He shrugged.

"They wouldn't want me to learn from you?"

"I don't know," Clevo said. "I suppose they're aware you're talking to me. They could stop it if they wanted."

"And if I learn from you?"

"Not from me, actually. From the past. From history, what other people have thought. I'm really not any more capable than you . . . but I know history, small portions of it. I won't teach you so much as guide."

"I did use your questions," Prufrax said. "But will I ever need to use them—think that way—again?"

Clevo nodded. "Of course."

—You're quiet.

—She's giving in to him.

—She gave in a long time ago.

—She should be afraid.

—Were you—we—ever really afraid of a challenge?

—No.

—Not Senexi, not forbidden knowledge.

Clevo first led her through the history of past wars, judging that was appropriate considering her occupation. She was attentive enough, though her mind wandered; sometimes he was didactic, but she found she didn't mind that much.

She saw that in all wars, the first stage was to dehumanize the enemy, reduce the enemy to a lower level so that he might be killed without compunction. When the enemy was not human to begin with, the task was easier. As wars progressed, this tactic frequently led to an underestimation of the enemy, with disastrous consequences. "We aren't exactly underestimating the Senexi," Clevo said. "The overs are too smart for that. But we refuse to understand them, and that could make the war last indefinitely."

"Then why don't the overs see that?"

"Because we're being locked into a pattern. We've been fighting for so long, we've begun to lose ourselves. And it's getting worse." He assumed his didactic tone, and she knew he was reciting something he'd formulated years before and repeated to himself a thousand times. "There is no war so important that, to win it, we must destroy our minds."

She didn't agree with that; losing the war with the Senexi would mean extinction, as she understood things.

Most often they met in the single unused weapons blister that had not been damaged. They met when the ship was basking in the real between sponge-space jaunts. He brought memory stores with him in portable modules, and they read, listened, experienced together. She never placed a great deal of importance in the things she learned; her interest was focused on Clevo. Still, she learned.

The rest of her time she spent training. She was aware of a growing isolation from the hawks, which she attributed to her uncertain rank status. Was her genotype going to be preserved or not? The decision hadn't been made. The more she learned, the less she wanted to be singled out for honor. Attracting that sort of attention might be dangerous, she thought. Dangerous to whom, or what, she could not say.

Clevo showed her how hero images had been used to indoctrinate birds and hawks in a standard of behavior that was ideal, not realistic. The results were not always good; some tragic blunders had been made by fighters trying to be more than anyone possibly could or refusing to be flexible.

The war was certainly not a fib. Yet more and more the overs seemed to be treating it as one. Unable to bring about strategic victories against the Senexi, the overs had settled in for a long war of attrition and were apparently bent on adapting all human societies to the effort.

"There are overs we never hear of, who make decisions that shape our entire lives. Soon they'll determine whether or not we're even born, if they don't already."

"That sounds paranoid," she said, trying out a new word and concept she had only recently learned.

"Maybe so."

"Besides, it's been like that for ages—not knowing all our overs."

"But it's getting worse," Clevo said. He showed her the projections he had made. In time, if trends continued unchanged, fighters and all other combatants would be treated more and more mechanically, until they became the machines the overs wished them to be.

—No.

—Quiet. How does he feel toward her?

It was inevitable that as she learned under his tutelage, he began to feel responsible for her changes. She was an excellent fighter. He could never be sure that what he was doing might reduce her effectiveness. And yet he had fought well—despite similar changes—until his billet switch. It had been the overs who had decided he would be more effective, less disruptive, elsewhere.

Bitterness over that decision was part of his motive. The overs had done a foolish thing, putting a fighter into research. Fighters were tenacious. If the truth were to be hidden, then fighters would be the ones likely to ferret it out. And pass it on. There was a code among fighters, seldom revealed to their immediate overs, much less to the supreme overs parsecs distant in their strategospheres. What one fighter learned that could be of help to another had to be passed on, even under penalty. Clevo was simply following that unwritten rule.

Passing on the fact that, at one time, things had been different. That war changed people, governments, societies, and that societies could effect an enormous change on their constituents, especially now—change in their lives, their thinking. Things could become even more structured. Freedom of fight was a drug, an illusion—

—No!

used to perpetuate a state of hatred.

"Then why do they keep all the data in stores?" she asked. "I mean, you study the data, everything becomes obvious."

"There are still important people who think we may want to find our way back someday. They're afraid we'll lose our roots, but—" His face suddenly became peaceful. She reached out to touch him, and he jerked slightly, turning toward her in the blister. "What is it?" she asked.

"It's not organized. We're going to lose the information. Ship overs are going to restrict access more and more. Eventually it'll decay, like some already has in these stores. I've been planning for some time to put it all in a single unit—"

—*He* built the mandate!

"and have the overs place one on every ship, with researchers to tend it. Formalize the loose scheme still in effect, but dying. Right now I'm working on the fringes. At least I'm allowed to work. But soon I'll have enough evidence that they won't be able to argue. Evidence of what happens to societies that try to obscure their histories. They go quite mad. The overs are still rational enough to listen; maybe I'll push it through." He looked out the transparent blister. The stars were smudging to one side as the cruiser began probing for entrances to sponge space. "We'd better get back."

"Where are you going to be when we return? We'll all be transferred."

"That's some time removed. Why do you want to know?"

"I'd like to learn more."

He smiled. "That's not your only reason."

"I don't need someone to tell me what my reasons are," she said testily.

"We're so reluctant," he said. She looked at him sharply, irritated and puzzled. "I mean," he continued, "we're hawks. Comrades. Hawks couple like *that*." He snapped his fingers. "But you and I sneak around it all the time."

Prufrax kept her face blank.

"Aren't you receptive toward me?" he asked, his tone almost teasing.

"It's just that that's not all," she said, her tone softening.

"Indeed," he said in a barely audible whisper.

In the distance they heard the alarms.

—It was never any different.

—What?

—Things were never any different before me.

—Don't be silly. It's all here.

—If Clevo made the mandate, then he put it here. It isn't true.

—Why are you upset?

—I don't like hearing that everything I believe is a . . . fib.

—I've never known the difference, I suppose. Eyes-open was never all that real to me. This isn't real, you aren't . . . this is eyes-shut. So why be upset? You and I . . . we aren't even whole people. I feel you. You wish the Zap, you fight, not much else. I'm just a shadow, even compared to you. But she is whole. She loves him. She's less a victim than either of us. So something has to have changed.

—You're saying things have gotten worse.

—If the mandate is a lie, that's all I am. You refuse to accept. I *have* to accept, or I'm even less than a shadow.

—I don't refuse to accept. It's just hard.

—You started it. You thought about love.

—You did!

—Do you know what love is?

—Reception.

They first made love in the weapons blister. It came as no surprise; if anything, they approached it so cautiously they were clumsy. She had become more and more receptive, and he had dropped his guard. It had been quick, almost frantic, far from the orchestrated and drawn-out ballet the hawks prided themselves for. There was no pretense. No need to play the roles of artists back once more into the past, through the dim gray millennia of repeating ages. History began to manifest again, differences in the record.

On the way back to Mercior, four skirmishes were fought. Prufrax did well in each. She carried something special with her, a thought she didn't even tell Clevo, and she carried the same thought with her through their last days at the Grounds.

Taking advantage of hawk liberty, she opted for a post-hardfought residence just outside the Grounds, in the relatively uncrowded Daughter of Cities zone. She wouldn't be returning to fight until several issues had been decided—her status most important among them.

Clevo began making his appeal to the middle overs. He was given Grounds duty to finish his proposals. They could stay together for the time being.

The residence was sixteen square meters in area, not elegant—*natural,* as rentOpts described it.

On the last day she lay in the crook of Clevo's arm. They had done a few hours of nature sleep. He hadn't come out yet, and she looked up at his face, reached up with a hand to feel his arm.

It was different from the arms of others she had been receptive toward. It was unique. The thought amused her. There had never been a reception like theirs. This was the beginning. And if both were to be duplicated, this love, this reception, would be repeated an infinite number of times. Clevo meeting Prufrax, teaching her, opening her eyes.

Somehow, even though repetition contributed to the death of history, she was pleased. This was the secret thought she carried into fight. Each time she would survive, wherever she was, however many duplications down the line. She would receive Clevo, and he would teach her. If not now—if one or the other died—then in the future. The death of history might be a good thing. Love could go on forever.

She had lost even a rudimentary apprehension of death, even with present pleasure to live for. Her functions had sharpened. She would please him by doing all the things he could not. And if he was to enter that state she frequently found him in, that state of introspection, of reliving his own battles and of envying her activity, then that wasn't bad. All they did to each other was good.

—*Was* good

—*Was*

She slipped from his arm and left the narrow sleeping quarter, pushing through the smoke-colored air curtain to the lounge. Two hawks and an over she had never seen before were sitting there. They looked up at her.

"Under," Prufrax said.

"Over," the woman returned. She was dressed in tan and green, Grounds colors, not ship.

"May I assist?"

"Yes."

"My duty, then?"

The over beckoned her closer. "You have been receiving a researcher."

"Yes," Prufrax said. The meetings could not have been a secret on the ship, and certainly not their quartering near the Grounds. "Has that been against duty?"

"No." The over eyed Prufrax sharply, observing her perfected fightform, the easy grace with which she stood, naked, in the middle of the small compartment. "But a decision has been reached. Your status is decided now."

She felt a shiver.

"Prufrax," said the elder hawk. She recognized him from fibs, and his companion: Kumnax and Arol. Once her heroes. "You have been accorded an honor, just as your partner has. You have a valuable genetic assortment—"

She barely heard the rest. They told her she would return to fight, until they deemed she had had enough experience and background to be brought into the polinstruc division. Then her fighting would be over. She would serve better as an example, a hero.

Heroes never partnered out of function. Hawk heroes could not even partner with exhawks.

Clevo emerged from the air curtain. "Duty," the over said. "The residence is disbanded. Both of you will have separate quarters, separate duties."

They left. Prufrax held out her hand, but Clevo didn't take it. "No use," he said.

Suddenly she was filled with anger. "You'll give it up? Did I expect too much? *How strongly?*"

"Perhaps even more strongly than you," he said. "I knew the order was coming down. And still I didn't leave. That may hurt my chances with the supreme overs."

"Then at least I'm worth more than your breeding history?"

"Now you are history. History the way they make it."

"I feel like I'm dying," she said, amazement in her voice. "What is that, Clevo? What did you do to me?"

"I'm in pain, too," he said.

"You're hurt?"

"I'm confused."

"I don't believe that," she said, her anger rising again. "You knew, and you didn't do anything?"

"That would have been counter to duty. We'll be worse off if we fight it."

"So what good is your great, exalted history?"

"History is what you have," Clevo said. "I only record."

—Why did they separate them?

—I don't know. You didn't like him, anyway.

—Yes, but now. . .

—I don't understand.

—We don't. Look what happens to her. They took what was best out of her. Prufrax

went into battle eighteen more times before dying as heroes often do, dying in the midst of what she did best. The question of what made her better before the separation—for she definitely was not as fine a fighter after— has not been settled. Answers fall into an extinct classification of knowledge, and there are few left to interpret, none accessible to this device.

—So she went out and fought and died. They never even made fibs about her. This killed her?

—I don't think so. She fought well enough. She died like other hawks died.

—And she might have lived otherwise.

—How can I know that, any more than you?

—They—we—met again, you know. I met a Clevo once, on my ship. They didn't let me stay with him long.

—How did you react to him?

—There was so little time, I don't know.

—Let's ask. . . .

In thousands of duty stations, it was inevitable that some of Prufrax's visions would come true, that they should meet now and then. Clevos were numerous, as were Prufraxes. Every ship carried complements of several of each. Though Prufrax was never quite as successful as the original, she was a fine type. She—

—She was never quite as successful. They took away her edge. They didn't even know it!

—They must have known.

—Then they didn't want to win!

—We don't know that. Maybe there were more important considerations.

—Yes, like killing history.

Aryz shuddered in his warming body, dizzy as if about to bud, then regained control. He had been pulled from the mandate, called to his own duty.

He examined the shapes and the human captive. There was something different about them. How long had they been immersed in the mandate? He checked quickly, frantically, before answering the call. The reconstructed Mam had malfunctioned. None of them had been nourished. They were thin, pale, cooling.

Even the bloated mutant shape was dying; lost, like the others, in the mandate.

He turned his attention way. Everything was confusion. Was he human or Senexi now? Had he fallen so low as to understand them? He went to the origin of the call, the ruins of the temporary brood chamber. The corridors were caked with ammonia ice, burning his pod as he slipped over them. The brood mind had come out of flux bind. The emergency support systems hadn't worked well; the brood mind was damaged.

"Where have you been?" it asked.

"I assumed I would not be needed until your return from the flux bind."

"You have not been watching!"

"Was there any need? We are so advanced in time, all our

actions are obsolete. The nebula is collapsed, the issue is decided."

"We do not know that. We are being pursued."

Aryz turned to the sensor wall—what was left of it—and saw that they were, indeed, being pursued. He had been lax.

"It is not your fault," the brood mind said. "You have been set a task that tainted you and ruined your function. You will dissipate."

Aryz hesitated. He had become so different, so tainted, that he actually *hesitated* at a direct command from the brood mind. But it was damaged. Without him, without what he had learned, what could it do? It wasn't reasoning correctly.

"There are facts you must know, important facts—"

Aryz felt a wave of revulsion, uncomprehending fear, and something not unlike human anger radiate from the brood mind. Whatever he had learned and however he had changed, he could not withstand that wave.

Willingly, and yet against his will—it didn't matter—he felt himself liquefying. His pod slumped beneath him, and he fell over, landing on a pool of frozen ammonia. It burned, but he did not attempt to lift himself. Before he ended, he saw with surprising clarity what it was to be a branch ind, or a brood mind, or a human. Such a valuable insight, and it leaked out of his permea and froze on the ammonia.

The brood mind regained what control it could of the fragment. But there were no defenses worthy of the name. Calm, preparing for its own dissipation, it waited for the pursuit to conclude.

The Mam set off an alarm. The interface with the mandate was severed. Weak, barely able to crawl, the humans looked at each other in horror and slid to opposite corners of the chamber.

They were confused: Which of them was the captive, which the decoy shape? It didn't seem important. They were both bone-thin, filthy with their own excrement. They turned with one motion to stare at the bloated mutant. It sat in its corner, tiny head incongruous on the huge thorax, tiny arms and legs barely functional even when healthy. It smiled wanly at them.

"We felt you," one of the Prufraxes said. "You were with us in there." Her voice was a soft croak.

"That was my place," it replied. "My only place."

"What function, what name?"

"I'm . . . I know that. I'm a researcher. In there, I knew myself in there."

They squinted at the shape. The head. Something familiar, even now. "You're a Clevo . . ."

There was noise all around them, cutting off the shape's weak words. As they watched, their chamber was sectioned like an orange, and the wedges peeled open. The illumination ceased. Cold enveloped them.

A naked human female, surrounded by tiny versions of herself, like an angel circled by fairy kin, floated into the chamber. She was thin as a snake. She wore nothing but silver rings on her wrists and a thin torque around her waist. She glowed blue-green in the dark.

The two Prufraxes moved their lips weakly but made no sound in the near vacuum. *Who are you?*

She surveyed them without expression, then held out her arms as if to fly. She wore no gloves, but she was of their type.

As she had done countless times before on finding such Senexi experiments—though this seemed older than most— she lifted one arm higher. The blue-green intensified, spread in waves to the mangled walls, surrounded the freezing, dying shapes. Perfect, angelic, she left the debris behind to cast its fitful glow and fade.

They destroyed every portion of the fragment but one. They left the mandate behind unharmed.

Then they continued, millions of them thick like mist, working the spaces between the stars, their only master the overness of the real.

They needed no other masters. They would never malfunction.

The mandate drifted in the dark and cold, its memory going on, but its only life the rapidly fading tracks where minds had once passed through it. The trails writhed briefly, almost as if alive, but only following the quantum rules of diminished energy states. Briefly, a small memory was illuminated.

Prufrax's last poem explained the mandate reflexively.

How the fires grow! Peace passes
All memory lost.
Somehow we always miss that single door,
Dooming ourselves to circle.

Ashes to stars, lies to souls,
Let's spin 'round the sinks and holes.

Kill the good, eat the young.
Forever and more
You and I are never done.

The track faded into nothing. Around the mandate, the universe grew old very quickly.

PRESS ENTER■

by John Varley

Press Enter■ *was purchased by Shawna McCarthy and appeared in the May 1984 issue of* IAsfm, *with an arresting cover by Hisaki Yasuda and interior illustrations by Laura Lakey. The response to* Press Enter■ *was immediate and wildly enthusiastic.* Press Enter■ *simply ran away with the awards in its category that year, sweeping both the Nebula and the Hugo Award, and was picked up by all three SF "Best of the Year" anthology series. And it remains one of the most popular stories that* IAsfm *has ever published.*

John Varley appeared on the SF scene in 1975, and by the end of 1976—in what was a meteoric rise to prominence even for a field known for meteoric rises—was already being recognized as one of the hottest new writers of the seventies. His books include the novels Ophiuchi Hotline, Titan, Wizard *and* Demon, *and the collections* The Persistence of Vision, The Barbie Murders, *and* Picnic on Nearside. *His most recent book is the collection* Blue Champagne. *In addition to the awards he earned for* Press Enter■, *he has also won another Nebula and Hugo for his short fiction.*

"This is a recording. Please do not hang up until—"

I slammed the phone down so hard it fell onto the floor. Then I stood there, dripping wet and shaking with anger. Eventually, the phone started to make that buzzing noise they make when a receiver is off the hook. It's twenty times as loud as any sound a phone can normally make, and I always wondered why. As though it was such a terrible disaster: "Emergency! Your telephone is off the hook!!!"

Phone answering machines are one of the small annoyances of life. Confess, do you really *like* talking to a machine? But what had just happened to me was more than a petty irritation. I had just been called by an automatic dialing machine.

They're fairly new. I'd been getting about two or three such calls a month. Most of them come from insurance companies. They give you a two-minute spiel and then a number to call if you are interested. (I called back, once, to give them a piece of my mind, and was put on hold, complete with Muzak.) They use lists. I don't know where they get them.

I went back to the bathroom, wiped water droplets from the plastic cover of the library book, and carefully lowered myself back into the water. It was too cool. I ran more hot water and was just getting my blood pressure back to normal when the phone rang again.

So I sat there through fifteen rings, trying to ignore it.

Did you ever try to read with the phone ringing?

On the sixteenth ring I got up. I dried off, put on a robe, walked slowly and deliberately into the living room. I stared at the phone for a while.

On the fiftieth ring I picked it up.

"This is a recording. Please do not hang up until the message has been completed. This call originates from the house of your next-door neighbor, Charles Kluge. It will repeat every ten minutes. Mister Kluge knows he has not been the best of neighbors, and apologizes in advance for the inconvenience. He requests that you go immediately to his house. The key is under the mat. Go inside and do what needs to be done. There will be a reward for your services. Thank you."

Click. Dial tone.

I'm not a hasty man. Ten minutes later, when the phone rang again, I was still sitting there thinking it over. I picked up the receiver and listened carefully.

It was the same message. As before, it was not Kluge's voice. It was something synthesized, with all the human warmth of a Speak'n'Spell.

I heard it out again, and cradled the receiver when it was done.

I thought about calling the police. Charles Kluge had lived next door to me for ten years. In that time I may have had a dozen conversations with him, none lasting longer than a minute. I owed him nothing.

I thought about ignoring it. I was still thinking about that when the phone rang again. I glanced at my watch. Ten minutes. I lifted the receiver and put it right back down.

I could disconnect the phone. It wouldn't change my life radically.

But in the end I got dressed and went out the front door, turned left, and walked toward Kluge's property.

My neighbor across the street, Hal Lanier, was out mowing the lawn. He waved to me, and I waved back. It was about seven in the evening of a wonderful August day. The shadows were long. There was the smell of cut grass in the air. I've always liked that smell. About time to cut my own lawn, I thought.

It was a thought Kluge had never entertained. His lawn was brown and knee-high and choked with weeds.

I rang the bell. When nobody came I knocked. Then I sighed, looked under the mat, and used the key I found there to open the door.

"Kluge?" I called out as I stuck my head in.

I went along the short hallway, tentatively, as people do when unsure of their welcome. The drapes were drawn, as always, so it was dark in there, but in what had once been the living room ten television screens gave more than enough light

for me to see Kluge. He sat in a chair in front of a table, with
his face pressed into a computer keyboard and the side of his
head blown away.

Hal Lanier operates a computer for the L.A.P.D., so I told
him what I had found and he called the police. We waited
together for the first car to arrive. Hal kept asking if I'd
touched anything, and I kept telling him no, except for the
front door knob.

An ambulance arrived without the siren. Soon there were
police all over, and neighbors standing out in their yards or
talking in front of Kluge's house. Crews from some of the
television stations arrived in time to get pictures of the body,
wrapped in a plastic sheet, being carried out. Men and women
came and went. I assumed they were doing all the standard
police things, taking fingerprints, collecting evidence. I would
have gone home, but had been told to stick around.

Finally I was brought in to see Detective Osborne, who
was in charge of the case. I was led into Kluge's living room.
All the television screens were still turned on. I shook hands
with Osborne. He looked me over before he said anything. He
was a short guy, balding. He seemed very tired until he looked
at me. Then, though nothing really changed in his face, he
didn't look tired at all.

"You're Victor Apfel?" he asked. I told him I was. He
gestured at the room. "Mister Apfel, can you tell if anything
has been taken from this room?"

I took another look around, approaching it as a puzzle.

There was a fireplace and there were curtains over the windows. There was a rug on the floor. Other than those items,
there was nothing else you would expect to find in a living
room.

All the walls were lined with tables, leaving a narrow aisle
down the middle. On the tables were monitor screens, key-
boards, disc drives—all the glossy bric-a-brac of the new age.
They were interconnected by thick cables and cords. Beneath
the tables were still more computers, and boxes full of electronic items. Above the tables were shelves that reached the
ceiling and were stuffed with boxes of tapes, discs, cartridges

. . . there was a word for it which I couldn't recall just then. It was software.

"There's no furniture, is there? Other than that . . ."

He was looking confused.

"You mean there was furniture here before?"

"How would I know?" Then I realized what the misunderstanding was. "Oh. You thought I'd been here before. The first time I ever set foot in this room was about an hour ago."

He frowned, and I didn't like that much.

"The medical examiner says the guy had been dead about three hours. How come you came over when you did, Victor?"

I didn't like him using my first name but didn't see what I could do about it. And I knew I had to tell him about the phone call.

He looked dubious. But there was one easy way to check it out, and we did that. Hal and Osborne and I and several others trooped over to my house. My phone was ringing as we entered.

Osborne picked it up and listened. He got a very sour expression on his face. As the night wore on, it just got worse and worse.

We waited ten minutes for the phone to ring again. Osborne spent the time examining everything in my living room. I was glad when the phone rang again. They made a recording of the message, and we went back to Kluge's house.

Osborne went into the back yard to see Kluge's forest of antennas. He looked impressed.

"Mrs. Madison down the street thinks he was trying to contact Martians," Hal said, with a laugh. "Me, I just thought he was stealing HBO." There were three parabolic dishes. There were six tall masts, and some of those things you see on telephone company buildings for transmitting microwaves.

Osborne took me to the living room again. He asked me to describe what I had seen. I didn't know what good that would do, but I tried.

"He was sitting in that chair, which was here in front of this table. I saw the gun on the floor. His hand was hanging down toward it."

"You think it was suicide?"

"Yes, I guess I did think that." I waited for him to comment, but he didn't. "Is that what you think?"

He sighed. "There wasn't any note."

"They don't always leave notes," Hal pointed out.

"No, but they do often enough that my nose starts to twitch when they don't." He shrugged. "It's probably nothing."

"That phone call," I said. "That might be a kind of suicide note."

Osborne nodded. "Was there anything else you noticed?"

I went to the table and looked at the keyboard. It was made by Texas Instruments, model TI-99/4A. There was a large bloodstain on the right side of it, where his head had been resting.

"Just that he was sitting in front of this machine." I touched a key, and the monitor screen behind the keyboard immediately filled with words. I quickly drew my hand back, then stared at the message there.

PROGRAM NAME: GOODBYE REAL WORLD
DATE: 8/20
CONTENTS: LAST WILL AND TESTAMENT; MISC.
FEATURES
PROGRAMMER: "CHARLES KLUGE"

TO RUN
PRESS ENTER■

The black square at the end flashed on and off. Later I learned it was called a cursor.

Everyone gathered around. Hal, the computer expert, explained how many computers went blank after ten minutes of no activity, so the words wouldn't be burned into the television screen. This one had been green until I touched it, then displayed black letters on a blue background.

"Has this console been checked for prints?" Osborne asked. Nobody seemed to know, so Osborne took a pencil and used the eraser to press the ENTER key.

The screen cleared, stayed blue for a moment, then filled with little ovoid shapes that started at the top of the screen and descended like rain. There were hundreds of them in many colors.

"Those are pills," one of the cops said, in amazement. "Look, that's gotta be a Quaalude. There's a Nembutal." Other cops pointed out other pills. I recognized the distinctive red stripe around the center of a white capsule that had to be a Dilantin. I had been taking them every day for years.

Finally the pills stopped failing, and the damn thing started to play music at us. "Nearer My God To Thee," in three-part harmony.

A few people laughed. I don't think any of us thought it was funny—it was creepy as hell listening to that eerie dirge —but it sounded like it had been scored for pennywhistle, calliope, and kazoo. What could you do but laugh?

As the music played, a little figure composed entirely of squares entered from the left of the screen and jerked spastically toward the center. It was like one of those human figures from a video game, but not as detailed. You had to use your imagination to believe it was a man.

A shape appeared in the middle of the screen. The "man" stopped in front of it. He bent in the middle, and something that might have been a chair appeared under him.

"What's that supposed to be?"

"A computer. Isn't it?"

It must have been, because the little man extended his arms, which jerked up and down like Liberace at the piano. He was typing. The words appeared above him.

SOMEWHERE ALONG THE LINE I MISSED SOME-
THING. I SIT HERE, NIGHT AND DAY, A SPIDER IN
THE CENTER OF A COAXIAL WEB. MASTER OF
ALL I SURVEY . . . AND IT IS NOT ENOUGH. THERE
MUST BE MORE.

ENTER YOUR NAME HERE■

"Jesus Christ," Hal said. "I don't believe it. An interactive suicide note."

"Come on, we've got to see the rest of this."

I was nearest the keyboard, so I leaned over and typed my name. But when I looked up, what I had typed was VICT9R.

"How do you back this up?" I asked.

"Just enter it," Osborne said. He reached around me and pressed enter.

DO YOU EVER GET THAT FEELING, VICT9R? YOU
HAVE WORKED ALL YOUR LIFE TO BE THE BEST
THERE IS AT WHAT YOU DO, AND ONE DAY YOU
WAKE UP TO WONDER WHY YOU ARE DOING IT/
THAT IS WHAT HAPPENED TO ME.

DO YOU WANT TO HEAR MORE, VICT9R/ Y/N■

The message rambled from that point. Kluge seemed to be aware of it, apologetic about it, because at the end of each forty or fifty-word paragraph the reader was given the Y/N option.

I kept glancing from the screen to the keyboard, remembering Kluge slumped across it. I thought about him sitting here alone, writing this.

He said he was despondent. He didn't feel like he could go on. He was taking too many pills (more of them rained down the screen at this point), and he had no further goal. He had done everything he set out to do. We didn't understand what he meant by that. He said he no longer existed. We thought that was a figure of speech

ARE YOU A COP, VICT9R? IF YOU ARE NOT, A COP
WILL BE HERE SOON. SO TO YOU OR THE COP; I
WAS NOT SELLING NARCOTICS. THE DRUGS IN
MY BEDROOM WERE FOR MY OWN PERSONAL
USE. I USED A LOT OF THEM. AND NOW I WILL
NOT NEED THEM ANYMORE.

PRESS ENTER■

Osborne did, and a printer across the room began to chatter, scaring the hell out of all of us. I could see the carriage zipping back and forth, printing in both directions, when Hal pointed at the screen and shouted.

"Look! Look at that!"

The compugraphic man was standing again. He faced us.

He had something that had to be a gun in his hand, which he now pointed at his head.

"Don't do it!" Hal yelled.

The little man didn't listen. There was a denatured gunshot sound, and the little man fell on his back. A line of red dripped down the screen. Then the green background turned to blue, the printer shut off, and there was nothing left but the little black corpse lying on its back and the word ★★DONE★★ at the bottom of the screen.

I took a deep breath and glanced at Osborne. It would be an understatement to say he did not look happy.

"What's this about drugs in the bedroom?" he said.

We watched Osborne pulling out drawers in dressers and bedside tables. He didn't find anything. He looked under the bed and in the closet. Like all the other rooms in the house, this one was full of computers. Holes had been knocked in walls for the thick sheaves of cables.

I had been standing near a big cardboard drum, one of several in the room. It was about thirty gallon capacity, the kind you ship things in. The lid was loose, so I lifted it. I sort of wished I hadn't.

"Osborne," I said. "You'd better look at this."

The drum was lined with a heavy-duty garbage bag. And it was two-thirds full of Quaaludes.

They pried the lids off the rest of the drums. We found drums of amphetamines, of Nembutals, of Valium. All sorts of things.

With the discovery of the drugs a lot more police returned to the scene. With them came the television camera crews.

In all the activity no one seemed concerned about me, so I slipped back to my own house and locked the door. From time to time I peeked out the curtains. I saw reporters interviewing the neighbors. Hal was there and seemed to be having a good time. Twice crews knocked on my door, but I didn't answer. Eventually they went away.

I ran a hot bath and soaked in it for about an hour. Then I turned the heat up as high as it would go and got in bed, under the blankets.

I shivered all night.

* * *

Osborne came over about nine the next morning. I let him in. Hal followed, looking very unhappy. I realized they had been up all night. I poured coffee for them.

"You'd better read this first," Osborne said and handed me the sheet of computer printout. I unfolded it, got out my glasses, and started to read.

It was in that awful dot-matrix printing. My policy is to throw any such trash into the fireplace, un-read, but I made an exception this time.

It was Kluge's will. Some probate court was going to have a lot of fun with it.

He stated again that he didn't exist, so he could have no relatives. He had decided to give all his worldly property to somebody who deserved it.

But who was deserving? Kluge wondered. Well, not Mr. and Mrs. Perkins, four houses down the street. They were child abusers. He cited court records in Buffalo and Miami, and a pending case locally.

Mrs. Radnor and Mrs. Polonski, who lived across the street from each other five houses down, were gossips.

The Andersons' oldest son was a car thief.

Marian Flores cheated on her high school algebra tests.

There was a guy nearby who was diddling the city on a freeway construction project. There was one wife in the neighborhood who made out with door-to-door salesmen, and two having affairs with men other than their husbands. There was a teenage boy who got his girlfriend pregnant, dropped her, and bragged about it to his friends.

There were no fewer than nineteen couples in the immediate area who had not reported income to the IRS, or who had padded their deductions.

Kluge's neighbors in back had a dog that barked all night.

Well, I could vouch for the dog. He'd kept me awake often enough. But the rest of it was *crazy!* For one thing, where did a guy with two hundred gallons of illegal narcotics get the right to judge his neighbors so harshly? I mean, the child abusers were one thing, but was it right to tar a whole family because their son stole cars? And for another . . . how did he *know* some of this stuff?

But there was more. Specifically, four philandering husbands. One was Harold "Hal" Lanier, who for three years had been seeing a woman named Toni Jones, a co-worker at the L.A.P.D. Data Processing facility. She was pressuring him for a divorce; he was "waiting for the right time to tell his wife."

I glanced up at Hal. His red face was all the confirmation I needed.

Then it hit me. What had Kluge found out about *me?*

I hurried down the page, searching for my name. I found it in the last paragraph.

". . . for thirty years Mr. Apfel has been paying for a mistake he did not even make. I won't go so far as to nominate him for sainthood, but by default—if for no other reason—I hereby leave all deed and title to my real property and the structure thereon to Victor Apfel."

I looked at Osborne, and those tired eyes were weighing me.

"But I don't *want* it!"

"Do you think this is the reward Kluge mentioned in the phone call?"

"It must be," I said. "What else could it be?"

Osborne sighed and sat back in his chair. "At least he didn't try to leave you the drugs. Are you still saying you didn't know the guy?"

"Are you accusing me of something?"

He spread his hands. "Mister Apfel, I'm simply asking a question. You're never one hundred percent sure in a suicide. Maybe it was a murder. If it was, you can see that, so far, you're the only one we know of that's gained by it."

"He was almost a stranger to me."

He nodded, tapping his copy of the computer printout. I looked back at my own, wishing it would go away.

"What's this . . . mistake you didn't make?"

I was afraid that would be the next question.

"I was a prisoner of war in North Korea," I said.

Osborne chewed that over for a while.

"They brainwash you?"

"Yes." I hit the arm of my chair, and suddenly had to be up and moving. The room was getting cold. "No. I don't . . . there's been a lot of confusion about that word. Did they 'brainwash' me? Yes. Did they succeed? Did I offer a confes-

sion of my war crimes and denounce the U.S. Government?
No."

Once more, I felt myself being inspected by those deceptively tired eyes.

"It's not something you forget."

"Is there anything you want to say about it?"

"It's just that it was all so . . . no. No, I have nothing further to say. Not to you, not to anybody."

"I'm going to have to ask you more questions about
Kluge's death."

"I think I'll have my lawyer present for those." Christ.
Now I am going to have to get a lawyer. I didn't know where
to begin.

Osborne just nodded again. He got up and went to the
door.

"I was ready to write this one down as a suicide," he said.
"The only thing that bothered me was there was no note. Now
we've got a note." He gestured in the direction of Kluge's
house and started to look angry.

"This guy not only write a note, he programs the fucking
thing into his computer, complete with special effects straight
out of Pac-Man.

"Now, I know people do crazy things. I've seen enough of
them. But when I heard the computer playing a hymn, that's
when I knew this was a murder. Tell you the truth, Mr. Apfel,
I don't think you did it. There must be two dozen motives for
murder in that printout. Maybe he was blackmailing people
around here. Maybe that's how he bought all those machines.
And people with that amount of drugs usually die violently.
I've got a lot of work to do on this one, and I'll find who did
it." He mumbled something about not leaving town, and that
he'd see me later, and left.

"Vic . . ." Hal said. I looked at him.

"About that printout," he finally said. "I'd appreciate it
. . . well, they said they'd keep it confidential. If you know
what I mean." He had eyes like a basset hound. I'd never
noticed that before.

"Hal, if you'll just go home, you have nothing to worry
about from me."

He nodded and scuttled for the door.

"I don't think any of that will get out," he said.

* * *

It all did, of course.

It probably would have even without the letters that began arriving a few days after Kluge's death, all postmarked Trenton, New Jersey, all computer-generated from a machine no one was ever able to trace. The letters detailed the matters Kluge had mentioned in his will.

I didn't know about any of that at the time. I spent the rest of the day after Hal's departure lying in my bed, under the electric blanket. I couldn't get my feet warm. I got up only to soak in the tub or to make a sandwich.

Reporters knocked on the door but I didn't answer. On the second day I called a criminal lawyer—Martin Abrams, the first in the book—and retained him. He told me they'd probably call me down to the police station for questioning. I told him I wouldn't go, popped two Dilantin, and sprinted for the bed.

A couple of times I heard sirens in the neighborhood. Once I heard a shouted argument down the street. I resisted the temptation to look. I'll admit I was a little curious, but you know what happened to the cat.

I kept waiting for Osborne to return, but he didn't. The days turned into a week. Only two things of interest happened in that time.

The first was a knock on my door. This was two days after Kluge's death. I looked through the curtains and saw a silver Ferrari parked at the curb. I couldn't see who was on the porch, so I asked who it was.

"My name's Lisa Foo," she said. "You asked me to drop by."

"I certainly don't remember it."

"Isn't this Charles Kluge's house?"

"That's next door."

"Oh. Sorry."

I decided I ought to warn her Kluge was dead, so I opened the door. She turned around and smiled at me. It was blinding.

Where does one start in describing Lisa Foo? Remember when newspapers used to run editorial cartoons of Hirohito and Tojo, when the *Times* used the word "Jap" without embarrassment? Little guys with faces wide as footballs, ears like jug handles, thick glasses, two big rabbity buck teeth, and pencil-thin moustaches . . .

Leaving out only the moustache, she was a dead ringer for a cartoon Tojo. She had the glasses, and the ears, and the teeth. But her teeth had braces, like piano keys wrapped in barbed wire. And she was five-eight or five-nine and couldn't have weighed more than a hundred and ten. I'd have said a hundred, but added five pounds each for her breasts, so improbably large on her scrawny frame that all I could read of the message on her T-shirt was "POCK LIVE." It was only when she turned sideways that I saw the esses before and after.

She thrust out a slender hand.

"Looks like I'm going to be your neighbor for a while," she said. "At least until we get that dragon's lair next door straightened out." If she had an accent, it was San Fernando Valley.

"That's nice."

"Did you know him? Kluge, I mean. Or at least that's what he called himself."

"You don't think that was his name?"

"I doubt it. 'Klug' means clever in German. And it's hacker slang for being tricky. And he sure was a tricky bugger. Definitely some glitches in the wetware." She tapped the side of her head meaningfully. "Viruses and phantoms and demons jumping out every time they try to key in, Software rot, bit buckets overflowing onto the floor . . ."

She babbled on it that vein for a time. It might as well have been Swahili.

"Did you say there were demons in his computers?"

"That's right."

"Sounds like they need an exorcist."

She jerked her thumb at her chest and showed me another half-acre of teeth.

"That's me. Listen, I gotta go. Drop in and see me anytime."

The second interesting event of the week happened the next day. My bank statement arrived. There were three deposits listed. The first was the regular check from the V.A., for

$487.00. The second was for $392.54, interest on the money my parents had left me fifteen years ago.

The third deposit had come in on the twentieth, the day Charles Kluge died. It was for $700,083.04.

A few days later Hal Lanier dropped by.

"Boy, what a week," he said. Then he flopped down on the couch and told me all about it.

There had been a second death on the block. The letters had stirred up a bit of trouble, especially with the police going house to house questioning everyone. Some people had confessed to things when they were sure the cops were closing in on them. The woman who used to entertain salesmen while her husband was at work had admitted her infidelity, and the guy had shot her. He was in the County Jail. That was the worst incident, but there had been others, from fistfights to rocks thrown through windows. According to Hal, the IRS was thinking of setting up a branch office in the neighborhood, so many people were being audited.

I thought about the seven hundred thousand and eighty-three dollars.

And four cents.

I didn't say anything, but my feet were getting cold.

"I suppose you want to know about me and Betty," he said, at last. I didn't. I didn't want to hear *any* of this, but I tried for a sympathetic expression.

"That's all over," he said with a satisfied sigh. "Between me and Toni, I mean. I told Betty all about it. It was real bad for a few days, but I think our marriage is stronger for it now." He was quiet for a moment, basking in the warmth of it all. I had kept a straight face under worse provocation, so I trust I did well enough then.

He wanted to tell me all they'd learned about Kluge, and he wanted to invite me over for dinner, but I begged off on both, telling him my war wounds were giving me hell. I just about had him to the door when Osborne knocked on it. There was nothing to do but let him in. Hal stuck around, too.

I offered Osborne coffee, which he gratefully accepted. He looked different. I wasn't sure what it was at first. Same old tired expression . . . no, it wasn't. Most of that weary look had been either an act or a cop's built-in cynicism. Today it was genuine. The tiredness had moved from his face to his shoulders, to his hands, to the way he walked and the way he slumped in the chair. There was a sour aura of defeat around him.

"Am I still a suspect?" I asked.

"You mean, should you call your lawyer? I'd say don't bother. I checked you out pretty good. That will ain't gonna hold up, so your motive is pretty half-assed. Way I figure it, every coke dealer in the Marina had a better reason to snuff Kluge than you." He sighed. "I got a couple questions. You can answer them or not."

"Give it a try."

"You remember any unusual visitors he had? People coming and going at night?"

"The only visitors I *ever* recall were deliveries. Post office. Federal Express, freight companies . . . that sort of thing. I suppose the drugs could have come in any of those shipments."

"That's what we figure, too. There's no way he was dealing nickel and dime bags. He must have been a middle man. Ship it in, ship it out." He brooded about that for a while and sipped his coffee.

"So are you making any progress?" I asked.

"You want to know the truth? The case is going in the toilet. We've got too many motives, and not a one of them that works. As far as we can tell, nobody on the block had the slightest idea Kluge had all that information. We've checked bank accounts and we can't find evidence of blackmail. So the neighbors are pretty much out of the picture. Though if he were alive, most people around here would like to kill him *now.*"

"Damn straight," Hal said.

Osborne slapped his thigh. "If the bastard was alive, *I'd* kill him," he said. "But I'm beginning to think he never *was* alive."

"I don't understand."

"If I hadn't seen the goddamn body . . ." He sat up a little straighter. "He said he didn't exist. Well, he practically didn't. PG&E never heard of him. He's hooked up to their lines and a meter reader came by every month, but they never billed him for a single kilowatt. Same with the phone company. He had a whole exchange in that house that was *made* by the phone company, and delivered by them, and installed by them, but they have no record of him. We talked to the guy who hooked it all up. He turned in his records, and the computer swallowed them. Kluge didn't have a bank account anywhere in California, and apparently he didn't need one. We've tracked down a hundred companies that sold things to him, shipped them out, and then either marked his account paid or forgot they ever sold him anything. Some of them have check numbers and account numbers in their books, for accounts or even *banks* that don't exist."

He leaned back in his chair, simmering at the perfidy of it all.

"The only guy we've found who ever heard of him was the guy who delivered his groceries once a month. Little store down on Sepulveda. They don't have a computer, just paper receipts. He paid by check. Wells Fargo accepted them and the checks never bounced. But Wells Fargo never heard of him."

I thought it over. He seemed to expect something of me at this point, so I made a stab at it.

"He was doing all this by computers?"

"That's right. Now, the grocery store scam I understand, almost. But more often than not, Kluge got right into the basic programming of the computers and wiped himself out. The power company was never paid, by check or any other way, because as far as they were concerned, they weren't selling him anything.

"No government agency has ever heard of him. We've checked him with everybody from the post office to the CIA."

"Kluge was probably an alias, right?" I offered.

"Yeah. But the FBI doesn't have his fingerprints. We'll find out who he was, eventually. But it doesn't get us any closer to whether or not he was murdered."

He admitted there was pressure to simply close the felony part of the case, label it suicide, and forget it. But Osborne would not believe it. Naturally, the civil side would go on for some time, as they attempted to track down all Kluge's deceptions.

"It's all up to the dragon lady," Osborne said. Hal snorted.

"Fat chance," Hal said and muttered something about boat people.

"That girl? She's still over there? Who is she?"

"She's some sort of giant brain from Cal Tech. We called out there and told them we were having problems, and she's what they sent." It was clear from Osborne's face what he thought of any help she might provide.

I finally managed to get rid of them. As they went down the walk I looked over at Kluge's house. Sure enough, Lisa Foo's silver Ferrari was sitting in his driveway.

I had no business going over there. I knew that better than anyone.

So I set about preparing my evening meal. I made a tuna casserole—which is not as bland as it sounds, the way I make it—put it in the oven and went out to the garden to pick the makings for a salad. I was slicing cherry tomatoes and thinking about chilling a bottle of white wine when it occurred to me that I had enough for two.

Since I never do anything hastily, I sat down and thought it over for a while. What finally decided me was my feet. For the first time in a week, they were warm. So I went to Kluge's house.

The front door was standing open. There was no screen. Funny how disturbing that can look, the dwelling wide open and unguarded. I stood on the porch and leaned in, but all I could see was the hallway.

"Miss Foo?" I called. There was no answer.

The last time I'd been here I had found a dead man. I hurried in.

Lisa Foo was sitting on a piano bench before a computer console. She was in profile, her back very straight, her brown legs in lotus position, her fingers poised at the keys as words sprayed rapidly onto the screen in front of her. She looked up and flashed her teeth at me.

"Somebody told me your name was Victor Apfel," she said.

"Yes. Uh, the door was open . . ."

"It's hot," she said, reasonably, pinching the fabric of her shirt near her neck and lifting it up and down like you do when you're sweaty. "What can I do for you?"

"Nothing, really." I came into the dimness and stumbled on something. It was a cardboard box, the large fat kind used for delivering a jumbo pizza.

"I was just fixing dinner, and it looks like there's plenty for two, so I was wondering if you . . ." I trailed off, as I had just noticed something else. I had thought she was wearing shorts. In fact, all she had on was the shirt and a pair of pink bikini underpants. This did not seem to make her uneasy.

". . . would you like to join me for dinner?"

Her smile grew even broader.

"I'd love to," she said. She effortlessly unwound her legs and bounced to her feet, then brushed past me, trailing the smells of perspiration and sweet soap. "Be with you in a minute."

I looked around the room again but my mind kept coming back to her. She liked Pepsi with her pizza; there were dozens of empty cans. There was a deep scar on her knee and upper thigh. The ashtrays were empty . . . and the long muscles of her calves bunched strongly as she walked. Kluge must have smoked, but Lisa didn't, and she had fine, downy hairs in the small of her back just visible in the green computer light. I heard water running in the bathroom sink, looked at a yellow notepad covered with the kind of penmanship I hadn't seen in decades, and smelled soap and remembered tawny brown skin and an easy stride.

She appeared in the hall, wearing cut-off jeans, sandals, and a new T-shirt. The old one had advertised BURROUGHS OFFICE SYSTEMS. This one featured Mickey Mouse and Snow White's Castle and smelled of fresh bleached cotton. Mickey's ears were laid back on the upper slopes of her incongruous breasts.

I followed her out the door. Tinkerbell twinkled in pixie dust from the back of her shirt.

"I like this kitchen," she said.

You don't really look at a place until someone says something like that.

The kitchen was a time capsule. It could have been lifted bodily from an issue of *Life* in the early fifties. There was the hump-shouldered Frigidaire, of a vintage when that word had been a generic term, like kleenex or coke. The counter tops were yellow tile, the sort that's only found in bathrooms these days. There wasn't an ounce of Formica in the place. Instead of a dishwasher I had a wire rack and a double sink. There was no electric can opener, Cuisinart, trash compacter, or microwave oven. The newest thing in the whole room was a fifteen-year-old blender.

I'm good with my hands. I like to repair things.

"This bread is terrific," she said.

I had baked it myself. I watched her mop her plate with a crust, and she asked if she might have seconds.

I understand cleaning one's plate with bread is bad manners. Not that I cared; I do it myself. And other than that, her manners were impeccable. She polished off three helpings of my casserole and when she was done the plate hardly needed washing. I had a sense of ravenous appetite barely held in check.

She settled back in her chair and I refilled her glass with white wine.

"Are you sure you wouldn't like some more peas?"

"I'd bust." She patted her stomach contentedly. "Thank you so much, Mister Apfel. I haven't had a home-cooked meal in ages."

"You can call me Victor."

"I just love American food."

"I didn't know there was such a thing. I mean, not like Chinese or . . . you *are* American, aren't you?" She just smiled. "What I mean—"

"I know what you meant, Victor. I'm a citizen, but not native-born. Would you excuse me for a moment? I know it's impolite to jump right up, with these braces I find I have to brush *instantly* after eating."

I could hear her as I cleared the table. I ran water in the sink and started doing the dishes. Before long she joined me, grabbed a dish towel, and began drying the things in the rack, over my protests.

"You live alone here?" she asked.

"Yes. Have ever since my parents died."

"Ever married? If it's none of my business, just say so."

"That's all right. No, I never married."

"You do pretty good for not having a woman around."

"I've had a lot of practice. Can I ask you a question?"

"Shoot."

"Where are you from? Taiwan?"

"I have a knack for languages. Back home, I spoke pidgin American, but when I got here I cleaned up my act. I also speak rotten French, illiterate Chinese in four or five varieties, gutter Vietnamese, and enough Thai to holler, 'Me wanna see American Consul, pretty-damn-quick, you!'"

I laughed. When she said it, her accent was thick.

"I been here eight years now. You figured out where home is?"

"Vietnam?" I ventured.

"The sidewalks of Saigon, fer shure. Or Ho Chi Minh's Shitty, as the pajama-heads renamed it, may their drinks rot off and their butts be filled with jagged punjee-sticks. Pardon my French."

She ducked her head in embarrassment. What had started out light had turned hot very quickly. I sensed a hurt at least as deep as my own, and we both backed off from it.

"I took you for a Japanese," I said.

"Yeah, ain't it a pisser? I'll tell you about it someday. Victor, is that a laundry room through that door there? With an electric washer?"

"That's right."

"Would it be too much trouble if I did a load?"

It was no trouble at all. She had seven pairs of faded jeans, some with the legs cut away, and about two dozen T-shirts. It could have been a load of boys' clothing except for the frilly underwear.

We went into the back yard to sit in the last rays of the setting sun, then she had to see my garden. I'm quite proud of it. When I'm well, I spend four or five hours a day working out there, year-round, usually in the morning hours. You can do that in southern California. I have a small greenhouse I built myself.

She loved it, though it was not in its best shape. I had spent most of the week in bed or in the tub. As a result, weeds were sprouting here and there.

"We had a garden when I was little," she said. "And I spent two years in a rice paddy."

"That must be a lot different than this."

"Damn straight. Put me off rice for *years*."

She discovered an infestation of aphids, so we squatted down to pick them off. She had that double-jointed Asian peasant's way of sitting that I remembered so well and could never imitate. Her fingers were long and narrow, and soon the tips of them were green from squashed bugs.

We talked about this and that. I don't remember quite how it came up, but I told her I had fought in Korea. I learned she was twenty-five. It turned out we had the same birthday, so some months back I had been exactly twice her age.

The only time Kluge's name came up was when she mentioned how she liked to cook. She hadn't been able to at Kluge's house.

"He has a freezer in the garage full of frozen dinners," she said. "He had one plate, one fork, one spoon, and one glass. He's got the best microwave oven on the market. And that's *it*, man. Ain't nothing else in his kitchen at *all*." She shook her head, and executed an aphid. "He was one weird dude."

When her laundry was done it was late evening, almost dark. She loaded it into my wicker basket and we took it out to the clothesline. It got to be a game. I would shake out a T-shirt and study the picture or message there. Sometimes I got it, and sometimes I didn't. There were pictures of rock groups, a map of Los Angeles, Star Trek tie-ins . . . a little of everything.

"What's the L5 Society?" I asked her.

"Guys that want to build these great big farms in space. I asked 'em if they were gonna grow rice, and they said they didn't think it was the best crop for zero gee, so I bought the shirt."

"How many of these things do you have?"

"Wow, it's gotta be four or five hundred. I usually wear 'em two or three times and then put them away."

I picked up another shirt, and a bra fell out. It wasn't the kind of bra girls wore when I grew up. It was very sheer, though somehow functional at the same time.

"You like, Yank?" Her accent was very thick. "You oughtta see my sister!"

I glanced at her, and her face fell.

"I'm sorry, Victor," she said. "You don't have to blush." She took the bra from me and clipped it to the line.

She must have misread my face. True, I had been embarrassed, but I was also pleased in some strange way. It had been a long time since anybody had called me anything but Victor or Mr. Apfel.

The next day's mail brought a letter from a law firm in Chicago. It was about the seven hundred thousand dollars. The money had come from a Delaware holding company which had been set up in 1933 to provide for me in my old age. My mother and father were listed as the founders. Certain long-term investments had matured, resulting in my recent windfall. The amount in my bank was *after* taxes.

It was ridiculous on the face of it. My parents had never had that kind of money. I didn't want it. I would have given it back if I could find out who Kluge had stolen it from.

I decided that, if I wasn't in jail this time next year, I'd give it all to some charity. Save the Whales, maybe, or the L5 Society.

I spent the morning in the garden. Later I walked to the market and bought some fresh ground beef and pork. I was feeling good as I pulled my purchases home in my fold-up wire basket. When I passed the silver Ferrari I smiled.

She hadn't come to get her laundry. I took it off the line and folded it, then knocked on Kluge's door.

"It's me. Victor."

"Come on in, Yank."

She was where she had been before, but decently dressed this time. She smiled at me, then hit her forehead when she saw the laundry basket. She hurried to take it from me.

"I'm sorry, Victor. I meant to get this—"

"Don't worry about it," I said. "It was no trouble. And it gives me the chance to ask if you'd like to dine with me again."

Something happened to her face which she covered quickly. Perhaps she didn't like "American" food as much as she professed to. Or maybe it was the cook.

"Sure, Victor, I'd love to. Let me take care of this. And why don't you open those drapes? It's like a tomb in here."

She hurried away. I glanced at the screen she had been

using. It was blank, but for one word: intercourse-p. I assumed it was a typo.

I pulled the drapes open in time to see Osborne's car park at the curb. Then Lisa was back, wearing a new T-shirt. This one said A CHANGE OF HOBBIT, and had a picture of a squat, hairy-footed creature. She glanced out the window and saw Osborne coming up the walk.

"I say, Watson," she said. "It's Lestrade of the Yard. Do show him in."

That wasn't nice of her. He gave me a suspicious glance as he entered. I burst out laughing. Lisa sat on the piano bench, poker-faced. She slumped indolently, one arm resting near the keyboard.

"Well, Apfel," Osborne started. "We've finally found out who Kluge really was."

"Patrick William Gavin," Lisa said.

Quite a time went by before Osborne was able to close his mouth. Then he opened it right up again.

"How the hell did you find that out?"

She lazily caressed the keyboard beside her.

"Well, of course I got it when it came into your office this morning. There's a little stoolie program tucked away in your computer that whispers in my ear every time the name Kluge is mentioned. But I didn't need that. I figured it out five days ago."

"Then why the . . . why didn't you tell me?"

"You didn't ask me."

They glared at each other for a while. I had no idea what events had led up to this moment, but it was quite clear they didn't like each other even a little bit. Lisa was on top just now and seemed to be enjoying it. Then she glanced at her screen, looked surprised, and quickly tapped a key. The word that had been there vanished. She gave me an inscrutable glance, then faced Osborne again.

"If you recall, you brought me in because all your own guys were getting was a lot of crashes. This system was brain-damaged when I got here, practically catatonic. Most of it was down and your guys couldn't get it up." She had to grin at that.

"You decided I couldn't do any worse than your guys were doing. So you asked me to try and break Kluge's codes without frying the system. Well, I did it. All you had to do was come by and interface and I would have downloaded N tons of wallpaper right in your lap."

Osborne listened quietly. Maybe he even knew he had made a mistake.

"What did you get? Can I see it now?"

She nodded and pressed a few keys. Words started to fill her screen, and one close to Osborne. I got up and read Lisa's terminal.

It was a brief bio of Kluge/Gavin. He was about my age, but while I was getting shot at in a foreign land, he was cutting a swath through the infant computer industry. He had been there from the ground up, working at many of the top research facilities. It surprised me that it had taken over a week to identify him.

"I compiled this anecdotally," Lisa said, as we read. "The first thing you have to realize about Gavin is that he exists nowhere in any computerized information system. So I called people all over the country—interesting phone system he's got, by the way; it generates a new number for each call, and you can't call back or trace it—and started asking who the top people were in the fifties and sixties. I got a lot of names. After that, it was a matter of finding out who no longer existed in the files. He faked his death in 1967. I located one account of it in a newspaper file. Everybody I talked to who had known him knew of his death. There is a paper birth certificate in Florida. That's the only other evidence I found of him. He was the only guy so many people in the field knew who left no mark on the world. That seemed conclusive to me."

Osborne finished reading, then looked up.

"All right, Ms. Foo. What else have you found out?"

"I've broken some of his codes. I had a piece of luck, getting into a basic rape-and-plunder program he'd written to attack *other* people's programs, and I've managed to use it against a few of his own. I've unlocked a file of passwords with notes on where they came from. And I've learned a few of his tricks. But it's the tip of the iceberg."

She waved a hand at the silent metal brains in the room.

"What I haven't gotten across to anyone is just what this *is*. This is the most devious electronic weapon ever devised. It's armored like a battleship. It has to be; there's a lot of very slick programs out there that grab an invader and hang on like a terrier. If they ever got this far Kluge could deflect them. But usually they never even knew they'd been burgled. Kluge'd come in like a cruise missile, low and fast and twisty. And he'd route his attack through a dozen cut-offs.

"He had a lot of advantages. Big systems these days are heavily protected. People use passwords and very sophisticated codes. But Kluge helped *invent* most of them. You need a damn good lock to keep out a locksmith. He helped *install* a lot of the major systems. He left informants behind, hidden in the software. If the codes were changed, the computer *itself* would send the information to a safe system that Kluge could tap later. It's like you buy the biggest, meanest, best-trained watchdog you can. And that night, the guy who *trained* the dog comes in, pats him on the head, and robs you blind."

There was a lot more in that vein. I'm afraid that when Lisa began talking about computers, ninety percent of my head shut off.

"I'd like to know something, Osborne," Lisa said.

"What would that be?"

"What is my status here? Am I supposed to be solving your crime for you, or just trying to get this system back to where a competent user can deal with it?"

Osborne thought it over.

"What worries me," she added, "is that I'm poking around in a lot of restricted data banks. I'm worried about somebody knocking on the door and handcuffing me. *You* ought to be worried, too. Some of these agencies wouldn't like a homicide cop looking into their affairs."

Osborne bridled at that. Maybe that's what she intended.

"What do I have to do?" he snarled. "Beg you to stay?"

"No. I just want your authorization. You don't have to put it in writing. Just say you're behind me."

"Look. As far as L.A. County and the State of California are concerned, this house doesn't exist. There is no lot here. It doesn't appear in the assessor's records. This place is in a legal limbo. If anybody can authorize you to use this stuff, it's me, because I believe a murder was committed in it. So you just keep doing what you've been doing."

"That's not much of a commitment," she mused.

"It's all you're going to get. Now, what else have you got?"

She turned to her keyboard and typed for a while. Pretty soon a printer started, and Lisa leaned back. I glanced at her screen. It said: osculate posterior-p. I remembered that osculate meant kiss. Well, these people have their own language. Lisa looked up at me and grinned.

"Not you," she said, quietly. *"Him."*

I hadn't the faintest notion of what she was talking about.

Osborne got his printout and was ready to leave. Again, he couldn't resist turning at the door for final orders.

"If you find anything to indicate he didn't commit suicide, let me know."

"Okay. He didn't commit suicide."

Osborne didn't understand for a moment.

"I want proof."

"Well, I have it, but you probably can't use it. He didn't write that ridiculous suicide note."

"How do you know that?"

"I knew that my first day here. I had the computer list the program. Then I compared it to Kluge's style. No *way* he could have written it. It's tighter'n a bug's ass. Not a spare line in it. Kluge didn't pick his alias for nothing. You know what it means?"

"Clever," I said.

"Literally. But it means...a Rube Goldberg device. Something overly complex. Something that works, but for the wrong reason. You 'kluge around' bugs in a program. It's the hacker's vaseline."

"So?" Osborne wanted to know.

"So Kluge's programs were really crocked. They were full of bells and whistles he never bothered to clean out. He was a genius, and his programs worked, but you wonder why they did. Routines so bletcherous they'd make your skin crawl. Real crufty bagbiters. But good programming's so rare, even his diddles were better than most people's super-moby hacks."

I suspect Osborne understood about as much of that as I did.

"So you base your opinion on his programming style."

"Yeah. Unfortunately, it's gonna be ten years or so before that's admissible in court, like graphology or fingerprints. But if you know anything about programming you can look at it and see it. Somebody else wrote that suicide note—somebody damn good, by the way. That program called up his last will and testament in a sub-routine. And he definitely *did* write that. It's got his fingerprints all over it. He spent the last five years spying on the neighbors as a hobby. He tapped into military records, school records, word records, tax files, and bank accounts. And he turned every telephone for three blocks into a listening device. He was one hell of a snoop."

"Did he mention anywhere why he did that?" Osborne asked.

"I think he was more than half crazy. Possibly he was suicidal. He sure wasn't doing himself any good with all those pills he took. But he was preparing himself for death, and Victor was the only one he found worthy of leaving it all to. I'd have *believed* he committed suicide if not for that note. But he didn't write it. I'll swear to that."

We eventually got rid of him, and I went home to fix the dinner. Lisa joined me when it was ready. Once more she had a huge appetite.

I fixed lemonade and we sat on my small patio and watched evening gather around us.

I woke up in the middle of the night, sweating. I sat up, thinking it out, and I didn't like my conclusions. So I put on my robe and slippers and went over to Kluge's.

The front door was open again. I knocked anyway. Lisa stuck her head around the corner.

"Victor? Is something wrong?"

"I'm not sure," I said. "May I come in?"

She gestured, and I followed her into the living room. An open can of Pepsi sat beside her console. Her eyes were red as she sat on her bench.

"What's up?" she said and yawned.

"You should be asleep, for one thing," I said.

She shrugged and nodded.

"Yeah. I can't seem to get in the right phase. Just now I'm in day mode. But Victor, I'm used to working odd hours, and long hours, and you didn't come over here to lecture me about that, did you?"

"No. You say Kluge was murdered."

"He didn't write his suicide note. That seems to leave murder."

"I was wondering why someone would kill him. He never left the house, so it was for something he did here with his computers. And now you're...well, I don't know *what* you're doing, frankly, but you seem to be poking into the same things. Isn't there a danger the same people will come after you?"

"People?" She raised an eyebrow.

I felt helpless. My fears were not well formed enough to make sense.

"I don't know...you mentioned agencies..."

"You notice how impressed Osborne was with that? You think there's some kind of conspiracy Kluge tumbled to, or you think the CIA killed him because he found out too much about something, or—"

"I don't know, Lisa. But I'm worried the same thing could happen to you."

Surprisingly, she smiled at me.

"Thank you so much, Victor. I wasn't going to admit it to Osborne, but I've been worried about that, too."

"Well, what are you going to do?"

"I want to stay here and keep working. So I gave some thought to what I could do to protect myself. I decided there wasn't anything."

"Surely there's something."

"Well, I got a gun, if that's what you mean. But think about it. Kluge was offed in the middle of the day. Nobody saw anybody enter or leave the house. So I asked myself, who can walk into a house in broad daylight, shoot Kluge, program that suicide note, and walk away, leaving no traces he'd ever been there?"

"Somebody very good."

"Goddamn good. So good there's not much chance one little gook's gonna be able to stop him if he decides to waste her."

She shocked me, both by her words and by her apparent lack of concern for her own fate. But she had said she was worried.

"Then you have to stop this. Get out of here."

"I won't be pushed around that way," she said. There was a

tone of finality to it. I thought of things I might say, and rejected them all.

"You could at least . . . lock your front door," I concluded, lamely.

She laughed and kissed my cheek.

"I'll do that, Yank. And I appreciate your concern. I really do."

I watched her close the door behind me, listened to her lock it, then trudged through the moonlight toward my house. Halfway there I stopped. I could suggest she stay in my spare bedroom. I could offer to stay with her at Kluge's.

No, I decided. She would probably take that the wrong way.

I was back in bed before I realized, with a touch of chagrin and more than a little disgust at myself, that she had every reason to take it the wrong way.

And me exactly twice her age.

I spent the morning in the garden, planning the evening's menu. I have always liked to cook, but dinner with Lisa had rapidly become the high point of my day. Not only that, I was already taking it for granted. So it hit me hard, around noon, when I looked out the front and saw her car gone.

I hurried to Kluge's front door. It was standing open. I made a quick search of the house. I found nothing until the master bedroom, where her clothes were stacked neatly on the floor.

Shivering, I pounded on the Laniers' front door. Betty answered and immediately saw my agitation.

"The girl at Kluge's house," I said. "I'm afraid something's wrong. Maybe we'd better call the police."

"What happened?" Betty asked, looking over my shoulder. "Did she call you? I see she's not back yet."

"Back?"

"I saw her drive away about an hour ago. That's quite a car she has."

Feeling like a fool, I tried to make nothing of it, but I caught a look in Betty's eye. I think she'd have liked to pat me on the head. It made me furious.

But she'd left her clothes, so surely she was coming back.

I kept telling myself that, then went to run a bath, as hot as I could stand it.

When I answered the door she was standing there with a grocery bag in each arm and her usual blinding smile on her face.

"I wanted to do this yesterday but I forgot until you came over, and I know I should have asked first, but then I wanted to surprise you, so I just went to get one or two items you didn't have in your garden and a couple of things that weren't in your spice rack . . ."

She kept talking as we unloaded the bags in the kitchen. I said nothing. She was wearing a new T-shirt. There was a big V, and under it a picture of a screw, followed by a hyphen and a small case "p." I thought it over as she babbled on. V, screw-p. I was determined not to ask what it meant.

"Do you like Vietnamese cooking?"

I looked at her and finally realized she was very nervous.

"I don't know," I said. "I've never had it. But I like Chinese, and Japanese, and Indian. I like to try new things." The last part was a lie, but not as bad as it might have been. I do try new recipes, and my tastes in food are catholic. I didn't expect to have much trouble with southeast Asian cuisine.

"Well, when I get through you *still* won't know," she laughed. "My momma was half-Chinese. So what you're gonna get here is a mongrel meal." She glanced up, saw my face, and laughed.

"I forgot. You've been to Asia. No, Yank, I ain't gonna serve any dog meat."

There was only one intolerable thing, and that was the chopsticks. I used them for as long as I could, then put them aside and got a fork.

"I'm sorry," I said. "Chopsticks happen to be a problem for me."

"You use them very well."

"I had plenty of time to learn how."

It was very good, and I told her so. Each dish was a revelation, not quite like anything I had ever had. Toward the end, I broke down halfway.

"Does the V stand for victory?" I asked.

"Maybe."

"Beethoven? Churchill? World War Two?"

She just smiled.

"Think of it as a challenge, Yank."

"Do I frighten you, Victor?"

"You did at first."

"It's my face, isn't it?"

"It's a generalized phobia of Orientals. I suppose I'm a racist. Not because I want to be."

She nodded slowly, there in the dark. We were on the patio again, but the sun had gone down a long time ago. I can't recall what we had talked about for all those hours. It had kept us busy, anyway.

"I have the same problem," she said.

"Fear of Orientals?" I had meant it as a joke.

"Of Cambodians." She let me take that in for a while, then went on. "When Saigon fell, I fled to Cambodia. It took me two years with stops when the Khmer Rouge put me in labor camps. I'm lucky to be alive, really."

"I thought they called it Kampuchea now."

She spat. I'm not even sure she was aware she had done it.

"It's the People's Republic of Syphilitic Dogs. The North Koreans treated you very badly, didn't they, Victor?"

"That's right."

"Koreans are pus suckers." I must have looked surprised, because she chuckled.

"You Americans feel so guilty about racism. As if you had invented it and nobody else—except maybe the South Africans and the Nazis—had ever practiced it as heinously as you. And you can't tell one yellow face from another, so you think of the yellow races as one homogeneous block. When in fact orientals are among the most racist peoples on the earth. The Vietnamese have hated the Cambodians for a thousand years. The Chinese hate the Japanese. The Koreans hate everybody. And *everybody* hates the 'ethnic Chinese'. The Chinese are the Jews of the East."

"I've heard that."

She nodded, lost in her own thoughts.

"And I hate all Cambodians," she said, at last. "Like you, I don't wish to. Most of the people who suffered in the camps were Cambodians. It was the genocidal leaders, the Pol Pot scum, who I should hate." She looked at me. "But sometimes we don't get a lot of choice about things like that, do we, Yank?"

The next day I visited her at noon. It had cooled down, but was still warm in her dark den. She had not changed her shirt.

She told me a few things about computers. When she let me try some things on the keyboard I quickly got lost. We decided I needn't plan on a career as a computer programmer.

One of the things she showed me was called a telephone modem, whereby she could reach other computers all over the world. She "interfaced" with someone at Stanford who she had never met, and who she knew only as "Bubble Sorter." They typed things back and forth at each other.

At the end, Bubble Sorter wrote "bye-p." Lisa typed T.

"What's T?" I asked.

"True. Means yes, but yes would be too straightforward for a hacker."

"You told me what a byte is. What's a byep?"

She looked up at me seriously.

"It's a question. Add p to a word, and make it a question. So bye-p means Bubble Sorter was asking if I wanted to log out. Sign off."

I thought that over.

"So how would you translate 'osculate posterior-p'?"

"'You wanna kiss my ass?' But remember, that was for Osborne."

I looked at her T-shirt again, then up to her eyes, which were quite serious and serene. She waited, hands folded in her lap.

Intercourse-p.

"Yes," I said. "I would."

She put her glasses on the table and pulled her shirt over her head.

We made love in Kluge's big waterbed.

I had a certain amount of performance anxiety—it had been a long, *long* time. After that, I was so caught up in the touch and smell and taste of her that I went a little crazy. She didn't seem to mind.

At last we were done, and bathed in sweat. She rolled over, stood, and went to the window. She opened it and a breath of air blew over me. Then she put one knee on the bed, leaned over me, and got a pack of cigarettes from the bedside table. She lit one.

"I hope you're not allergic to smoke," she said.

"No. My father smoked. But I didn't know you did."

"Only afterwards," she said with a quick smile. She took a deep drag. "Everybody in Saigon smoked, I think." She stretched out on her back beside me and we lay like that, soaking wet, holding hands. She opened her legs so one of her bare feet touched mine. It seemed enough contact. I watched the smoke rise from her right hand.

"I haven't felt warm in thirty years," I said. "I've been hot, but I've never been warm. I feel warm now."

"Tell me about it," she said.

So I did, as much as I could, wondering if it would work this time. At thirty years remove, my story does not sound so horrible. We've seen so much in that time. There were people in jails at that very moment, enduring conditions as bad as any I encountered. The paraphernalia of oppression is still pretty much the same. Nothing physical happened to me that would account for thirty years lived as a recluse.

"I *was* badly injured," I told her. "My skull was fractured. I still have . . . problems from that. Korea can get very cold, and I was never warm enough. But it was the other stuff. What they call brainwashing now.

"We didn't know what it was. We couldn't understand that even after a man had told them all he knew they'd keep on at us. Keeping us awake. Disorienting us. Some guys signed confessions, made up all sorts of stuff, but even that wasn't enough. They'd just keep on at you.

"I never did figure it out. I guess I couldn't understand an evil that big. But when they were sending us back and some of the prisoners wouldn't go . . . they really didn't *want* to go, they really believed . . ."

I had to pause there. Lisa sat up, moved quietly to the end of the bed, and began massaging my feet.

"We got a taste of what the Vietnam guys got, later. Only

for us it was reversed. The G.I.'s were heroes, and the prisoners were . . ."

"You didn't break," she said. It wasn't a question.

"No, I didn't."

"That would be worse."

I looked at her. She had my foot pressed against her flat belly, holding me by the heel while her other hand massaged my toes.

"The country was shocked," I said. "They didn't understand what brainwashing was. I tried telling people how it was. I thought they were looking at me funny. After a while, I stopped talking about it. And I didn't have anything else to talk about.

"A few years back the Army changed its policy. Now they don't expect you to withstand psychological conditioning. It's understood you can say anything or sign anything."

She just looked at me, kept massaging my foot, and nodded slowly. Finally she spoke.

"Cambodia was hot," she said. "I kept telling myself when I finally got to the U.S. I'd live in Maine or someplace, where it snowed. And I did go to Cambridge, but I found out I didn't like snow."

She told me about it. The last I heard, a million people had died over there. It was a whole country frothing at the mouth and snapping at anything that moved. Or like one of those sharks you read about that, when its guts are ripped out, bends in a circle and starts devouring itself.

She told me about being forced to build a pyramid of severed heads. Twenty of them working all day in the hot sun finally got it ten feet high before it collapsed. If any of them stopped working, their own heads were added to the pile.

"It didn't mean anything to me. It was just another job. I was pretty crazy by then. I didn't start to come out of it until I got across the Thai border."

That she had survived it at all seemed a miracle. She had gone through more horror than I could imagine. And she had come through it in much better shape. It made me feel small. When I was her age, I was well on my way to building the prison I have lived in ever since. I told her that.

"Part of it is preparation," she said wryly. "What you expect out of life, what your life has been so far. You said it yourself. Korea was new to you. I'm not saying I was ready for Cambodia, but my life up to that point hadn't been what you'd call sheltered. I hope you haven't been thinking I made a living in the streets by selling apples."

She kept rubbing my feet, staring off into scenes I could not see.

"How old were you when your mother died?"

"She was killed during Tet, 1968. I was ten."

"By the Viet Cong?"

"Who knows? Lot of bullets flying, lot of grenades being thrown."

She sighed, dropped my foot, and sat there, a scrawny Buddha without a robe.

"You ready to do it again, Yank?"

"I don't think I can, Lisa. I'm an old man."

She moved over me and lowered herself with her chin just below my sternum, settling her breasts in the most delicious place possible.

"We'll see," she said and giggled. "There's an alternative sex act I'm pretty good at, and I'm pretty sure it would make you a young man again. But I haven't been able to do it for about a year on account of these." She tapped her braces. "It'd be sort of like sticking it in a buzz saw. So now I do this instead. I call it 'touring the silicone valley.'" She started moving her body up and down, just a few inches at a time. She blinked innocently a couple times, then laughed.

"At last, I can see you," she said. "I'm awfully myopic."

I let her do that for a while, then lifted my head.

"Did you say silicone?"

"Uh-huh. You didn't think they were real, did you?"

I confessed that I had.

"I don't think I've ever been so happy with anything I ever bought. Not even the car."

"Why did you?"

"Does it bother you?"

It didn't, and I told her so. But I couldn't conceal my curiosity.

"Because it was safe to. In Saigon I was always angry that I never developed. I could have made a good living as a prostitute, but I was always too tall, too skinny, and too ugly. Then in Cambodia I was lucky. I managed to pass for a boy some of the time. If not for that I'd have been raped a lot more than I was. And in Thailand I knew I'd get to the West one way or another, and when I got there, I'd get the best car there was, eat anything I wanted any time I wanted to, and purchase the best tits money could buy. You can't imagine what the West looks like from the camps. A place where you can buy tits!"

She looked down between them, then back at my face.

"Looks like it was a good investment," she said.

"They do seem to work okay," I had to admit.

We agreed that she would spend the nights at my house. There were certain things she had to do at Kluge's, involving equipment that had to be physically loaded, but many things she could do with a remote terminal and an armload of software. So we selected one of Kluge's best computers and about a dozen peripherals and installed her at a cafeteria table in my bedroom.

I guess we both knew it wasn't much protection if the people who got Kluge decided to get her. But I know I felt better about it, and I think she did, too.

The second day she was there a delivery van pulled up outside and two guys started unloading a king-size waterbed. She laughed and laughed when she saw my face.

"Listen, you're not using Kluge's computers to—"

"Relax, Yank. How'd you think I could afford a Ferrari?"

"I've been curious."

"If you're really good at writing software you can make a lot of money. I own my own company. But every hacker picks up tricks here and there. I used to run a few Kluge scams, myself."

"But not anymore?"

She shrugged. "Once a thief, always a thief, Victor. I told you I couldn't make ends meet selling my bod."

Lisa didn't need much sleep.

We got up at seven, and I made breakfast every morning. Then we would spend an hour or two working in the garden. She would go to Kluge's and I'd bring her a sandwich at noon, then drop in on her several times during the day. That was for my own peace of mind; I never stayed more than a minute. Sometime during the afternoon I would shop or do household chores, then at seven one of us would cook dinner. We alternated. I taught her "American" cooking, and she taught me a little of everything. She complained about the lack of vital ingredients in American markets. No dogs, of course, but she claimed to know great ways of preparing monkey, snake, and rat. I never knew how hard she was pulling my leg, and didn't ask.

After dinner she stayed at my house. We would talk, make love, bathe.

She loved my tub. It is about the only alteration I have made in the house, and my only real luxury. I put it in—having to expand the bathroom to do so—in 1975, and never regretted it. We would soak for twenty minutes or an hour, turning the jets and bubblers on and off, washing each other, giggling like kids. Once we used bubble bath and made a mountain of suds four feet high, then destroyed it, splashing water all over the place. Most nights she let me wash her long black hair.

She didn't have any bad habits—or at least none that clashed with mine. She was neat and clean, changing her clothes twice a day and never so much as leaving a dirty glass on the sink. She never left a mess in the bathroom. Two glasses of wine was her limit.

I felt like Lazarus.

Osborne came by three times in the next two weeks. Lisa met him at Kluge's and gave him what she had learned. It was getting to be quite a list.

"Kluge once had an account in a New York bank with nine *trillion* dollars in it," she told me after one of Osborne's visits. "I think he did it just to see if he could. He left it in for one day, took the interest, and fed it to a bank in the Bahamas, then destroyed the principal. Which never existed anyway."

In return, Osborne told her what was new on the murder investigation—which was nothing—and on the status of Kluge's property, which was chaotic. Various agencies had sent people out to look the place over. Some FBI men came, wanting to take over the investigation. Lisa, when talking about computers, had the power to cloud men's minds. She did it first by explaining exactly what she was doing, in terms so abstruse that no one could understand her. Sometimes that was enough. If it wasn't, if they started to get tough, she just moved out of the driver's seat and let them try to handle Kluge's contraption. She let them watch in horror as dragons leaped out of nowhere and ate up all the data on a disc, then printed "You Stupid Putz!" on the screen.

"I'm cheating them," she confessed to me. "I'm giving them stuff I *know* they're gonna step in, because I already stepped in it myself. I've lost about forty percent of the data Kluge had stored away. But the others lose a hundred percent. You ought to see their faces when Kluge drops a logic bomb into their work. That second guy threw a three thousand printer clear across the room. Then tried to bribe me to be quiet about it."

When some federal agency sent out an expert from Stanford, and he seemed perfectly content to destroy everything in sight in the firm belief that he was *bound* to get it right sooner or later, Lisa showed him how Kluge entered the IRS main computer in Washington and neglected to mention how Kluge had gotten out. The guy tangled with some watchdog program. During his struggles, it seemed he had erased all the tax records from the letter S down into the W's. Lisa let him think that for half an hour.

"I thought he was having a heart attack," she told me. "All the blood drained out of his face and he couldn't talk. So I showed him where I had—with my usual foresight—arranged for that to be recorded, told him how to put it back where he found it, and how to pacify the watchdog. He couldn't get out of that house fast enough. Pretty soon he's gonna realize you *can't* destroy that much information with anything short of dynamite because of the backups and the limits of how much can be running at any one time. But I don't think he'll be back."

"It sounds like a very fancy video game," I said.

"It is, in a way. But it's more like Dungeons and Dragons. It's an endless series of closed rooms with dangers on the other side. You don't dare take it a step at a time. You take it a *hundredth* of a step at a time. Your questions are like, 'Now this isn't a question, but if it entered my mind to *ask* this question—which I'm not about to do—concerning what might happen if I looked at this door here—and I'm not touching it, I'm not even in the next room—what do you suppose you might do?' And the program crunches on that, decides if you fulfilled the conditions for getting a great big cream pie in the face, then either throws it or allows as how it might just move from step A to step A prime. Then you say, 'Well, maybe I *am* looking at that door.' And sometimes the program says 'You looked, you looked, you dirty crook!' And the fireworks start."

Silly as all that sounds, it was very close to the best explanation she was ever able to give me about what she was doing.

"Are you telling everything, Lisa?" I asked her.

"Well, not *every*thing. I didn't mention the four cents."

Four cents? Oh my god.

"Lisa, I didn't want that, I didn't ask for it, I wish he'd never—"

"Calm down, Yank. It's going to be all right."

"He kept records of all that, didn't he?"

"That's what I spend most of my time doing. Decoding his records."

"How long have you known?"

"About the seven hundred thousand dollars? It was in the first disc I cracked."

"I just want to give it back."

She thought that over and shook her head.

"Victor, it'd be more dangerous to get rid of it now than it would be to keep it. It was imaginary money at first. But now it's got a history. The IRS thinks it knows where it came from. The taxes are paid on it. The State of Delaware is convinced that a legally chartered corporation disbursed it. An Illinois law firm has been paid for handling it. Your bank has been paying you interest on it. I'm not saying it would be impossible to go back and wipe all that out, but I wouldn't like to try. I'm good, but I don't have Kluge's touch."

"How could he *do* all that? You say it was imaginary money. That's not the way I thought money worked. He could just pull it out of thin air?"

Lisa patted the top of her computer console and smiled at me.

"This is money, Yank," she said, and her eyes glittered.

* * *

At night she worked by candlelight so she wouldn't disturb me. That turned out to be my downfall. She typed by touch and needed the candle only to locate software.

So that's how I'd go to sleep every night, looking at her slender body bathed in the glow of the candle. I was always reminded of melting butter dripping down a roasted ear of corn. Golden light on golden skin.

Ugly, she had called herself. Skinny. It was true she was thin. I could see her ribs when she sat with her back impossibly straight, her tummy sucked in, her chin up. She worked in the nude these days, sitting in lotus position. For long periods she would not move, her hands lying on her thighs, then she would poise, as if to pound the keys. But her touch was light, almost silent. It looked more like yoga than programming. She said she went into a meditative state for her best work.

I had expected a bony angularity, all sharp elbows and knees. She wasn't like that. I had guessed her weight ten pounds too low, and still didn't know where she put it. But she was soft and rounded, and strong beneath.

No one was ever going to call her face glamorous. Few would even go so far as to call her pretty. The braces did that, I think. They caught the eye and held it, drawing attention to that unsightly jumble.

But her skin was wonderful. She had scars. Not as many as I had expected. She seemed to heal quickly, and well.

I thought she was beautiful.

I had just completed my nightly survey when my eye was caught by the candle. I looked at it, then tried to look away.

Candles do that sometimes. I don't know why. In still air, with the flame perfectly vertical, they begin to flicker. The flame leaps up then squats down, up and down, up and down, brighter and brighter in regular rhythm, two or three beats to the second—

—and I tried to call out to her, wishing the candle would stop its regular flickering, but already I couldn't speak—

—I could only gasp, and I tried once more, as hard as I could, to yell, to scream, to tell her not to worry, and felt the nausea building . . .

* * *

I tasted blood. I took an experimental breath, did not find the smells of vomit, urine, feces. The overhead lights were on.

Lisa was on her hands and knees leaning over me, her face very close. A tear dropped on my forehead. I was on the carpet, on my back.

"Victor, can you hear me?"

I nodded. There was a spoon in my mouth. I spit it out.

"What happened? Are you going to be all right?"

I nodded again and struggled to speak.

"You just lie there. The ambulance is on its way."

"No. Don't need it."

"Well, it's on its way. You just take it easy and—"

"Help me up."

"Not yet. You're not ready."

She was right. I tried to sit up and fell back quietly. I took deep breaths for a while. Then the doorbell rang.

She stood up and started to the door. I just managed to get my hand around her ankle. Then she was leaning over me again, her eyes as wide as they would go.

"What is it? What's wrong now?"

"Get some clothes on," I told her. She looked down at herself, surprised.

"Oh. right."

She got rid of the ambulance crew. Lisa was a lot calmer after she made coffee and we were sitting at the kitchen table. It was one o'clock and I was still pretty rocky. But it hadn't been a bad one.

I went to the bathroom and got the bottle of Dilantin I'd hidden when she moved in. I let her see me take one.

"I forgot to do this today," I told her.

"It's because you hid them. That was stupid."

"I know." There must have been something else I could have said. It didn't please me to see her look hurt. But she was hurt because I wasn't defending myself against her attack, and that was a bit too complicated for me to dope out just after a grand mal.

"You can move out if you want to," I said. I was in rare form.

So was she. She reached across the table and shook me by the shoulders. She glared at me.

"I won't take a lot more of that kind of shit," she said, and I nodded and began to cry.

She let me do it. I think that was probably best. She could have babied me, but I do a pretty good job of that myself.

"How long has this been going on?" she finally said. "Is that why you've stayed in your house for thirty years?"

I shrugged. "I guess it's part of it. When I got back they operated, but it just made it worse."

"Okay. I'm mad at you because you didn't tell me about it, so I didn't know what to do. I want to stay, but you'll have to tell me how. Then I won't be mad anymore."

I could have blown the whole thing right there. I'm amazed I didn't. Through the years I'd developed very good methods for doing things like that. But I pulled through when I saw her face. She really did want to stay. I didn't know why, but it was enough.

"The spoon was a mistake," I said. "If there's time, and if you can do it without risking your fingers, you could jam a piece of cloth in there. Part of a sheet, or something. But nothing hard." I explored my mouth with a finger. "I think I broke a tooth."

"Serves you right," she said. I looked at her and smiled, then we were both laughing. She came around the table and kissed me, then sat on my knee.

"The biggest danger is drowning. During the first part of the seizure, all my muscles go rigid. That doesn't last long. Then they all start contracting and relaxing at random. It's *very* strong."

"I know. I watched, and I tried to hold you."

"Don't do that. Get me on my side. Stay behind me and watch out for flailing arms. Get a pillow under my head if you can. Keep me away from things I could injure myself on." I looked her square in the eye. "I want to emphasize this. Just *try* to do all those things. If I'm getting too violent, it's better you stand off to the side. Better for both of us. If I knock you out, you won't be able to help me if I start strangling on vomit."

I kept looking at her eyes. She must have read my mind, because she smiled slightly.

"Sorry, Yank. I am not freaked out. I mean, like, it's totally gross, you know, and it barfs me out to the max, you could—"

"—gag me with a spoon, I know. Okay, right, I know I was dumb. And that's about it. I might bite my tongue or the inside of my cheek. Don't worry about it. There is one more thing."

She waited and I wondered how much to tell her. There wasn't a lot she could do, but if I died on her I didn't want her to feel it was her fault.

"Sometimes I have to go to the hospital. Sometimes one seizure will follow another. If that keeps up for too long, I won't breathe, and my brain will die of oxygen starvation."

"That only takes about five minutes," she said, alarmed.

"I know. It's only a problem if I start having them frequently, so we could plan for it if I do. But if I don't come out of one, start having another right on the heels of the first, or if you can't detect any breathing for three or four minutes, you'd better call an ambulance."

"Three or four minutes? You'd be dead before they got here."

"It's that or live in a hospital. I don't like hospitals."

"Neither do I."

The next day she took me for a ride in her Ferrari. I was nervous about it, wondering if she was going to do crazy things. If anything, she was too slow. People behind her kept honking. I could tell she hadn't been driving long from the exaggerated attention she put into every movement.

"A Ferrari is wasted on me, I'm afraid," she confessed at one point. "I never drive it faster than fifty-five."

We went to an interior decorator in Beverly Hills and she bought a low-watt gooseneck lamp at an outrageous price.

I had a hard time getting to sleep that night. I suppose I was afraid of having another seizure, though Lisa's new lamp wasn't going to set it off.

Funny about seizures. When I first started having them,

everyone called them fits. Then, gradually, it was seizures, until fits began to sound dirty.

I guess it's a sign of growing old, when the language changes on you.

There were rafts of new words. A lot of them were for things that didn't even exist when I was growing up. Like software. I always visualized a limp wrench.

"What got you interested in computers, Lisa?" I asked her.

She didn't move. Her concentration when sitting at the machine was pretty damn good. I rolled onto my back and tried to sleep.

"It's where the power is, Yank." I looked up. She had turned to face me.

"Did you pick it all up since you got to America?"

"I had a head start. I didn't tell you about my Captain, did I?"

"I don't think you did."

"He was strange. I knew that. I was about fourteen: He was an American, and he took an interest in me. He got me a nice apartment in Saigon. And he put me in school."

She was studying me, looking for a reaction. I didn't give her one.

"He was surely a pedophile, and probably had homosexual tendencies, since I looked so much like a skinny little boy."

Again the wait. This time she smiled.

"He was good to me. I learned to read well. From there on, anything is possible."

"I didn't actually ask you about your Captain. I asked why you got interested in computers."

"That's right. You did."

"Is it just a living?"

"It started that way. It's the future, Victor."

"God knows I've read that enough times."

"It's true. It's already here. It's power, if you know how to use it. You've seen what Kluge was able to do. You can make money with one of these things. I don't mean earn it, I mean *make* it, like if you had a printing press. Remember Osborne mentioned that Kluge's house didn't exist? Did you think what that means?"

"That he wiped it out of the memory banks."

"That was the first step. But the lot exists in the county plat books, wouldn't you think? I mean, this country hasn't *entirely* given up paper."

"So the county really does have a record of that house."

"No. That page was torn out of the records."

"I don't get it. Kluge never left the house."

"Oldest way in the world, friend. Kluge looked through the L.A.P.D. files until he found a guy known as Sammy. He sent him a cashier's check for a thousand dollars, along with a letter saying he could earn twice that if he'd go to the hall of records and do something. Sammy didn't bite, and neither did McGee, or Molly Unger. But Little Billy Phipps did, and he got a check just like the letter said, and he and Kluge had a wonderful business relationship for many years. Little Billy drives a new Cadillac now, and hasn't the faintest notion who Kluge was or where he lived. It didn't matter to Kluge how much he spent. He just pulled it out of thin air."

I thought that over for a while. I guess it's true that with enough money you can do just about anything, and Kluge had all the money in the world.

"Did you tell Osborne about Little Billy?"

"I erased that disc, just like I erased your seven hundred thousand. You never know when you might need somebody like Little Billy."

"You're not afraid of getting into trouble over it?"

"Life is risk, Victor. I'm keeping the best stuff for myself. Not because I intend to use it, but because if I ever needed it badly and didn't have it, I'd feel like such a fool."

She cocked her head and narrowed her eyes, which made them practically disappear.

"Tell me something, Yank. Kluge picked you out of all your neighbors because you'd been a Boy Scout for thirty years. How do you react to what I'm doing?"

"You're cheerfully amoral, and you're a survivor, and you're basically decent. And I pity anybody who gets in your way."

She grinned, stretched, and stood up.

"'Cheerfully amoral', I like that." She sat beside me, making a great sloshing in the bed. "You want to be amoral again?"

"In a little bit." She started rubbing my chest. "So you got into computers because they were the wave of the future.

Don't you ever worry about them . . . I don't know, I guess it sounds corny . . . do you think they'll take over?"

"Everybody thinks that until they start to use them," she said. "You've got to realize just how stupid they are. Without programming they are good for nothing, literally. Now, what I do believe is that the people who *run* the computers will take over. They already have. That's why I study them."

"I guess that's not what I meant. Maybe I can't say it right."

She frowned. "Kluge was looking into something. He'd been eavesdropping in artificial intelligence labs and reading a lot of neurological research. I think he was trying to find a common thread."

"Between human brains and computers?"

"Not quite. He was thinking of computers and neurons. Brain cells." She pointed to her computer. "That thing, or any other computer, is light-years away from being a human brain. It can't generalize, or infer, or categorize, or invent. With good programming it can appear to do some of those things, but it's an illusion.

"There's an old speculation about what would happen if we finally built a computer with as many transistors as the human brain has neurons. Would there be a self-awareness? I think that's baloney. A transistor isn't a neuron, and a quintillion of them aren't any better than a dozen.

"So Kluge—who seems to have felt the same way—started looking into the possible similarities between a neuron and an 8-bit computer. That's why he had all that consumer junk sitting around his house, those Trash-80's and Atari's and TI's and Sinclair's, for chrissake. He was used to *much* more powerful instruments. He ate up the home units like candy."

"What did he find out?"

"Nothing, it looks like. An 8-bit unit is more complex than a neuron, and no computer is in the same galaxy as an organic brain. But see, the words get tricky. I said an Atari is more complex than a neuron, but it's hard to really compare them. It's like comparing a direction with a distance, or a color with a mass. The units are different. Except for one similarity."

"What's that?"

"The connections. Again, it's different, but the concept of networking is the same. A neuron is connected to a lot of others. There are trillions of them, and the way messages pulse through them determines what we are and what we think and what we remember. And with that computer I can reach a million others. It's bigger than the human brain, really, because the information in that network is more than all humanity could cope with in a million years. It reaches from Pioneer Ten, out beyond the orbit of Pluto, right into every living room that has a telephone in it. With that computer you can tap tons of data that has been collected but nobody's even had the time to look at.

"That's what Kluge was interested in. The old 'critical mass computer' idea, the computer that becomes aware, but with a new angle. Maybe it wouldn't be the size of the computer, but the *number* of computers. There used to be thousands of them. Now there's millions. They're putting them in cars. In wristwatches. Every home has several, from the simple timer on a microwave oven up to a video game or home terminal. Kluge was trying to find out if critical mass could be reached that way."

"What did he think?"

"I don't know. He was just getting started." She glanced down at me. "But you know what, Yank? I think you've reached critical mass while I wasn't looking."

"I think you're right." I reached for her.

Lisa liked to cuddle. I didn't, at first, after fifty years of sleeping alone. But I got to like it pretty quickly.

That's what we were doing when we resumed the conversation we had been having. We just lay in each others' arms and talked about things. Nobody had mentioned love yet, but I knew I loved her. I didn't know what to do about it, but I would think of something.

"Critical mass," I said. She nuzzled my neck and yawned.

"What about it?"

"What would it be like? It seems like it would be such a vast intelligence. So quick, so omniscient. God-like."

"Could be."

"Wouldn't it . . . run our lives? I guess I'm asking the same questions I started off with. Would it take over?"

She thought about it for a long time.

"I wonder if there would be anything to take over. I mean,

why should it care? How could we figure what its concerns would be? Would it want to be worshipped, for instance? I doubt it. Would it want to 'rationalize all human behavior, to eliminate all emotions,' as I'm sure some sci-fi film computer must have told some damsel in distress in the fifties.

"You can use a word like awareness, but what does it mean? An amoeba must be aware. Plants probably are. There may be a level of awareness in a neuron. Even in an integrated circuit chip. We don't even know what our own awareness really is. We've never been able to shine a light on it, dissect it, figure out where it comes from or where it goes when we're dead. To apply human values to a thing like this hypothetical computer-net consciousness would be pretty stupid. But I don't see how it could interact with human awareness at all. It might not even notice us, any more than we notice cells in our bodies, or neutrinos passing through us, or the vibrations of the atoms in the air around us."

So she had to explain what a neutrino was. One thing I always provided her with was an ignorant audience. And after that, I pretty much forgot about our mythical hyper-computer.

"What about your Captain?" I asked, much later.

"Do you really want to know, Yank?" she mumbled sleepily.

"I'm not afraid to know."

She sat up and reached for her cigarettes. I had come to know she sometimes smoked them in times of stress. She had told me she smoked after making love, but that first time had been the only time. The lighter flared in the dark. I heard her exhale.

"My Major, actually. He got a promotion. Do you want to know his name?"

"Lisa, I don't want to know any of it if you don't want to tell it. But if you do, what I want to know is did he stand by you."

"He didn't marry me, if that's what you mean. When he knew he had to go, he said he would, but I talked him out of it. Maybe it was the most noble thing I ever did. Maybe it was the most stupid.

"It's no accident I look Japanese. My grandmother was raped in '42 by a Jap soldier of the occupation. She was Chinese, living in Hanoi. My mother was born there. They went south after Dien Bien Phu. My grandmother died. My mother had it hard. Being Chinese was tough enough, but being half Chinese and half Japanese was worse. My father was half French and half Annamese. Another bad combination. I never knew him. But I'm sort of a capsule history of Vietnam."

The end of her cigarette glowed brighter once more.

"I've got one grandfather's face and the other grandfather's height. With tits by Goodyear. About all I missed was some American genes, but I was working on that for my children.

"When Saigon was falling I tried to get to the American Embassy. Didn't make it. You know the rest, until I got to Thailand, and when I finally got Americans to notice me, it turned out my Major was still looking for me. He sponsored me over here, and I made it in time to watch him die of cancer. Two months I had with him, all of it in the hospital."

"My God," I had a horrible thought. "That wasn't the war, too, was it? I mean, the story of your life—"

"—is the rape of Asia. No, Victor. Not that war, anyway. But he was one of those guys who got to see atom bombs up close, out in Nevada. He was too Regular Army to complain about it, but I think he knew that's what killed him."

"Did you love him?"

"What do you want me to say? He got me out of hell."

Again the cigarette flared, and I saw her stub it out.

"No," she said. "I didn't love him. He knew that. I've never loved anybody. He was very dear, very special to me. I would have done almost anything for him. He was fatherly to me." I felt her looking at me in the dark. "Aren't you going to ask how old he was?"

"Fiftyish," I said.

"On the nose. Can I ask you something?"

"I guess it's your turn."

"How many girls have you had since you got back from Korea?"

I held up my hand and pretended to count on my fingers.

"One," I said, at last.

"How many before you went?"

"One. We broke up before I left for the war."

"How many in Korea?"

"Nine. All at Madame Park's jolly little whorehouse in Pusan."

"So you've made love to one white and ten Asians. I bet none of the others were as tall as me."

"Korean girls have fatter cheeks, too. But they all had your eyes."

She nuzzled against my chest, took a deep breath, and sighed.

"We're a hell of a pair, aren't we?"

I hugged her, and her breath came again, hot on my chest. I wondered how I'd lived so long without such a simple miracle as that.

"Yes. I think we really are."

Osborne came by again about a week later. He seemed subdued. He listened to the things Lisa had decided to give him without much interest. He took the printout she handed him and promised to turn it over to the departments that handled those things. But he didn't get up to leave.

"I thought I ought to tell you, Apfel," he said, at last. "The Gavin case has been closed."

I had to think a moment to remember Kluge's real name had been Gavin.

"The coroner ruled suicide a long time ago. I was able to keep the case open quite a while on the strength of my suspicions." He nodded toward Lisa. "And on what she said about the suicide note. But there was just no evidence at all."

"It probably happened quickly," Lisa said. "Somebody caught him, tracked him back—it can be done; Kluge was lucky for a long time—and did him the same day."

"You don't think it was suicide?" I asked Osborne.

"No. But whoever did it is home free unless something new turns up."

"I'll tell you if it does," Lisa said.

"That's something else," Osborne said. "I can't authorize you to work over there anymore. The county's taken possession of house and contents."

"Don't worry about it," Lisa said softly.

There was a short silence as she leaned over to shake a cigarette from the pack on the coffee table. She lit it, exhaled, and leaned back beside me, giving Osborne her most inscrutable look. He sighed.

"I'd hate to play poker with you, lady," he said. "What do you mean, 'don't worry about it'?"

"I bought the house four days ago. And its contents. If anything turns up that would help you reopen the murder investigation, I will let you know."

Osborne was too defeated to get angry. He studied her quietly for a while.

"I'd like to know how you swung that."

"I did nothing illegal. You're free to check it out. I paid good cash money for it. The house came onto the market. I got a good price at the Sheriff's sale."

"How'd you like it if I put my best men on the transaction? See if they can dig up some funny money? Maybe fraud. How about I get the F.B.I. in to look it all over?"

She gave him a cool look.

"You're welcome to. Frankly, Detective Osborne, I could have stolen that house, Griffith Park, and the Harbor Freeway and I don't think you could have caught me."

"So where does that leave me?"

"Just where you were. With a closed case, and a promise from me."

"I don't like you having all that stuff, if it can do the things you say it can do."

"I didn't expect you would. But that's not your department, is it? The county owned it for a while, through simple confiscation. They didn't know what they had, and they let it go."

"Maybe I can get the Fraud detail out here to confiscate your software. There's criminal evidence on it."

"You could try that," she agreed.

They stared at each other for a while. Lisa won. Osborne rubbed his eyes and nodded. Then he heaved himself to his feet and slumped to the door.

Lisa stubbed out her cigarette. We listened to him going down the walk.

"I'm surprised he gave up so easy," I said. "Or did he? Do you think he'll try a raid?"

"It's not likely. He knows the score."

"Maybe you could tell it to me."

"For one thing, it's not his department, and he knows it."

"Why did you buy the house?"

"You ought to ask *how*."

I looked at her closely. There was a gleam of amusement behind the poker face.

"Lisa. What did you do?"

"That's what Osborne asked himself. He got the right answer, because he understands Kluge's machines. And he knows how things get done. It was no accident that house going on the market, and no accident I was the only bidder. I used one of Kluge's pet councilmen."

"You bribed him?"

She laughed and kissed me.

"I think I finally managed to shock you, Yank. That's gotta be the biggest difference between me and a native-born American. Average citizens don't spend much on bribes over here. In Saigon, everybody bribes."

"Did you bribe him?"

"Nothing so indelicate. One has to go in the back door over here. Several entirely legal campaign contributions appeared in the accounts of a State Senator, who mentioned a certain situation to someone, who happened to be in the position to do legally what I happened to want done." She looked at me askance. "Of *course* I bribed him, Victor. You'd be amazed to know how cheaply. Does that bother you?"

"Yes," I admitted. "I don't like bribery."

"I'm indifferent to it. It happens, like gravity. It may not be admirable, but it gets things done."

"I assume you covered yourself."

"Reasonably well. You're never entirely covered with a bribe, because of the human element. The councilman might geek if they got him in front of a grand jury. But they won't, because Osborne won't pursue it. That's the second reason he walked out of here without a fight. *He* knows how the world wobbles, he knows what kind of force I now possess, and he knows he can't fight it."

There was a long silence after that. I had a lot to think about, and I didn't feel good about most of it. At one point Lisa reached for the pack of cigarettes, then changed her mind. She waited for me to work it out.

"It is a terrific force, isn't it," I finally said.

"It's frightening," she agreed. "Don't think it doesn't scare me. Don't think I haven't had fantasies of being superwoman. Power is an awful temptation, and it's not easy to reject. There's so much I could do."

"Will you?"

"I'm not talking about stealing things, or getting rich."

"I didn't think you were."

"This is political power. But I don't know how to wield it . . . it sounds corny, but to use it for good. I've seen so much evil come from good intentions. I don't think I'm wise enough to do any good. And the chances of getting torn up like Kluge did are large. But I'm wise enough to walk away from it. I'm still a street urchin from Saigon, Yank. I'm smart enough not to use it unless I have to. But I can't give it away, and I can't destroy it. Is that stupid?"

I didn't have a good answer for that one. But I had a bad feeling.

My doubts had another week to work on me. I didn't come to any great moral conclusions. Lisa knew of some crimes, and she wasn't reporting them to the authorities. That didn't bother me much. She had at her fingertips the means to commit more crimes, and that bothered me a lot. Yet I really didn't think she planned to do anything. She was smart enough to use the things she had only in a defensive way— but with Lisa that could cover a lot of ground.

When she didn't show up for dinner one evening, I went over to Kluge's and found her busy in the living room. A nine-foot section of shelving had been cleared. The discs and tapes were stacked on a table. She had a big plastic garbage can and a magnet the size of a softball. I watched her wave a tape near the magnet, then toss it in the garbage can, which was almost full. She glanced up, did the same operation with a handful of discs, then took off her glasses and wiped her eyes.

"Feel any better now, Victor?" she asked.

"What do you mean? I feel fine."

"No, you don't. And I haven't felt right, either. It hurts me to do it, but I have to. You want to go get the other trash can?"

I did, and helped her pull more software from the shelves.

"You're not going to wipe it all, are you?"

"No. I'm wiping records, and . . . something else."

"Are you going to tell me what?"

"There are things it's better not to know," she said darkly.

I finally managed to convince her to talk over dinner. She had said little, just eating and shaking her head. But she gave in.

"Rather dreary, actually," she said. "I've been probing around some delicate places the last couple days. These are places Kluge visited at will, but they scare the hell out of me. Dirty places. Places where they know things I thought I'd like to find out."

She shivered, and seemed reluctant to go on.

"Are you talking about military computers? The CIA?"

"The CIA is where it starts. It's the easiest. I've looked around at NORAD—that's the guys who get to fight the next war. It makes me shiver to see how easy Kluge got in there. He cobbled up a way to start World War Three, just as an exercise. That's one of the things we just erased. The last two days I was nibbling around the edges of the big boys. The Defense Intelligence Agency and the National Security . . . something. DIA and NSA. Each of them is bigger than the CIA. Something knew I was there. Some watchdog program. As soon as I realized that I got out quick, and I've spent the last five hours being sure it didn't follow me. And now I'm sure, and I've destroyed all that, too."

"You think they're the ones who killed Kluge?"

"They're surely the best candidates. He had tons of their stuff. I know he helped design the biggest installation at NSA, and he'd been poking around in there for years. One false step is all it would take."

"Did you get it all? I mean, are you sure?"

"I'm sure they didn't track me. I'm not sure I've destroyed all the records. I'm going back now to take a last look."

"I'll go with you."

We worked until well after midnight. Lisa would review a tape or a disc, and if she was in any doubt, toss it to me for the magnetic treatment. At one point, simply because she was unsure, she took the magnet and passed it in front of an entire shelf of software.

It was amazing to think about it. With that one wipe she

had randomized billions of bits of information. Some of it might not exist anywhere else in the world. I found myself confronted by even harder questions. Did she have the right to do it? Didn't knowledge exist for everyone? But I confess I had little trouble quelling my protests. Mostly I was happy to see it go. The old reactionary in me found it easier to believe There Are Things We Are Not Meant To Know.

We were almost through when her monitor screen began to malfunction. It actually gave off a few hisses and pops, so Lisa stood back from it for a moment, then the screen started to flicker. I stared at it for a while. It seemed to me there was an image trying to form in the screen. Something three-dimensional. Just as I was starting to get a picture of it I happened to glance at Lisa, and she was looking at me. Her face was flickering. She came to me and put her hands over my eyes.

"Victor, you shouldn't look at that."

"It's okay," I told her. And when I said it, it was, but as soon as I had the words out I knew it wasn't. And that is the last thing I remembered for a long time.

I'm told it was a very bad two weeks. I remember very little of it. I was kept under high dosage of drugs, and my few lucid periods were always followed by a fresh seizure.

The first thing I recall clearly was looking up at Doctor Stuart's face. I was in a hospital bed. I later learned it was in Cedars-Sinai, not the Veteran's Hospital. Lisa had paid for a private room.

Stuart put me through the usual questions. I was able to answer them, though I was very tired. When he was satisfied as to my condition he finally began to answer some of my questions. I learned how long I had been there, and how it had happened.

"You went into consecutive seizures," he confirmed. "I don't know why, frankly. You haven't been prone to them for a decade. I was thinking you were well under control. But nothing is ever really stable, I guess."

"So Lisa got me here in time."

"She did more than that. She didn't want to level with me at first. It seems that after the first seizure she witnessed she read everything she could find. From that day, she had a syringe and solution of Valium handy. When she saw you couldn't breathe she injected you with 100 milligrams, and there's no doubt it saved your life."

Stuart and I had known each other a long time. He knew I had no prescription for Valium. Though we had talked about it the last time I was hospitalized. Since I lived alone, there would be no one to inject me if I got in trouble.

He was more interested in results than anything else, and what Lisa did had the desired result. I was still alive.

He wouldn't let me have any visitors that day. I protested but soon was asleep. The next day she came. She wore a new T-shirt. This one had a picture of a robot wearing a gown and mortarboard, and said "Class of 11111000000." It turns out that was 1984 in binary notation.

She had a big smile and said, "Hi, Yank!" and as she sat on the bed I started to shake. She looked alarmed and asked if she should call the doctor.

"It's not that," I managed to say. "I'd like it if you just held me."

She took off her shoes and got under the covers with me. She held me tightly. At some point a nurse came in and tried to shoo her out. Lisa gave her profanities in Vietnamese, Chinese, and a few startling ones in English, and the nurse left. I saw Doctor Stuart glance in later.

I felt much better when I finally stopped crying. Lisa's eyes were wet, too.

"I've been here every day," she said. "You look awful, Victor."

"I feel a lot better."

"Well, you look better than you did. But your doctor says you'd better stick around another couple of days, just to make sure."

"I think he's right."

"I'm planning a big dinner for when you get back. You think we should invite the neighbors?"

I didn't say anything for a while. There were so many things we hadn't faced. Just how long could it go on between us? How long before I got sour about being so useless? How long before she got tired of being with an old man? I don't know just when I had started to think of Lisa as a permanent part of my life. And I wondered how I could have thought that.

"Do you want to spend more years waiting in hospitals for a man to die?"

"What do you want, Victor? I'll marry you if you want me to. Or I'll live with you in sin. I prefer sin, but if it'll make you happy—"

"I don't know why you want to saddle yourself with an epileptic old fart."

"Because I love you."

It was the first time she had said it. I could have gone on questioning—bringing up her Major again, for instance—but I had no urge to. I'm very glad I didn't. So I changed the subject.

"Did you get the job finished?"

She knew which job I was talking about. She lowered her voice and put her mouth close to my ear.

"Let's don't be specific about it here, Victor. I don't trust any place I haven't swept for bugs. But, to put your mind at ease, I did finish, and it's been a quiet couple of weeks. No one is any wiser, and I'll never meddle in things like that again."

I felt a lot better. I was also exhausted. I tried to conceal my yawns, but she sensed it was time to go. She gave me one more kiss, promising many more to come, and left me.

It was the last time I ever saw her.

At about ten o'clock that evening Lisa went into Kluge's kitchen with a screwdriver and some other tools and got to work on the microwave oven.

The manufacturers of those appliances are very careful to insure they can't be turned on with the door open, as they emit lethal radiation. But with simple tools and a good brain it is possible to circumvent the safety interlocks. Lisa had no trouble with them. About ten minutes after she entered the kitchen she put her head in the oven and turned it on.

It is impossible to say how long she held her head in there. It was long enough to turn her eyeballs to the consistency of boiled eggs. At some point she lost voluntary muscle control and fell to the floor, pulling the microwave down with her. It shorted out, and a fire started.

The fire set off the sophisticated burglar alarm she had installed a month before. Betty Lanier saw the flames and called the fire department as Hal ran across the street and into the burning kitchen. He dragged what was left of Lisa out onto the grass. When he saw what the fire had done to her upper body, and in particular her breasts, he threw up.

She was rushed to the hospital. The doctors there amputated one arm and cut away the frightful masses of vulcanized silicone, pulled all her teeth, and didn't know what to do about the eyes. They put her on a respirator.

It was an orderly who first noticed the blackened and bloody T-shirt they had cut from her. Some of the message was unreadable, but it began, "I can't go on this way anymore . . ."

There is no other way I could have told all that. I discovered it piecemeal, starting with the disturbed look on Doctor Stuart's face when Lisa didn't show up the next day. He wouldn't tell me anything, and I had another seizure shortly after.

The next week is a blur. I remember being released from the hospital, but I don't remember the trip home. Betty was very good to me. They gave me a tranquilizer called Tranxene, and it was even better. I ate them like candy. I wandered in a drugged haze, eating only when Betty insisted, sleeping sitting up in my chair, coming awake not knowing where or who I was. I returned to the prison camp many times. Once I recall helping Lisa stack severed heads.

When I saw myself in the mirror, there was a vague smile on my face. It was Tranxene, caressing my frontal lobes. I knew that if I was to live much longer, me and Tranxene would have to become very good friends.

I eventually became capable of something that passed for rational thought. I was helped along somewhat by a visit from Osborne. I was trying, at that time, to find reasons to live, and wondered if he had any.

"I'm very sorry," he started off. I said nothing. "This is on my own time," he went on. "The department doesn't know I'm here."

"Was it suicide?" I asked him.

"I brought along a copy of the . . . the note. She ordered it from a shirt company in Westwood, three days before the . . . accident."

He handed it to me, and I read it. I was mentioned, though not by name. I was "the man I love." She said she couldn't cope with my problems. It was a short note. You can't get too much on a T-shirt. I read it through five times, then handed it back to him.

"She told you Kluge didn't write his note. I tell you she didn't write this."

He nodded reluctantly. I felt a vast calm, with a howling nightmare just below it. Praise Tranxene.

"Can you back that up?"

"She saw me in the hospital shortly before she died. She was full of life and hope. You say she ordered the shirt three days before. I would have felt that. And that note is pathetic. Lisa was never pathetic."

He nodded again.

"Some things I want to tell you. There were no signs of a struggle. Mrs. Lanier is sure no one came in the front. The crime lab went over the whole place and we're sure no one was in there with her. I'd stake my life on the fact that no one entered or left that house. Now, *I* don't believe it was suicide, either, but do you have any suggestions?"

"The NSA," I said.

I explained about the last things she had done while I was still there. I told him of her fear of the government spy agencies. That was all I had.

"Well, I guess they're the ones who could do a thing like that, if anyone could. But I'll tell you, I have a hard time swallowing it. I don't know why, for one thing. Maybe you believe those people kill like you and I'd swat a fly." His look made it into a question.

"I don't know what I believe."

"I'm not saying they wouldn't kill for national security, or some such shit. But they'd have taken the computers, too. They wouldn't have let her alone, they wouldn't even have let her *near* that stuff after they killed Kluge."

"What you're saying makes sense."

He muttered on about it for quite some time. Eventually I offered him some wine. He accepted thankfully. I considered joining him—it would be a quick way to die—but did not. He drank the whole bottle, and was comfortably drunk when he suggested we go next door and look it over one more time. I was planning on visiting Lisa the next day, and knew I had to start somewhere building myself up for that, so I agreed to go with him.

We inspected the kitchen. The fire had blackened the counters and melted some linoleum, but not much else. Water had made a mess of the place. There was a brown stain on the floor which I was able to look at with no emotion.

So we went back to the living room, and one of the computers was turned on. There was a short message on the screen.

IF YOU WISH TO KNOW MORE
PRESS ENTER█

"Don't do it," I told him. But he did. He stood, blinking solemnly, as the words wiped themselves out and a new message appeared.

YOU LOOKED

The screen started to flicker and I was in my car, in darkness, with a pill in my mouth and another in my hand. I spit out the pill and sat for a moment, listening to the old engine ticking over. In my other hand was the plastic pill bottle. I felt very tired but opened the car door and shut off the engine. I felt my way to the garage door and opened it. The air outside was fresh and sweet. I looked down at the pill bottle and hurried into the bathroom.

When I got through what had to be done there were a dozen pills floating in the toilet that hadn't even dissolved. There were the wasted shells of many more, and a lot of other stuff I won't bother to describe. I counted the pills in the bottle, remembered how many there had been, and wondered if I would make it.

I went over to Kluge's house and could not find Osborne. I was getting tired, but I made it back to my house and stretched out on the couch to see if I would live or die.

* * *

The next day I found the story in the paper. Osborne had gone home and blown out the back of his head with his revolver. It was not a big story. It happens to cops all the time. He didn't leave a note.

I got on the bus and rode out to the hospital and spent three hours trying to get in to see Lisa. I wasn't able to do it. I was not a relative and the doctors were quite firm about her having no visitors. When I got angry they were as gentle as possible. It was then I learned the extent of her injuries. Hal had kept the worst from me. None of it would have mattered, but the doctors swore there was nothing left in her head. So I went home.

She died two days later.

She had left a will, to my surprise. I got the house and contents. I picked up the phone as soon as I learned of it, and called a garbage company. While they were on the way I went for the last time into Kluge's house.

The same computer was still on, and it gave the same message.

PRESS ENTER■

I cautiously located the power switch and turned it off. I had the garbage people strip the place to the bare walls.

I went over my own house very carefully, looking for anything that was even the first cousin to a computer. I threw out the radio. I sold the car, and the refrigerator, and the stove, and the blender, and the electric clock. I drained the waterbed and threw out the heater.

Then I bought the best propane stove on the market and hunted a long time before I found an old icebox. I had the garage stacked to the ceiling with firewood. I had the chimney cleaned. It would be getting cold soon.

One day I took the bus to Pasadena and established the Lisa Foo Memorial Scholarship fund for Vietnamese refugees and their children. I endowed it with seven hundred thousand eighty-three dollars and four cents. I told them it could be used for any field of study except computer science. I could tell they thought me eccentric.

* * *

And I really thought I was safe, until the phone rang.

I thought it over for a long time before answering it. In the end, I knew it would just keep on going until I did. So I picked it up.

For a few seconds there was a dial tone, but I was not fooled. I kept holding it to my ear and finally the tone turned off. There was just silence. I listened intently. I heard some of those far-off musical tones that live in phone wires. Echoes of conversations taking place a thousand miles away. And something infinitely more distant and cool.

I do not know what they have incubated out there at the NSA. I don't know if they did it on purpose, or if it just happened, or if it even has anything to do with them, in the end. But I know it's out there, because I heard its soul breathing on the wires. I spoke very carefully.

"I do not wish to know any more," I said. "I won't tell anyone anything. Kluge, Lisa, and Osborne all committed suicide. I am just a lonely man, and I won't cause you any trouble."

There was a click, and a dial tone.

Getting the phone taken out was easy. Getting them to remove all the wires was a little harder, since once a place is wired they expect it to be wired forever. They grumbled, but when I started pulling them out myself, they relented, though they warned me it was going to cost.

PG&E was harder. They actually seemed to believe there was a regulation requiring each house to be hooked up to the grid. They were willing to shut off my power—though hardly pleased about it—but they just weren't going to take the wires away from my house. I went up on the roof with an axe and demolished four feet of eaves as they gaped at me. Then they coiled up their wires and went home.

I threw out all my lamps, all things electrical. With hammer, chisel, and handsaw I went to work on the drywall just above the baseboards.

As I stripped the house of wiring I wondered how many times why I was doing it. Why was it worth it? I couldn't have very many more years before a final seizure finished me off. Those years were not going to be a lot of fun.

Lisa had been a survivor. She would have known why I was doing this. She had once said I was a survivor, too. I survived the camp. I survived the death of my mother and father and managed to fashion a solitary life. Lisa survived the death of just about everything. No survivor expects to live through it all. But while she was alive, she would have worked to stay alive.

And that's what I did. I got all the wires out of the walls, went over the house with a magnet to see if I had missed any metal, then spent a week cleaning up, fixing the holes I had knocked in the walls, ceiling, and attic. I was amused trying to picture the real-estate agent selling this place after I was gone.

It's a great little house, folks. No electricity . . .

Now I live quietly, as before.

I work in my garden during most of the daylight hours. I've expanded it considerably, and even have things growing in the front yard now.

I live by candlelight and kerosene lamp. I grow most of what I eat.

It took a long time to taper off the Tranxene and the Dilantin, but I did it, and now take the seizures as they come. I've usually got bruises to show for it.

In the middle of a vast city I have cut myself off. I am not part of the network growing faster than I can conceive. I don't even know if it's dangerous, to ordinary people. It noticed me, and Kluge, and Osborne. And Lisa. It brushed against our minds like I would brush away a mosquito, never noticing I had crushed it. Only I survived.

But I wonder.

It would be very hard . . .

Lisa told me how it can get in through the wiring. There's something called a carrier wave that can move over wires carrying household current. That's why the electricity had to go.

I need water for my garden. There's just not enough rain here in southern California, and I don't know how else I could get the water.

Do you think it could come through the pipes?

BLOODCHILD

by Octavia E. Butler

*"Bloodchild" was purchased by Shawna McCarthy, and
appeared in the June 1984 issue of* IAsfm, *with a striking abstract cover by Wayne Barlowe and dramatic interior illustrations by Nicholas Jainschigg. "Bloodchild"
was Butler's second sale to* IAsfm; *her first IAsfm story,
"Speech Sounds," had already won her a Hugo Award
the previous year, but "Bloodchild" was to prove even
more popular, going on to win both the Hugo and the
Nebula Award. "Bloodchild" was another controversial
story. In my headnote for it in* The Year's Best Science
Fiction *I wrote: "Here's as powerful a story as you're
likely to see this (or any other) year," and although
IAsfm lost a few subscribers over it, it was more than
worth it. Primarily known as a prolific and popular
novelist, Butler rarely writes short fiction, but when she
does, it's worth the wait. As you are about to discover...*

*Octavia E. Butler sold her first novel in 1976 and
has subsequently emerged as one of the foremost writers
of her generation. Her critically acclaimed novels include* Patternmaster, Mind of My Mind, Survivor,

Kindred *and* Wild Seed. *Her most recent novel was*
Clay's Ark. *She is currently at work on a new novel,*
tentatively entitled Exogenesis. *Born in Pasadena, Cali-*
fornia, she now lives and works in Los Angeles.

My last night of childhood began with a visit home. T'Gatoi's
sisters had given us two sterile eggs. T'Gatoi gave one to my
mother, brother, and sisters. She insisted that I eat the other
one alone. It didn't matter. There was still enough to leave
everyone feeling good. Almost everyone. My mother
wouldn't take any. She sat, watching everyone drifting and
dreaming without her. Most of the time she watched me.

I lay against T'Gatoi's long, velvet underside, sipping from
my egg now and then, wondering why my mother denied herself such a harmless pleasure. Less of her hair would be gray
if she indulged now and then. The eggs prolonged life, prolonged vigor. My father, who had never refused one in his
life, had lived more than twice as long as he should have.
And toward the end of his life, when he should have been
slowing down, he had married my mother and fathered four
children.

But my mother seemed content to age before she had to. I
saw her turn away as several of T'Gatoi's limbs secured me
closer. T'Gatoi liked our body heat, and took advantage of it
whenever she could. When I was little and at home more, my
mother used to try to tell me how to behave with T'Gatoi—
how to be respectful and always obedient because T'Gatoi was
the Tlic government official in charge of the Preserve, and
thus the most important of her kind to deal directly with Terrans. It was an honor, my mother said, that such a person had
chosen to come into the family. My mother was at her most
formal and severe when she was lying.

I had no idea why she was lying, or even what she was
lying about. It *was* an honor to have T'Gatoi in the family, but
it was hardly a novelty. T'Gatoi was not interested in being
honored in the house she considered her second home. She
simply came in, climbed onto one of her special couches and
called me over to keep her warm. It was impossible to be

formal with her while lying against her and hearing her complain as usual that I was too skinny.

"You're better," she said this time, probing me with six or seven of her limbs. "You're gaining weight finally. Thinness is dangerous." The probing changed subtly, became a series of caresses.

"He's still too thin," my mother said sharply.

T'Gatoi lifted her head and perhaps a meter of her body off the couch as though she were sitting up. She looked at my mother, and my mother, her face lined and old-looking, turned away.

"Lien, I would like you to have what's left of Gan's egg."

"The eggs are for the children," my mother said.

"They are for the family. Please take it."

Unwillingly obedient, my mother took it from me and put it to her mouth. There were only a few drops left in the now-shrunken, elastic shell, but she squeezed them out, swallowed them, and after a few moments some of the lines of tension began to smooth from her face.

"It's good," she whispered. "Sometimes I forget how good it is."

"You should take more," T'Gatoi said. "Why are you in such a hurry to be old?"

My mother said nothing.

"I like being able to come here," T'Gatoi said. "This place is a refuge because of you, yet you won't take care of yourself."

T'Gatoi was hounded on the outside. Her people wanted more of us made available. Only she and her political faction stood between us and the hordes who did not understand why there was a Preserve—why any Terran could not be courted, paid, drafted, in some way made available to them. Or they did understand, but in their desperation, they did not care. She parceled us out to the desperate and sold us to the rich and powerful for their political support. Thus, we were necessities, status symbols, and an independent people. She oversaw the joining of families, putting an end to the final remnants of the earlier system of breaking up Terran families to suit impatient Tlic. I had lived outside with her. I had seen the desperate eagerness in the way some people looked at me. It was a little frightening to know that only she stood between us and that desperation that could so easily swallow us. My mother would look at her sometimes and say to me, "Take care of her." And I would remember that she too had been outside, had seen.

Now T'Gatoi used four of her limbs to push me away from her onto the floor. "Go on, Gan," she said. "Sit down there with your sisters and enjoy not being sober. You had most of the egg. Lien, come warm me."

My mother hesitated for no reason that I could see. One of my earliest memories is of my mother stretched alongside T'Gatoi, talking about things I could not understand, picking me up from the floor and laughing as she sat me on one of T'Gatoi's segments. She ate her share of eggs then. I wondered when she had stopped, and why.

She lay down against T'Gatoi, and the whole left row of T'Gatoi's limbs closed around her, holding her loosely, but securely. I had always found it uncomfortable to lie that way but, except for my older sister, no one else in the family liked it. They said it made them feel caged.

T'Gatoi meant to cage my mother. Once she had, she moved her tail slightly, then spoke. "Not enough egg, Lien. You should have taken it when it was passed to you. You need it badly now."

T'Gatoi's tail moved once more, its whip motion so swift I wouldn't have seen it if I hadn't been watching for it. Her sting drew only a single drop of blood from my mother's bare leg.

My mother cried out—probably in surprise. Being stung doesn't hurt. Then she sighed and I could see her body relax. She moved languidly into a more comfortable position within the cage of T'Gatoi's limbs. "Why did you do that?" she asked, sounding half asleep.

"I could not watch you sitting and suffering any longer."

My mother managed to move her shoulders in a small shrug. "Tomorrow," she said.

"Yes. Tomorrow you will resume your suffering—if you must. But for now, just for now, lie here and warm me and let me ease your way a little."

"He's still mine, you know," my mother said suddenly. "Nothing can buy him from me." Sober, she would not have permitted herself to refer to such things.

"Nothing." T'Gatoi agreed, humoring her.

"Did you think I would sell him for eggs? For long life? My son?"

"Not for anything," T'Gatoi said stroking my mother's shoulders, toying with her long, graying hair.

I would like to have touched my mother, shared that moment with her. She would take my hand if I touched her now. freed by the egg and the sting, she would smile and perhaps say things long held in. But tomorrow, she would remember all this as a humiliation. I did not want to be part of a remembered humiliation. Best just to be still and know she loved me under all the duty and pride and pain.

"Xuan Hoa, take off her shoes," T'Gatoi said. "In a little while I'll sting her again and she can sleep."

My older sister obeyed, swaying drunkenly as she stood up. When she had finished, she sat down beside me and took my hand. We had always been a unit, she and I.

My mother put the back of her head against T'Gatoi's underside and tried from that impossible angle to look up into the broad, round face. "You're going to sting me again?"

"Yes, Lien."

"I'll sleep until tomorrow noon."

"Good. You need it. When did you sleep last?"

My mother made a wordless sound of annoyance. "I should have stepped on you when you were small enough," she muttered.

It was an old joke between them. They had grown up together, sort of, though T'Gatoi had not, in my mother's lifetime, been small enough for any Terran to step on. She was nearly three times my mother's present age, yet would still be young when my mother died of age. But T'Gatoi and my mother had met as T'Gatoi was coming into a period of rapid development—a kind of Tlic adolescence. My mother was only a child, but for a while they developed at the same rate and had no better friends than each other.

T'Gatoi had even introduced my mother to the man who became my father. My parents, pleased with each other in spite of their very different ages, married as T'Gatoi was going into her family's business—politics. She and my mother saw each other less. But sometime before my older sister was born, my mother promised T'Gatoi one of her children. She would have to give one of us to someone, and she preferred T'Gatoi to some stranger.

Years passed. T'Gatoi traveled and increased her influence. The Preserve was hers by the time she came back to my mother to collect what she probably saw as her just reward for her hard work. My older sister took an instant liking to her and wanted to be chosen, but my mother was just coming to term with me and T'Gatoi liked the idea of choosing an infant and watching and taking part in all the phases of development. I'm told I was first caged within T'Gatoi's many limbs only three minutes after my birth. A few days later, I was given my first taste of egg. I tell Terrans that when they ask whether I was ever afraid of her. And I tell it to Tlic when T'Gatoi suggests a young Terran child for them and they, anxious and ignorant, demand an adolescent. Even my brother who had somehow grown up to fear and distrust the Tlic could probably have gone smoothly into one of their families if he had been adopted early enough. Sometimes, I think for his sake he should have been. I looked at him, stretched out on the floor across the room, his eyes open, but glazed as he dreamed his egg dream. No matter what he felt toward the Tlic, he always demanded his share of egg.

"Lien, can you stand up?" T'Gatoi asked suddenly.

"Stand?" my mother said. "I thought I was going to sleep."

"Later. Something sounds wrong outside." The cage was abruptly gone.

"What?"

"Up, Lien!"

My mother recognized her tone and got up just in time to avoid being dumped on the floor. T'Gatoi whipped her three meters of body off her couch, toward the door, and out at full speed. She had bones—ribs, a long spine, a skull, four sets of limbbones per segment. But when she moved that way, twisting, hurling herself into controlled falls, landing running, she seemed not only boneless, but aquatic—something swimming through the air as though it were water. I loved watching her move.

I left my sister and started to follow her out the door, though I wasn't very steady on my own feet. It would have been better to sit and dream, better yet to find a girl and share a waking dream with her. Back when the Tlic saw us as not much more than convenient big warm-blooded animals, they would pen several of us together, male and female, and feed us only eggs. That way they could be sure of getting another generation of us no matter how we tried to hold out. We were lucky that didn't go on long. A few generations of it and we would have *been* little more than convenient big animals.

"Hold the door open, Gan," T'Gatoi said. "And tell the family to stay back."

"What is it?" I asked.

"N'Tlic."

I shrank back against the door. "Here? Alone?"

"He was trying to reach a call box, I suppose." She carried the man past me, unconscious, folded like a coat over some of her limbs. He looked young—my brother's age perhaps—and he was thinner than he should have been. What T'Gatoi would have called dangerously thin.

"Gan, go to the call box," she said. She put the man on the floor and began stripping off his clothing.

I did not move.

After a moment, she looked up at me, her sudden stillness a sign of deep impatience.

"Send Qui," I told her. "I'll stay here. Maybe I can help."

She let her limbs begin to move again, lifting the man and pulling his shirt over his head. "You don't want to see this," she said. "It will be hard. I can't help this man the way his Tlic could."

"I know. But send Qui. He won't want to be of any help here. I'm at least willing to try."

She looked at my brother—older, bigger, stronger, certainly more able to help her here. He was sitting up now, braced against the wall, staring at the man on the floor with undisguised fear and revulsion. Even she could see that he would be useless.

"Qui, go!" she said.

He didn't argue. He stood up, swayed briefly, then steadied, frightened sober.

"This man's name is Bram Lomas," she told him, reading from the man's arm band. I fingered my own arm band in sympathy. "He needs T'Khotgif Teh. Do you hear?"

"Bram Lomas, T'Khotgif Teh," my brother said. "I'm going." He edged around Lomas and ran out the door.

Lomas began to regain consciousness. He only moaned at first and clutched spasmodically at a pair of T'Gatoi's limbs. My younger sister, finally awake from her egg dream, came close to look at him, until my mother pulled her back.

T'Gatoi removed the man's shoes, then his pants, all the while leaving him two of her limbs to grip. Except for the final few, all her limbs were equally dexterous. "I want no argument from you this time, Gan," she said.

I straightened. "What shall I do?"

"Go out and slaughter an animal that is at least half your size."

"Slaughter? But I've never—"

She knocked me across the room. Her tail was an efficient weapon whether she exposed the sting or not.

I got up, feeling stupid for having ignored her warning, and went into the kitchen. Maybe I could kill something with a knife or an ax. My mother raised a few Terran animals for the table and several thousand local ones for their fur. T'Gatoi would probably prefer something local. An achti, perhaps. Some of those were the right size, though they had about three times as many teeth as I did and a real love of using them. My mother, Hoa, and Qui could kill them with knives. I had never killed one at all, had never slaughtered any animal. I had spent most of my time with T'Gatoi while my brother and sisters were learning the family business. T'Gatoi had been right. I should have been the one to go to the call box. At least I could do that.

I went to the corner cabinet where my mother kept her larger house and garden tools. At the back of the cabinet there was a pipe that carried off waste water from the kitchen—except that it didn't anymore. My father had rerouted the waste water before I was born. Now the pipe could be turned so that one half slid around the other and a rifle could be stored inside. This wasn't our only gun, but it was our most easily accessible one. I would have to use it to shoot one of the biggest of the achti. Then T'Gatoi would probably confiscate it. Firearms were illegal in the Preserve. There had been incidents right after the Preserve was established—Terrans shooting Tlic, shooting N'Tlic. This was before the joining of families began, before everyone had a personal stake in keeping the peace. No one had shot a Tlic in my lifetime or my mother's, but the law still stood—for our protection, we were told. There were stories of whole Terran families wiped out in reprisal back during the assassinations.

I went out to the cages and shot the biggest achti I could find. It was a handsome breeding male and my mother would not be pleased to see me bring it in. But it was the right size, and I was in a hurry.

I put the achti's long, warm body over my shoulder—glad that some of the weight I'd gained was muscle—and took it to the kitchen. There, I put the gun back in its hiding place. If T'Gatoi noticed the achti's wounds and demanded the gun, I would give it to her. Otherwise, let it stay where my father wanted it.

I turned to take the achti to her, then hesitated. For several seconds, I stood in front of the closed door wondering why I was suddenly afraid. I knew what was going to happen. I hadn't seen it before but T'Gatoi had shown me diagrams, and drawings. She had made sure I knew the truth as soon as I was old enough to understand it.

Yet I did not want to go into that room. I wasted a little time choosing a knife from the carved, wooden box in which my mother kept them. T'Gatoi might want one, I told myself, for the tough, heavily furred hide of the achti.

"Gan!" T'Gatoi called, her voice harsh with urgency.

I swallowed. I had not imagined a simple moving of the feet could be so difficult. I realized I was trembling and that shamed me. Shame impelled me through the door.

I put the achti down near T'Gatoi and saw that Lomas was unconscious again. She, Lomas, and I were alone in the room, my mother and sisters probably sent out so they would not have to watch. I envied them.

But my mother came back into the room as T'Gatoi seized the achti. Ignoring the knife I offered her, she extended claws from several of her limbs and slit the achti from throat to anus. She looked at me, her yellow eyes intent. "Hold this man's shoulders, Gan."

I stared at Lomas in panic, realizing that I did not want to touch him, let alone hold him. This would not be like shooting an animal. Not as quick, not as merciful, and, I hoped, not as final, but there was nothing I wanted less than to be part of it.

My mother came forward. "Gan, you hold his right side,"

she said. "I'll hold his left." And if he came to, he would throw her off without realizing he had done it. She was a tiny woman. She often wondered aloud how she had produced, as she said, such "huge" children.

"Never mind," I told her, taking the man's shoulders. "I'll do it."

She hovered nearby.

"Don't worry," I said. "I won't shame you. You don't have to stay and watch."

She looked at me uncertainly, then touched my face in a rare caress. Finally, she went back to her bedroom.

T'Gatoi lowered her head in relief. "Thank you, Gan," she said with courtesy more Terran than Tlic. "That one . . . she is always finding new ways for me to make her suffer."

Lomas began to groan and make choked sounds. I had hoped he would stay unconscious. T'Gatoi put her face near his so that he focused on her.

"I've stung you as much as I dare for now," she told him. "When this is over, I'll sting you to sleep and you won't hurt anymore."

"Please," the man begged. "Wait . . ."

"There's no more time, Bram. I'll sting you as soon as it's over. When T'Khotgif arrives she'll give you eggs to help you heal. It will be over soon."

"T'Khotgif!" the man shouted, straining against my hands.

"Soon, Bram." T'Gatoi glanced at me, then placed a claw against his abdomen slightly to the right of the middle, just below the last rib. There was movement on the right side— tiny, seemingly random pulsations moving his brown flesh, creating a concavity here, a convexity there, over and over until I could see the rhythm of it and knew where the next pulse would be.

Lomas's entire body stiffened under T'Gatoi's claw, though she merely rested it against him she wound the rear section of her body around his legs. He might break my grip, but he would not break hers. He wept helplessly as she used his pants to tie his hands, then pushed his hands above his head so that I could kneel on the cloth between them and pin them in place. She rolled up his shirt and gave it to him to bite down on.

And she opened him.

His body convulsed with the first cut. He almost tore him-

self away from me. The sounds he made . . . I had never heard
such sounds come from anything human. T'Gatoi seemed to
pay no attention as she lengthened and deepened the cut, now
and then pausing to lick away blood. His blood vessels con-
tracted, reacting to the chemistry of her saliva, and the bleeding slowed.

I felt as though I were helping her torture him, helping her
consume him. I knew I would vomit soon, didn't know why I
hadn't already. I couldn't possibly last until she was finished.

She found the first grub. It was fat and deep red with his
blood—both inside and out. It had already eaten its own egg
case, but apparently had not yet begun to eat its host. At this
stage, it would eat any flesh except its mother's. Let alone, it
would have gone on excreting the poisons that had both sickened and alerted Lomas. Eventually it would have begun to
eat. By the time it ate its way out of Lomas's flesh, Lomas
would be dead or dying—and unable to take revenge on the
thing that was killing him. There was always a grace period
between the time the host sickened and the time the grubs
began to eat him.

T'Gatoi picked up the writhing grub carefully, and looked
at it, somehow ignoring the terrible groans of the man.

Abruptly, the man lost consciousness.

"Good," T'Gatoi looked down at him. "I wish you Terrans
could do that at will." She felt nothing. And the thing she
held . . .

It was limbless and boneless at this stage, perhaps fifteen
centimeters long and two thick, blind and slimy with blood. It
was like a large worm. T'Gatoi put it into the belly of the
achti, and it began at once to burrow. It would stay there and
eat as long as there was anything to eat.

Probing through Lomas' flesh, she found two more, one of
them smaller and more vigorous. "A male!" she said happily.
He would be dead before I would. He would be through his
metamorphosis and screwing everything that would hold still
before his sisters even had limbs. He was the only one to
make a serious effort to bite T'Gatoi as she placed him in the
achti.

Paler worms oozed to visibility in Lomas's flesh. I closed
my eyes. It was worse than finding something dead, rotting,

and filled with tiny animal grubs. And it was far worse than any drawing or diagram.

"Ah, there are more," T'Gatoi said, plucking out two long, thick grubs. "You may have to kill another animal, Gan. Everything lives inside you Terrans."

I had been told all my life that this was a good and necessary thing Tlic and Terran did together—a kind of birth. I had believed it until now. I knew birth was painful and bloody, no matter what. But this was something else, something worse. And I wasn't ready to see it. Maybe I never would be. Yet I couldn't *not* see it. Closing my eyes didn't help.

T'Gatoi found a grub still eating its egg case. The remains of the case were still wired into a blood vessel by their own little tube or hook or whatever. That was the way the grubs were anchored and the way they fed. They took only blood until they were ready to emerge. Then they ate their stretched, elastic egg cases. Then they ate their hosts.

T'Gatoi bit away the egg case, licked away the blood. Did she like the taste? Did childhood habits die hard—or not die at all?

The whole procedure was wrong, alien. I wouldn't have thought anything about her could seem alien to me.

"One more, I think," she said. "Perhaps two. A good family. In a host animal these days, we would be happy to find one or two alive." She glanced at me. "Go outside, Gan, and empty your stomach. Go now while the man is unconscious."

I staggered out, barely made it. Beneath the tree just beyond the front door, I vomited until there was nothing left to bring up. Finally, I stood shaking, tears streaming down my face. I did not know why I was crying, but I could not stop. I went farther from the house to avoid being seen. Every time I closed my eyes I saw red worms crawling over redder human flesh.

There was a car coming toward the house. Since Terrans were forbidden motorized vehicles except for certain farm equipment, I knew this must be Lomas's Tlic with Qui and perhaps a Terran doctor. I wiped my face on my shirt, struggled for control.

"Gan," Qui called as the car stopped. "What happened?" He crawled out of the low, round, Tlic-convenient car door. Another Terran crawled out the other side and went into the house without speaking to me. The doctor. With his help and a few eggs, Lomas might make it.

"T'Khotgif Teh?" I said.

The Tlic driver surged out of her car, reared up half her length before me. She was paler and smaller than T'Gatoi—probably born from the body of an animal. Tlic from Terran bodies were always larger as well as more numerous.

"Six young," I told her. "Maybe seven, all alive. At least one male."

"Lomas?" she said harshly. I liked her for the question and the concern in her voice when she asked it. The last coherent thing he had said was her name.

"He's alive," I said.

She surged away to the house without another word.

"She's been sick," my brother said, watching her go. "When I called, I could hear people telling her she wasn't well enough to go out even for this."

I said nothing. I had extended courtesy to the Tlic. Now I didn't want to talk to anyone. I hoped he would go in—out of curiosity if nothing else.

"Finally found out more than you wanted to know, eh?"

I looked at him.

"Don't give me one of *her* looks," he said. "You're not her. You're just her property."

One of her looks. Had I picked up even an ability to imitate her expressions?

"What'd you do, puke?" He sniffed the air. "So now you know what you're in for."

I walked away from him. He and I had been close when we were kids. He would let me follow him around when I was home and sometimes T'Gatoi would let me bring him along when she took me into the city. But something had happened when he reached adolescence. I never knew what. He began keeping out of T'Gatoi's way. Then he began running away—until he realized there was no "away." Not in the Preserve. Certainly not outside. After that he concentrated on getting his share of every egg that came into the house, and on looking out for me in a way that made me all but hate him—a way that clearly said, as long as I was all right, he was safe from the Tlic.

"How was it, really?" he demanded, following me.

"I killed an achti. The young ate it."

"You didn't run out of the house and puke because they ate an achti."

"I had . . . never seen a person cut open before." That was true, and enough for him to know. I couldn't talk about the other. Not with him.

"Oh," he said. He glanced at me as though he wanted to say more, but he kept quiet.

We walked, not really headed anywhere. Toward the back, toward the cages, toward the fields.

"Did he say anything?" Qui asked. "Lomas, I mean."

Who else would he mean? "He said 'T'Khotgif.'"

Qui shuddered. "If she had done that to me, she'd be the last person I'd call for."

"You'd call for her. Her sting would ease your pain without killing the grubs in you."

"You think I'd care if they died?'"

No. Of course he wouldn't. Would I?

"Shit!" He drew a deep breath. "I've seen what they do. You think this thing with Lomas was bad? It was nothing."

I didn't argue. He didn't know what he was talking about.

"I saw them eat a man," he said.

I turned to face him. "You're lying!"

"*I saw them eat a man.*" He paused. "It was when I was little. I had been to the Hartmund house and I was on my way home. Halfway here, I saw a man and a Tlic and the man was N'Tlic. The ground was hilly. I was able to hide from them and watch. The Tlic wouldn't open the man because she had nothing to feed the grubs. The man couldn't go any farther and there were no houses around. He was in so much pain he told her to kill him. He begged her to kill him. Finally, she did. She cut his throat. One swipe of one claw. I saw the grubs eat their way out, then burrow in again, still eating."

His words made me see Lomas's flesh again, parasitized, crawling. "Why didn't you tell me that?" I whispered.

He looked startled, as though he'd forgotten I was listening. "I don't know."

"You started to run away not long after that, didn't you?"

"Yeah. Stupid. Running inside the Preserve. Running in a cage."

I shook my head, said what I should have said to him long ago. "She wouldn't take you, Qui. You don't have to worry."

"She would . . . if anything happened to you."

"No. She'd take Xuan Hoa. Hoa . . . wants it." She wouldn't if she had stayed to watch Lomas.

"They don't take women," he said with contempt.

"They do sometimes." I glanced at him. "Actually, they prefer women. You should be around them when they talk among themselves. They say women have more body fat to protect the grubs. But they usually take men to leave the women free to bear their own young."

"To provide the next generation of host animals," he said, switching from contempt to bitterness.

"It's more than that!" I countered. Was it?

"If it were going to happen to me, I'd want to believe it was more, too."

"It is more!" I felt like a kid. Stupid argument.

"Did you think so while T'Gatoi was picking worms out of that guy's guts?"

"It's not supposed to happen that way."

"Sure it is. You weren't supposed to see it, that's all. And his Tlic was supposed to do it. She could sting him unconscious and the operation wouldn't have been as painful. But she'd still open him, pick out the grubs, and if she missed even one, it would poison him and eat him from the inside out."

There was actually a time when my mother told me to show respect for Qui because he was my older brother. I walked away, hating him. In his way, he was gloating. He was safe and I wasn't. I could have hit him, but I didn't think I would be able to stand it when he refused to hit back, when he looked at me with contempt and pity.

He wouldn't let me get away. Longer-legged, he swung ahead of me and made me feel as though I were following him.

"I'm sorry," he said.

I strode on, sick and furious.

"Look, it probably won't be that bad with you. T'Gatoi likes you. She'll be careful."

I turned back toward the house, almost running from him.

"Has she done it to you yet?" he asked, keeping up easily.

"I mean, you're about the right age for implantation. Has she—"

I hit him. I didn't know I was going to do it, but I think I meant to kill him. If he hadn't been bigger and stronger, I think I would have.

He tried to hold me off, but in the end, had to defend himself. He only hit me a couple of times. That was plenty. I don't remember going down, but when I came to, he was gone. It was worth the pain to be rid of him.

I got up and walked slowly toward the house. The back was dark. No one was in the kitchen. My mother and sisters were sleeping in their bedrooms—or pretending to.

Once I was in the kitchen, I could hear voices—Tlic and Terran from the next room. I couldn't make out what they were saying—didn't want to make it out.

I sat down at my mother's table, waiting for quiet. The table was smooth and worn, heavy and well-crafted. My father had made it for her just before he died. I remembered hanging around underfoot when he built it. He didn't mind. Now I sat leaning on it, missing him. I could have talked to him. He had done it three times in his long life. Three clutches of eggs, three times being opened and sewed up. How had he done it? How did anyone do it?

I got up, took the rifle from its hiding place, and sat down again with it. It needed cleaning, oiling.

All I did was load it.

"Gan?"

She made a lot of little clicking sounds when she walked on bare floor, each limb clicking in succession as it touched down. Waves of little clicks.

She came to the table, raised the front half of her body above it, and surged onto it. Sometimes she moved so smoothly she seemed to flow like water itself. She coiled herself into a small hill in the middle of the table and looked at me.

"That was bad," she said softly. "You should not have seen it. It need not be that way."

"I know."

"T'Khotgif—Ch'Khotgif now—she will die of her disease. She will not live to raise her children. But her sister will provide for them, and for Bram Lomas." Sterile sister. One fertile female in every lot. One to keep the family going. That sister owed Lomas more than she could ever repay.

"He'll live then?"

"Yes."

"I wonder if he would do it again."

"No one would ask him to do that again."

I looked into the yellow eyes, wondering how much I saw and understood there, and how much I only imagined. "No one ever asks us," I said. "You never asked me."

She moved her head slightly. "What's the matter with your face?"

"Nothing. Nothing important." Human eyes probably wouldn't have noticed the swelling in the darkness. The only light was from one of the moons, shining through a window across the room.

"Did you use the rifle to shoot the achti?"

"Yes."

"And do you mean to use it to shoot me?"

I stared at her, outlined in moonlight—coiled, graceful body. "What does Terran blood taste like to you?"

She said nothing.

"What are you?" I whispered. "What are we to you?"

She lay still, rested her head on her topmost coil. "You know me as no other does," she said softly. "You must decide."

"That's what happened to my face," I told her.

"What?"

"Qui goaded me into deciding to do something. It didn't turn out very well." I moved the gun slightly, brought the barrel up diagonally under my own chin. "At least it was a decision I made."

"As this will be."

"Ask me, Gatoi."

"For my children's lives?"

She would say something like that. She knew how to manipulate people, Terran and Tlic. But not this time.

"I don't want to be a host animal," I said. "Not even yours."

It took her a long time to answer. "We use almost no host animals these days," she said. "You know that."

"You use us."

"We do. We wait long years for you and teach you and join our families to yours." She moved restlessly. "You know you aren't animals to us."

I stared at her, saying nothing.

"The animals we once used began killing most of our eggs after implantation long before your ancestors arrived," she said softly. "You know these things, Gan. Because your people arrived, we are relearning what it means to be a healthy, thriving people. And your ancestors, fleeing from their home-world, from their own kind who would have killed or enslaved them—they survived because of us. We saw them as people and gave them the Preserve when they still tried to kill us as worms."

At the word "Worms" I jumped. I couldn't help it, and she couldn't help noticing it.

"I see," she said quietly. "Would you really rather die than bear my young, Gan?"

I didn't answer.

"Shall I go to Xuan Hoa?"

"Yes!" Hoa wanted it. Let her have it. She hadn't had to watch Lomas. She'd be proud . . . not terrified.

T'Gatoi flowed off the table onto the floor, startling me almost too much.

"I'll sleep in Hoa's room tonight," she said. "And some-time tonight or in the morning, I'll tell her."

This was going too fast. My sister. Hoa had had almost as much to do with raising me as my mother. I was still close to her—not like Qui. She could want T'Gatoi and still love me.

"Wait! Gatoi!"

She looked back, then raised nearly half her length off the floor and turned it to face me. "These are adult things, Gan. This is my life, my family!"

"But she's . . . my sister."

"I have done what you demanded. I have asked you!"

"But—"

"It will be easier for Hoa. She has always expected to carry other lives inside her."

Human lives. Human young who would someday drink at her breasts, not at her veins.

I shook my head. "Don't do it to her, Gatoi." I was not Qui. It seemed I could become him, though, with no effort at all. I could make Xuan Hoa my shield. Would it be easier to know that red worms were growing in her flesh instead of mine?

"Don't do it to Hoa," I repeated.

She stared at me, utterly still.

I looked away, then back at her. "Do it to me."

I lowered the gun from my throat and she leaned forward to take it.

"No," I told her.

"It's the law," she said.

"Leave it for the family. One of them might use it to save my life someday."

She grasped the rifle barrel, but I wouldn't let go. I was pulled into a standing position over her.

"Leave it here!" I repeated. "If we're not your animals, if these are adult things, accept the risk. There is risk, Gatoi, in dealing with a partner."

It was clearly hard for her to let go of the rifle. A shudder went through her and she made a hissing sound of distress. It occurred to me that she was afraid. She was old enough to have seen what guns could do to people. Now her young and this gun would be together in the same house. She did not know about our other guns. In this dispute, they did not matter.

"I will implant the first egg tonight," she said as I put the gun away. "Do you hear, Gan?"

Why else had I been given a whole egg to eat while the rest of the family was left to share one? Why else had my mother kept looking at me as though I were going away from her, going where she could not follow? Did T'Gatoi imagine I hadn't known?

"I hear."

"Now!" I let her push me out of the kitchen, then walked ahead of her toward my bedroom. The sudden urgency in her voice sounded real. "You would have done it to Hoa tonight!" I accused.

"I must to do it to someone tonight."

I stopped in spite of her urgency and stood in her way. "Don't you care who?"

She flowed around me and into my bedroom. I found her waiting on the couch we shared. There was nothing in Hoa's room that she could have used. She would have done it to Hoa on the floor. The thought of her doing it to Hoa at all disturbed me in a different way now, and I was suddenly angry.

Yet I undressed and lay down beside her. I knew what to do, what to expect. I had been told all my life. I felt the familiar sting, narcotic, mildly pleasant. Then the blind probing of her ovipositor. The puncture was painless, easy. So easy going in. She undulated slowly against me, her muscles forcing the egg from her body into mine. I held on to a pair of her limbs until I remembered Lomas holding her that way. Then I let go, moved inadvertently, and hurt her. She gave a low cry of pain and I expected to be caged at once within her limbs. When I wasn't, I held on to her again, feeling oddly ashamed.

"I'm sorry," I whispered.

She rubbed my shoulders with four of her limbs.

"So you care?" I asked. "Do you care that it's me?"

She did not answer for some time. Finally, "You were the one making choices tonight, Gan. I made mine long ago."

"Would you have gone to Hoa?"

"Yes. How could I put my children into the care of one who hates them?"

"It wasn't . . . hate."

"I know what it was."

"I was afraid."

Silence.

"I still am." I could admit it to her here, now.

"But you came to me . . . to save Hoa."

"Yes." I leaned my forehead against her. She was cool velvet, deceptively soft. "And to keep you for myself," I said. It was so. I didn't understand it, but it was so.

She made a soft hum of contentment. "I couldn't believe I had made such a mistake with you," she said. "I chose you. I believed you had grown to choose me."

"I had, but . . ."

"Lomas."

"Yes."

"I have never known a Terran to see and take it well. Qui has seen one, hasn't he?"

"Yes."

"Terrans should be protected from seeing."

I didn't like the sound of that—and I doubted that it was possible. "Not protected," I said. "Shown. Shown when we're young kids, and shown more than once. Gatoi, no Terran ever sees a birth that goes right. All we see is N'Tlic—pain and terror and maybe death."

She looked down at me. "It is a private thing. It has always been a private thing."

Her tone kept me from insisting—that and the knowledge that if she changed her mind, I might be the first public example. But I had planted the thought in her mind. Chances were it would grow, and eventually she would experiment.

"You won't see it again," she said. "I don't want you thinking anymore about shooting me."

The small amount of fluid that came into me with her egg relaxed me as completely as a sterile egg would have, so that I could remember the rifle in my hands and my feelings of fear and revulsion, anger and despair. I could remember the feelings without reviving them. I could talk about them.

"I wouldn't have shot you," I said. "Not you." She had been taken from my father's flesh when he was my age.

"You could have," she insisted.

"Not you." She stood between us and her own people, protecting, interweaving.

"Would you have destroyed yourself?"

I moved carefully, uncomfortably. "I could have done that. I nearly did. That's Qui's 'away,' I wonder if he knows."

"What?"

I did not answer.

"You will live now."

"Yes." *Take care of her*, my mother used to say. Yes.

"I'm healthy and young," she said. "I won't leave you as Lomas was left—alone, N'Tlic. I'll take care of you."

BESTSELLING
Science Fiction
and
Fantasy

Fantasy from Ace fanciful and fantastic!